PRAISE FOR THE COVERT-ONE SERIES

THE GENEVA STRATEGY

"[Freveletti's] grasp of fast-action suspense and understanding of international politics, as well as martial arts combat training, brings real-life action to a continuance of Robert Ludlum's original creations."   —BookReporter.com

"Exciting . . . Freveletti offers a savory mix of intense action and cynical politics."   —*Publishers Weekly*

THE UTOPIA EXPERIMENT

"Mills offers an interesting new premise for action-adventure . . . [and] rockets the action around the world."   —*Kirkus Reviews*

"Ludlum fans will enjoy the frantic pace and dramatic shifts in plot . . . Mills's genius is making 'extra-human capabilities' seem not merely possible but almost already available, echoing the prescience of Jules Verne. We are all headed into this brave new world. Here, Mills helps us enjoy the ride while we consider the consequences."
     —*Fredericksburg Free Lance-Star* (VA)

"Well-written . . . This book is a winner."
     —BookReporter.com

"A fast-paced book with great characters . . . Mills is a very good writer."   —Bubblews.com

THE JANUS REPRISAL

"From the opening sentence that literally starts with a bang, the latest Covert-One novel speeds along at a breakneck pace . . . Freveletti, who has an amazing talent for action scenes, has written one of the top entries in the Covert-One series, which has established itself as the best of the numerous series based on Ludlum characters." —*Booklist*

"Wonderful . . . Award-winning novelist Freveletti lends her imaginative talents to the Covert-One series with a book that is nearly impossible to put down and moves at the speed of light without pause . . . [It] races forward with the energy of a super-charged Bourne film." —BookReporter.com

"A fast-moving, well-written thriller." —*Oklahoman*

"Freveletti turbocharges tension to nonstop levels in this Covert-One thriller." —*Kirkus Reviews*

"Masterful . . . The action is quite cinematic, the characters well-drawn, and the plot as tight as they come." —CriminalElement.com

"Exciting . . . Great read, really well-done, and a great finish." —BestsellersWorld.com

THE ARES DECISION

"The action never flags . . . Mills nicely integrates relevant military and scientific details into the story line, while his skill at

characterization will leave many hoping he'll become a permanent posthumous collaborator with Ludlum."

—*Publishers Weekly*

"A tight and tense page-turner . . . Mills does the large-scale
thriller better than anyone else working the genre today."

—*Booklist*

"Fast-paced and action-filled, with iconic characters and contemporary themes, the story is a stand-alone-worthy entry in
the Covert-One series . . . Fans of Ludlum and Mills thrillers
will find *The Ares Decision* right on target."

—*Fredericksburg Free Lance-Star* (VA)

"Plenty of comfort food for those with an appetite for the
thriller genre."

—*Kirkus Reviews*

"It should have the dual effect of sustaining interest in the series and moving Mills onto the must-read list of many. If your
boat is floated by thriller novels that are set in the real world
and have the ability to scare the pants off you, you will absolutely love this one . . . I can think of no greater compliment
than to tell you that portions of the novel made my skin crawl.
And I loved every minute of it."

—BookReporter.com

"The pacing and the premise are pure Ludlum."

—WomanAroundTown.com

"Filled with action, intrigue, and a plot that puts the team in a
tight spot and their lives in constant danger. The end result is
an exciting read."

—TheSunDaily.my

THE PATRIOT ATTACK

ROBERT LUDLUM'S™

THE
PATRIOT ATTACK

A COVERT-ONE NOVEL

SERIES CREATED BY ROBERT LUDLUM
WRITTEN BY KYLE MILLS

GRAND CENTRAL
PUBLISHING

NEW YORK   BOSTON

Copyright © 2015 by Myn Pyn, LLC

Excerpt from *The Janson Equation* copyright © 2015 by Myn Pyn, LLC

Grand Central Publishing
Hachette Book Group
1290 Avenue of the Americas
New York, NY 10104

www.HachetteBookGroup.com

Printed in the United States of America

RRD-C

First Edition: September 2015
10 9 8 7 6 5 4 3 2 1

Grand Central Publishing is a division of Hachette Book Group, Inc.
The Grand Central Publishing name and logo is a trademark of Hachette Book Group, Inc.

The Hachette Speakers Bureau provides a wide range of authors for speaking events. To find out more, go to www.hachettespeakersbureau.com or call (866) 376-6591.

Library of Congress Cataloging-in-Publication Data has been applied for.

ISBN 978-1-4555-7762-0 (regular edition)
ISBN 978-1-4555-3633-7 (large print edition)

THE PATRIOT ATTACK

Prologue

Fukushima Daiichi Nuclear Power Plant
Northeastern Japan
March 11, 2011

D r. Hideki Ito felt the floor shift and braced himself against the elaborate control console in front of him. He waited for the earthquake to subside, reminding himself that the structure had weathered a number of powerful tremors two days before with no issues.

Still, he could feel the tension creeping into his stomach the way it always did when the earth decided to move. There was no reason for concern, he told himself again. The general had chosen to shut down Reactor Four and use it as a research facility, ostensibly because of its ability to contain a radiation leak in the face of just these kinds of shocks. It wasn't radiation they were asking it to hold in check, though. The work Ito had dedicated his life to was far more dangerous and difficult to control.

The vibrations seemed reluctant to subside as they had in the past, and he glanced nervously behind him. The room itself was unremarkable—a nine-meter cube of treated concrete lined with insulated pipes of every imaginable diameter. The only access was through a small titanium hatch centered between tables covered in computer equipment. His two research assistants had pulled back from their keyboards and sat holding the edges of their chairs, feet spread wide to keep from toppling to the rubber-coated floor.

The young man had the same stoic expression he'd been wearing since Ito had recruited him two years ago. The woman, a brilliant postdoc recently coaxed from the University of Tokyo, was searching the stark bunker with quick, birdlike movements of her head. Looking for cracks, Ito mused sympathetically. He felt compelled to do the same thing a thousand times a day.

The elderly physicist faced forward again, squinting through ten-centimeter-thick glass at the tiny room beyond. At its center was a secondary glass enclosure containing samples of concrete, plastic, and steel. Interspersed were organic materials—various dirt and stone specimens, as well as a few carefully chosen plants. And hovering above it all was a disinterested white rat stretching lazily on one of the robotic arms that serviced the enclosure.

The electron microscope reacted to the joystick in Ito's hand as he tried to compensate for the continuing tremors and maneuver it over a patch of moss. The deep-green color suggested that it, like the rat, had been unharmed by his experiments. Of course, that hypothesis would have to be confirmed at the atomic level. To the naked eye, none of the human-made materials in the enclosure had suffered any damage either. The deeper truth, though, was very different.

With the scope finally over its subject, Ito was able to examine its fundamental structure on a monitor set into the wall. It looked precisely as it always had. A thriving biological specimen unaffected by the war being silently fought around it.

After so many years of failure, Ito was having a difficult

time adjusting to his recent string of triumphs. Were they real or was there a fatal error hidden somewhere in the thousands of calculations he'd made? Were his carefully designed safety protocols as foolproof as they seemed? Was his sense of control just an illusion?

The euphoria he'd experienced when he first realized that he was influencing the fundamental forces of nature had slowly turned to a sense of dread. Had Einstein felt this way when his equations were used to create the bombs that had been dropped on Ito's own country so many years ago? Had Einstein understood that, while intoxicating to explore, nature would never allow itself to be mastered by something so trivial as the human mind?

As if reacting to his thoughts, the intensity of the earthquake began to grow. This time, though, something was different. Within a few seconds, Ito was struggling to stay upright, even with both hands gripping the console in front of him. The roar of the tremors filled his ears, making it impossible to understand the high-pitched shouts of his new assistant.

A pipe snaking across the ceiling burst, showering him in a stream of frigid seawater powerful enough to finally knock him off his feet. He crawled across the heaving floor toward a cutoff valve, eyes burning from the salty spray as a wave of panic began to take hold. By the time he made it to the wall, he could no longer keep his eyes open. He was forced to feel along the wet concrete until he found the metal wheel he'd been searching for.

It didn't move with the first effort, but his adrenaline-fueled muscles finally managed to break it free. He spun it right and when it stopped, so did everything else—the tremors, the water, the light. Chaos had suddenly turned to silence.

Ito pressed his back against the wall, struggling to fight off the disorientation brought about by the unexpected collapse of sensory input. He focused on the sound of dripping water, eyes now open but seeing only blackness.

Power had been lost. That was why the lights were out. No electricity.

That simple bit of analysis was enough to build on, and he clung to it as he evaluated his situation. Beyond the sound of falling water, he could make out the erratic breathing of his two assistants. The room was stable, so the earthquake was over. Aftershocks were possible—even likely—but when and how powerful could only be guessed at.

In the rest of the plant emergency protocols would be under way. Active reactors would go into automatic shutdown, and backup generators would be brought online to keep the cooling systems running. None of this was of any importance, though. The only thing that mattered was his own lab's security.

"Isami!" Ito called into the darkness. "The emergency lights! Can you reach them?"

A grunted affirmative was followed by the splash of lurching footsteps. They'd trained for this situation and after only a few seconds, the room was bathed in a dull-red glow. Isami was predictably at the switch, but Mikiko was huddled beneath a table, her eyes locked on the thick glass wall that ran the length of the room's north side.

The dust and water vapor hanging in the air created a kaleidoscopic effect, but not enough to hide what she was fixated on: a jagged, lightning-shaped crack that ran from floor to ceiling.

Mikiko suddenly bolted for the door, slamming into it and clawing for the handle. Ito moved more quickly than he would have thought possible, leaping to his feet and shoving her out of the way before sliding back the cover from a keypad. He managed to enter only two digits of his personal lockdown code before she grabbed him from behind. His air was cut off as she snaked an arm around his throat but he kept one hand wrapped around the door's handle and refused to be torn away. Her terrified shouts filled the room as he fought to get the remaining sequence into the pad.

Isami managed to get to them and pulled the woman off, dragging her back as the metal-against-metal grinding of the lockdown bolts filled the room. The sound prompted the woman to fight even harder and Isami finally threw her to the floor, grabbing a fallen stapler and slamming it twice into the side of her head.

Ito stared down in horror at the blood flowing from her temple but then turned away. There had been no choice. Their lives were meaningless when weighed against the devastation that would ensue if his creation escaped into the world.

Once again silence descended, broken only by the gentle drip of water and the rhythm of their breathing.

Ito walked hesitantly to a hatch in the cracked glass wall, opening it as his heart pounded painfully in his chest. He slid through, having already forgotten about the unconscious woman on the floor and the emotionless man standing over her.

The glass cube containing his experiment was supported by hydraulic shock absorbers and thick rubber pads—additional insurance against eventualities exactly like this one. They were all intact, as was the glass upon first inspection. He went around it slowly, running a bare hand carefully along its sides. His heart rate began to regulate as he moved, but then his finger hit something. It was nearly imperceptible—nothing more than a slight roughness in the meticulously ground surface. He held his breath, moving his head back and forth in the red light, praying to the Christian god he'd adopted so many years before that the imperfection was just a trick of perception.

But like so many times before, his prayers weren't answered. The crack was only a few centimeters long, and there was no way to determine with any certainty if it had fully penetrated. Not that it mattered. No chance of a loss of containment, no matter how remote, could be tolerated.

"We have a possible breach," Ito said, his voice shaking audibly as he passed back through the hatch.

It took the combined efforts of both him and his assistant to open the bent locker that held their radiation gear. They put it on without speaking. There was nothing to be said.

Ito secured his face mask and connected it to an oxygen supply as Isami went to the unconscious girl and began trying to get her limp body into a bright yellow hazmat suit similar to the ones they were wearing. The safety gear would be sufficient to keep them from being killed outright by the radiation-driven sterilization process, but that was all. They would trade a relatively quick death for a drawn-out, painful one.

Ito used the key around his neck to unlock a cage protecting a fluorescent orange lever. He put his gloved hand on it and closed his eyes. In that place, in that moment, it was impossible not to look backward and question his entire adult life. To wonder if he had spent the last forty-five years shining a light into a place that God intended to remain dark.

1

Northwestern Japan
Present Day

Lieutenant Colonel Jon Smith had parked his rental car in the trees about a mile back, negotiating the remaining descent on foot. The dirt road was steep as hell and turned slick near the bottom, but there was no other way into the remote fishing village without a boat.

Behind him the mountains had swallowed the stars, but ahead the clear sky above the Sea of Japan was dotted with tiny pricks of light. Combined with a few salt-encrusted bulbs still burning below, there was just enough illumination to make out the sloped roofs of buildings hugging the shore and the long skiffs beached in front of them. The haphazard paths among the tightly packed homes, boathouses, and processing buildings, thankfully, were inky black.

He skirted the hazy glow of a porch light and eased along the edge of a shed that smelled of fresh diesel and rotten fish. The simple rhythm of his surroundings remained unchanged: the quiet lapping of waves, a southern wind just strong enough to get hold of the occasional loose board, the nearly imperceptible hum of power lines. Beyond that, nothing.

Smith followed the dim arrow on his GPS watch toward

a narrow passageway between buildings, still wondering why he'd been chosen for this job. While his complexion and military-cut hair were relatively dark, a six-foot-tall, blue-eyed American slinking around rural Japan at 2:00 a.m. had the potential to attract more attention than would be desirable under the circumstances. And then there was the matter of his Japanese-language skills, which consisted of a few phrases incorrectly remembered from reading *Shogun* in high school.

There was just no way Covert-One didn't have access to Japanese operatives. Hell, even Randi would have been a vast improvement. A little makeup and hair dye would be good enough to make her 90 percent invisible, and while most of her operational experience had been China-based, Japan was at least somewhere in the general vicinity of her area of expertise.

No doubt Klein had his reasons—he always did. And the job itself didn't seem all that difficult. Meet a man, get a standard-sized briefcase weighing in at a manageable twelve pounds, and bring it back to Maryland on a military transport out of Okinawa.

Piece of cake, right? Hell, he'd probably have time to grab a little sushi and have his spine walked on.

The darkness deepened as he entered the narrow space between the buildings, forcing him to slow to a crawl. The GPS said he was only twenty yards from the rendezvous point, and he slid a silenced Glock from beneath his sweatshirt. Not that he thought he'd be needing it, but you never knew.

The passage came to a T and Smith poked his head around the side of a warehouse to quickly scan both directions. Nothing but darkness. He was starting to regret not bringing light amplification equipment, but as hard as it was for a six-foot, blue-eyed American to remain anonymous in this part of the world, cover those blue eyes with an elaborate set of night-vision goggles and he might as well be juggling chain saws in a top hat.

He turned right, inching along for a few seconds, unable to completely silence the sound of his boots crunching on something he swore was fish bones.

"I'm here!"

The whisper was heavily accented and barely audible. Smith froze, squinting into the darkness as a vague human outline appeared from behind a stack of wooden pallets. He resisted the urge to speed up, keeping his steps careful as he approached with his gun held loosely by his side. Even in what little starlight could filter between the buildings, he could see from the man's body language that he was scared. No point in making things worse by leading with a suppressor-tipped semiautomatic.

Unfortunately, his attempt to project as much casual calm as circumstances would allow seemed to be failing. By the time he eased alongside the man, it sounded like he was starting to hyperventilate. On the bright side, no discussion was necessary and the briefcase exchanged hands without problems—other than the fact that it was probably twice as heavy as Smith had been told. A rare error in detail by Fred Klein.

"Are you all right to get out of here on your own?" Smith said quietly.

The man nodded as a gust of wind kicked up. The old buildings around them protested, but there was something about the sound that didn't seem to follow the pattern it had before. Something out of place.

Smith grabbed the man by the front of the shirt and tried to jerk him back behind the pallets, but he panicked and resisted. A moment later there was a dull thunk followed by the man's legs collapsing.

Smith followed his injured contact to the ground and dragged him behind cover. The man was still breathing, but there was a wet sucking sound to it that Smith had heard too many times in his years as a combat doctor. A crude examination—while he was trying to watch both directions for people moving in on their position—turned up a crossbow bolt sunk to the fletching between two ribs. The man started to choke on his own blood, and Smith felt a rare moment of hesitation. The physician in him was finding it impossible to just abandon the man despite the fact that there was nothing he or anyone else could do to save him. The covert operative in him was screaming that he was being boxed in and if he didn't get out soon, he wasn't going to fare any better than the man fighting for breath on the ground in front of him.

Knowing in excruciating detail what the remaining minutes of the man's life would be like, Smith pressed his suppressor against the man's chest and fired a single round into his heart. The muffled crack of the round was followed by a now familiar thunk from the opposite direction of the first. Smith threw himself backward and slammed into the weathered boards behind him as a crossbow bolt hissed past his face.

That confirmed his fear that whoever these sons of bitches were, they were coming in from both directions. And they were good. He still hadn't heard either one, and that last shot had been threaded through a gap in the pallets.

Smith grabbed the briefcase and held it behind him as he broke cover and darted toward the unseen man who had just shot at him. Crossbows were accurate, quiet, and hit like a runaway train, but they weren't fast to reload.

A rickety staircase that ran up the side of the warehouse to his right was only a few yards away and he adjusted his trajectory toward it. Not that he had a chance in hell of getting up it, but he'd seen the outline of a single window beneath it on his way in and filed its location away in the event of a situation just like this.

The heavy briefcase hung over his shoulder was slowing him down as he tried to run, but the trade-off proved a good one when he heard a bolt slam into it from behind. With his right hand, he grabbed the support for the stairs and swung beneath them, throwing the briefcase through the window and leaping after it.

The remaining glass in the frame raked across his torso and the landing was a pile of wooden crates, but he was still breathing and a few scrapes and bruises weren't anything that would hinder him.

Smith stayed low, tripping awkwardly across the warehouse interior toward a door warped badly enough to let the starlight bleed around it. Instead of bursting through, though, he ran his hand desperately along the wall next to it. When he found what he was looking for, he went completely motionless, trying to blend into the rough-hewn boards and watching the shattered window he'd entered through. While he'd elected to leave his night-vision gear at home, he was willing to bet that the men coming after him hadn't.

When a dim human outline slipped cautiously into the empty window frame, Smith hit the lights. As expected, the man grabbed for his goggles, and at that moment Smith squeezed off a single round. Even for him it was a low-percentage shot—the sudden glare of the overhead lights, a partially obscured moving target, a heart rate running in the

160s. So he was surprised when the man's head jerked back and he sank from view. Like his dad used to be fond of saying: better to be lucky than good.

Smith shoved through the door and, as suspected, someone was waiting for him out front. Also as expected, the man had lost a good second pulling off his night-vision goggles and now had to hit a backlit opponent with a medieval weapon. Advantage lost.

Smith fired a round into his chest as he sprinted away from the warehouse and toward the water. The man went down hard but immediately started to get back to his feet. The body armor that was beneath his black sweater wasn't as effective at stopping the close-range round that Smith pumped into his face when he ran past.

Another bolt released behind him and he instinctively went into a crouch, hearing it hiss by just to his right. Too close. It was another fifteen yards to the edge of the water and the chance of him making it alive was starting to look remote.

He abruptly cut left and sprinted toward an open fishing boat pulled halfway onto the sand, diving headfirst into it. The brief illusion of safety, though, exploded in the crack of shattering wood and a powerful impact to his right shoulder blade. There was a stainless steel cooler in front of him and he crawled behind it, aware of the strength draining from his limbs. As he rolled painfully onto his side, he heard the crossbow bolt jutting from his back scrape against the bottom of the boat.

A few lights had snapped on in the buildings around the shore, and the shadows were dissipating at about the same rate as the adrenaline that was keeping him going. He could hear cautious footsteps moving toward him in the sand and he unscrewed the suppressor from his gun, firing a few blind rounds in the general direction of his attackers.

The unsilenced Glock would be enough to wake the rest of the town, but probably not in time to scare off the men who were about to kill him. The water was clearly his best chance for survival.

The briefcase was too heavy to swim with so he pressed his thumb against a hidden screen behind the handle and was surprised when the locks actually popped open. Klein had redeemed himself.

Smith wasn't sure what he was going to find, but a ziplock bag full of what looked like garbage wasn't high on his list. An odd thing to die for, he mused as he stuffed the bag into a pocket in his cargo pants and fired a few more noisy rounds over the cooler.

The pain in his back was becoming debilitating and it took him more than five seconds to slither to the back of the boat. Gritting his teeth, he grabbed hold of the outboard motor and used the leverage to throw himself over the stern.

The water was deeper than he anticipated—good for cover, bad for drowning—but the pain was so intense that he wasn't sure he'd be able to swim. Finally, he forced himself to start kicking and managed to pull with the arm that would still move. The gun dropped from his hand as he tried to parallel the surface, not sure how deep he was but hearing impacts in the water. Crossbow bolts at the very least, but probably also bullets now. Stealth had been lost and there was no reason for the men hunting him to be bashful.

He went deeper. Or at least he thought he did. His sense of direction was being swallowed by blood loss, pain, and lack of oxygen. When his head started to spin, he followed the bubbles up, breaking the surface only with his mouth as he gulped desperately at the sea air. When his mind started to clear, he brought his head far enough above the surface to look back in the direction of the beach. Three men. All wading in after him.

Smith dived again, swimming awkwardly and trying to ignore the drag from the bolt in his back as it carved into muscle and bone. He came up only when he began to feel consciousness slipping away and to make sure that he was still heading in the right direction. Unfortunately, that direction was out to sea.

He had no idea how long he'd been in the water when he finally had to admit that he couldn't go any farther. Surfacing, he rolled onto his back and bobbed helplessly in the swells. Based on the lights that were still coming to life on shore, he'd only made it about four hundred yards. The silhouettes of people coming out of their homes were easily discernible, but all he could hear was the hypnotic whisper of the water.

A quiet grunt brought Smith back to alertness and he swam away from it, using a modified sidestroke with his right arm floating uselessly below the surface. He was barely moving, though, and it was only a few seconds before a hand closed around his ankle.

Smith flipped onto his back in time to see an arm burst from the water, knife in hand. He kicked at his attacker's head, connecting solidly enough to make the man miss but not enough to do any damage. With no other option, Smith took a deep breath and grabbed the man's knife hand. Then he dragged him under.

The man started to fight, but Smith was too weak to do anything but try to control the knife. He wrapped his legs around the man's waist, their proximity and the density of the water taking the sting out of the blows he was absorbing.

The advantage Smith was counting on was that he had been floating motionless for some time while his opponent had been swimming as hard as he could in pursuit. The hope was that he'd already been in oxygen debt when they'd gone under.

His lungs started to burn, melding with the rest of the pain racking his body, and he looked in the direction he thought was up to see only blackness. Eventually, the pain started to fade and he felt an unfamiliar sense of peace taking hold of him.

The air was bubbling slowly from his mouth when he became aware that the man had stopped fighting. What did that mean again? What was he supposed to do?

Primal instinct more than anything prompted him to push the limp body away and kick. He felt himself floating gently upward toward...what?

The air flooding back into his lungs was accompanied by the return of the unbearable pain in his back and the reality of the hopelessness of his situation. The silhouetted crowd on the bank had grown, but there were still two men in the water coming toward him. Neither seemed to be as good a swimmer as their friend whom he'd sent to the bottom, though.

Smith rolled onto his side again, moving away from shore and into the darkness.

When he couldn't go on anymore, the lights from shore had disappeared—either turned off or lost in the swells. He floated on his back, feeling the crossbow bolt being tugged by the current. The pain had faded. Like everything else. Blood loss, most likely. His head felt like it was full of gauze, and he was having a hard time remembering where he was. In the ocean, but which one? Or was it a sea? What was the difference between the two again?

A sudden burst of light appeared in front of him and he

squinted into it. Not particularly bright, but startling in the complete darkness. Voices. The lapping of water against a wooden hull.

A final, weak burst of adrenaline brought him momentarily back to the present. The contents of the briefcase were still in his pocket and he had no idea what they were or of their importance. No idea what kind of threat they could pose in the wrong hands. But the fact that he'd been sent, that Klein was involved, suggested that capture wasn't an option.

He had no strength left to escape the boat or to fight the men in it. And that left him very few alternatives.

Smith exhaled, reducing his buoyancy, and felt the water close in on top of him.

One mission too many.

2

al Qababt
Egypt

The street market was packed with people, jostling, laughing, and haggling for everything from rugs to Tupperware to stuffed animals. It was late morning and the heat of the day was already descending, mixing the stench of sweat with the aroma of spices and cooking meat to create an atmosphere that felt oddly comfortable to Randi Russell.

It was ironic that Muslim countries had become the easiest environments for her to operate in. Covered head to toe in a hijab, surrounded by the constant roar of Middle Eastern life, she could move around with almost ghostlike anonymity. For all the chauvinistic morons looking right through her knew, she could have a rocket launcher strapped to her back. But why would they worry? What could they possibly have to fear from a woman?

"Okay, Randi. He's right in front of you. No more than four or five yards."

She acknowledged the voice in her earpiece with a short nod, though she wasn't sure it would be visible from her teammates' position in a multistory hotel to the east.

She felt sweat break across her forehead, but it wasn't from the sun beating on her black headgear. It was a mouth-drying, heart-pounding sense of childlike excitement. Four or five yards. She'd started to doubt whether she'd ever get this close.

Charles Hashem had grown into a top al-Qaeda operative whose evil was matched only by his infuriating competence. It had taken the CIA two years even to place him in Egypt and her another five grueling months to find her way to this particular market on this particular morning.

"Got him."

His gray shirt, sunglasses, and average-length black hair didn't provide much to differentiate him from any other man in the street, but she'd had every existing photo of him stuck to her wall for the last year and a half. Oddly similar to her bedroom as an early teenager except that fantasies of being whisked away by Luke Perry on horseback had been replaced with dreams of ending the life of the man hurrying toward a narrow souq in front of her.

It was a shame she didn't actually have that rocket launcher. Seeing his burning body parts cartwheeling down the cobblestones would have been one of the happiest moments of her life. And she had her camera phone with her. Best CIA Christmas card photo ever.

"Can we get him to a viable extraction point?" the voice in her ear said. An unwelcome reminder that her mission was significantly different from her fantasy.

"Are you kidding?" Randi mumbled, counting on her throat mike to pick it up. "Look around me. Eight hundred people would see us toss him in the van and then where would we go? Traffic's moving slower than I am."

She lost sight of him and panicked for a moment, pushing ineffectually through the unbroken mass of people ahead. She was stronger and faster than most men, but her 125 pounds just didn't provide sufficient inertia to penetrate.

A man whose coffee she jostled looked down at the stain on his shirt and grabbed her arm. A moment later he found himself falling backward over an enormous bag of pistachios with that hot coffee now in his face. She slipped away in the commotion, knowing that no one would ever think a woman could have done such a thing to a big strong Muslim man.

"Damn it! Where is he, Bill? Talk to me!"

"Don't get your panties bunched up, Randi. He went under the awnings to your left while you were screwing around with that guy at the nut stand. We're temporarily blind, so get your ass in there. If we lose him after getting this close, *we're going* to be the ones getting water boarded."

Again she felt the panic rising in her. Hashem was not only brilliant at staying out of America's crosshairs, he had a master's in biology from Stanford, where he'd graduated with a 3.95 average. Losing him was not an option.

A familiar profile flashed into view behind a pile of colorful scarves and she had her target again. "I see him. Moving in."

"To do what?" The wariness was audible in Bill's voice amid the static. "Like you said, we have no shot at an extraction here. You're just going to have to stay with him until we get to a workable location."

Despite the fact that there were numerous women on the street who were utterly indistinguishable from her, Hashem was eventually going to figure out that he was being followed. And when he did, his six-foot, two-hundred-pound frame was going to cut through the crowd at a speed she simply couldn't match.

"Come on, Bill. You know as well—"

Randi fell silent when a powerful hand clamped onto her arm and spun her violently around. She went reflexively for a knife hidden beneath her hijab, but then recognized the coffee-stained shirt and burned cheeks. Pistachio man.

Normally she'd have used her considerable language skills and a little groveling to quietly extricate herself from the situation, but today she just didn't have time to screw around.

In a smooth motion not quite fast enough to look unnatural, she grabbed one of the fingers wrapped around her upper arm and broke it. The man howled in pain and dropped to one knee, cradling his mangled digit.

"Someone help!" Randi shouted in Arabic. "I think he's having a heart attack!"

People surged in, once again ignoring her and allowing her to back away.

"Where is he?" Randi said when she broke free. Ahead of her the souq split. "Which way?"

The fact that there was no immediate reply was understandable. An assassination had specifically not been authorized, for two reasons. The first was hard to argue with: an opportunity for an extended interrogation would likely turn up all kinds of interesting information. The second, though, was more bureaucratic. Charles Hashem was an American citizen.

And not just some disaffected naturalized immigrant. He'd been born in Cleveland to a nice Persian couple who were grateful as hell to America for giving them the opportunity to escape Iran. In fact they were the ones who had originally tipped off the government about their son's increasingly radical political and religious leanings.

The next words she heard were muffled, as though Bill was talking to his partner. "No, no. About an hour from now."

Randi smiled. An hour from now would be 11:00 a.m. Hashem was at her eleven o'clock.

She weaved gracefully, using skill to make up for her lack of heft, until she was right behind him. In place of the RPG she was sadly lacking, she retrieved a pen from her pocket and clicked the top, making sure to keep it pointed away from the innocent people jostling by.

Hashem jerked at the sudden sting in his lower back but by the time he looked back, Randi had put two people between them and was heading for a stand lined with barrels of olives.

The pain would subside in a few seconds and the tiny red mark in a few minutes. The microscopic pellet, though, would be slowly dissolving in his bloodstream. When it finally broke down it would release a poison that would cause what she had been assured was an extremely unpleasant death.

Word was that the whole thing was based on some kind of ocean-dwelling predatory snail. What would those guys at Langley think of next?

3

Northeastern Japan

White.

The color of heaven, right?

If so, Jon Smith could come to only two possible conclusions: either he was still alive or God had made a serious clerical error.

His vision came into focus slowly, but it didn't take him long to realize that the second hypothesis was correct. No angelic choirs. Just a ceiling.

Smith tried to sit up but the throb in his back became an excruciating dagger, forcing him to ease back onto the mattress. His torso seemed to move more or less the way it was supposed to, and after a quick evaluation he confirmed that his fingers and toes did the same. No paralysis. He carefully rotated his head through the few degrees it would move, taking in his surroundings and trying to get a read on his injuries from the nature and severity of the pain.

His new home wasn't a hospital room. Too nice. Gracefully curved and scrupulously finished wood beams framed a modern take on Japanese paper screens, the expensive contemporary furniture was tastefully sparse, and the artwork was bright and incomprehensible. There were no windows to tell him if it was day or night and little sound but the humming of the machines to his left.

He squinted at the monitor next to his bed and noted the heart rate and blood pressure numbers. Neither was great, but neither suggested he was flirting with death.

Smith closed his eyes for a moment and then tried to take a deep breath, hardly getting any air in at all before the pain forced him to stop. So he could add a few shattered ribs and possibly a broken scapula to the crossbow-bolt-size puncture wound in his back.

As his mind continued to sharpen, he examined the IV running into his arm and tried unsuccessfully to read the label on the bag. Antibiotics, fluids, and probably an opiate-based painkiller judging from the familiar nausea he was feeling. More concerning was the tube inserted between his ribs and draining into a jar on the floor. Collapsed lung. Outstanding.

He reached weakly for a stethoscope hanging from the IV stand and put it in his ears. Steeling himself for the pain, he forced himself to take a moderate breath with the instrument pressed to his side. It sounded like the lung was inflating. Not exactly news worth celebrating, but better than the alternative.

He'd given up his job as a MASH doctor in favor of microbiology a long time ago, but they weren't skills that faded easily Given the facts, his prognosis was solid. With a lot of time, a lot of rest, and proper care, he could potentially make a full recovery. The fact that he wasn't in a hospital, though, made him doubt he'd ever get those things.

There was a rustling on the other side of the only door to the room and Smith watched it slide open. He considered feigning unconsciousness, but it seemed likely that he was being monitored by video and that his mysterious benefactor wouldn't be so easily fooled. Besides, what was the point? Daring escapes were pretty much off the table—he'd be lucky to crawl out of there in his condition. Better to figure out where he stood than to lie there and wonder.

The Japanese man who entered was in his midforties with a compact frame, intermittent gray hair, and a waistline barely being held in check. His suit and haircut were both extremely expensive but neither looked natural on him. Even through a morphine fog, Smith could see that this guy hadn't been a beneficiary of the prep school and private university upbringing he was trying to project. More likely, he'd risen to the top the old-fashioned way: by killing his competitors.

"Who are you?" Smith said. His voice came out little more than a croak and the man picked up a cup, holding it while Smith sucked on the straw.

"I was going to ask you the same thing."

His English was better than expected. Maybe he'd actually outsmarted a few of those competitors after all.

Smith eased himself back into the pillows, letting the pain play out on his face to provide an excuse not to volunteer information.

"You're very interesting to me," the man said, also declining to contribute an introduction. "My doctor says it would be virtually impossible for someone with a crossbow bolt in his back to swim as far out into the ocean as you did. And yet there you were."

"High school breaststroke champion," Smith managed to get out and then let out a weak cough. The pain that action unleashed would have been truly breathtaking if he could actually breathe.

"Indeed."

Smith pointed to the cup and the man examined him for a moment before holding it up so he could get another drink. Likely less an act of kindness than an effort to get his guest's voice working again.

"Even more fascinating to me were the men chasing you. They were quite motivated. Not a single one of them gave up the search until he drowned."

Smith tried to get his hazy mind to focus. Could that be true? And if this man was making these kinds of observations, did it suggest that he wasn't involved in the attack? The fancy house, the men floating off remote beaches in quiet boats. Some kind of smuggler? A simple drug runner?

"You'll understand that I like to keep abreast of things that happen in my waters."

Smith knew that he wasn't in any condition to play cat and mouse with this man and was getting ready to fake losing consciousness, but it was a piece of theater that turned out to be unnecessary. His vision began to swim and his eyes fluttered uncontrollably. There was no reason to fight it so he just let the darkness come.

When the man spoke again, his voice sounded a thousand miles away. "Of course. You rest. We have all the time in the world to talk."

4

R andi Russell ran her fingers through her short hair, moving closer to the showerhead and watching the black dye swirl down the drain. The fake tanner darkening the skin visible from beneath her hijab would just have to wear off on its own.

When the water turned clear, she shut off the faucet and stepped out onto the tile floor. The mirror was fogged, displaying only a hazy image of her thin, toned body and dark eyes beneath a shock of blonde hair. Her athletic beauty had always been an asset—opening doors, keeping men off balance, causing people to dismiss her as a piece of arm candy.

The last few years had been a solid run, gaining her the gratitude of multiple heads of state and generating a serious legend at the CIA, MI6, and a few other acronyms. The problem was that the dead enemies and friends, the blur of missions, and the constant moving were starting to get a little depressing. It was something she once again promised herself that she'd work on when she got back to the States. And with Charles Hashem finally rotting in hell, maybe she'd actually do it this time.

She pulled on a pair of old sweats and a T-shirt with a giant smiley face and the slogan "Have a Nice Day." A gift from a Mossad operative with a sense of humor.

All she needed now was a drink, a comfortable bed, and ten solid hours of unconsciousness. Tomorrow she'd mix in with the tourists and businesspeople for a midmorning flight to Reagan and then a hysterical reaming for killing an American who everyone agreed needed to be dead. In the end, though, it would be little more than a bunch of bureaucratic ass covering. Nothing she needed to worry about any more than last time or the time before that.

Sure, one day they'd throw her under the bus, but not yet. They'd wait until she slowed down and wasn't as useful anymore. For now, though, she had the comfort of knowing they needed her to do the things that they didn't have the skills for, or that they thought could come back to bite them at a confirmation hearing. People with her talents and track record were hard to replace.

Randi rubbed the towel over her head a few more times and then pushed through the bathroom door into her hotel suite.

One of the things that had kept her alive for so long was the fact that there was no loss in translation between what her mind commanded and what her body did. By the time the man sitting in the leather chair next to the bar looked up, she'd pulled a knife from the pocket in her sweats and drawn her hand back to throw it.

He just frowned disapprovingly and looked at her over his wire-rimmed glasses.

"Mr. Klein," Randi said, not yet lowering the knife. "What are you doing here?"

Fred Klein was the mastermind behind a loose confederation of independent operators that went by the intentionally vague designation Covert-One. The president of the United States—a childhood friend of Klein's—had quietly authorized the formation of the organization years ago in the face of the government's increasing paralysis. Covert-One had become an organization of last resort, brought into play only when time had run out and the consequences of failure were too dire to contemplate.

Randi had been recruited only recently based on the recommendation of Jon Smith, but she still didn't have a strong sense of what she'd gotten herself into. What she did know, though, was that when Fred Klein showed up unexpectedly in your hotel room, something hadn't gone to plan. And that brought her own survival into question.

"I needed to talk to you," Klein responded simply.

"That's why they invented phones." She moved subtly away from the windows. The curtains were drawn, but there were other ways for a sniper to line up a shot.

Klein wasn't particularly impressive to look at. Thinning hair, mediocre suit, slightly jutting brow. But in the short time she'd known him, she'd developed a healthy respect for the man. He had a disconcerting way of thinking ten steps ahead and rarely made mistakes. Great if he was on your team, but in her business team affiliation tended to be hazy and subject to sudden changes.

"This is something I felt we should discuss face-to-face." He wiped away some imaginary sweat from his upper lip. "We've lost contact with Jon."

"Lost contact?"

"In a fishing village northeast of Toyama, Japan."

"I know that area," she said, finally lowering the knife. "I'll go find him."

Klein rose suddenly enough that her grip on the blade tightened involuntarily, but he just went to the bar and poured two scotches. After handing one to her, he returned to the chair.

"He was hit in the back with a crossbow bolt and was last seen swimming out to sea with at least three men pursuing. I've had people out there for two days looking for him and we're continuing the effort..." His voice trailed off.

The implication was clear. She made her way a bit unsteadily to a small sofa across from him.

"I wanted to tell you before you heard somewhere else," he said as she sat. "The story we're going with is that he was cave diving off the coast of Okinawa. That there was an accident and he's missing."

Typically clever, Randi thought numbly. No one would expect to recover a body under those circumstances.

"My understanding is that your mission in Egypt is finished and you're flying back to DC tomorrow." He seemed a bit bowed when he stood again and started for the door. "We need to talk when you get back. About what Jon was working on."

She watched him leave in silence and then just stared at the closed door. For a moment she thought she was going to throw up but then it passed, replaced by an unexpected sense of loneliness that was even worse.

No. Jon had been in tough scrapes before and he always made it out. Klein's people just hadn't found him yet. Or for that matter, the man could be lying. What did she really know about him?

Randi forced herself to her feet and picked up the phone on the nightstand. Scrolling through an encrypted list of contacts with a shaking finger, she finally came to the one she was looking for—an unattributed number with a Japanese prefix.

5

Being chosen as XO of Japan's new state-of-the-art battleship had been the proudest moment in a life that Gaku Akiyama had always considered charmed. He'd been an exceptional athlete, earned a master's in history from Oxford, and then joined Japan's naval defense forces as his father had before him. His efforts to honor his family for everything they'd done for him had succeeded beyond his wildest dreams.

Like so many dreams, though, this one had finally revealed its dark side.

He was standing at the edge of the deck watching the setting sun backlight a Chinese missile cruiser sailing at an intentionally provocative and impossibly dangerous half-kilometer distance. Beyond were the deep-orange silhouettes of eight more Chinese warships showcasing that country's resolve and the superiority of its arsenal. Finally, at the very edge of his vision were the jagged outlines of a group of useless rocks known to the Japanese as the Senkaku Islands and to the Chinese as the Diaoyus.

Akiyama looked behind him at the men going about their duties, at the helicopters lined up on the deck awaiting orders, and at the 250-meter flat deck that had caused so much anger on the part of China.

Despite considering himself a great patriot—perhaps even a nationalist—he found himself in the rare and uncomfortable position of sympathizing with his opponent's position on this topic. Retrofitting the *Izumo* to launch offensive weapons would be a relatively trivial task that could be carried out in a matter of months.

On the other hand, his own country's leadership was correct when it pointed out that there would be no point to such an operation. While it was true that Japan had overwhelmed China in World War II, those days were long past. Their increasingly belligerent neighbor to the west now had a standing army of over two million men, a budget three times that of Japan, and a navy boasting more than seven hundred vessels. In fact, credible rumors were circulating that the Chinese were sending their new aircraft carrier into the area in an effort to humiliate the Japanese further by physically dwarfing the crown jewel of their fleet.

And for what? A few rocks sticking out of the ocean? Some oil beneath the ocean floor? Fishing rights?

No, in truth none of those things really mattered. This dispute was entirely about the past: The atrocities perpetrated by his own grandfathers on the Chinese people so many decades ago. The humiliation felt by the Japanese people at their eventual surrender. The newfound conviction of his own generation that they should not be damned to a life of penitence for things that occurred years before they were even born.

The Americans felt understandably justified at having fashioned the Japanese constitution in a way that forbade military force and limited the country to defensive troops. His ancestors had been a warlike and often even brutal people. But that world existed now only in the books he'd studied in school. Japan had become an incredibly wealthy country built on a fragile foundation of stability and economic cooperation. It had become one of humanity's great innovators and a responsible world citizen that spent billions aiding its less fortunate neighbors.

Despite this transformation, though, the threats from China and the Koreas were real and growing. Could the United States be trusted to protect them in the current world order? And even more important, should this even be America's responsibility any longer? In Akiyama's mind, the answer was a resounding no. It was time for Japan to stand on its own feet.

This was, however, a seismic shift that would have to be handled with the utmost political skill and cultural sensitivity. The events unfolding around him were anything but the careful first steps that he'd imagined. No, this was a senseless escalation engineered by politicians concerned only with retaining their power. It had played out in history so many times but no one ever learned. Once the nationalist flame rose to a certain height, it could only be quenched with blood.

The breeze picked up and Akiyama raised the collar on his jacket, continuing to watch the sun sink into the ocean to the west. He was about to head belowdecks when the deceptive peace was broken by a high-pitched wail. The executive officer spun and saw the men on deck behind him freeze for a split second and then begin sprinting in every direction.

"Battle stations!" Akiyama shouted, dodging the men rushing by. "Battle stations!"

Over his headset he could hear a nearly unintelligible

patchwork of voices. For the moment he ignored the calm drone of the captain's orders and instead focused on the more panicked voice of a junior officer stating the reason for the alarm. A Chinese *Luzhou*-class guided missile destroyer had locked on their targeting radar.

Akiyama started to run the length of the deck, checking his men's positions, offering words of encouragement, and shouting harsh criticisms when warranted. Above all, though, he did everything in his power to encourage calm.

"No one lifts a finger without direct orders!" he yelled repeatedly. "Is that clear? I don't care what the circumstances are. No one acts without specific instructions from an officer!"

He clamped a hand on the shoulder of a terrified-looking boy who couldn't have been more than nineteen. "You're going to be all right. Do you understand? You've trained for this and you wouldn't be on the *Izumo* if you weren't one of Japan's finest."

The boy nodded weakly and Akiyama continued on. He felt a great sense of pride at the efficiency and speed with which his men were carrying out their duties, but much more than that he felt fear. The irony of a peaceful Asia was that neither player in this conflict had access to battle-hardened troops. The best he could do was stagger the younger sailors with those who had years in the defense forces. That meant very little, though, if those older men had never been in a combat situation.

There was simply no way to turn away from the fact that there were hundreds of terrified young people precariously balanced on opposite sides of a razor blade.

6

Good to see you, Mr. Klein," the head of the president's protection detail said.

"Dave," Klein said, returning the greeting.

He'd known David McClellan since the man had joined the Secret Service almost twenty years ago, and there was no more tight-lipped operative in the entire government. The perfect man for the job.

President Sam Adams Castilla was alone—it was nearly midnight and his wife, Cassie, would have gone to bed hours ago. He didn't rise, instead watching his old friend approach with a cold Coors in his hand.

In the past, they'd been more open about their meetings, casting themselves as two childhood friends getting together to talk about old times. Lately, though, Klein had become concerned that the intelligence background that had made him an ideal choice to head Covert-One would raise suspicion. Now he flew as far beneath the radar as possible.

Castilla took a sip of his beer before speaking. "It hasn't hit the papers yet but yesterday a Chinese missile cruiser targeted

Japan's new battleship with attack radar."

"The Senkakus, I assume?"

The president nodded. "I've already got Russia, North Korea, the economy, and the entire Middle East to deal with. Now this."

"It's a lot of ships and a lot of bad blood in a very small area."

"It's World War Three in the making is what it is," Castilla said, his voice rising in volume.

Klein pointed to the door behind which Castilla's wife was sleeping, and the president lowered his voice. "It's a lot worse than most people know. Look, I like Prime Minister Sanetomi and I'm sympathetic to the fact that what happened during the war is ancient history. But it frankly doesn't matter what I think. It matters what the *Chinese* think. And to those assholes, the Rape of Nanking might as well have been last Tuesday."

It was yet another of those impossibly complicated problems, this time made worse by both countries handling it in the most destructive way possible. Nationalism was on the rise in Asia, and every day it seemed to grow in pitch. Politicians who until recently had been calling for calm were now seeing the writing on the wall and allowing themselves to be swept up in the fervor. The question was, where would it end?

"Did you know that almost half of Chinese television shows revolve around the killing of enormous numbers of Japanese?" Castilla asked.

"No, I didn't know that."

"Seven hundred million people just last season, Fred. That's what? Six times the population of the whole country? I think the CIA told me it pencils out to twenty-two Japanese people per second, twenty-four hours a day, three hundred and sixty-five days a year. You take that kind of hate, add a faltering economy, an oversize military-industrial complex, and some rocks sticking out of the ocean, and you've written the recipe for disaster."

"What did Takahashi do?"

Masao Takahashi was the chief of staff in command of Japan's defense forces. A brilliant military man but not exactly a dove.

"About the television shows? I doubt he watches them."

Klein frowned. "I was referring to the attack radar, Sam."

"To his credit, nothing. The *Izumo* went to battle stations and then backed the hell away."

"He defused the situation, then? I'm honestly surprised. Maybe he's getting a little perspective in his old age."

"Yeah. Just enough perspective that now I have to worry that the son of a bitch is thinking about getting into politics. You know he's one of the richest men in Japan, right?"

Klein nodded. "Technology, energy, defense contracting, gaming, and I don't even know what else. His family's built quite an empire since the war."

"And make no mistake, he's the patriarch. People will tell you that his siblings run the companies, but take it from me, they don't take a piss without asking Masao first."

Klein leaned back and looked at his old friend thoughtfully. The United States was not a country accustomed to being caught up in the current, but this might be one of those rare occasions. Tensions between Japan and China went back to well before America was even a twinkle in Thomas Jefferson's eye.

"So now we've got two of the world's largest economies staring at each other over the brink," Castilla continued. "China's got the second-largest military in the world, including nukes. Japan technically doesn't have an army but has the fifth-largest defense budget on the planet and a quarter million active-duty soldiers."

The Japanese constitution prevented the country from building a military or projecting power by force, but that clause had always been open to interpretation and now was coming under increasing criticism. In reality, Japan was one constitutional convention away from tossing three-quarters of a century of codified pacifism into the dustbin of history—something China would not take sitting down.

Castilla waved his beer can a little frantically. "And do you know who's right in the middle of this shit storm? Me. Because we have a treaty saying in no uncertain terms that the United States will protect Japan if it's ever attacked. If the Chinese decide they don't like the direction the political winds are blowing in Japan—even though they're partially to blame— what then? Do they sink that fancy new battleship? Mark my words, Fred, I'm in the process of getting painted into a very tight corner."

The strength seemed to go out of him and he fell back into the cushions. He didn't speak again for almost a minute. "Still no word on Jon?"

Klein hadn't been prepared for the sudden change in subject and he didn't immediately respond. Thoughts of Smith continued to tie knots in his stomach. Klein was responsible for sending him to Japan and now he found himself second-guessing that decision. Smith had been his best man, but he'd had no real experience operating in that theater. Had Klein made an error sending him there? Was Jon Smith's disappearance his fault?

"Nothing yet."

"I'm sorry."

Castilla stared down at the can in his hand, but he was clearly just waiting for the right moment to speak again. The president of the United States didn't have the luxury of dwelling on the fate of a single man. Even one like Jon Smith.

"Where does this leave your investigation into the Fukushima nuclear disaster, Fred?"

"It's been a serious setback," Klein admitted. "Our informant's dead and the evidence he brought out of Reactor Four is missing along with Jon. After more than two years, I'm afraid we're back to square one."

7

"Ow are you doing?"

Maggie Templeton stood from behind her impressive bank of computer monitors, concern deepening the lines etched into her face by time.

"Good. Why wouldn't I be?" Randi said, continuing toward an open door at the back of the spacious outer office.

Fred Klein also stood when she entered—a reflex bred into him at a time when formality and manners still mattered.

"How are you?"

"Fine. I'm fine, okay?"

Randi fell into a chair and examined the man. He looked like he always did—like he had in Cairo. Nondescript at first glance but upon closer inspection hiding something behind those wire-rimmed glasses. Cunning. Enough that it made Randi feel like she wasn't in control of her own life—an unfamiliar sensation that she despised. Of course, Smith would have reminded her that Klein had never used his considerable power or intellect to do anything but stand behind her. Then again, the last time he'd been heard from, he'd been swimming out to sea with an arrow in his back.

"So why am I here, Mr. Klein?"

He settled back behind his government-surplus desk. "What do you know about Fukushima?"

"The nuclear disaster? Just what I saw on TV like everyone else. Earthquake, waves, explosions, radiation. Not really my area of expertise."

He pulled out a pipe and went through his normal OCD ritual lighting it while the elaborate ventilation system that Maggie had installed started up.

"The plant had six reactors. One through Three were active, Five and Six were in cold shutdown for maintenance, and Four had been defueled. After the earthquake, One, Two, and Three went into automatic shutdown mode. Emergency generators came on to run the cooling system."

"Then the wave hit."

He nodded. "Forty feet high. It came over the seawall and knocked out the diesel generators. When the battery backups ran down, things got hot and the explosions started..."

"Causing the radiation leaks," she said, completing his thought. "That was years ago, Mr. Klein. What's it to Covert-One?"

"Some things have come to light about the disaster that don't completely make sense."

Randi shrugged. "That's not terribly surprising. Whenever a screwup that big happens the only people working harder than the disaster relief teams are the corporate hacks and politicians covering their asses. They'd probably have had enough power to cool the thing down if it weren't for all the paper shredders firing up in Tokyo."

"A fair assessment, but it goes beyond that," Klein said. "The highest levels of radiation were measured in Reactor Four."

Randi pondered that for a moment. "Didn't you say that had been defueled?"

"I did."

"I'm no nuclear engineer but defueled sounds safe."

"It should have been. And setting aside the radiation levels for a moment, why, four days after the tsunami, was there an explosion in that reactor?"

She shrugged again. "Jon's the scientist. But someone must have an explanation."

"Oh, there are a number of them. Not one is even remotely plausible, though."

"And that's what Jon was working on?"

Klein took a long pull on his pipe. "I managed to make contact with a man who had smuggled out some suspicious samples right after the tsunami. He was passing them on to Jon when   when things went wrong."

"I assume you misplaced the samples, too?"

He didn't answer immediately, but her phrasing was clearly not lost on him. "The samples are gone."

"I guess I don't understand what we're trying to get at here. Are you saying that the Japanese nuclear contractors might have cut corners and built an unsafe reactor? Or are you—"

"The man I was in contact with suspected some kind of sabotage," Klein interjected. "And he was scared. He wouldn't talk about it on the phone or even via encrypted e-mail. He suddenly decided he wanted to be rid of that sample and told me if I didn't get someone over there in twenty-four hours, he was going to destroy it and disappear."

"So that's what got Jon sent to a remote fishing village in Japan."

"There was no time to bring someone up to speed. Jon was my top operative so I sent him."

Touché, Randi thought, keeping her face impassive. While she was closer to Smith than she was to anyone else in the world, she was also competitive. That was Klein's subtle way of telling her that he thought Smith was better.

"Okay, sabotage," she said. "Nuclear reactors are pretty well secured and pretty sturdy. Attacking them isn't easy to do. Who? An antinuke group?"

"Maybe, but I'm more concerned about the possibility of foreign actors."

"China."

Klein took another pull on his pipe. "You know better than I do how the Chinese feel about Japan, and the situation in the East China Sea is headed nowhere good. The president is putting pressure on the Japanese prime minister to calm things down but, frankly, it's easier said than done."

"That's an understatement," Randi said. "Sanetomi is the Zen master of politicians, but the position he's in is impossible. If he goes far enough to appease the Chinese, his own people are going to see him as selling them down the river. And if he stands his ground firmly enough to keep his job, the Chinese are going to start polishing up their ICBMs. The Buddha himself would fall off the tightrope he's stuck on."

"And then there's General Takahashi," Klein said. "While he's being typically clever about it, he seems to be going out of his way to provoke China."

"Okay, but why a nuclear plant? And why years ago before things got really hot between them? Are they concerned that the Japanese might be using Fukushima to create a nuclear arsenal?"

"We have assurances from Sanetomi that they're not, and the intelligence community seems satisfied by that."

"So maybe the Chinese were just trying to create an incident? Make the Japanese lose face and give them something internal to focus on. Or do you think they actually could have been trying to soften them up for an attack?"

"An outright attack on Japan would be a serious enterprise. It would drag in the US and the rest of the world from the first salvo."

Randi tapped her fingers absently on the arm of her chair. "Leads?"

"Like I told you, the man I was in contact with in Japan is dead, the samples are gone, and there's nothing but silence coming out of China. But I know you're well connected there."

Before turning her focus to the Middle East, she'd operated a great deal in China and spoke fluent Mandarin. "Okay. Let me nose around a little bit."

"You have an idea?"

She stood and started for the door. "I just might."

8

Near Imizu
Japan

Jon Smith took as deep a breath as he could, gritting his teeth as he pushed himself into a sitting position. He closed his eyes for a moment to let the pain subside, then opened them again in order to examine the shackle anchoring his ankle to the bed.

He'd have actually laughed if he didn't know how excruciating it would be. Of all the desperate situations he'd extricated himself from over his career, this was almost insulting. The strap was fashioned from a simple strip of leather, and the flimsy padlock securing it looked like it came off a piece of tourist luggage.

He eased himself back into the pillows to assess his situation one more time. According to the machine he was attached to, his vitals had stabilized. Generally good news. The chest tube was gone and the hole between his ribs had been closed with a few neat sutures. Even better. On the downside, though, the pain in his back was as bad as ever and now he had confirmation as to why.

The doctor caring for him didn't speak much English—probably by design—but with some universal medical jargon and a couple of X-ray films, Smith had been able to put together a mental list of what had happened to him: five broken ribs, two of which were smashed beyond recognition, a precariously reinflated lung, massive initial blood loss, a near-fatal case of hypothermia, a scapula held together with a couple of screws, and a sutured hole where the crossbow bolt had been extracted. Actually, *extracted* sounded better than the pantomime the doctor had used to describe the procedure. Two hands on the shaft and a foot in the small of his back. In the man's defense, though, combat medicine sometimes rewarded those willing to just dive right in.

So he was technically on the mend, but not so much that the chintzy ankle restraint didn't look both a mile away and a little like Fort Knox. He scanned the medical cart next to him, but there was nothing sharp enough to cut with or small enough to turn into a pick. And even if there had been, what then? The only escape he could realistically envision involved him shuffling along, dragging an IV cart behind him. Any obstacle more formidable than an unarmed Girl Scout or, God forbid, a set of stairs would be completely insurmountable.

He reached out and carefully retrieved the cup next to his bed, sucking thoughtfully on the straw. No matter how many angles he examined the problem from, he always came to the same conclusion: he was completely, irretrievably screwed. Whoever the man was who had locked him to this bed and called in the medical team hadn't done it out of the goodness of his heart. He wanted answers and he'd do whatever was necessary to get them.

There was a creak outside that Smith had determined was a loose floorboard ten feet or so down the hallway. He counted to three and right on cue the sound of a key turning in the door disturbed the monotonous beeping of the machine monitoring his heart. Another one-count and it began to swing open.

The unusually tall Asian woman who entered had an athletic grace that in another place and time he would have stopped to admire. A simple brown dress clung loosely to her curves, and a broad-brimmed hat completely shadowed her face. She set a small satchel on the medical cart but didn't immediately come any closer.

Smith tried to tell himself she was a nurse, but she had a predatory way of moving that suggested something very different. This wasn't a woman who cared for the sick and helpless. This was a woman who extracted information from the sick and helpless.

He looked away, staring up at the perfect white of the ceiling. He'd never been interrogated by a woman before and that worried him. Since he'd regained consciousness, he'd been preparing himself for a clumsy Japanese guy with a lot of tattoos and a rubber hose. In the shape he was in, he figured he wouldn't have to hold out long. Death would quickly intervene on his behalf.

This woman was almost certainly a very different animal. She'd be aware of his injuries, inflicting pain carefully and only when necessary. She'd confuse him, drug him, try to make him psychologically dependent on her. And she'd keep him alive for as long as it took.

Smith started going over the story he'd concocted, trying to imprint it into his mind with enough force to make it real. He was a drug addict. An American military doctor from the base in Okinawa who had written one too many bogus prescriptions for himself and had the army's investigators breathing down his neck. He'd been trying to find another supplier when the man he'd been there to meet was killed. Smith was just in the wrong place at the wrong time—an innocent bystander in a war between his new dealer and the Japanese mafia.

The woman moved soundlessly to the foot of his bed and looked down at him. Her face was still shadowed by the hat, so he looked for hints in her body language about what was to come. Even in his situation, it was hard to ignore the perfection of her outline beneath the utilitarian dress. With a little luck she'd start by trying to use her beauty to play his emotions.

When she lifted her hand and he saw the matte-black blade, though, it was clear that Lady Luck had once again turned her back on him.

9

Yasukuni Shrine
Tokyo
Japan

General Masao Takahashi looked up from the classified documents he was reviewing when his limousine began to slow. Outside, the street was filled with demonstrators numerous enough to force his driver to come almost to a stop in order to pick his way through. To the right, the crowd was dominated by older men carrying the Rising Sun flag, some in deteriorating Imperial Japanese uniforms. Takahashi nodded respectfully toward them, though he knew he was invisible behind the tinted windows. Patriots who still remembered the meaning of courage and service.

Their opposition, fittingly on his left, consisted mostly of college-age representatives of an entitled and self-absorbed generation who had never experienced the slightest hardship. Despite that, all they did was complain about an economy that allowed them to live at a standard he could have never even imagined as a child. Not a single one of these cowards would have survived a week of his youth. The hunger. The cold. The fear and confusion of being a defeated people in a country under occupation.

His driver glided to a stop and Takahashi looked away from

the protesters in disgust. Their obscene placards dishonored the men who had fought and died for the country that they now believed owed them so much.

He ignored the chants penetrating his vehicle and looked out over the well-tended grounds of Yasukuni. The leaves had taken on a reddish-gold color, contrasting the unbroken blue sky. The shrine lay just beyond, adding the deep-green sweep of its traditional roof and the graceful white of the banner guarding the entrance. It had originally been built by Emperor Meiji in 1869, and it now honored the almost 2.5 million men who had served and died for Japan.

He wasn't surprised when his phone rang, nor that the screen identified the caller as Prime Minister Fumio Sanetomi. He considered ignoring it, but his plans were advancing at a pace that was already at the edge of control. Keeping the country's politicians complacent was desirable, though not absolutely critical to carrying out those plans. Sanetomi and his hangers-on continued to wrap themselves in the illusion that they were relevant, and for now that was convenient. Soon, though, the politicians would be revealed for what they were: weak and honorless men who had spent three-quarters of a century slowly bleeding their own people.

"Good afternoon, Prime Minister," Takahashi said, putting the phone to his ear.

"And to you, General. It's my understanding that you're at Yasukuni."

"You're well informed, as it seems is everyone else. It was my hope to make this a reflective, private affair."

"I'm certain it was," Sanetomi replied. His voice was typically even, reverberating with a solemnity that the electorate found hypnotic but Takahashi found insufferable.

"Unfortunately, anonymity is difficult for a man of your stature and accomplishments," the prime minister continued. "Because of this I must ask you to remain in your car and order your driver to turn around immediately."

Takahashi's jaw tightened at the smooth attempt to manipulate him with flattery. Prior to his career as a politician, Sanetomi had been a schoolteacher, and what he'd learned handling children had proved extremely useful in dealing with the sheep he surrounded himself with. But the general wasn't one of them. He had been defending Japan since Sanetomi was crying at his mother's breast.

"General? Are you still there?"

Takahashi let his silence draw out. In recent years the shrine had become one of many flashpoints in Japan's declining relationship with China. The Chinese, instead of wielding their growing power and wealth to break free of the past, had decided to use it to reopen old wounds and humiliate their smaller neighbor to the east.

The shrine housed men who had been judged war criminals for their service to the emperor during World War II—a judgment that he found not only a disgrace, but personally offensive. The quote "History is written by the victors" had been widely attributed to Winston Churchill, and it seemed fitting in this case. While Japanese soldiers who had killed in the throes of war were labeled monsters, the Americans were held up as heroes for using nuclear weapons against Japanese civilians and the Chinese continued to worship the butcher Mao.

Even the textbooks used in Japanese schools had been rewritten to reflect the perpetual guilt of Takahashi's people and to heap that shame on children who had nothing to do with the events of the past. Still, it wasn't enough for a rising China. They were putting political pressure on Sanetomi's government to rewrite the books again—to eradicate any allusion to who the Japanese people were and how a tiny island had become feared by the entire world.

"I'm sorry, Mr. Prime Minister, but you must understand that if I were to turn around now, it would be seen as a dismissal of the sacrifice made by the men honored in this place. I—"

"General, please," Sanetomi interrupted. This time, his voice wasn't quite as even. Most people would mistake the subtle change in tone as irritation, but Takahashi saw it was something very different. Fear.

"After what just happened in the Senkakus, you more than anyone should understand that this isn't the time for provocations. We're stepping very close to the brink, Masao. Very close to the point where the posturing could..." His voice petered out for a moment. "Could become something more."

War, Takahashi mouthed silently, relishing the feel of the word on his lips. How could a politician who wouldn't even speak the word be trusted to protect Japan? These men's lives were ruled entirely by fear. Of confrontation, insult, embarrassment. Of anything that could affect their soft and privileged lives.

Sanetomi liked very much to talk about the greatness of Japan and his own patriotism, but it was just theater. He would use back channels to Beijing to do whatever was necessary to appease his Chinese masters and de-escalate the standoff in the East China Sea. To quietly return Japan to the pathetic state that its people had come to accept as normal.

"I don't understand," Takahashi said, feigning respectfulness. "We demonstrated no aggression whatsoever in defending islands that virtually the entire international community agrees are ours. Further, I ordered the *Izumo* to retreat when the Chinese targeted it, even though that craft is more than capable of defending itself. How is it the responsibility of the Japanese people to de-escalate a situation that we didn't create?"

"You are entirely aware that this isn't a matter of fault," Sanetomi responded. "In addition to a substantial nuclear arsenal, the Chinese military has ten times our manpower, ten times our tanks and artillery, and four times our combat aircraft. I understand and respect your efforts over the last thirty years to update the capabilities of our defense forces, General. But this isn't the time for arrogance."

Takahashi resisted the urge to laugh. Sanetomi understood nothing. It was very much the time for arrogance.

"Of course, I sympathize with your position, Prime Minister. But you must understand that I'm not a politician. I'm a soldier. I won't turn my back on these brave men and the sacrifices they made for our country."

"Even if the people of Japan have to suffer the consequences of your actions?"

"I doubt any discomfort they might experience would compare to what was suffered by the men whose souls rest here, Prime Minister."

Takahashi cut off the call and stepped from the vehicle, barely aware of the competing shouts from the protesters on either side. He walked the barricaded corridor between them, focused on the Shinto priest waiting on the other end. The holy man wore the white robe demanded by tradition, and it flowed gracefully in the breeze as the general approached.

The countries that pretended to rule the world had become weak. Europe was fractured and useless. Russia was sinking into a disastrous kleptocracy that would inevitably lead to another revolution. China's corruption continued to grow as it destroyed everything it laid its hands on in the name of unfettered greed.

Even the United States, which had been such a force for stability in the world, had been transformed into a bickering, bankrupt shadow of its former self. It could no longer be trusted to govern itself, let alone show leadership to a rising Asia or control the Middle East as it descended into chaos.

Nature abhorred a vacuum and America was leaving one that would prove catastrophic. Only he and his closest advisers understood it yet, but a new era was dawning. This was to be Japan's time.

Takahashi stopped and bowed respectfully to the priest, the hair standing on the back of his neck as it always did in this place. One day he too would be honored here. People would remember him as the man who changed Japan—and the world—forever.

10

Tokyo
Japan

C an I get you another cup of coffee?"
Kaito Yoshima—his name when he was in Japan—
answered the young waitress with a smile and flawless Japanese. Even if she'd been a student of subtle accents she would have placed him in the northeastern part of the island. Certainly she would never have dreamed that he'd been born and raised outside Dingxi, China.

He admired her as she weaved through the crowded coffee shop, dodging the knots of animated conversation with practiced agility. His preferences leaned more toward the exotic, but even he had to admit that there was something special about this girl. French wasn't one of his four languages and he strained to remember the phrase. A certain *je ne sais quoi*.

Yoshima turned back to the massive window, ignoring the crowded street scene beyond and instead focusing on his reflection. In addition to his perfect accent, there would also be no way for the people surrounding him to determine his foreign birth from his features. They were a gift from the Japanese soldier who had raped his grandmother during the war—a strange trick of genetics that had not gone unnoticed by the Chinese government.

He'd been taken from his family just before his fourth birthday under the cover that he'd been identified as deeply gifted and would be educated at an exclusive boarding school. To this day his family had no idea that the school he'd been shipped off to was actually a training facility for spies and assassins.

From before he could even clearly remember, he had been immersed in the Japanese language and culture, the subtle art of espionage, and of course the shining glory of the Communist Party. Upon reaching adolescence, he'd been issued a forged passport and begun traveling to Japan on a regular basis, honing his ability to blend in under the watchful eye of his trainers and classmates.

There had been thirty of them in all, split equally between male and female. Friendships had been a luxury none of them could afford, and the endless competition had been both cruel and brutal. Mistakes, weakness, and even the slightest hint of a lack of patriotism or resolve were all severely punished. If enough of these usually trivial violations were incurred, that student was expelled.

Of course he knew now that this was just a euphemism. The level of secrecy that had to be maintained around a program that stole children and turned them into anti-Japanese weaponry was oppressive, to say the least. No, it was clear that the children born without the necessary intelligence or physical capability—and even the gentle ones whose nature was unsuited to the tasks they would be charged with—now inhabited a series of unmarked graves in the Chinese countryside.

Only nine of the thirty had survived their training, and those nine went on to become China's top covert operatives.

Or at least that's what he was told. He'd never seen any of them again, and that separation generated a strange emptiness in him that he'd never been able to completely fill. His teachers had in some ways done their jobs too well. Now he straddled two different countries, two different cultures. Which did he really belong to? Certainly his loyalty to Beijing had been beaten into him throughout his childhood, but he was a man now and his allegiance to that country was beginning to feel more like a habit than anything else.

The pretty waitress returned and he smiled at her as she slid the latte onto the table in front of him.

"Do you speak English?" she asked, pointing to the copy of *1984* he'd been rereading to pass the time.

"I try," Yoshima responded easily. "But I don't think anyone could really understand me."

It was a lie, of course. While slightly accented, his English was nearly perfect. Another gift from the Chinese government.

"I'm taking a class," she said. "It's *really* hard. So don't feel bad. I can't even understand myself!"

Her laugh was engaging enough to turn his thoughts to using the skills he'd been provided to disappear. Maybe somewhere in Japan. Maybe with this very girl.

She turned and he watched her walk away again, the fantasy fading as the physical distance between them grew. There had been so many women like her, so many daydreams of a normal life where his Japanese features didn't make him the constant target of hatred by the very people he had been charged with protecting.

A bitter smile crossed his lips. *The very people he had been charged with protecting.*

In truth, the only people he protected were his country's

politicians. And that task was getting harder and harder as they pushed China further toward the brink. The runaway economic growth was slowing, information was becoming increasingly difficult to control, and his hopelessly corrupt masters were feeling their grip on the population weakening.

With all other avenues exhausted and religion unavailable to them, they had chosen Japan as a focal point for the Chinese people's anger. They dredged up atrocities that had happened generations ago and skillfully transformed a group of useless islands into a beacon of national pride. All the while arrogantly believing that they could control the carefully cultivated rage of a billion human beings.

He scanned the street out front again, finally letting his gaze settle on a small Honda parked parallel to the curb. It looked almost laughably normal—Japan's most common car in Japan's most common color. Neither old nor new, neither clean nor dirty, it might as well have been invisible.

Within that mundane exterior, though, it was really quite remarkable. Six kilos of crudely formulated but still potent plastic explosive were hidden inside the driver's-side door. The body had been cleverly reinforced with steel plate in order to channel and amplify the power of the blast into a force that its Chinese designer struggled to describe without invoking the frowned-upon concept of God.

No mistakes would be tolerated. No chances taken. General Masao Takahashi wouldn't be injured or even killed. He would be vaporized.

A text popped up on the phone in front of him and he took a casual sip of his coffee as he looked down at it. Three minutes.

There was no excitement, no dread, and no adrenaline. Those responses had been deemed to dampen logical faculties and had been eradicated from him long ago. He was not to think or feel, and certainly not to question. He was a tool of men far greater than him. Nothing more.

For a long time, he'd believed all of it. Now, though, he saw things much more clearly.

There was no question that Masao Takahashi was an extremely dangerous man. He refused to bend with the wind, to acknowledge that the Chinese government's saber rattling was just a bit of political showmanship for the benefit of the masses who granted it power. Because of this, Yoshima's masters had decided that if the general's influence was removed, the Japanese people would sink back into their mumbled apologies and averted gazes.

Ironically, it was the training he'd been given by these men that made him certain they were wrong. Nationalism was on the rise in Japan, and Takahashi's death would do nothing but strengthen it. All he would accomplish here today would be to inch the two countries a little closer to the point of no return.

Another text came in warning him that the ETA of the general's limousine was now one minute. He carefully inserted a set of custom earbuds and plugged the cord into his phone. Anyone looking would think he was listening to music, but the headphones were actually designed for hearing protection.

A drop of sweat ran down his forehead and he wiped it away. His masters had carefully designed the assassination to look like the work of the Japanese Patriotic Front, a left-wing group that had recently set off bombs in Yokohama and Nagoya. The subtle poison he'd suggested had been deemed too exotic and easily traced to a foreign source if discovered. And the sniper bullet that was his backup plan had been deemed too professional looking.

So he was sitting in a coffee shop waiting to unleash hell. Yoshima looked at the faces of the pedestrians walking by the colorful shop windows and at the drivers on their way home from work. How many would be disfigured or carry debilitating injuries for the rest of their lives? How many would die?

He bobbed his head to imaginary music and watched out of the corner of his eye as Takahashi's opulent personal limousine came into view. Waiting until it was almost even with the Honda, he reached out and pushed the "volume" button on his phone three times in quick succession. A two-second delay had been programmed in, and he used the time to force himself to relax. It was important that he not flinch before the blast. The modern world was riddled with cameras, and every second of footage would be examined by the Japanese authorities.

Even after being briefed by the engineers in Beijing, he was stunned by the power of the blast. People around him screamed and dived to the floor, as did he, covering his head and making sure that panic read clearly on his face. He surreptitiously watched the people around him, not wanting to be the first, or the last, to look up.

When others started to move, he lifted his head and peered through the cracked window in front of him. As promised, the explosion had indeed been tightly concentrated. The entire front of the building across the street was caved in and starting to burn. People who weren't lying motionless were fleeing desperately in every direction. Mangled cars, one still spinning on its roof, were scattered like a child's discarded toys.

Yoshima stared into the smoke and dust billowing from the hole in the building across from him and felt his brow furrow involuntarily. The wind was pulling at the cloud, providing brief glimpses of what was behind. It took a moment for his mind to knit together the patchwork but when it did, he forgot the cameras and rose to his feet.

There should have been no more left of Takahashi's car than a few small pieces of twisted metal and burning rubber. But there it was, lying intact on its side in the rubble.

Impossible.

11

Tokyo
Japan

General Masao Takahashi could no longer make sense of a world he thought he understood. There was no sound but the ringing in his ears and there was no light beyond a few muted rays coming from above. The only thing that seemed familiar was the ache in his shoulder, though he didn't know why it hurt or when the pain had started.

After a few moments his equilibrium came back enough for him to realize that he wasn't sitting upright. His arm was jammed between the back of the vehicle's front seat and the door. The light filtering in was coming through a window. The car was on its side.

"Genzo," he called out, but his driver didn't answer.

Takahashi freed his arm, finally feeling his mind start to come back online. He was crumpled against the driver's-side rear window, and through the glass he could see a mix of bright floor tiles and rubble.

"Genzo," he said louder, righting himself to the best of his ability and leaning forward through the seats. His driver hadn't been wearing a seat belt and lay motionless with one hand hanging loosely through the steering wheel. There was a blood smear about ten centimeters in diameter on the undamaged windshield, and when Takahashi reached for his man he discovered the stain had come from what had once been Genzo's forehead.

He stood on the door panel and reached up to try to open the door above him. The latch worked and he managed to crack it, only enough to let in a wave of black smoke and terrified screams.

The handle was suddenly torn from his grasp and he threw an arm up against the filtered glare of the afternoon sun. Someone was shouting at him but the buzzing in his ears and crackle of flames made it impossible to understand anything that was being said.

He felt a powerful hand grip him under his injured arm and he was immediately dragged out of the vehicle.

"General!" the man shouted directly in his ear. "Are you hurt?"

Takahashi just shook his head, still dazed.

"Come on! We have to get out of here!"

From his elevated position on the side of the limousine, Takahashi could finally take in his surroundings. The building was thick with smoke but still recognizable as some kind of store. He remembered the roar and the flash now. An explosion. His vehicle had come partially through a cement wall and partially through a display window. The burning figures that had at first looked like mannequins were, he now realized, corpses strewn among shattered brick and shredded clothing.

"Let's go, General! Now!"

He was pulled off the car and his arm was thrown painfully over a broad set of shoulders. Men from his chase car, some bleeding badly, others visibly burned, fell in around him as he was swept deeper into the wrecked building.

As they progressed, the still bodies were replaced by ones writhing in agony or trying pathetically to escape the approaching flames. He saw a small child, half his body charred black, wailing next to a motionless young woman. Someone running past scooped the child up and disappeared like a ghost into the choking smoke.

They slammed through a metal door and the open space turned into a dark hallway. His head continued to clear and after a few more moments he forcibly slowed. "Where are we going?"

"The fire exit," one of his men said.

"Are you sure there is one?" Takahashi asked, feeling himself being pushed forward again. "We could get trapped by the fire."

"We're certain, sir. We've been through all the buildings on your normal travel routes. This has a rear exit that opens onto the next street."

He had no reason to doubt what he was being told. His security detail had been handpicked from the best men the country had to offer.

"My vehicle," Takahashi said.

"Sir, we need to focus on getting you out of here."

The man ahead of him had a hand against his earpiece as they ran, nodding at whatever was coming over it. "General, I have confirmation that a helicopter is on its way and will be airlifting the car out."

Takahashi didn't respond. Justifying the urgency of the salvage operation would be difficult but significantly simpler than the explanations necessary if the police got hold of the limousine.

They burst through another door and came out onto a relatively quiet secondary street. Pedestrians were talking in frightened tones and pointing at the smoke just starting to clear the tightly packed buildings. Takahashi's men barreled right through them, going for a half-unloaded truck parked at the curb.

Its owners were too stunned to offer any resistance, instead watching in silence as the head of Takahashi's security detail shoved the general through the driver's door and then leaped in after him.

In the rearview mirror Takahashi saw his remaining men stepping in front of cars and forcing their occupants out into the street. Within thirty seconds two of his men had pulled a commandeered Prius in front of the truck and another three had a BMW a few meters off its rear bumper.

"Please get down, General!"

He ignored the suggestion. The likelihood that there was a secondary team looking to finish the failed assassination attempt was remote at best. And even if it hadn't been, he was not going to cower like a child in the face of it.

"What's the ETA on that chopper, Lieutenant?"

"I'm being told it should be on-site within half an hour, sir. After that, it'll take another fifteen minutes to hook up the cables. Where should the vehicle be taken, sir?"

Takahashi didn't immediately respond, looking at the stunned expressions of the people they passed while trying to calculate exactly what had happened and who was responsible. "I'll give you a destination when it's in the air."

12

Near Imizu
Japan

I'm going to give you the benefit of the doubt and assume you were having an off day when you let this happen."

Jon Smith's eyes rose from the blade in the woman's hand to her face, still shadowed by the brim of her hat. The voice was familiar, but the drugs flowing into him through the IV made it hard to concentrate.

She used the knife to cut through the leather strap securing his ankle and then stepped back into better light.

The hair was an unfamiliar black, but the dark eyes and arrogant smile were unmistakable.

"Randi? How...how the hell did you find me? Did Fred—"

She scowled and shook her head. "Fred's the reason you got a crossbow bolt in your back. I thought we should talk before I let him in on where you were."

He let her words sink in for a moment. Had they increased his pain meds? He still hurt like hell but his processing speed seemed to be crawling. "The guy I talked to...the one in charge..."

"Noboru Ueno. One of Japan's most successful..." She paused for a moment to consider her word choice. "Entrepreneurs."

Smith shook his head weakly. "Jesus, Randi. Is there an organized crime boss on the planet you don't have a relationship with?"

She shrugged noncommittally. "Count yourself lucky that I have friends in low places. Noboru's plans for you weren't exactly all sunshine and lollipops. Unless I miss my guess, they'd have ended with you getting mixed in with the cat food at one of his meatpacking plants."

"And you trust this guy, but not Fred?"

"I don't trust anyone. You know that. But Noboru and I go way back and we have some shared interests. With Klein I'm never quite sure."

Smith forced himself into a sitting position. She watched him struggle, silently calculating how his condition would affect her plans but not offering any help.

"I take it you're here to spring me?"

She nodded. "The doc says you're in pretty bad shape but that it should be okay to move you if we're careful. They're bringing a wheelchair and I'll take you to an apartment I rented through a dummy corporation. No way to trace it to either one of us. We can lay low there until you're a little more mobile and we figure out how to get you back to the States."

"Fred can send a jet."

"We'll see. No need to jump into anything blind."

He didn't bother to protest, instead pointing to a pair of cargo pants folded in the corner. He rarely won an argument with her even when he was firing on all cylinders. Better to concentrate on getting the hell out of there before their host changed his mind.

While he was struggling to get his zipper up with dead-feeling fingers, the door opened and the man he'd spoken with when he'd first woken up entered, followed by three very serious-looking companions.

"Randi," Noboru Ueno said, examining her from bottom to top, finally stopping at the black-dyed hair. "What have you done to yourself?"

"You know how I hate to attract attention."

He reached for her hand and kissed it. "Impossible. You look radiant as always."

"Such a charmer," she said with a barely perceptible smile. "Now where's the wheelchair you promised me?"

"And where are the items you promised me?"

Randi pointed to the satchel lying on the table. Ueno opened it and flipped approvingly through what from Smith's position appeared to be bearer bonds.

"I could have just wired the money to your account in Croatia."

He shook his head. "I've come to enjoy the feel of paper in my hand."

Smith was too drugged to generate any meaning from Ueno's subtle nod, but Randi wasn't similarly handicapped.

The men moved on her with blinding speed, but it wasn't fast enough. Instead of backing away like they expected, she charged at the lead man, the blade reappearing in her hand and sinking to the hilt in his side. She spun, catching the second man in the head with an elbow as Smith threw himself out of the bed. He had the vague sensation of the IVs ripping out of his hand as he went for Ueno, but when his feet hit the floor, his legs wouldn't support him. He collapsed at the man's feet, pain and nausea washing over him as he tried desperately to get up and help Randi.

The man who'd caught the elbow was shaken but didn't

go down. He managed to block the knife from getting him in the throat but the gash it put in his forearm looked to be six inches long and down to the bone. She feinted high on the only uninjured man left but she was off balance and he knew it. A foot sweep took her down hard onto the wood floor and the man with the wounded forearm managed to drop a knee on her arm, splattering her with blood and trapping the knife.

And then it was over. Each man probably outweighed her by fifty pounds and both were now on top of her. In a standing fight, Randi's uncanny speed and accuracy made her a force to be reckoned with. On the ground, though, her size was an insurmountable disadvantage.

Smith managed to get to all fours but his head was spinning so badly he could no longer determine which way was up. Ueno used a foot to shove him onto his side and then stared down at him. The Japanese man's mouth was moving, but Smith had to concentrate to decipher his words.

"The doctor assured me that your injuries were too serious for you to even get out of bed without help, but Randi's friends tend to be very resilient. In light of that, I had him add a little something to your IV."

Ueno adjusted the dead guard leaking all over his expensive teak floor and then walked over to Randi and kicked her hard in the side. "He was one of my best."

She thrashed wildly against the men holding her, prompting Ueno to take a cautious step backward.

"Not good enough, you son of a bitch! And these two won't be either!"

He let out a long, frustrated breath. "I spent millions on my security. I was guaranteed that it would be impossible to smuggle a weapon past my entry hall. And now this."

Ueno stepped over the expanding crimson puddle at his feet and opened the door, waving in five more men. A moment later Smith had been rolled onto his stomach and his numb limbs were being wound with duct tape. From his position he could see that Randi was getting the same treatment, though at least she was putting up a respectable—if completely point-less—fight.

Smith barely managed not to vomit from nausea and pain when he was thrown over a man's shoulder and carried out into the hallway. Randi was right behind him, still kicking and shouting threats as they went through the front doors and were deposited into the trunk of a waiting vehicle.

"You better just kill me now, Noboru. Because if you don't, I'll be back."

Smith couldn't see the man from his position with Randi on top of him but when the Japanese man spoke, he sounded genuinely shaken.

"This was very difficult for me, Randi. I've always liked you and to be completely honest, I'm afraid of you and your Central Intelligence Agency. But the men who want you..." His voice faded for a moment. "I'm afraid of them more."

13

Randi Russell realized she was hyperventilating and forced herself to get control. Her mouth was taped shut and her face was crammed into the trunk lid, so the deep, cleansing breaths she normally used to keep her rage in check weren't an option. She tried to picture a peaceful landscape dappled with sun, but Noboru Ueno's face kept intruding. Fantasies of his death filled her mind—from the classic simplicity of a bullet between the eyes to more exotic scenarios involving stampeding cattle and Rube Goldberg dismemberment machines.

Pull it together, Randi!

The white heat of her anger was one of her greatest strengths. It could keep her going when everyone else collapsed from exhaustion, and it could keep her locked on a target when everyone else had given up in frustration. But it could also run out of control and make it impossible for her to think. That's where Jon usually stepped in with a calm assessment and well-thought-out plan. From the looks of him when they were being carried out by Ueno's men, though, about the best he could do at this point was not drool down the front of his shirt.

She held her breath for a moment, silencing the loud rush of air coming through her nose and trying to orient herself to her surroundings.

The trunk they were stuffed into wasn't as spacious as the grandeur of the car would have suggested. She was wedged in hard and beneath her Jon must have been worse off. Ueno's men had left little to chance, winding the better part of a roll of duct tape around each of them and then securing them back-to-back. That made getting to the trunk latch or the electrical wires threaded behind the carpet pretty much out of the question.

The sound of the engine was smooth and even, suggesting that the driver was a pro who knew enough not to get nervous and attract attention. After a number of turns and stops getting out of Ueno's property, they'd been going mostly straight and steady for the last fifteen minutes.

Other than that, there was nothing but darkness. And for some reason that bothered her. It took a moment to figure out why.

Jon.

He had always been an immovable object. Unflappable no matter how bad the shit hit the fan, unkillable even in the most dire situations. Now he wasn't moving at all.

A jolt of adrenaline coursed through Randi when she realized that despite being crushed up against him, she couldn't feel him breathing. She jerked backward and felt a rush of relief when he grunted weakly. He was alive. But for how much longer?

If he died, it would be her fault. She'd come there with no backup at all. Klein didn't know anything about Ueno and no one at the agency had any idea where she was or that Covert-One even existed.

That left it up to her to bail their asses out. But how?

She tried to slide forward, planning to search the dark space for something sharp—a protruding bolt, a disconnected wire—but didn't have the leverage to move more than half an inch. She pulled harder but it didn't get her any farther and Jon wasn't even groaning anymore when she yanked on him. Had he lost consciousness? Or was he...

Pull it together! She scolded herself again. There was precisely nothing she could do about his condition until she got them out of there. If he was dead, he was dead.

The vehicle began to slow and finally rolled to a stop. For a moment she feared they'd reached their destination but then the car moved, gliding along for a few seconds before once again coming to a standstill. Traffic.

Maybe someone with their window open would hear her if she started shouting. She ground her face on the inside of the trunk, trying to scrape the tape off her mouth. The carpet covering the surface was too soft to have any effect on the powerful adhesive.

She kept at it, straining until her neck muscles were on the verge of giving out and the skin felt like it was being torn from her cheeks. Then just let her body go slack. There was no way out. She'd killed them.

Randi didn't know how long she drifted like that, thinking about Jon and Klein. About her dead husband and Ueno. The traffic didn't get any better and the gentle rocking kept pulling her further into oblivion.

The car stopped again, but this time there was a deafening crash and she was thrown violently to the side. The trunk lid bent outward enough to let in a little light and she rammed her knees into it, trying to get it to open the rest of the way. The latch held, but flexed enough to give her hope.

Randi had pulled back for another try when the gunfire started—controlled bursts from three, maybe four separate automatic weapons. She tensed, but none of the rounds sounded like they were hitting metal. Just glass and flesh.

After only a few seconds the guns went silent and all she could hear was the revving of motors and the crumpling of bodywork as people tried to escape on the packed road.

A steel bar slid into the gap in the trunk near her feet and another appeared above her head. A moment later the lid had been pried open and she was squinting at a Japanese man with a straight razor in his hand.

She tried unsuccessfully to dodge when he swung it at her, but instead of going for her throat, he cut her loose from Jon. After a few more deft waves of his blade, she was free enough to pull herself out of the trunk under her own power. He pointed to an SUV stopped near the overturned delivery truck that was backing up traffic, but she refused to move until he'd pulled Jon from the trunk and was carrying him toward the waiting vehicle.

Through the windshields of the cars blocked in around them, she could see that most people were just staring at her in horror. A few others were shaking their phones in frustration as they tried to film the scene. She counted three men still standing, all sweeping MP5s smoothly back and forth, searching for targets. The four men who were in the car she'd been trapped in were all dead. None had even managed to get his door open before taking multiple shots to the head.

She stood behind the man shoving Jon into the back of the SUV, trying to figure out who the hell she was dealing with. By the precision of their attack and the classy setup with the delivery truck, there was no question they were pros—an assumption that was supported by the fact that no one's phone seemed to be working. The type of gear you needed for that kind of jamming wasn't something you picked up at Walmart.

But whose pros? Should she make a break for it and let them take Jon with the idea of living long enough to track him down again? Or should she throw in with them?

The SUV started backing up with the rear door still open. There was no more time.

Running awkwardly with her hands still taped behind her, she dived through the open door and landed on top of Jon, who was sprawled unconscious across the seat. As soon as she was in, the driver floored it into the grass median, speeding around the crippled van and onto the open road beyond. She barely managed to pull her feet in before the acceleration slammed the door closed.

The straight razor was on the floorboard and she slid down to pick it up. A moment later her hands were free and she was carefully cutting the tape off Jon.

The good news was that he was breathing. The bad news was that it was creating a wet, sucking sound that came not only from his throat, but from a reopened wound between his ribs.

"Jon! Can you hear me?"

His eyes fluttered momentarily, but that was about it. She tore his shirt fully open and pressed a wad of cloth against the hole in his side. Beyond that, she wasn't sure what else she could do.

"Who the hell are you people?" she said, turning to look at the man calmly piloting the vehicle up the road.

By way of an answer, he passed a phone back. It was already in the process of connecting to a number that came up all zeros.

"Hello?" she said, putting it to her ear.

"Hello, Randi." The voice was unmistakable and not entirely unexpected. Fred Klein.

"You had me followed," she said, her indignation ringing a bit hollow.

"When I found out you were on your way to the area where Jon was presumed to have died, I was concerned you were looking for revenge instead of pursuing the mission I assigned you."

She had to admit that it wasn't a completely unreasonable supposition.

"I have to say," he continued, "I'm so pleased with what you turned up I can't even bring myself to be angry at you for doing one of the stupidest and most careless things I've ever had the misfortune to witness. Now, tell me about Jon's condition."

Her mouth tightened but she didn't protest. In light of what had happened, she was forced to silently admit that Klein might have a small point. "He doesn't look good."

"Understood. I have a jet with a medical team waiting not far away. For now our priorities have shifted. We need to get Jon out of harm's way and stabilized. We'll talk about the rest later."

14

Outside Tokyo
Japan

General Masao Takahashi stood on the broad deck of his home watching the sun set over meticulously tended gardens that seemed to extend to the horizon. The pain in his shoulder throbbed in time with his heartbeat but other than that his injuries had turned out to be trivial. Nothing more than a few deep bruises and four stitches above his right knee.

His enemies had made a great error in failing to kill him. Takahashi had always drawn strength from adversity, and this event was already an example of that. It demonstrated to him that he had become careless with his own life—something a man in his position could not afford.

The unavoidable weakness in the elaborate operation beginning to unfold across the world stage was its dependence on a single man. No one else had the combination of history, knowledge, and authority necessary to carry out his plan. No one else had the resolve it would take to change the world order at its very foundation.

If he had been killed, everything he and so many others had spent their lives working toward would collapse. His great country and its people would be doomed to continue their descent into irrelevance.

He had doubled his security detail and would from now on take varied routes and modes of transportation when he was forced to travel. The men allowed close to him had been whittled down to those whose loyalty was entirely beyond question. Even his food was now being purchased from randomly selected suppliers by a man who had been with his family for the last thirty-five years.

Momentum was building at an exponential rate, and soon it would be beyond anyone's ability to control. Until then he needed to keep his hand firmly on the rudder.

Takahashi descended the time-worn steps to a gravel pathway, limping along it as he admired the perfect order of the landscape. The property had originally belonged to his father and he'd changed nothing since the man's death. In many ways he saw it as a shrine not that different from Yasukuni a place to honor not the soldiers, but the industrialists who had transformed a defeated island nation into a power that would once again challenge the entire world.

As he walked through the flowering trees and stone gardens, it was still hard to believe that it all belonged to him. His father had suffered a rare moment of speechlessness when young Masao had told him his plans to join Japan's fledgling defense forces. Of course his father had been a great patriot and had given everything to the war effort, but the defense forces were weak and would be kept that way by the obscene constitution forced on the country by Douglas MacArthur. A brilliant man, Takahashi's father saw the future of Japan as economic and wanted his eldest son by his side, helping him build a new kind of world power.

In the end, though, he had given his blessing. There were

many ways to serve and he'd respected his son's decision to choose his own path.

It was a great tragedy that he'd died when he had. Japan was still mired in a decades-long recession, its people continued to bow and scrape over long-dead history, and China was becoming a superpower in its own right with a massively expanding economy and military. After a lifetime of devotion, he had passed with eyes filled by Japan's weakness.

Now, though, things were finally changing. The recession was finally losing its grip and a generation with no firsthand knowledge of the war was refusing to take responsibility for the supposed sins of their fathers. Most important, though, Japan's ability to defend itself—so long abdicated to America—was quietly reemerging.

For centuries the Japanese had been the masters of their own destiny, and soon they would be again. His plans didn't end there, though. The mistakes of the past would not be repeated. This time Japan would take its rightful place as the planet's supreme power.

Takahashi heard footsteps approaching from behind and turned to watch Akio Himura, the director of Japan's intelligence apparatus, moving quickly along the path.

"The trees are very beautiful this afternoon," he said, bowing.

Takahashi returned the bow. "Walk with me, Akio."

They remained silent for a few moments, admiring the evening light fading around them. It was Takahashi who finally spoke. "What has the media been able to obtain?"

"Very little, sir. There appears to be no video of the actual explosion—though as you know, significant documentation of the aftermath *does* exist. It's gotten extensive coverage on both national and international news networks."

The general nodded. The advent of cell phones and the Internet made it virtually impossible to prevent the dissemination of information. Instead, it was necessary to master the much more subtle art of shaping it.

"And my limousine?"

"The clearest images are relatively low resolution, and the car is intermittently hidden by smoke. It is, however, possible to see the lack of damage compared with the completely destroyed vehicles around it as well as the destruction of the front of the building it was thrown through."

"Has anyone publicly spoken to that?"

"Not specifically. The assumption is that the blast wasn't properly focused. People tend to see what they expect to see and only look for familiar explanations. The media's calling it a miracle you survived, and my people are building on that to further increase your stature."

Takahashi gave a silent nod, losing himself for a moment in the rhythm of their footsteps. His survival had been anything but a miracle—something that would be painfully obvious to anyone willing to open their eyes. His personal vehicle had been built from a next-generation carbon fiber–ceramic alloy. For its weight, the new material was an order of magnitude stronger than steel and six times as resistant to heat.

A far lesser version of it had been sold for hundreds of millions to the Americans for inclusion in their laughable F-35 fighter program, but they were completely unaware of its inferiority. And that ignorance was something Takahashi was very interested in maintaining. For now.

"Its removal went smoothly, then?"

"As soon as the fire was under control, our men covered it with tarps so no more photographs could be taken. Less than twenty more minutes passed before we airlifted it out."

"And the reaction to that?"

"As expected, we've had a few complaints that the defense forces seemed to be prioritizing the vehicle over casualties, but rescue efforts were well in hand and we've told the press that we needed it for the investigation. The complaints are already largely buried and the car is safe at the north base."

"I trust that you'll continue to handle the situation with your normal competence," Takahashi said. "Now tell me about this investigation. Where has it led?"

Himura smoothed his tie nervously. "To the Japanese Patriotic Front."

The general's expression darkened. The JPF was a far-left terrorist group responsible for a series of recent bombings. Among other things, they demanded the immediate defunding of the defense forces, the nationalization of numerous businesses including those owned by Takahashi's family, and the continued penitence of the Japanese people.

The JPF was the only group of people in the world Takahashi despised more than the Chinese. They sabotaged their own homeland, attacked their own people, and insulted the men who had worked tirelessly to build the country that kept them safe and put food in their bellies.

Himura's people had expended considerable resources hunting them over the past two years, all to no avail. It was suspected that these traitors lived almost entirely off the grid, perhaps even abroad. The possibility of foreign funding had also been broached but no evidence of that existed. In truth, nothing existed. Despite the combined efforts of Himura, the police, and Interpol, the JPF remained a ghost.

"I don't know, Akio. Based on their history, this seems too bold for them. And the civilian casualties are far beyond what they've tolerated in the past."

"I agree, but we have to acknowledge that the severity of their attacks has been escalating. At first it was just unoccupied buildings. But their bombing of the defense force convoy last year killed two soldiers and injured eight others. You're a significant target. Perhaps they thought the costs were justifiable."

"You believe this?"

"What I know is that all leads thus far point in their direction. Having said that, they are denying responsibility, which is also unprecedented. The press is speculating that it's because collateral damage was worse than they'd expected."

"It would be hard not to anticipate the casualties."

"Again, I agree. And these things lead me to be skeptical of their involvement."

"China, then."

"I think that's the most likely answer, but finding sufficient evidence to make an accusation may be impossible."

"What about fabricating evidence?"

Himura was understandably surprised by the question. "It would be dangerous. Tensions are running higher than they have since the war. I fear we're in danger of crossing a line from which we won't be able to return. I'm not sure we're ready—"

"I'm not interested in your analysis of our tactical situation," Takahashi said, letting a hint of anger creep into his voice. "I asked only if it was possible."

"Please accept my apologies for overstepping my boundaries," Himura said with a submissive bow. "It was inexcusable. Yes, I believe it's possible."

Takahashi took a deep breath and let it out slowly. "There's more, isn't there? I know you too well, Akio. I can see it in your face."

"Yes, sir. Randi Russell and the injured man . . ." His voice faltered.

"Go on."

"They escaped."

Takahashi stopping short, feeling the pain flare in his injured knee. "What? How?"

"The car transporting them was attacked. It was a professional job. Our chase cars were blocked by traffic and four of our men were killed. It appears that the entire assault lasted only a few seconds and that there was sufficient electronic interference to prevent anyone from recording it."

"Were you able to track them?"

Himura's fearful silence answered the question.

"And the debris from Reactor Four?"

"Noboru Ueno didn't have it. Either the injured man lost it in the sea or he had it on him when he escaped."

Takahashi felt the rage building inside him but allowed only a hint of it to read on his face. The Americans now had samples from Fukushima, and there was no way to predict how long it would take for them to understand what they were looking at.

He felt the sweat break on his forehead and began walking again, letting the breeze cool what felt like a sudden fever. "Find them, Akio. Find them now."

15

Outside Busan
South Korea

*J*on? Can you hear me? Jon!"

A woman's voice. Familiar, but too distant to place.

"Jon!"

Smith opened his eyes and squinted against the fluorescent lights. Randi's face was hovering above him and he could feel the warmth of her hand in his.

"Good to have you back. I swear you've been nothing but trouble lately."

"You get what you pay for," he mumbled, trying to figure out where he was and how he'd gotten there. He remembered Randi coming to rescue him and the wheels falling off that operation pretty quickly. Then a car trunk and after that nothing.

"Jon? How are you feeling?"

A man's voice. This time he was able to process it without too many skipped beats. He let his head loll to the left and saw Fred Klein standing there in his ever-present rumpled suit. His mouth was curled into a disapproving frown but Smith sensed it wasn't aimed at him.

"I think...I think I'm okay."

"My people had to do a little more work on your back

and reinflate your lung again but they said the screws in your shoulder blade were fine and the broken ribs will heal on their own. Until they do, though, I'm told they'll hurt like hell."

Smith nodded weakly and turned back to Randi, who seemed genuinely worried. "Stop looking at me like that. It's making me nervous. How did you get us out of the trunk?"

She released his hand and backed away, the expression of concern turning uncertain.

"I was having her followed," Klein said when it became clear she wasn't going to answer. "We set up an ambush, took out the men in the car, and then flew you here."

Smith looked around him at the windowless hospital room. "Are we back in the States?"

"I'm afraid not. We had a doctor and equipment on the jet but you were having a lot of trouble breathing. We had to make an emergency landing in South Korea."

"Seoul? What hospital are we at? I know the director of..."

He fell silent when Klein shook his head and walked to the door. Smith leaned forward as far as he could when the director of Covert-One opened it. The building beyond was nothing more than the rotting carcass of an abandoned warehouse. Rain fell through the collapsed roof, and the rusted top of a crane jutted from the floor twenty feet below. A dangerous-looking man with Eastern European features and an Israeli assault rifle glanced back at them and then returned his attention to the warehouse floor.

Klein quietly closed the door and took a seat next to a table, its only purpose seeming to be to hold an enormous flower arrangement. "We have places like this set up all around the world specifically for these kinds of situations. It's the first time we've used this one."

"The president will be happy his money wasn't wasted," Smith managed to get out.

Klein nodded. "We just need you to concentrate on healing, Jon. No one can get to you here, so you don't have anything else to worry about."

Smith tried to sit up, but the attempt wasn't as successful as he'd hoped. He motioned to Randi and she helped ease him forward. A few extra pillows kept him there.

"I'm still not clear on how we got out of the trunk. Your guys just started shooting on a public road?"

Klein's irritation was immediately visible and Randi retreated again.

"Not only a public road, but a crowded public road. Randi discovered you were alive and went after you without telling me. By the time I found out, I didn't have the luxury of anything subtle."

"You sent Jon to Japan," Randi said, defensively. "You implied he was dead."

"I implied that because I believed it to be likely."

"What you believed doesn't make any difference. How could I be sure you didn't set him up? That you weren't setting me up?"

Klein let out a long, frustrated breath. "Randi, you're as talented as anyone I've ever worked with, but without trust this relationship isn't going to work."

"You're lecturing me about trust? I notice you were having me watched."

"And where would you be if I hadn't? In my experience, trips that start in car trunks rarely end well."

"Fred's right," Smith said. "And he walks the walk, Randi. He's always been there for me. And frankly he's always been there for you, too."

"The past is no guarantee of the future."

"If you want guarantees, you're in the wrong business."

Her face tightened as though she'd just swallowed something toxic. "Fine. I screwed up and I apologize."

Klein nodded. "Apology accepted. Now let's put it behind us and start fresh."

She crossed the room and offered her hand. "Deal. But if you ever decide to cross me or Jon, make sure you finish the job."

He held her hand in his grip. "And if you ever decide to cross me, I suggest you do the same."

She gave an almost imperceptible nod and it was done.

"Now that we finally have that out of the way," Smith said. "Could someone tell me what the docs said about my prognosis?"

"Sorry," Klein responded. "You should have a full recovery but it's going to take time and a fair amount of work. There's a medical rundown in the folder on the table next to you. You'll understand it better than I would. Having said that, I don't need a medical degree to know that you were lucky as hell."

Smith nodded. "The bolt got slowed down by a boat hull before I got hit. If it hadn't been, it would have gone right through me."

"And that reminds me," Klein said. "One issue we haven't discussed is that you had some fairly highly radioactive material in your pocket for an undetermined amount of time. It's all in the folder, but the doctor said it could cause problems with reproduction and that you should get regular cancer screenings going forward."

Smith would have laughed if he didn't know how excruciating it would be. "I think the family ship has sailed for me, Fred.

And if I keep working for you, I doubt I'll live long enough to have to worry about cancer."

Klein seemed a little bothered by that and changed the subject. "I appreciate you getting the evidence out. There was no second chance on this."

"What happened to it?"

"I have it locked down at the marina waiting for you."

"Any thoughts on who attacked me? And who convinced Randi's friend to turn on her?"

"We don't need to talk about this right now, Jon. You should save your strength."

"I'm awake and I'm guessing the TV's in Korean. Give me something I can think about to take my mind off my back."

"It had to be someone powerful," Randi offered. "Noboru isn't some small-time crook. I'd put his net worth at around a quarter of a billion dollars and his IQ high enough to know better than to piss me off. Now that I know you're okay, I'll be going back to Japan so he and I can have a little chat."

"That might be problematic," Klein said, retrieving an iPad from the table next to him. He tapped in a few commands and the television bolted near the ceiling came to life with video of a sprawling mansion overlooking the ocean. The flames consuming it looked to be rising more than a hundred feet in the air.

"This was captured by a Japanese news helicopter. Randi, I think you'll recognize the building."

"Noboru's house."

Klein nodded. "The blaze started about fifteen minutes after you were taken away."

"Can I assume that he and his men were inside?"

"It would appear so. Obviously, the bodies are badly damaged but an initial autopsy suggests no sign of smoke inhalation. They were dead before the blaze started."

"What about the men driving the car we were in?" Smith asked. "Did they work for Noboru?"

"I don't think so. There wasn't much time, but I had one of my men take a photo and the index finger of the driver—"

"The index finger?" Randi said, sounding impressed.

"I like to be thorough. Unfortunately, neither the photo, nor the fingerprint, nor a DNA analysis has revealed anything. Beyond his being of Japanese descent, I can't tell you anything about that man. He doesn't seem to exist."

"What about the Japanese authorities?"

"Complete silence on the issue. My men shot up a car in heavy traffic, killing four men, and it's like it never happened."

"Like it never happened?" Smith said. "That takes a lot of juice in an age of cell phones and Twitter."

He started coughing and put a hand to his mouth. It came back spattered with blood. Not much, though. It looked residual.

"Look, Jon. We're going to get out of here and let you sleep. You focus on getting well and when the doctor gives the okay—hopefully in a few days—I'll put you on a jet home. We can talk more then."

16

Beijing
China

The military had closed the road to cars but pedestrians were being allowed to pass freely through the barricades.

The angry crowd had grown to over ten thousand people and Randi Russell was pretty sure that she'd collided with at least half of them. The wind direction changed and the familiar smog was reinforced by the smoke from a series of burning Japanese flags. The spike heels she was wearing weren't exactly her first choice for massive political demonstrations, but she still managed to avoid getting run over by a pedal-powered food cart before finding some relatively clear sidewalk to the north.

Protests like this were breaking out all over China, driven by social media posts that were being selectively ignored by the government censors who spent their lives eradicating any hint of dissent from the Internet.

Of course the requisite soldiers had still been sent. There was no way the corrupt old men who ran China would let a gathering this size develop without the presence of the military. As long as the anger was aimed at their neighbor to the east, though, there would be no interference. In fact, a few soldiers had joined in and were shouting anti-Japanese slogans with at least as much gusto as the civilians around them. The difference was that instead of pumping their fists in the air, they were pumping rifles. It was an image that even Randi found disturbing. This situation had been heading nowhere good for a long time, and now the recent Senkaku standoff had combined with the attempt on Masao Takahashi's life to fan the flame. It was time for the politicians on both sides to dump a bucket of cold water on this thing—but she doubted that would happen anytime soon. There was nothing like a little xenophobic paranoia to keep the rabble motivated.

She skirted a banner with a Photoshop-generated picture of Takahashi's corpse and made a beeline for a high-rise condo building across the street.

A security guard nervously watching the demonstration through glass doors let her in and then quickly locked them inside. The shouts and bullhorn-amplified diatribes subsided a bit, but enough still penetrated to stave off any illusion of calm or normalcy.

Two more security guards admired her as she teetered toward their desk, digging a lipstick from the huge leather bag on her arm.

"Hey, y'all," she said, further reddening already garish lips. "I'm here to visit Li Wong."

She purposely mangled the pronunciation of Kaito Yoshima's Chinese name, but the guards just smiled. His passion for Western blondes would be well-known to them.

They told her in Chinese to go up and she squinted at them, affecting a deep expression of concentration. That got another grin from the men and they just motioned toward the back of the lobby.

"You're sweethearts," she said, starting toward the elevators. "Have a terrific day, now!"

She could feel them staring but who could blame them? She'd gone all out with the miniskirt—glittery silver and short enough that it took all her discipline not to keep tugging it down. The look was completed by huge silver hoop earrings and a vest made of a fur she couldn't identify. Considering the market she'd bought it at, rat was her best guess.

Randi watched the numbers light up as she rode to the top floor, grateful that no one else got on. Though she'd been blessed with the body and face for it, she found this persona exhausting. The hijab disguise had made her lazy.

When the doors opened, no one was in sight. There were only four condos on this floor, keeping traffic to a minimum. Of course there were cameras and she had no doubt the guards were watching, probably entertaining themselves with graphic speculation about what Yoshima's evening with this particular blonde would involve. She guessed that their imaginations were probably a lot less interesting than what reality would hold.

Randi dug in her bag for a key card and then pulled out her cell phone, pretending to pick up a call as she shoved the key into the lock. She feigned annoyance and bent over to examine the doorknob, presenting what she calculated would be a fair amount of the white thong she'd purchased for that very purpose.

It would keep the men's attention away from the thin wire connecting her phone to the key card and the fact that it was taking the algorithm longer than normal to find the entry code. Leave it to Yoshima to upgrade his damn security.

After an excruciating ten seconds, the red light on the door flickered to green.

"Show's over," she said under her breath as she straightened up and stepped into the dark condo.

Her heart rate rose noticeably when she slid the silenced Glock from her purse and pushed the door quietly closed with her back.

She'd run into Yoshima on a number of occasions but they'd never had any reason to go at it. He was a bit of an odd guy—a unique combination of intellectual, philosophical, and ridiculously dangerous. She imagined that it was the result of him being forced into the spy business as a child as opposed to choosing the profession himself. It was a background that could create personalities pretty far from the norm. She had a pretty good nose for people in her business and even she would have probably pegged him as a history professor or engineer if they happened to meet in a bar.

There was no sound at all and the place had the smell of having been closed up for a while. After almost a minute of complete motionlessness, she felt along the wall for a light switch. A moment later the expansive room was illuminated in a subdued glow.

The Chinese clearly compensated their covert operatives better than the Americans. The decor was a vague take on ancient Rome but managed to avoid kitsch. The art tended more toward the modern and looked original to her eye. Sofas were unblemished leather, and the crystal lined up on the bar looked like high-end Czech. The thing that jumped out, though, wasn't what was there but what was missing. There wasn't so much as a hint of anything Asian.

She kept the gun in her hand as she crossed the living room, turning down a hallway and heading for a small study that she knew was there from his CIA file. It was a little messier and more personal than the rest of the space, and she leafed disinterestedly through the papers lying on the desk. There was a laptop too, but she didn't bother to turn it on. There wouldn't be anything of interest on it.

Finally she turned her attention to a photograph of Yoshima and what she guessed was his mother. There was no denying that he was a good-looking guy. Beneath glasses his file said he didn't need were eyes that always seemed to be looking at something he couldn't quite fathom. A thin scar running along his left cheek gave his delicate features a certain ruggedness. If she recalled correctly, the man who gave it to him hadn't lived long enough to see it bleed.

Yoshima had an undergraduate degree in physics that he'd gotten by going to school between missions. No one at the CIA had ever figured out why he'd bothered, but having met him a few times Randi suspected it was out of simple interest in the subject.

And that brought her to an interesting hypothesis: If China needed someone to mess with a Japanese nuclear plant, who could possibly be more perfect for the mission than Kaito Yoshima?

She wandered out of the study and into his bedroom, giving it a cursory search before peeking into the bathroom to admire a travertine shower that could have fit ten people comfortably.

The truth was that she felt a little sorry for Yoshima. He'd been torn from his family, brought up in a brutal government facility, and now regularly risked his life for a country where his Japanese features made him the target of racism, suspicion, and even hate. No wonder he liked Western blondes. They just saw Asian. Ninety-nine percent of them wouldn't be able to tell Chinese from Japanese if you put a gun to their hair spray–encrusted heads.

She wandered back out into the living room, finding another photo of him. In this one, he was with a group of laughing people outside a bar. His smile wasn't entirely convincing, and the eyes seemed to look right through the camera.

The agency's analysts pegged him as clinically depressed, and based on her experience they were probably right. It was one of the things that made him such a dangerous opponent. He genuinely didn't seem to care if he lived or died.

Randi considered riffling though a few more drawers and shelves, but then decided against it. That wasn't why she was here.

She was here to send a message.

17

Beijing Airport
China

Kaito Yoshima handed his passport through the window and smiled easily as the control officer examined him with unveiled contempt. The standoff in the Senkaku Islands had calmed somewhat with the withdrawal of Japan's new battleship, but his unsuccessful attempt on General Takahashi's life had inflamed both countries. Just as he'd predicted.

Of course his superiors would run for cover. They would blame his inexplicable failure for the escalation between the two countries. As though a successful assassination would have been more palatable to the Japanese people and China would treat Takahashi's death with solemnity instead of celebrating it in the streets.

"What is your purpose here?" the man said in halting English.

Yoshima pulled out a piece of paper covered with Chinese characters. The document said that he was an economic consultant under contract to the Chinese government. A convenient cover story for when it was impractical for him to travel under his Chinese identity.

In the past the document had made these low-level workers

snap to pretty quickly, but that power seemed to be waning. Instead of handing it back to him with a curt nod, the man examined it with an expression turning from contempt to disgust.

Finally he slammed his stamp into the well-worn Japanese passport and looked past him to the German tourist next in line.

Yoshima walked through the crowded hallway toward baggage claim, spirited along by the flow of people around him.

It had been impossible to know how to react to his situation, so he'd done what he always did: taken the most dangerous course.

Now, though, he was beginning to regret his decision. There had been nothing but silence from his masters after Takahashi's survival was confirmed by the press. And while he was confident that he would soon find himself in the role of scapegoat, there was some question as to what that meant exactly. After the inevitable flurry of politicians looking to leverage the failed assassination to further their careers, would it be quietly acknowledged that he had followed his orders to the letter and that Takahashi's survival was a bizarre fluke? Would he receive a formal reprimand that would be completely meaningless in a profession as clandestine as his? Or would he disappear like so many of his classmates before him?

In truth, though, that wasn't what was causing him to hang back and obsessively scan the crowd surrounding him.

No, at least in the short term, he had a much more dangerous situation to contend with.

Of course he had cameras and other security devices hidden in his condominium, each uploading to its own secure site on the Internet. He knew Randi Russell had been there, but he also knew that she'd made no effort to disable his security, disguise her identity, or even make her search look workmanlike. Why? Was this her idea of a request for a parley? Or was that just what she wanted him to think? Perhaps her real goal was to draw him close enough to kill.

Yoshima felt someone press a hand against the back of his neck and then a sudden weight in his jacket pocket. He spun violently only to find the startled face of an old woman who quickly scurried into the crowd. A quick brush of his fingers beneath his collar turned up a strip of tape stuck to his skin and the small, hard bump beneath it.

A search for who had put it there would be futile, he knew. It could have been anyone—even the old woman. Randi loved criminals and he had no doubt that in a scenario like this, she would have employed one of the finest pickpockets in the country.

His jacket vibrated and he reached for the phone that had been placed there, once again letting himself be swept forward. There was little point in further caution or worry. He was entirely at the mercy of the person on the other end of the line.

"Hello, Randi."

"Kaito—or should I say Li? Who are you today?"

"I'm Kaito."

"The thing stuck to the back of your neck is an explosive. It's one of our latest. Tiny, subtle, surprisingly quiet. Not qualities you appreciate apparently, but enough to snap your spine."

He sighed quietly. Undoubtedly her words were an allusion to the massive explosion in Tokyo and the admittedly unconscionable number of innocent victims. "I suspected as much."

"It's one of the things I've always liked about you, Kaito. You're not stupid. Did you check luggage?"

"No."

"Come out through baggage claim. I'm in a blue BMW."

When he stepped out onto the sidewalk, Randi leaped from the car in a silver miniskirt that bordered on the obscene. She had long blonde hair that Yoshima suspected was a wig and narrow heels that he noted would make it hard for her to move quickly—a detail he filed away in the chance it might become useful in the future.

She threw her arms around him and kissed him hard on the lips. She was hardly the first blonde to pick him up from the airport this way, and it would look completely normal to anyone who might be watching.

She had a cell phone in one hand, and he focused on it for a moment while playing along with the charade she'd crafted. Undoubtedly the detonator for the device on his neck was integrated into the phone but he had no way of knowing how it worked. Did she have to push a button? Or perhaps she was already pushing the button, and it was releasing it that would separate his vertebrae.

"Why don't you drive, sweetie?" she said, climbing into the passenger seat and closing the door.

It started to rain while he was standing there and he walked deliberately around the back of the vehicle, tossing his hand luggage into the backseat and then slipping behind the wheel.

"It's good to see you," she said as they merged into traffic. "How long has it been? Four years?"

He shook his head. "You're forgetting Cambodia."

"Oh, God, you're right. It was a hundred and six degrees with ninety percent humidity. And don't even get me started on the snakes."

"Is the car clean?" he asked.

"I got it out of the lot, so I assume it is. But with this police state you live in, it's hard to say for sure."

"You stole it?"

"Me? You're the one driving." She flashed a broad smile. "Relax. I'll return it when I catch my flight tomorrow morning."

"After you've killed me?"

"For God's sake, Kaito. Can't a girl visit an old friend? Catch up a little?"

He didn't respond.

"Is your condo clean?"

"Yes."

"Great. We'll do our catching up there."

18

General Masao Takahashi sat silently in the open vehicle, looking ahead at the rail it rode on disappearing into the gloom.

The tunnel was almost perfectly round and five meters in diameter, dug into a mountainside in a remote part of Japan. Widely spaced overhead lights intermittently illuminated the rock walls and the security detail seated around him. Beyond that, there was nothing.

They would descend nearly a kilometer into the earth before arriving at a set of blast doors leading to what had originally been conceived as a storage facility for Japan's nuclear waste. After the Fukushima disaster, though, many of the country's plants had been shut down, leaving the complex largely idle.

It was then that he'd had control transferred to the defense forces under the cover of making certain the radioactive refuse was secure. The real reason was that he needed a replacement for the Reactor Four lab that had been lost. A replacement that offered both foolproof containment and distance from prying eyes.

It took another ten minutes to reach the entrance, and

Takahashi could feel the cold from the cave beginning to penetrate his uniform. Or maybe it wasn't the temperature at all. Maybe it was something more.

The massive doors opened automatically as the vehicle approached and they glided to a stop inside. Before his takeover of the facility, this section had been lined with concrete. All that was gone now, replaced by the natural dirt and rock.

As they continued deeper into the earth on foot, the passageway constricted until it was only two meters across. Ahead, one of his men paused at a turn and then signaled that it was safe to proceed. Living surrounded by constant security made Takahashi feel like a coward, but there was little choice at this point. Most of his meetings were now being held at his heavily secured home. This trip, though, had been unavoidable. Moving Dr. Ito was becoming too difficult to do with the required efficiency and anonymity.

They finally came to a door made of a reddish woven material—the same material his limousine had been constructed of. His men fanned out, taking up strategic positions along the corridor while he pressed his thumb against a screen set into the wall.

Inside, the light was much better, though the walls remained the necessarily unadorned dirt and rock. The only furniture was a wooden table surrounded by similarly constructed chairs. The two men seated in them immediately stood and bowed.

Takahashi returned the bow, nodding at his intelligence czar, Akio Himura, and then walking over to Hideki Ito. He put a hand warmly on the scientist's back. "How are you, Doctor?"

"I'm well, General. Thank you for asking."

Of course it wasn't true—a reality that was very unfortunate for their cause. Ito was entirely bald from successive rounds of chemotherapy, and his face seemed to have collapsed in places, creating strange hollows where the muscles had selectively atrophied. The pigmentation in his skin also seemed to have been short-circuited by the massive dose of radiation he'd received in Reactor Four, leaving light and dark splotches of various sizes on his cheeks and bare scalp.

The two people assisting him that day were dead—though not by natural causes as Ito had been told. They'd simply not been valuable enough to warrant the cost of dealing with their radiation injuries. Hideki Ito was quite a different matter, though. There were no limits to what Takahashi would do to keep the man alive and working.

"I'm pleased to hear it," the general said, pulling out a chair and holding it as the frail scientist sat, a grateful smile on his peeling lips.

Takahashi took his place at the head of the table and looked at Himura. He seemed nervous. As he should be.

"It's my understanding that you've identified the man who escaped with Randi Russell?"

"Yes, sir. His name is Jon Smith. Though we found him through his personal connection with Russell and not through the CIA."

"He's not an agent, then?"

"No, sir. He's an army doctor stationed at Fort Detrick. A microbiologist and virus hunter."

"What was a virus hunter doing in a Japanese fishing village collecting reactor samples?"

"We don't know, sir. He has a Special Forces background, which explains how he was able to kill a number of our men and make it to the water, but there's very little additional information available on him. Suspiciously little."

"Military intelligence?"

"That's my assumption, though we can't find any connection between him and that division in the US Army's computer files."

Takahashi's first order of business when he'd begun designing Japan's clandestine remilitarization program over thirty years ago had been building Japan's cyber warfare unit. Computers were still crude and largely unconnected at the time, but he'd predicted with uncanny accuracy their proliferation and how critical they would become to modern warfare. He'd pulled together Japan's top minds and, with that head start, put together a system that was now a decade beyond anything even America's NSA could bring to bear. With a few notable exceptions, Himura's people could bypass the security of any private or government database in the world. Or so he'd thought.

"Maybe our abilities aren't as advanced as I've been led to believe."

"I don't think that's the case, sir. While our access fluctuates when our targets upgrade or change systems, it's quite good right now. More likely Smith is involved in a unit that's kept off the books."

The danger signals continued to grow.

"Any leads on finding either him or Russell?"

Himura's mouth tightened. "Not yet. Russell is on paid leave awaiting an inquiry relating to the killing of an American citizen in Egypt. Smith is on paid medical leave for injuries that officially occurred in a scuba accident. He has not, however, received care at any army facility."

Takahashi nodded. "Why him? Why Smith?"

"He's a scientist," Himura responded.

"But not in this field."

"Nanotechnology has many similarities to virology," Ito interjected.

"Agreed," Himura said. "The specific field of nanotech is fairly obscure. It's unlikely that the Americans would have anyone with the exact mix of skills necessary. Smith may have been their best choice."

"So it's possible that the Americans suspect nanotechnology was present at Fukushima," Takahashi said, trying to keep his voice calm.

"I've gone back through every security protocol and haven't been able to find a breach that could have led to that kind of knowledge," Himura said. "But anything is possible."

"All right, then. Who would he take it to, Doctor? Who are America's top people in the field?"

"There are a number of them. Most are pure academics working at universities."

"Dr. Ito's already provided us with the names, General, and we're watching all of them as well as the military's top materials engineers in case they don't suspect what caused the damage and are just looking for a starting point. Nothing so far."

Takahashi knew that there was no point in raising his voice or making threats. Despite his recent string of failures, Himura was eminently competent and would do everything in his power to perform his duty. Even laying down his life if necessary.

"And the assassination attempt?"

His intelligence czar didn't bother to hide his relief at the change of subject. "The JPF continues to deny involvement. The evidence against them is solid, but it's all circumstantial.

Certainly nothing that couldn't be fabricated by the Chinese intelligence apparatus."

"Do you believe that's what happened?"

"I'm becoming increasingly convinced. But it will be extremely difficult to prove. Despite our penetration into their information systems, there is no indication of any move against you. When it comes to operations this sensitive, the Chinese tend to work completely off the grid. Orders are given in whispers to men with no official government positions."

Takahashi leaned back in his chair and stared blankly at the stone walls for a moment. "The Chinese are obviously getting bolder. The Americans are doing what they can to broker peace, but I'm not convinced they're going to succeed. And frankly, I'm not sure we can trust them. The time has come to face the possibility of war and to assess our readiness."

"Surely passions can be calmed," Ito said, obviously shaken by the thought of a military confrontation. The man's unparalleled genius had allowed him to rise from a small, largely experimental cog in Takahashi's machine to his chief technological officer. There was no denying, though, that Ito was weak. It had been easy to ply him—indeed, blind him—with unlimited research funds and unfettered access to cutting-edge technology, but he had no real patriotism or political conviction. He was a man whose interests lay only in the things his magnificent mind could create.

"Of course we will do everything possible to promote peace, Doctor. But while it's comfortable to hope for the best, it's wise to plan for the worst, no?"

"Of course. I understand."

"And on that subject, is the demonstration of our drone technology still on schedule for this week?"

"It is," Ito said submissively. "I think you'll find the software to be an order of magnitude more sophisticated than prior generations. We've also made intermediate strides in range, speed, and maneuverability."

"I look forward to it. Now I don't think there's any reason to keep you from your work any longer. It's been good seeing you as always. I'm glad you're well."

Ito was typically anxious to go and stood quickly, giving a short bow before leaving the room. Takahashi remained silent for a long time, considering the dangers and opportunities presented by the quickly shifting landscape.

"You told me it would be possible to fabricate evidence that implicates the Chinese in the attempt on my life, Akio."

"Yes, sir."

"Can I assume you've created a plan to do just that?"

"I have."

"Good. Leak just enough to get the press speculating about a possible link to Beijing."

Himura wiped a hand nervously across his mouth before responding. "I would advise against it."

"Why?"

"First, creating something like this out of whole cloth was extremely complicated. Our efforts could be discovered. And second..." His voice faded.

"Speak up," Takahashi prompted.

The intelligence chief gave a jerky nod. "Sir, you understand that this..." Again he hesitated. "Dr. Ito is right. Passions are running high. Very high."

"I trust it's not lost on you that US military intelligence has physical evidence from Fukushima. And just as important, Ito's health is failing. I don't know how much longer our doctors can keep him alive. I assume that you agree his presence would be desirable in case there are problems with the deployment of his weapon?"

"Yes, sir. But—"

"We don't have the luxury of waiting any longer," Takahashi said, standing and smoothing his uniform. "Do it immediately."

19

Beijing
China

Kaito Yoshima walked to the bar in the corner of his living room and poured two drinks. Randi hung back. She had her phone in her hand and her thumb hovering over the touchscreen but was still starting to regret suggesting coming back to the condo. Who knew what surprises he'd built into the place? She'd given him the home-field advantage.

He walked over to her and held out a crystal glass filled with what was undoubtedly very good scotch. She just shook her head.

"It's not drugged, Randi. You have my word."

"It's not that I don't trust you, Kaito. Of course not. It's the calories, you know?"

He smiled and fell onto a sofa, patting the cushion next to him. She took a chair opposite, keeping a heavy coffee table between them.

"So can I assume you're here because the CIA suspects that I had something to do with the attempt on Masao Takahashi?"

It was a good bet, but she actually had no idea what agency analysts had come up with on that. It did provide a convenient way into this interrogation, though. A bit of misdirection.

"Shouldn't we?"

He waved a hand dismissively as though the attempted assassination of Japan's ranking soldier was too trivial a topic to dwell on. "We don't get paid enough for this, Randi. More and more we've become the eminently expendable pawns of insane and stupid men whose only interest is to cling to power."

"You won't get any argument from me."

"Have you ever thought about leaving the government and taking your skills private?"

"It occasionally crosses my mind."

"I think about it more and more every day. And now..." He fell silent for a moment. "They're going to lose control of this situation, Randi. And when they do, millions are going to die. For nothing. For a piece of political theater meant to keep people's minds off their real problems."

"Pick a category of people and tell the masses that everything wrong with their lives is that group's fault," Randi said. "It's been a winning message for thousands of years."

"With terrible consequences even when humans were limited to swords and clubs." He took a sip of his drink. "My country has always been difficult to govern. Too big, too diverse, too opportunistic. Frankly, too racist. The government has bribed the population with economic growth but that growth is unsustainable. And now that it's beginning to falter we face a very dangerous situation. Perhaps even the breakup of China. It wouldn't be the first time."

"And if your country broke up, where would you go, Kaito?"

He crossed his legs and spread his arms across the back of the sofa. "I thought perhaps Japan, but I don't belong there either. I don't belong anywhere."

"So, a mercenary."

"What better job for a man without a country?"

Randi nodded silently. As was so often the case with Yoshima, what was most interesting about this conversation was what was missing: a denial of his involvement in the Takahashi assassination attempt.

"China's banging the war drum," Randi said. "But like you say, it's only for show. Everybody knows it except—"

"General Takahashi," Yoshima said, finishing her thought. "He's a brilliant man. His grasp of technology, strategy, history, and the art of war is unparalleled. In many ways he's a perfect military being. If he'd led the Japanese during World War Two, I wonder if things would have gone as well for America."

"Lucky we were allies by the time he enlisted."

Yoshima finished his drink and reached for the one he'd poured Randi. "His family was one of the wealthiest and most powerful in Japan before the war. MacArthur considered them part of the feudal system that had created Imperial Japan and stripped them of everything. Did you know that? Takahashi's childhood was one of cold and hunger. His family was forced to find shelter with former servants and do hard labor just to survive."

"I guess you can't keep a good man down."

"Clearly. His father began rebuilding his empire almost immediately—during the American occupation. At first his business affairs were less than legal but eventually he managed to legitimize them. Now the family is once again one of the wealthiest and most powerful in Japan."

"I'm not sure I understand, Kaito. If Takahashi's as smart as you make out, why isn't he playing the game? Why is he courting a confrontation that would turn into a disaster for his country?"

"I admit that it's perplexing. Perhaps his mind is going. Sometimes the past looms large to the elderly. The defeat at the hands of the Americans, the years of humiliation, the loss of self-determination." He smiled. "All things too complex to be considered by crude weapons like ourselves, right, Randi? Now, where were we before I was diverted into this subject? I believe it was our business enterprise."

"And what enterprise is that?"

"Think about it, Randi. You and me. Hanging out our...roof tile."

"Shingle."

"Of course. Shingle. We would name our own price and be turning away work within twenty-four hours of moving into our luxury office suite. I was thinking Dubrovnik. Lovely place. But of course I'm open to suggestion. Paris? Rome? Istanbul? The world is our...Help me. I find American idioms so challenging. It's not clam..."

"Oyster."

"Precisely."

The dull thump of helicopter rotors became audible and Yoshima laid down his drink to walk to the window. "We'd have the power to choose our jobs. Think of it. Nothing we aren't interested in. Nothing we don't believe in. I'd rather trust my own conscience than—"

Suddenly he was in motion, diving to the right and slamming a hand into what looked like a blank section of wall. A moment later a series of steel curtains fell from the ceiling, covering the windows.

Startled, Randi grabbed the Glock from her bag but then spun at the sound of a battering ram hitting the front door. The crack of splintering wood accompanied the first impact, but the second blow generated the dull ring of steel on steel. Clearly not the stock condo door.

When she turned back, Yoshima was calmly punching a code into a safe set into the floor. He pulled out a Sig Sauer and a small bag that Randi assumed was full of passports, fake credit cards, and cash. She had similar bags stashed all over the world.

"You must have been recognized at the airport. I was afraid that might happen."

"Then why the hell did we come back here?"

"Where better? Besides, I thought perhaps we'd have a few drinks, some conversation..." He studied her for a moment. "Who knows where it might have led?"

The hammering on the door continued, growing louder as the men holding the ram became increasingly frustrated. The sound of machine-gun fire erupted outside and the metal curtains billowed inward with the impact. She dived over a chair and flattened herself against the floor, slithering forward to see if Yoshima had been hit.

He was just standing there, looking calmly down at her.

"It's an internal security helicopter," he shouted over the sound of bullets slamming into steel. "I assure you that I'm quite familiar with them and they don't have anything on board powerful enough to penetrate." He pointed toward the door behind her. "That, though, could be a problem."

She stood and looked back, seeing that the door was now bowing dangerously with every impact.

"Can I assume you have a way out?"

"Maybe," he said, starting for the kitchen with her close behind. "But more important, what do you think about my proposal?"

"Which? Going into business together or going to bed together?"

He paused for what seemed like an inordinately long time in their current situation. "Both."

She had to admit that he was an attractive guy and intriguing as hell. "Bed, maybe. But I'm thinking no on the business idea."

He smiled and went for a pantry-sized cabinet next to the stove. "It's an answer I can live with."

The machine guns out front fell silent but the hammering on the door got even louder, and the shouts of the men on the other side were no longer fully muffled.

"That remains to be seen, Kaito."

20

Jon Smith eased himself from the car and then reached back in to retrieve his duffel.

"I can get that, Jon," the driver said, running around the front bumper.

Smith waved him off. "I'm good, Eric. Thanks."

He hefted the strap onto his good shoulder and turned toward the house, breathing the pine-scented air as deeply as the shattered bones across his back would allow. It smelled like home. Something he was more grateful for than he'd ever thought possible.

The house was the way he remembered it. Casual Western modern with no expense spared to make it look deeply weathered and just a bit haphazard in design. The closest neighbor was a mile down a steep, winding road, providing a silence that at that moment he found extraordinarily appealing.

Smith started up the gravel driveway, concentrating on not hunching when he walked. Not because he didn't need to, but because he knew Eric was watching. Pride could be a bitch.

The door was ajar and the elaborate security system was

flashing green to indicate that it had been disarmed. Before stepping inside, Smith glanced back at the man who'd brought him there. "Hey, I forgot to say congratulations."

"Thanks."

He put his duffel on the kitchen counter and went to the refrigerator for a beer. Getting one off the bottom shelf required a difficult knee bend, but it was worth it. Snake River Lager tasted just as good as he remembered.

The house had been unoccupied for a while and he wiped away some dust before putting his beer down on the granite counter. It had originally been a pretty rustic place belonging to Randi's college roommate. After it got burned down with the help of an Afghan assassin, Klein had made the mistake of giving Randi a blank check for its reconstruction.

Then came the attack by a special ops team and the maddeningly difficult-to-eradicate smell of knockout gas. Apparently that was the last straw for the former roommate, and Randi had bought the house through a maze of offshore corporations. While it still wasn't impossible for a motivated party with substantial resources to track the place down, it would be difficult enough that he felt safe there. At least safer than he would have at his own house.

"Jon!" Karen Ivers called as she appeared in the hallway. "How are you doing?"

"I've seen better days. But you look great. Domestic bliss must agree with you."

She and Eric had gotten married a month before. He knew it drove Klein nuts that two of his operatives had walked down the aisle, but even the old man wasn't willing to stand in the way of true love.

"And you look...not dead."

He laughed painfully and took another swig of his beer. "Hey, the smell of gas is gone."

"New carpet, new paint, refinished woodwork, and we've had the windows open for a month. Seems to have worked. Look, I've checked the place out and everything's fine. The cell tower is still unreliable for some reason, but Randi's put in a satellite link. We've upgraded your phone so it will automatically connect. Just dial normally. The fridge is stocked with beer, as I see you've noticed, and the meds you asked for are in the bathroom. Is there anything else Eric and I can do for you?"

He shook his head. "Nah. Why don't you guys get out of here. I'm good."

"You're sure?"

In truth, he wasn't. He should have stayed in Korea a few more days, but this job needed to get done and Randi wasn't going to be able to handle it on her own.

"Absolutely. I feel better than I look. Really."

"Okay. You know that this place is pretty far off the radar but not a hundred percent, right?"

"Yeah, but I couldn't bear the thought of holing up in some fleabag safe house. It's not my own bed, but it's second best."

She slid a thumb drive onto the counter next to his beer. "Fred wanted me to give you this."

He nodded, scooping up the nondescript storage device. As the Internet became increasingly compromised by hackers and even America's own National Security Agency, Covert-One's communication was being done this way more and more. What did Marty call it? An air gap.

"Let us know if you need anything," she said, heading for the door.

"I will."

"I'm serious, Jon. None of that male stubbornness."

He smiled. "Thanks, but you don't need to worry about me. I'll be fine."

When she'd closed the door behind her, Smith sagged a bit. Too much standing in one stint.

He shuffled to the small office at the back of the house and turned on the desktop computer, holding a series of keys in order to boot to an alternate operating system.

It had been designed specifically for Covert-One—ultra-simple, ultrasecure, and completely incapable of connecting to the Internet or any other peripheral except for Covert-One–supplied USB sticks.

Despite its lack of complexity, the OS took five minutes to start up, scan for anomalies, and declare itself secure. He inserted the drive and entered his password, then went for another beer. It would take another few minutes for the processor to unravel the heavy encryption.

When he returned, he washed down a few ibuprofen and watched the progress bar crawl along. Not as effective as the OxyContin he'd been taking but a hell of a lot easier to think on.

The report finally opened and his stomach tightened when he saw that Randi was in China making contact with Kaito Yoshima. There was no question that she could hold her own against anyone on the planet, but Yoshima was particularly dangerous when he was in the mood to be. He'd been trained from infancy for this kind of work and, frankly, seemed a little mentally unbalanced.

Smith continued to scan the text on screen, discovering that the bag of radioactive debris he'd been sent to retrieve was once part of the Fukushima nuclear power plant. That explained Randi's line of investigation. Not only was Yoshima an experienced saboteur who could pass for Japanese, but he also had a degree in physics.

The rest related mostly to the suspicious radiation levels at Reactor Four. Beyond that, there wasn't a lot. Despite him getting shot with a crossbow, nearly drowned, and thrown in the back of a vehicle, they didn't seem much further along than when Klein had first called.

He pulled the thumb drive and went back into the kitchen, putting it in the microwave and watching it spark on the rotisserie. A good night's sleep. That's what he needed. Then it would be time to get off his ass and help figure this thing out.

21

Beijing
China

Kaito Yoshima pulled open the pantry door and began yanking shelves out, strewing canned goods and cleaning products across the floor. Randi had her back against the wall next to the kitchen's entrance and was watching the front door as it slowly buckled under the force of the battering ram.

"Anytime now would be good, Kaito!"

"Patience, Randi. I'm going as quickly as I can."

She glanced at the gun in her hand and let out a long, frustrated breath. What exactly was it she thought she was going to do with that weapon? She was one of the CIA's top operatives, and as such there was no way in hell she could start shooting at Chinese authorities. If she got caught and identified there was no telling what kind of damage it could do to the delicate relationship between the two countries. Reluctantly, she stuffed it back in her purse along with all the other deadly toys she couldn't use.

The helicopter could still be heard hovering outside the barricaded windows but at least it had stopped shooting. On a less positive note, a chunk of door frame about the size of a basketball had been dislodged and a man's arm was already through it feeling around for the interior locks. The temptation to wing him and slow down the assault was almost unbearable. Just a nick above the elbow . . .

"Kaito—" she said, but then fell silent when she turned. The back of the cabinet was on the floor, and in its place was a dark shaft bisected by a single vertical cable.

"You son of a bitch!" she shouted, running to the cabinet. "If you've left me—"

"Be calm, Randi. I'm here."

The voice echoed a bit but when she looked down into the shaft, she saw him hanging from a climbing harness only a few feet below floor level.

"They used this to transport construction materials when the structure was being built," Yoshima said. "Unfortunately, it's small enough that the only way this has a chance of working is for you to stand on my shoulders."

She reached down and twisted the heel on her shoe, unlocking the mechanism that held it on and then repeating the process on the other foot. She'd have to remember to send the machinist who'd done the modifications a nice bonus. If she lived that long.

Randi grabbed a kitchen towel to protect her hands from the thin metal cable and stepped onto Yoshima's shoulders. The front door finally gave way, followed immediately by excited shouts and the sound of combat boots running in their direction.

"Close the cabinet door, Randi."

When she did a dim red light came on, providing just enough illumination to see.

"There's a latch on the left side. Can you find it?"

She squinted into the gloom, finally spotting it as the voices grew louder and the footfalls grew closer. At least one man was in the kitchen. Probably two.

The mechanism was completely silent and she managed to engage it right before someone jerked on the handle from outside. The impacts of a rifle butt against the cabinet door started a moment later.

Yoshima looked up at her. "I take it you found it."

"Yes. Can we leave now?"

"Of course, but first I'd like to thank you for wearing a skirt."

She was about to kick him in the side of the head when the sound of automatic fire erupted. Randi threw her hands up reflexively, but the bullets didn't penetrate, instead ringing off the cabinet door's steel reinforcements. She cursed under her breath when she heard a pained scream from one of the men trying to get at them. He'd clearly been caught with a ricochet. There was no way to hold her responsible for that, was there? Technically the moron shot himself.

"Can I safely remove the explosive taped to the back of my neck?" Yoshima asked calmly.

"Oh, for Christ's sake," she shouted as another deafening volley hit the cabinet door. "It's piece of tape with a Tic Tac in it."

Yoshima sighed as they started sliding down the cable. "Of course it is."

The ride down took only a few seconds, which still felt like an eternity to Randi. If the men above managed to get through, they would spray bullets down into the shaft. There would be nowhere to run.

Randi crammed her knees onto the wall, taking the weight off Yoshima as he flicked on another red light and opened a panel that led to the underground garage. They climbed out, weaving through the cars parked there and watching for any sign of the Chinese authorities. Beyond the security cameras bolted near the ceiling, though, it looked clear.

Yoshima crept around a battered delivery van and waved her up as he threw a leg over a beefy BMW motorcycle that looked like it had been designed for the Baja 500.

She jumped on the back as he fired up the motor, barely getting her arms around his waist before the front wheel lifted and they started up the garage's ramp.

They dodged around the exit gate, nearly scraping the wall as a startled attendant looked on. Yoshima put the bike into a well-practiced slide and she tried to keep her weight neutral enough to allow him to turn onto the sidewalk. Pedestrians dived in every direction as they accelerated, but to his credit Yoshima managed to miss each of them.

Behind, two unmarked cars started after them, leaving a cloud of tire smoke as they forced their way into traffic. The pursuing vehicles were bigger and less nimble than Yoshima's bike, though, and were doing little more than racking up serious body-panel damage as they receded into the distance.

"Tell me about Fukushima!" Randi shouted as they shot up the white line between two lanes of crawling traffic. The bike's speedometer read almost eighty as they crossed an intersection against the light, nearly taking out a group of cyclists.

"The nuclear plant?" he yelled back. "What about it?"

The regular police had joined the chase and she saw one turn into the intersection they'd just blown though. Traffic got denser and Yoshima grabbed the brakes, putting the bike into a nose wheelie that barely kept them from going broadside into an SUV. Behind, the sirens were multiplying and getting louder.

"What happened there?"

"I don't understand what you're asking me, Randi. A tsunami hit it and knocked out their power. I don't think now is the time for an explanation of how nuclear reactors overheat."

"You didn't have anything to do with it?"

They managed to get around the SUV and were accelerating again. Distracted by her questions, Yoshima didn't see the car door opening in front of them until it was too late. He tried to cut left, but clipped the right side of his bars and the bike went out from under them. He hit the asphalt and she was catapulted onto the much softer hood of a Ford, sliding across it and managing to land on her feet.

"Kaito!" she shouted, running between cars and lifting the dazed man to his feet. She could hear the screeching of tires behind her but there was no time to look back. People were getting out of their vehicles, calling to the police, pointing at them. From experience, she knew that the situation could devolve quickly. It would only take one bystander to decide he was John Wayne and try to grab them for this disaster to turn into complete chaos.

"Get on!" she said, lifting the still-running bike and jumping on. Yoshima wrapped his arms around her waist and she twisted the throttle, going right for an angry-looking man blocking their path. He briefly held his ground but then thought better of it when she goosed the throttle and lifted the front wheel in preparation for running straight over him.

"Kaito! Which way do we—"

She heard a single shot and a moment later the grip on her waist lost its strength. Yoshima's mouth brushed her ear. "I'm sorry we won't spend that night together."

Randi tried to get hold of him but he was already toppling

backward off the bike. She slammed on the rear brake and skidded into a ninety-degree stop, looking back at him lying in the street. Two men were running in their direction from a black Audi parked horizontally across the road. One stopped to take aim at her.

Yoshima managed to prop himself on an elbow and wave her off with a smile full of bloody teeth.

Her purse was hanging across her back and she instinctively reached for it but, again, stopped herself. She couldn't shoot these sons of bitches, and that made getting to Yoshima impossible.

With no other alternative, she planted a foot and twisted the throttle again, spinning the bike 180 degrees before accelerating toward an alleyway. Hopefully, it would give her cover from the chopper she could hear approaching from the north.

22

Jon Smith kept his pace slow and steady as he walked down the hallway. The woman at the front desk had told him the man he was looking for would be in the first lab past the offices, but who knew there would be so many damn offices?

Ironically, the stitched-up hole and titanium screws in his back weren't bothering him all that much. It was the shattered ribs. Deep breaths were completely impossible, and just get ting out of bed was a project that involved him sliding off the mattress and onto the floor.

Still, it was good to be out and moving around—particularly with no one trying to kill him.

He stopped in front of an open door and tapped quietly on the frame. The woman inside glanced up from her computer. "Can I help you?"

"I'm looking for Dr. Greg Maple."

"You're on the right track," she responded with a smile. "Keep going. First lab you come to."

"Is it much farther?"

She seemed confused by the question, examining his broad

shoulders, narrow waist, and tan face. "About twenty-five yards. Do you consider that far?"

Yes, he thought. His favorite twenty-five-mile trail-running loop suddenly seemed easy by comparison.

"Thanks for the info."

It was right where she said it would be. The wall on the right turned to glass, displaying a large room tangled with unfathomable machinery, insulated pipes, and electrical cables. Maple was alone at the center wearing an old pair of slacks and an even older sweater. It was impossible to see what was spread out on the table in front of him, but he was tapping himself in the head with a pencil, pondering it intensely.

Smith went through the door and closed it behind him. "Hey, Greg."

"Jon? Man, I haven't seen you in forever!" Maple said, throwing his arms wide and approaching with a broad smile.

Smith held out a cautionary hand. "Whoa, Greg. Broken ribs and stitches."

He stopped. "What the hell happened to you?"

"I was doing some diving off the coast of Japan and got hit by a boat. Spent some time in a coma as a John Doe in a hospital near the coast."

It wasn't a perfect cover story, but so far everyone was buying it.

"Jesus, man. I'm sorry. Not as bad as that time I went overboard in the strait, though. At least the Sea of Japan's warm."

Smith grinned by way of response. Maple was a naval academy graduate and former sub driver who had gone on to get a PhD in nuclear engineering. Now he consulted for various defense contractors designing the power plants for a variety of seagoing weapons systems. If anyone understood the ways atomic containment could fail, it was Greg Maple.

"Hey, what do you say I take you to lunch, Jon? Celebrate your narrow escape from the Grim Reaper?"

"Sounds great," Smith said, holding up the briefcase gripped in his good hand. "But before that, I was hoping you could look at something for me."

"Sure. What is it?"

"First, you have to agree that this is just between us."

"Okay."

"Seriously, Greg. You can't talk to anyone about this. Not your wife, not your mother, not your priest. Are we clear?"

"Jesus, Jon. Fine. Scout's honor."

Smith handed him the case and he was about to open it when Smith stopped him. "It's radioactive."

"Radioactive? A little out of your wheelhouse, isn't it?"

"Let's just say I'm branching out."

"Okay. No problem."

They walked to the other end of the lab and Maple put the briefcase into a lead glass enclosure. He used a couple of joysticks to control the mechanical arms inside with impressive precision. A moment later the latches were popped and the case was open.

"It looks like garbage," he said, raising the bag of debris and laying it on a small platform.

"It's steel, concrete, and plastic," Smith said. "Try to break it. Hit it with something."

Maple glanced at him, a little confused, but then he used the mechanical claw to tap a piece of concrete about the size of a golf ball. It immediately crumbled. Similar tests on the steel and plastic provided the same results.

"What happened to it?" Maple asked.

"You tell me."

He put a few pieces of debris on a tray. "Let's take a look through the scope."

There was a monitor and keyboard next to the joysticks and Maple punched in a few commands. A moment later a hazy image came up.

"This is the steel," Maple said, tapping the screen. "High-quality stuff. But look to the left where the texture changes. Let's zoom in a little more."

Oddly, as the magnification increased the image came into better focus. What had looked like haze from a distance read as countless individual pockmarks up close.

"Hello..." Maple said, squinting at the image.

"So that's what's causing the structural weakness in the material, Greg? All those little holes?"

"It's a good bet. This kind of steel should appear pretty smooth at this magnification."

"Could radiation have done the damage?"

"No," Maple said, absently. He increased the scope's power again and the uniformity of the damage disappeared. Some of the pockmarks were round and milky in appearance, while others appeared to have collapsed in on themselves.

"Let's take a look at the concrete."

They found the same kind of damage in both it and the plastic samples.

"Where did you get this?" Maple asked, panning the scope back to the steel.

"It's not really important."

"It would help to give me some context."

"I'm concerned it might influence your conclusion."

He let out a long breath, still staring at the screen. "Can I bring some other people in on this?"

"Absolutely not."

Finally he dropped into a chair and looked up at Smith. "You're not giving me much to work with, Jon. You're starting to sound like those military intel guys."

"Call me a utility infielder."

"Uh-huh."

"Look, if it wasn't hard, I wouldn't need you, Greg. Why don't you just give me your first impression?"

The engineer chewed his lip for a moment. "It's not radiation damage. You can take that to the bank. I've never seen anything quite like this, and I can guarantee you I've seen everything radiation can do to construction materials. It's weird that the damage is so similar in such different mediums. Can you tell me if they all came from the same place?"

"They did," Smith said. "Is it possible that it was sabotage?"

"With what? A death ray?"

"You tell me."

Maple pointed to the screen again. "Look at the pattern of damage. It's from the outside in on some samples and coming from a single side on others. Nothing from the inside out."

"So it was attacked by something. Like it was facing a radiation source and that source slowly penetrated."

"It's not radiation, Jon."

Smith leaned into the screen. "In a way, it looks like a biological attack. An infection. A bacteria attacks the tissue and multiplies, moving inward as it goes."

"So you think your concrete got a cold?"

"Just thinking out loud. What about some kind of corrosive

liquid—an acid. It gets on the material and essentially soaks in, weakening it as it goes."

"A reasonable guess, but there's no real indication of that kind of fluid movement. And again, the damage in all three materials looks so similar. If you dump the same acid on concrete, steel, and plastic, you don't get the same result, right? The plastic maybe gets melted, the steel gets etched, and the concrete just gets a stain. Obviously, I'll run some tests but I can tell you that this isn't like any chemical agent I've run across. My gut says no."

"What else does your gut say?"

He leaned back in his chair and stared at the image on the screen. "That you've found something very new. And very dangerous."

23

912 Miles Northeast of Papua New Guinea

General Masao Takahashi stood on the bridge of the cargo ship and looked out over the deck. Longer than that of an American aircraft carrier, it was empty with the exception of three massive containers directly beneath his position. As forecasted, the weather had come in, creating a perfect environment for the test they were about to run. The thick layer of clouds was high enough not to hamper visibility, but it would still blind the American satellites that were becoming virtually impossible to schedule around. An intermittent mist was collecting on the glass in front of him and winds were gusting to forty knots, creating what he considered realistic battle conditions. Wars were not won only under temperate skies.

He looked behind him at the five men on the bridge and at the banks of equipment far too sophisticated for this type of ship. Dr. Hideki Ito, wearing a wool hat and dark glasses to obscure his radiation injuries, was talking quietly to the captain. The other men were glued to their computer screens making the necessary preparations.

"Is everything ready?" Takahashi asked.

Ito gave a jerky nod. "Yes, of course, sir. The planes are being uncrated as we speak."

"I'd like to meet the pilots."

The scientist looked through the window, suddenly seeming a bit pensive. He was not a man to brave the elements, or indeed to leave his lab if he could avoid it.

"Akifumi," Takahashi said. "Perhaps you would like to join me?"

Captain Akifumi Watanbe gave a short bow and motioned toward the bridge's exit. He was a man of few words who, despite current appearances, had never been involved in the merchant marine. He had retired from Japan's naval defense forces five years ago, and it was unlikely that there was a more patriotic or competent officer in the country.

The wind lashed the stairs as they descended, but the rain began to dissipate. On deck, crews from the air defense force were preparing two Mitsubishi F-15 Eagle fighter jets. Another crew was farther forward setting up an aircraft carrier–style catapult that had been specifically designed and built for that vessel.

The two pilots were standing together at the front of the planes, and both snapped to attention when they saw Takahashi approaching. There were no words spoken. None were necessary. He bowed deeply and then backed away to watch them climb into their cockpits.

Automation was the future of warfare, particularly for a country with as few resources as his own. It was a reality he both accepted and despised. There was a time when wars created heroes. When loyalty and courage rose to unparalleled heights. When men came to understand who they were and form bonds stronger than anything civilian life could ever hope to produce.

It was nothing more than nostalgia now. Let the Americans and Chinese bankrupt their countries with weapons and tactics that were nothing more than incremental improvements over those used against his own country so many decades ago. Neither he nor Japan could afford such childish illusions.

Another smaller crate had been opened behind him and Takahashi walked to it with the ever-silent Watanbe trailing close behind.

The next-generation missile it contained was finally small enough, though he frowned as he passed a hand over its titanium shell. At two meters, it was at the very limit of the guidelines he'd set out. The mantra "Small, cheap, and independent" had been coined by his mentor, and Takahashi had remained loyal to its spirit for more than thirty years now.

He moved around the weapon, careful not to interfere with the men preparing it for launch. There were two flexible forward wings and a set of oversized tail wings that allowed for the extremely high level of maneuverability the system demanded.

When all this began so long ago, Takahashi had wondered if he would see this class of weapon operational during his lifetime. It had been made a reality only by an advance in solid propellant that made it three times as energy dense for the weight as the most sophisticated fuel used by the Americans.

His people had focused first on an underwater version— a rocket-propelled torpedo that was crucial to the defense of an island nation and relatively easy to develop in secrecy. The air-to-air system they were testing today was based on that technology and, while not originally prioritized, would become a critical piece in the overhaul of Japan's military capability.

Ultimately, the goal would be to shrink the projectiles down to a meter and reduce the cost to the point that he could unleash swarms numbering in the thousands. Japan's enemies would have no answer.

Takahashi felt a hand on his shoulder. "I'm being told we're nearly ready, Masao."

He turned and smiled warmly at the captain. "Lead the way, old friend."

When they reentered the bridge, Dr. Ito was rushing around with a level of nervous energy that belied his age and physical condition.

"Doctor," Takahashi said. "I'm told we're ready to proceed?"

"Yes, sir," he said, spinning and giving an awkward bow. "We're in the process of rebooting the water-launched unit. Less than a minute."

One of the missiles was currently lying on the seafloor—another advance borrowed from their torpedo technology. And another capability that greatly benefited an island nation.

Outside, the engines of the two fighter planes began spooling up, and Takahashi leaned into the windows to watch one being attached to the catapult. He heard Watanbe announce that there were no other craft within radar range and clear the pilot for takeoff. A moment later the F-15 was speeding down the makeshift runway.

"What are the final numbers, Doctor?" Takahashi asked as the second fighter prepared for launch.

"I think it's most instructive to make comparisons to the American F-16. Our weapon has five times the operational range, partially due to more advanced propellant and lower weight but also because they can simply be destroyed when their fuel is expended as opposed to having to return to base. In mass production we're estimating a unit cost of four million US dollars as compared with twenty-five million for the F-16, not including the pilot and an order of magnitude more maintenance. Our maximum speed is approximately Mach eight compared with Mach two for the plane. And we can pull twenty-three g's in a turn whereas the most a human pilot can endure is nine."

"But a pilot can think," Takahashi said.

"So can our computers, General. In fact, our systems are consistently outperforming human pilots."

"In simulations."

"I know you have a great bias against simulations, General, but they've become quite sophisticated." He looked down at the floor for a moment and then raised his head, daring to meet the general's gaze. "I want to say again that this test isn't nece—"

Takahashi held up a hand, silencing the man. Ito's concern for the two pilots demonstrated his complete inability to look past his tiny world of equations and experiments. These pilots had been honored with an opportunity to sacrifice for their country. Their courage would be remembered for generations.

"Proceed," Takahashi said, leaning into the glass in order to track the two F-15s as they flew loops around the massive container ship.

Ito tapped the shoulder of a young man sitting at a computer terminal. Almost immediately the rocket on deck began to smoke. A moment later flame exploded from the back, blackening the deck and sending it streaking into the air. It leveled off and entered a holding pattern above them.

"Please keep your eyes starboard," Ito said. Takahashi turned and watched a second missile burst from the water and join its mate arcing lazily around the ship.

"To be clear, it's my understanding that these weapons are completely autonomous," Takahashi said. "You and your people will not be controlling them in any way."

"That's correct, General. Once they're given the order to engage, ongoing human involvement is unnecessary."

He nodded. While giving machines this much autonomy had its dangers, there was little choice. America's drones could be controlled from remote locations due to the weakness of their opponents. A sophisticated enemy would have the ability to jam, and perhaps even co-opt, control signals.

"Can we begin the attack protocol, sir?"

Takahashi nodded.

"In this first demonstration, we'll be flying the units in their basic mode. To use video game terminology, this is level one."

It was an apt analogy. The computer control system had been created by a former video game designer who had specialized in building computer-generated opponents for human players. The man was undeniably brilliant, but Takahashi still had his doubts. It seemed impossible that a pile of transistors and silicon chips could compete with human instinct, ingenuity, and courage.

The missiles broke from their holding pattern and went directly for the fighter aircraft, which immediately took evasive action. The rockets had no offensive weapons per se. They were ramming devices. Kamikazes.

"In basic mode, we've exactly matched the missiles' capabilities to those of the planes," Ito said as the general watched one of the fighters go into a steep dive in order to avoid being hit. The pilot barely managed to pull up before impacting the water while his electronic opponent broke off and lined up for a second attack.

"So what you're seeing here is a direct comparison between the abilities of the pilots. Human against machine."

Takahashi noticed that he was leaning against the ship's

controls and righted himself, standing straight as the battle played out before him. It was difficult not to let his expression reflect what he was feeling as he watched. Next to him, even the stoic Watanbe seemed disturbed at what he was seeing. The pilots—two of their best—were completely outmatched. They were surviving by flying at the ragged edge of their abilities, using guns and air-to-air missiles to try to keep their electronic opponents off them.

"There's simply no way they can compete," Ito said, seeming to read the general's mind. "You've created an unfair test. The computer can monitor hundreds of different variables, calculate millions of possibilities, and make nanosecond decisions that are translated into action instanta—"

"Go to full capability," Takahashi said.

"But, sir, haven't we already proved—"

"You've proved nothing!" the general shouted. "Do it now."

"Yes, sir," Ito said, shrinking back, clearly unable to understand the general's sudden anger.

One of the pilots fired a missile and despite himself, Takahashi felt a moment of elation when it locked onto one of Ito's missiles. The precisely executed evasive maneuvers he'd come to expect of the cutting-edge weapon weren't materializing. Perhaps these computers weren't as superior as their creator believed.

But then the engines flared and Ito's rocket increased its speed to what seemed an impossible level.

"The fighters' AAM-3s have a top speed of only Mach two point five and a range of thirteen kilometers," Ito explained. "The computer's determined that it will be more efficient to just stay ahead of it until it runs through its fuel."

The pilot banked to try to take out the other autonomous

missile as it skimmed the waves in pursuit of the other fighter, but there was no chance. It was too fast to even reliably track with the human eye.

The plane exploded into a fireball just as Takahashi spotted the imminent return of Ito's second weapon. The pilot saw it too and with no other recourse, aimed straight for it with guns firing a constant stream of tracer bullets. They collided less than a second later, another fireball filling the air before breaking up and falling lazily toward the sea.

Takahashi took a hesitant step back from the windows. The test had been a resounding success, but his only sensation was one of numbness. He had set out to change the world and done just that. He had created a new reality in which men like him, men like those magnificent pilots, were of no importance.

"They're ready to be put into full production?" he asked finally.

"Yes, sir."

"Then do it."

"Right away," Ito said.

"And the Fukushima project?" Takahashi asked. "We're on track again?"

The loss of the Reactor Four lab had been a setback, but the new facility in the north was proving to be a more effective—and more private—setting for what needed to be done.

Ito licked his cracked lips. The damage to the flesh on his face normally made his expression difficult to read. Today, though, his fear was on full display.

"Progress is difficult, General. We're trying to control the underlying forces of nature."

"It's my understanding that all your tests have been one hundred percent successful."

"Yes, sir. My error correction systems have functioned flaw-lessly to date. But those are only small-scale simulations. We—"

"Weren't you just telling me that I should rely on simula-tions?"

Ito became even more uncomfortable. "In this case, I'm not sure that reliance is wise."

"You sell yourself short, Doctor. You've succeeded. You've succeeded beyond anyone's wildest dreams."

24

Prince George's County, Maryland
USA

F red Klein rose from his chair when Randi charged into his office, but Smith had finally managed to find a comfortable position and stayed put.

"Is Yoshima dead?" she asked by way of greeting.

"We believe so. Reports are that his body was taken away by Chinese authorities, but we haven't been able to find out anything more."

She stood frozen in the middle of the floor. "And me?"

"It appears that you were identified, but the Chinese government isn't sure yet how to handle the situation. After all, you were the one who was attacked and you showed impressive restraint. My guess is that the Chinese will be happy to let this just fade away."

"You said we had to move on this thing," Randi explained unnecessarily. "Yoshima seemed like our best lead."

"I agree."

It was clear that she was blaming herself for the man's death, and Smith sympathized. He'd been in the same position more times than he wanted to remember. "It's not your fault,

Randi. If anyone understood the risks of this kind of life it was Kaito. I'm not even sure he cared."

Her face fell a bit and she eased silently into a chair.

"Were you able to learn anything?" Klein prompted.

"I'd say he was behind the attempt on Takahashi's life. But he didn't know anything about Fukushima."

"You're sure?"

"Not a hundred percent. He could have been playing me but my gut says he wasn't."

Klein let out a long breath and reached for his pipe. "So not back to square one, but close."

"None of this makes sense to me," Smith said. "No matter how many ways I look at it, I can't get the pieces to fit."

"How so?" Klein said.

"According to your people, there's no damage at the other Japanese nuclear plants, right?"

"We went over all of them looking for any sign of the kind of structural weakness you and Greg Maple described and came up empty."

"So the Chinese develop some kind of new weapon and they use it on that particular plant and *only* that plant."

"It could have just been the first one," Randi interjected. "Then the tsunami hit."

"But why Japanese nuclear power plants? What was their play?"

"To discredit them?" Klein said. "Make them lose face?"

"A serious nuclear incident would also keep the Japanese pretty well occupied," Randi added. "And let's not forget that killing Takahashi would throw a wrench into their defense forces' readiness. Maybe they were setting up an attack."

Klein shook his head. "The Japanese have other competent

generals—and let's not forget our treaty. In a war with Japan, the Japanese defense forces are the least of China's problem. I can tell you that the president intends to honor our agreement to protect the Japanese in the event of an attack. We already have two carrier groups in the area as a display of that commitment."

"I agree," Smith said. "The Chinese government is drumming up all this hysteria to divert attention from the slowdown in their economy, not because they want to go to war. But they're not entirely wrong to be worried about Takahashi. A remilitarized Japan would completely disrupt the balance of power in the Pacific, and the general isn't exactly a dove."

"So you think they could have been trying to quiet things down by taking out Takahashi?" Randi said.

"There's a certain twisted logic to it."

They sat in silence for almost a minute before Klein spoke again. "Something we need to remember is that whatever happened at Fukushima, it wasn't seen through to its conclusion. The tsunami intervened. Could it have been a terrorist group? The JPF has been escalating their attacks. What about an antinuke group? Japan has their share of those for obvious reasons."

"It's unlikely," Smith said. "We'll know more after Greg finishes his analysis, but at this point the technology used looks well beyond what you'd expect from a terrorist group." He leaned forward to ease the pressure on his back. "Hell, from what I've seen so far, it may be beyond us."

25

Tokyo
Japan

When General Takahashi entered the office, the two men inside immediately stood. Prime Minister Fumio Sanetomi walked quickly toward him and bowed before extending his hand—an American custom he'd adopted in recent years.

"How are you, General? I'm happy to see that you look well despite your recent ordeal."

"I'm fine, thank you for asking, sir. I was extremely lucky. Many others weren't."

Sanetomi nodded gravely and swept a hand toward the other man in the room. "You know Akio Himura."

Takahashi bowed respectfully to Japan's intelligence czar. Of course, the prime minister had no idea of their close relationship. Politicians were men without honor who came and went with the whims of the Japanese people. Admittedly, Sanetomi was better than most. His economic policies had accelerated Japan's escape from recession, and he seemed to have at least a vague notion of his country's potential to again rise to world prominence. Like his predecessors, he had supported the growth of Japan's defense forces—but also like his predecessors, he had been kept in the dark as to the full scope of that growth. In the end, neither his conviction nor his courage could be counted on.

"Please," the prime minister said. "Sit with me."

Takahashi and Himura did as they were told. Sanetomi poured them tea.

"I think you both know that I believe it's time for Japan to step out of America's shadow to pursue its own interests. And I've taken whatever political risks are necessary to start us down that path."

Takahashi fought back a smirk. *Political risks.*

It was considered the grandest of sacrifices by people in Sanetomi's profession. Takahashi thought of the two pilots who had happily died to carry out the test of their new air defense system and felt sickened by the man sitting before him.

While the veneer of politeness demanded by their culture obscured it, Takahashi despised the prime minister and was certain that the politician felt the same way about him. It mattered little, though. The power and wealth of the Takahashi family combined with his popularity would make it political suicide to try to remove him from his position as the commander of the defense forces.

The prime minister put down the teapot and continued his thought, choosing his words carefully. "You're pushing too hard, General. You're fanning flames that could consume us all."

Takahashi responded only with a brief, properly contrite nod.

"And you," Sanetomi said, shifting his gaze to Himura. "The

leak from your organization that China may have been involved in the attempt on the general's life was unforgivable. Demonstrations in China and at home have grown in size and intensity. There are concerns of civil unrest."

"My apologies, Prime Minister. I assure you that we're doing everything in our power to track the source of the leak."

Sanetomi leaned back in his chair and examined both men for a moment. "It matters very little at this point. The damage is done and I find myself forced to be the first to pull back from the brink. After all, we can't have the Chinese making another attempt on the general's life. He is far too important to Japan for us to lose."

Takahashi nodded the appropriate acknowledgment of the man's words, but saw them as a hollow piece of flattery. "And what will that entail, Prime Minister?"

"I'm working directly with President Castilla to put together a series of concessions on both sides in order to calm the situation."

"Concessions?" Himura said.

"We will propose that the Chinese use their censorship capabilities to extinguish anti-Japanese sentiment on the Internet and to crack down on demonstrations. They'll pull back their military from the Senkakus and agree to join us in face-to-face talks regarding those islands. They'll also cancel their most offensive anti-Japanese television programs and agree to work with some of our entertainment people to develop ones with a more modern outlook."

Takahashi didn't bother hiding his contempt. After everything that had happened, the prime minister's answer was to develop television programs? It was beyond absurd.

"I assume we will have to provide similar concessions,"

Himura said, clearly concerned that Takahashi wouldn't be able to control his tongue. And on this occasion, the intelligence chief might have been right.

"It's the nature of politics, I'm afraid," Sanetomi said calmly. "We will publicly remove a number of the people they consider war criminals from the Yasukuni Shrine. We will work with their historians to rewrite the sections of our school history books in order to..." His voice faded for a moment as he again considered his phrasing. "To more neutrally reflect our soldiers' actions during the war."

Takahashi opened his mouth to protest, but the politician silenced him with a raised hand. "Further, we'll promise to agree to some level of resource sharing with regard to the Senkaku Islands. And finally, we will agree to scrap our new battleship out of respect for their concerns about its offensive potential."

General Takahashi's jaw clenched, but beyond that he kept his face opaque. More apologies. More crawling. Mao had eradicated the opium dens from his worthless country, but his people had simply replaced that addiction with a new one: endless Japanese penitence. And like all addicts, the more they filled their veins, the more they needed.

"Am I to understand that you find this arrangement acceptable?" Takahashi said.

"I find it inescapable," Sanetomi replied. "And if you'll excuse my frankness, your behavior is not an insignificant part of what put me in this position."

"My behavior? The Chinese government creates a constant stream of lies to divert attention from their own towering incompetence and corruption, and *I* am responsible? For what? For believing in my country? For honoring those who've given their lives for it? For not having the courtesy to die at the hands of their assassins?"

Himura gave him a cautioning stare and he knew the man was right. Soon, none of this would be of any importance. Still, some insults were too great to swallow.

Sanetomi stared into his teacup as silence once again returned to the room. "You must accept my apologies, General. I did not call this meeting to assign blame. I called it to discuss a situation that's spiraling out of control more quickly and more dangerously than either of you know."

"Sir?" Himura prompted.

"I recently received a disturbing call from the Americans. They've found evidence of possible sabotage at Fukushima Reactor Four. The structure was weakened in a way that they don't yet fully understand."

"Do we have samples for our own analysis?" Himura asked smoothly.

"Unfortunately, no. The debris on our end has been disposed of and the Americans haven't offered to provide any of theirs. We've examined all the other reactors in the country, though, and found no problems. So for now it appears to have been isolated to that single reactor at Fukushima."

Takahashi remained silent, satisfied to let the intelligence man control the conversation. The prime minister was completely ignorant of the fact that Dr. Ito had been using Reactor Four as a lab and of what was being developed there.

"This is most serious," Himura said. "It could have been an attack by Chinese sa—"

"We cannot allow ourselves to jump to conclusions," Sanetomi interrupted. "The Americans haven't yet determined the cause of the damage. It could have been some kind of chemical or radiation issue, or even some unexpected result of the tsunami."

"How did they get these samples?" Himura probed.

"I'm not sure why that's important, Akio. The Americans are our allies and are keeping us fully informed."

Takahashi leaned forward in his chair. "Both Akio and I would be negligent not to bring up the possibility that this was the first salvo in a Chinese attack. It's completely plausible that the tsunami interrupted their plans and that now, with the attempt on my life, they're moving forward again."

"Again, I caution you about jumping to conclusions. Having said that, I've spoken to President Castilla about that very possibility and he's reaffirmed America's commitment to us. In fact, he's moving another carrier group into the area to join the two here already."

"So you trust the Americans to intervene on our behalf against their most significant trading partner and the country whose loans keep their government from collapsing?"

Sanetomi gave a short, confident nod. "I do. But I'm not as naïve as you believe me to be, General. It's clearly time to do a detailed assessment of your forces' ability to defend us from a Chinese attack. While I believe that President Castilla is a man of his word, the Americans have a limited presence in this part of the world. Even with them fully committed, we will not abdicate our right—and our responsibility—to defend ourselves."

"I will begin immediately," Takahashi said, surprised that the politician was even willing to go this far.

"But quietly, General. No. Silently. I'm not ready to put our defense forces on any kind of alert. The Chinese have agreed in principle to talks that I believe may de-escalate this situation. We can't afford to do anything to jeopardize that."

"I believe that to be extraordinarily unwise," Takahashi said, only because Sanetomi would expect it. The idea of putting their forces on alert in the traditional sense was a quaint anachronism now that they consisted largely of computer networks and autonomous systems. "The Chinese may just be agreeing to negotiations in order to further lull us into complacency."

"It's a risk worth taking, General. And I'm sure that I don't have to remind you that it's my decision to make."

Takahashi gave another contrite nod. The prime minister could play whatever political games he wished. They no longer had any meaning. While it appeared that the Americans hadn't yet discovered the truth about Fukushima, they would soon enough.

The point of no return had been crossed.

26

J on Smith opened the cardboard container and scooped an unidentifiable tangle of Chinese food onto his plate. Across the coffee table from him, Randi was gnawing on an egg roll with one hand and compulsively spinning a chopstick across the backs of her fingers with the other.

"I'm empty," Smith said. "You want another beer?"

"I'll get them."

He managed to stand before she did and started toward the kitchen. "No, it's good for me to get up and move around."

"Doctor's orders?" she said sarcastically.

He ignored her and dug around in the fridge, finding a couple of Fat Tires at the back.

"Thanks again for putting me up," he said, popping the tops and starting back for the living room.

"Mi casa es su casa."

She was wearing an old Columbia University sweatshirt and a pair of military-issue boxer shorts that he suspected had belonged to her late husband. Her bare feet were propped on a fossil stone coffee table—one of the many expensive upgrades Klein had signed off on out of guilt for getting her shot in the back.

"Interesting choice of cuisine," he said, easing back onto the couch and shoveling some noodles into his mouth.

"Don't get Freudian on me, Jon. I was in the mood, okay?"

"Absolutely."

They ate in silence for a while, him trying to find a comfortable position on the sofa and her staring off into space. She'd hardly said anything on the drive over from their meeting with Klein, which was unusual. When in the throes of an operation, she was usually a ball of nervous energy.

"You okay, Randi?"

The sound of his voice snapped her back into the present. "Why wouldn't I be?"

"I don't know. You seem a little...detached."

"Maybe being stuck in the middle of something that could turn into World War Three has me a little on edge."

Doubtful, he knew. She thrived on this kind of thing. The bigger and uglier the better.

"It's Kaito, isn't it?"

The egg roll stopped short on its way to her mouth. "Yoshima? What about him?"

"He's dead."

"I'm aware of that."

Smith went back to eating. Pushing would just piss her off. And he was in no condition to deal with a pissed-off Randi Russell.

She was the first to break the silence. "Maybe going to see him wasn't such a great idea."

Smith shrugged. "Sometimes you just have to close your eyes and charge."

"I guess." She scooped some food from the carton onto her plate. "As much as I hate to admit it, I kind of liked the guy.

He wasn't a scumbag like a lot of them. I honestly don't know what he was."

"Bat-shit insane as near as I could ever tell."

"Yeah. But who wouldn't be if they'd grown up like that?" She kicked her feet back up onto the table. "Klein was stuck for the first time I've ever seen and I had an angle. I keep asking myself if I was just showing off. If I dived in without completely thinking through what I was doing."

Smith chewed thoughtfully. Her willingness to throw herself at things full guns was her greatest strength. In truth, though, sometimes a hammer wasn't the right tool for the job.

"He wasn't involved in Fukushima," she said. "So I got him killed for nothing."

"Jesus, Randi. You're acting like he was the pope or something. On top of everything else he's done in his career, he just tried to assassinate the head of Japan's military and managed to take out a lot of innocent people in the process."

"Yeah. But I'm guessing a bunch of Chinese politicians came up with the bomb idea. Not his style. And I'm not sure Takahashi doesn't need killing. All he seems interested in doing is throwing gas on this thing."

Smith shrugged. "Are you even sure you got Kaito killed? He botched the assassination. You might have just been in the wrong place at the wrong time. Another blonde bimbo holed up in his apartment when the Chinese government decided he'd outlived his usefulness."

She threw a fortune cookie at him, bouncing it off his chest. "Bimbo, huh?"

"I meant that in the most positive way possible."

"I have a bad feeling about all this, Jon. You know how

these things can go: one minute everyone's flipping each other the bird from the deck of their ship, and the next a million people are dead. Delicate situations just aren't my forte."

When he laughed, the pain wasn't quite as bad as it had been over the last few days. "You said a mouthful there."

27

Off the Coast of the Senkaku Islands
East China Sea

ontacts?" Captain Isao Matsuoka asked.
      "No change, sir."
   He looked out at the calm water for a few more seconds, then turned to scan the bridge of Japan's newest battleship. It was magnificent even by American standards—a testament to flawless design manned by sailors he believed to be unparalleled in all the world. And yet it meant nothing.

   The truth was that the JDS *Izumo* was little more than twenty thousand tons of scrap metal—an antique before the first steel plate had been welded into place at the shipyard. Still, it had been his honor to command her. And it would be an even greater honor die with her.

   He returned his gaze to the glass, examining the helicopters lined up on the flight deck and the open sea beyond. The sun had risen from the water only half an hour ago and he squinted into it, searching for the enemy along the horizon.

   Both Japan's forces and those of the Chinese had retreated to safer distances on the orders of their governments. It created a deceptively peaceful scene of blue skies and gentle swells. The calm before the storm.

"Captain," his XO said, coming up behind him. "We have a secure call coming in for you on the satellite link."

Matsuoka nodded. "I'll take it in my cabin."

He walked quickly, giving respectful nods and even a few smiles and clapped shoulders to his men as he passed. It wasn't his normal custom—poor for discipline in his experience. But this day was different. A captain was only as good as the men beneath him and this was the finest crew he'd ever had the privilege to command. He was confident that they would face what was to come with courage and resolve that would be remembered for centuries.

He entered his cabin and closed the door behind him before retrieving the satellite phone from his desk.

"This is Matsuoka."

"Good morning, Captain."

He stood a little straighter, suddenly feeling the urge to look around his utilitarian quarters for anything out of place. It would be a pointless exercise, of course. There had been nothing out of place in his life since he was a child. "Good morning, General Takahashi."

"Situation report?"

"Calm seas under clear skies, sir. The Chinese have retreated from their forward positions and are holding at the locations outlined in my last report."

"Can you confirm for me that there's still a single Song-class submarine within torpedo range?"

"As of two minutes ago, that was correct, General."

Matsuoka lowered himself into the cabin's only chair, suddenly feeling an unfamiliar weakness in his legs. Was this to be the moment? The beginning of a new Japan?

"It has been a great honor to serve with you, Isao."

"The honor has been mine, sir."

The line went dead and Matsuoka switched off the handset. He didn't understand the general's plan. In fact, he knew almost nothing of it. All he could be certain of was that Takahashi was the greatest patriot and most brilliant military man he had ever known. His family had served Japan for centuries and after the war had been one of the driving forces behind the country's rise to economic power. It was only fitting that a Takahashi would be the one to lead Japan into a new era.

Matsuoka reached for a photo on his desk—one of the few personal items visible in the room. It depicted his wife and his two young boys. He wouldn't see them grow up or have a hand in what they would become. But they'd remember him. And everyone they ever met would know that they were the sons of Captain Isao Matsuoka.

28

Northeastern Japan

General Masao Takahashi stepped into the room and paused while the head of his security detail took a position against the dirt-and-stone wall. The two other men in the room were so absorbed by the monitor they were staring into, neither noticed them enter.

The engineer sitting behind the console that dominated the room was Rentaro Fujii. He had been with the defense forces for more than twenty-five years and was largely responsible for designing their autonomous torpedo technology and the air-to-air system that had been so successfully tested the day before. Leaning over his shoulder was the hunched and increasingly deformed figure of Dr. Hideki Ito.

"Is everything ready?" Takahashi said, breaking the silence.

The two scientists spun and Fujii leaped to his feet in order to deliver a respectful bow. "All systems are online and showing green, General."

Takahashi nodded and turned to his guard. "I'll be fine. Please wait outside."

His reluctant expression was expected but, as always, he followed his orders without question. Takahashi trusted the man with his life, but knowledge of what was about to happen in that room could never be revealed and had to be limited to a few critical people. Ito's condition made him easy to control and, unknown to him, his doctors were confident that he wouldn't live another year. The man returning to his position in front of the console was nearing the end of his usefulness and would be watched obsessively until it was practical to implement a more permanent solution. Takahashi even considered himself a potential threat. In a few years, age would catch up to him as it did all men. He couldn't afford to let his mind weaken. At the first signs that it was happening, he would take his own life.

"The Chinese submarine is still within range of our battleship," Ito said. "We have a torpedo resting on the seafloor less than six hundred meters from it."

"The Song carries Yu-4 torpedoes," Takahashi said. "Will this be convincing?"

"As we've discussed, our technology is significantly different, sir."

It was a wild understatement. Their system was based on the Soviet VA-111 Shkval—a rocket-propelled torpedo. Gas released from the nose cone allowed the weapon to fly inside a bubble and achieve speeds in excess of two hundred knots. The Soviet version was still available on the international arms market but had never fully made the jump from theoretical to practical. Maneuverability was extremely poor, range was limited to about twelve kilometers, and the archaic guidance system could neither compensate for the sea's unpredictable currents nor distinguish the enemy from natural geological features.

Fujii and his people had overcome all those problems and more. Range was now 90 kilometers at over 350 knots, pinpoint maneuverability had been achieved using subtle distortions of the bubble's shape, and targeting was handled by a purpose-built computer connected to a state-of-the-art sensor array. It couldn't just differentiate a submarine from an underwater volcano, it could differentiate the USS *Ronald Reagan* from the *Stennis*.

"You're still confident that we can mimic the Chinese torpedo?"

"As I told you," Ito started hesitantly. "Even with our modifications, this technology is going to make a different sound from the Yu-4. We have, however, dialed its speed back to match the Yu-4's, and we're using the appropriate explosive payload. Still, I'm concerned that it won't bear careful scrutiny by naval experts."

Takahashi looked at the unfathomable readouts on the computer monitor and let out a long breath. They had more than seven hundred of these weapons on the ocean floor, covering not only Japanese waters but also Chinese ports and sea-lanes. The torpedoes lay dormant waiting for the signal to activate, and then their artificial brains would take over—scanning the sea around them, prioritizing targets, coordinating with other units. In a matter of hours they could decimate the entire Chinese fleet and make conventional naval warfare obsolete forever. Still, this was a dangerous game. As it had three-quarters of a century before, everything hinged on the reaction of the Americans. Takahashi's bias was to not repeat the mistake of his predecessors and provoke the United States. But if it became necessary, he would crush that country just as it had crushed Japan.

"Is the Song submarine in a plausible attack position?"

Ito wiped a film of perspiration from his damaged skin. "General, please accept my apologies, but I don't understand what we're doing here. The situation—"

"I asked you a question, Doctor," Takahashi said, raising his voice for the first time in the presence of the scientist. Ito tensed visibly, as did the man sitting in the chair next to him.

"Yes, General. The submarine is in an acceptable position. But the consequences of this..."

Takahashi wasn't accustomed to being challenged, but understood that Ito wasn't a soldier and couldn't be treated as one.

"Doctor, every year the Chinese increase their military spending. They whip their people into an anti-Japanese frenzy by using the memory of events from a time before most of them were even born. More recently, they tried to assassinate me. And why wouldn't they? There are never any consequences for their actions. In fact, they were rewarded with an offer of negotiations and further concessions by our prime minister. The more we give, the more they take. What we do here today will focus the world's eyes where they should be— on a country positioning itself to create an Asian hegemony. The situation is getting out of control, and this, while distasteful, may be the only thing that can de-escalate it."

Of course, it was all a lie. The dogs that made up the Chinese government would never back down. Their lives of power and privilege depended on their ability to blind their population to the fact that far from being a rising power, China was rotting from within. Income disparity, the reliance on slave wages, environmental destruction, sleight of hand in the financial industry. Like the Soviet Union before it, China was drowning. And like a drowning man, there was nothing and no one they wouldn't drag under for one last gasp of air.

"I understand, General. But surely there's another option."

Takahashi had appeased the scientist as much as he was willing to. The man was becoming increasingly unfocused, spending valuable time thinking about things that were none of his affair.

"Launch the weapon."

Ito stood frozen, but Fujii didn't hesitate. "The torpedo is away, General."

Takahashi straightened, standing at attention. His order would end in the death of many fine Japanese sailors. It would be a weight he would bear until the day he died.

29

President's Private Residence
The White House
Washington, DC, USA

A nd so there it is, Fred."
President Sam Adams Castilla sat on the sofa while Klein watched a flat screen on the wall. The image of a massive battleship on fire was shaky and clearly cobbled together from numerous sources.

Flames and smoke obscured the scene as the wind whipped across the slowly listing deck. Japanese sailors were running in every direction, trying to contain the fire, rescue their comrades, and retrieve bodies. Some were forced to throw themselves overboard, and Klein watched in horror as they took the long fall to the waves.

His ability to immediately analyze and make accurate predictions about any situation was one of the things that made him the president's most trusted confidant. But what to make of this? How to calculate the potential ramifications?

"Does the media have access to this footage, Sam?"

"Not yet. Sanetomi's clamped down on it, but it's only a matter of time. By tomorrow, the entire world will be watching

Japan's brand-new battleship heading for the bottom of the sea with its captain and a lot of young kids still aboard."

"Jesus," Klein muttered as the screen faded to black. "What are our naval analysts saying about it?"

"We don't have anything more than the video at this point," Castilla said, taking a seat behind a modest desk. "But their initial reaction is that the damage is consistent with what you'd expect from a well-placed torpedo. In fact, just the kind that the Song-class sub in the area would be carrying."

"And the Chinese?"

"They're denying the attack. They insist that their sub has all torpedoes on board and accounted for. Of course, the Japanese say that means nothing. If China planned this, they'd have been smart enough to carry an extra and make everything look innocent."

"What's the public reaction been?"

"Hundreds of thousands of people taking to the streets in Japan. The prime minister's trying to calm them down, to tell people all the facts aren't in yet, but about all that's accomplished is to get people calling for his resignation. Of course, there are similar riots in China, but to their credit the leadership is trying to crack down on them. The question is whether it's too little too late."

He let his head sink into his hands. "I'm ordering two more carrier groups into the area, Fred. The Chinese are backpedaling and Sanetomi is calling for calm, but General Takahashi isn't. He's been on Japanese TV five times today with enough fiery rhetoric that I told the CIA to stop sending me translations. I talked personally with the prime minister but he's completely lost control of the man."

"Could he ask for the general's resignation?"

"Not a chance in hell. Beyond being one of the wealthiest men in the world, Takahashi's also one of the most powerful men in Japan. He's been with their defense forces for more than forty years, and the leaks about the Chinese being behind the attempt on his life have given him even more credibility. The people trust him and according to our analysts, it's for good reason. While they all agree that he's a nationalistic bastard, they also agree that he's a brilliant nationalistic bastard. After this, he could probably stage a coup and end up with a better approval rating than I've got right now. I swear to God I'm starting to wish that explosion had incinerated the son of a bitch."

Klein frowned.

"What?" Castilla said, eyeing him.

"We're getting some confusing information about the assassination attempt."

"Confusing how?"

"We're confident that Kaito Yoshima was the Chinese operative behind it and that he framed the Japanese Patriotic Front. What's been leaked from Japan's intelligence agency, though, relates to hired Eastern European mercenaries and we can't confirm any of it. The whole story seems to have come out of nowhere. Another in a long list of pieces that just don't fit."

"That's the least of my problems," Castilla said. "This was bad before but now we're looking at a potential full-scale war that the US is obligated by treaty to fight in. The secretary of state is on his way to Asia to sit down with both Sanetomi and the president of China. The hope is that we can portray this as a collision or some other kind of accident and that the Chinese will make enough concessions for everyone to save face and step away from the gun."

"Do you think it'll work?"

"It has to. A war between the US and China just plain can't happen. Whenever I ask anyone about how it would play out, all they can do is curl up into the fetal position."

Klein completely understood that reaction. While he found the words hard to utter, what they were talking about was World War III. There was no way the Europeans and Russians could sit out a confrontation involving the world's two largest economies and two most powerful militaries. The situation would spiral out of control, and in the context of modern technology that could mean turning the planet into an irradiated cinder.

"Sam, I'm convinced that there is more to this than meets the eye. You need to keep things at a slow boil until Jon and Randi can figure out what happened at Fukushima. My gut says that there's something critical there. That it's the piece we're missing in all of this."

Castilla nodded, but his stare was a bit distant. "You've known me for a long time, Fred. My decision-making style isn't that complicated. I gather the facts, listen to the experts, and hire the best people available to execute the solution we come up with. But do you know what I'm going to do tonight? I'm going to have a few too many drinks and then I'm going to get on my knees and pray."

30

J on Smith parked away from the lights in the empty lot and eased himself out of his classic Triumph. A chill immediately went through him, but it wasn't just the fall air. It was also the memory of the panicked 4:00 a.m. call he'd received from Greg Maple. After multiple unheeded warnings that the line wasn't secure, he'd finally had no choice but to tell the man he was on his way and hang up.

Smith managed to achieve a slow jog as he approached the front of the concrete bunker of a building. Inside, the lights were dim, but he could see a shadow moving on the other side of the glass. By the time he made it up the steps, one of the doors was swinging open and he was being motioned inside.

"Are you all right, Greg?"

The scientist didn't answer, instead scanning the lot before closing the door and locking it again.

"Did you find contamination somewhere else?"

Maple had examined the samples Klein's contacts had collected from the other Japanese nuclear power plants and pronounced them clean. Smith was concerned that the man had discovered he'd missed something and that another Asian nuclear disaster was in the offing. Maybe more than one.

Maple just shook his head and started back into the building at a hurried walk. "They're fine. The first samples you gave me are unique."

The ribs in Smith's back felt like they were grinding a bit as he caught up, but not anywhere near as badly as they had been. "What the hell's going on, then? What am I doing here at five thirty in the morning?"

"They're from a nuclear plant, aren't they?" Maple said, pushing through the door to his lab.

He'd been bound to figure it out. Frankly, if he hadn't, Smith would have started to wonder if he'd come to the right man.

"Yes."

"Japanese?"

"Fukushima Reactor Four."

Maple gave a short nod and sat in front of a computer screen that contained the same hazy, pockmarked image that had been on it when Smith left four days ago. This time, though, Maple seemed to know what he was looking at. He tapped the screen with his finger, and Smith couldn't help noticing the smear of sweat it left.

"This is nanotechnology, Jon. It's goddamn molecular manufacturing."

As a biologist, Smith had a better-than-average grasp on nanotech. The problem was that it was an ever-shifting category that had come to include basically everything human made and small. He'd never heard the term "molecular manufacturing."

"Explain."

Maple let out a frustrated rush of air. "It's the holy grail,

Jon. But even if the government decided to throw truckloads of money at it, we're twenty, maybe twenty-five years away from coming up with anything that would work. Jesus, man, it—"

"Greg! Calm down and start from the beginning. What am I looking at on the screen?"

The scientist paused for a moment to get control of himself. "Okay...listen...nanotech has all kinds of applications. The most basic is creating next-generation materials, right? If you can put the individual molecules—even atoms—in a certain structure, you get a material that does what you want on a very fundamental level."

"I'm familiar with that kind of research. Basically making stuff harder than diamond, improving heat dissipation, electrical conductivity. That kind of thing."

"Exactly. The next step would be making very tiny, very simple machines."

"I'm with you," Smith said. "I've worked with some experimental nanoscale machines that can close battlefield wounds. Amazing stuff with a lot of potential."

"Yes. Right. The holy grail, though, is machines that can replicate themselves. The best analogy is a 3-D printer that can print out a working copy of itself."

Maple tapped the screen again, and again left a sweaty fingerprint. "See the pockmarks? The tiny voids? They're not really voids. They're microscopic, self-replicating machines."

"You're losing me again."

The nuclear engineer brought up a complex diagram that didn't really clarify anything.

"There's a lot of damage to the machines themselves, but after examining a few hundred, I was able to come up with this rough sketch of what we're looking at."

"Which is?"

"A microscopic machine that was built up atom by atom."

"For what purpose?"

"It uses the material it's in—either concrete, plastic, or steel—as fuel to make copies of itself."

"Okay. But what's it do once it's made enough copies? What's its *purpose?*"

"As near as I can tell, that *is* its purpose. There are structures on it that seem to have other functions, but I can't say yet what they are. Probably some kind of command and control system."

Smith let that process for a moment. "Okay, let me get this straight. If I set a bunch of these loose on a piece of concrete, they'll eat the concrete and spit out replicas of themselves. One will become two. Two will become four. Four will become eight. And so on until they run out of concrete."

"Unless some of those command and control structures are designed to shut it off, yes."

"So the weakness in the material is caused by these little robots eating holes in it for fuel."

"Exactly. The structural problems are just a by-product. The machines aren't as strong as the surrounding material. It's like drilling holes in a piece of steel and filling them with Styrofoam. Eventually you'd be able to just break it apart with your fingers."

"But if these things can eat concrete, plastic, and steel, why not rock? Why not people?"

"There are actually three distinct versions here, each designed to use one—and only one—of those fuels. So if you put them on rock or a person they'd just lie dormant. Like a car with no gas."

Smith nodded silently. The potential for this as a weapon was obvious. Toss a handful on a tank and eventually it would fall apart as the steel and plastic degraded. Like biological weapons, though, they would create logistical problems. What would happen if a stiff wind blew them back onto your own tank?

"Jon," Maple started again, reaching out and gripping Smith's forearm. "I can't stress enough how dangerous these machines are. I'm not exaggerating when I say they make nukes look like wooden clubs. Remember what I was saying about how these can't use dirt as fuel? Well, what if I changed the design to make them do just that? They'd start making copies of themselves and their numbers would climb at a geometric rate. Depending on how fast they work, in a few months—maybe even a few weeks—the only thing left of the planet would be endless trillions of microscopic robots fighting over the last bit of fuel to make another copy."

31

Above the Senkaku Islands
East China Sea

General Masao Takahashi peered out the window of the air defense transport plane, following the sun as it began to rise from the horizon. He squinted into the glare, searching the sea below for the US carrier group holding to the northeast. It was the fourth such armada to steam into Asian waters—a display of power and resolve meant to counterbalance the growing threat to what the Americans assumed was still the helpless country they had created so many decades ago.

China would take a half step back, Japan would continue to grovel over its past, and Western economic interests—the only interests that mattered to the United States—would be preserved.

Takahashi could still remember the day he'd seen the great man. The day that Douglas MacArthur's motorcade had roared through the irrelevant little village his family had been left to rot in. The American commander had been exactly as the news reels depicted: a uniformed statue sitting in the back of a jeep, hidden by his hat, pipe, and sunglasses. He hadn't even bothered to look at the poverty-stricken farmers lined up alongside the muddy road, showing complete indifference to the people whose pride and dignity he'd stolen.

Ironically, the people there that day saw him as a god. A supernatural entity who would restore Japan and teach it the arcane secrets of Western democracy. The savior of a backward race that could not be trusted to create its own future.

Takahashi's mother hadn't come to see the spectacle. A woman of wealth and grace before the war, she had been in the middle of a fourteen-hour day working the fields. It had been hot, backbreaking labor that she wasn't suited for, but she never complained. She'd died just as his father was beginning to lay the foundations for the revival of the empire the Americans had stripped from him. And even with that last breath, she had spoken only of her concern for her sons.

Takahashi had been just a boy at the time with no concept of what was happening. No understanding that the treats she had given him and his brothers were from her own rations and that she hadn't left herself enough to survive. Or maybe he had understood. Maybe he had just been unwilling to look beyond his own empty belly.

His headphones crackled to life with the voice of the pilot, pulling him back into the present. "General, we have a visual on our target."

Takahashi went forward, stopping in the doorway to the cockpit. Through the windscreen he could see the vague shape of no fewer than five ships. The JDS *Isi* helicopter carrier and two Takanami-class destroyers were the only ones identifiable at this distance. The *Izumo*, though, was gone. She had dropped beneath the waves for the last time hours ago with forty-three men still aboard.

China's ships had immediately retreated from the Sen-

kakus at the orders of their confused government. Denials had
been quickly and emphatically delivered, but the world was
skeptical. The Chinese people, weaned on a diet of violent
anti-Japanese rhetoric, had once again taken to the streets, this
time with a fervor that the Communist Party was proving unable to control.

Despite their despotic tendencies, the truth was that the
members of the politburo ruled their country at the pleasure of
the billion people surrounding them. And those people's pleasure was blood.

The pilot arced the plane to the west and Takahashi braced
himself as they closed in on the massive rescue effort. After
a few moments he could see individual divers working from
rafts and the men standing at attention on the deck of the *Isi*,
watching over the rows of flag-draped bodies.

He had spent most of his adult life studying Japan and
the complex nature of its people. How could a small island in
the Pacific have taken on the world? Why were Japanese children consistently slotted at the very top of academic achieve-
ment? How had his people acquired their unparalleled levels
of courage and discipline?

At first he had focused on history and culture, but it hadn't
taken him long to realize that there were no satisfying answers
there. Japan had been a relatively primitive and inward-looking
feudal state, and in some ways that philosophy had persisted
well into the nineteenth century. When his country finally decided to modernize, though, it had done so at a pace that the
rest of the world could only marvel at. It was solely the failure
of Japan's nuclear weapons program that had kept the tiny island from taking control of Asia.

Even after its defeat at the hands of America, Japan had

quickly risen to become the leader of technological innovation and the second-largest economy in the world—relegated to that subordinate position only by their relatively small population and lack of natural resources.

How had all this been possible?

The answer was finally revealed by the fledgling science of genetics. Isolated from their neighbors, the Japanese had not only changed in physical appearance, but had evolved the superior intelligence, discipline, and loyalty that elevated them above the other races. In a very real sense, they were born to rule.

"General," the pilot said, twisting in his seat and pulling one of his earphones off. "You have a call from the prime minister."

Takahashi nodded and pointed through the windscreen at the bodies on the *Isi*'s flight deck. "Get a picture of that."

It would be a powerful image for his people to rally around. Of course, it wouldn't be difficult to determine who had leaked the photo to the press, but what could the government do? Every day he got stronger and the Japanese people came to see their politicians for the useless theater troupe they were.

He took a seat in the back and plugged his headset into the plane's communications system. "This is Takahashi."

"What's your assessment, General?"

Sanetomi tried to make his voice sound commanding but he couldn't obscure his apprehension. There was nothing in his life that could have prepared him for what he now found himself faced with. He had been a simple schoolteacher before he'd gone to law school and discovered his gift for public speaking and making powerful friends. This was a situation that demanded leadership, and in the end Sanetomi was just a man who looked good on television.

"The Chinese sank the *Izumo* in waters the entire international community agrees are ours," Takahashi said.

The prime minister tried to respond, but Takahashi talked over him. "According to the Americans it's also likely that they attempted to sabotage the Fukushima nuclear plant. And according to our own intelligence people, they almost certainly tried to assassinate me."

"Chinese involvement in the problems at Fukushima is little more than conjecture, General."

And of course that's all it ever would be.

"My apologies, Mr. Prime Minister. Of course you're right."

"We must step back," Sanetomi said. "This can't go any further."

"And how would you have us do that, sir? Should I tell our captains to scuttle our ships? Would that satisfy the Chinese? Or perhaps we could just reward them for their unprovoked attacks by giving them—"

"I won't be spoken to in that tone, General! Do you *want* to fight a war? Do you think it would be glorious? Even with the Americans' help and the paltry toys you've developed, the destruction would be beyond anything we experienced during World War Two. Is that your goal? To die with your family's sword in your hand while our country burns? Is that your idea of honor?"

Takahashi didn't immediately respond, instead looking out the window at the rescue efforts that were quickly becoming futile. No survivors had been found for more than six hours.

"Sometimes destruction is needed before creation is possible."

Sanetomi's stunned silence wasn't entirely unexpected. "You've been out there long enough, General. Return. Now."

"As you wish," Takahashi said, cutting off the link.

He leaned back in his chair and listened to the drone of the aircraft's engines. They were on the inevitable path to the world's first—and perhaps last—postmodern war. Technology would eventually progress to the point where battles between advanced nations would be unthinkable. At that point, the world order would likely be fixed for generations. It was his duty to make sure Japan led that world order.

Takahashi felt the plane level out and he assumed that they were on their way back to Japan at Prime Minister Sanetomi's hysterical bidding.

It was impossible to know how long it would take for the Americans to understand the meaning of the Reactor Four samples. Perhaps they already did.

And if that was the case, they would do anything in their power to stop him from using Ito's weapon. They might even go so far as to warn the Chinese or even join them in a preemptive attack on Japan. He needed just a little longer to prepare. To ensure that his plan would succeed. Soon there would be no one who could stop what was to come.

32

J on Smith wandered around the lab looking at the stainless steel tables, computers, and other machinery, but not
really seeing any of it. Maple watched him with a confused,
helpless expression that was more than a little worrying.
When a guy who made his living marrying advanced weaponry
with nuclear power got scared, the shit had officially hit the
fan.

"How would you develop something like this?" Smith said,
finally coming to a stop in the middle of the floor.

"With a lot of dedication, brains, and funding."

"So, in your opinion, this is not the work of a terrorist
group."

"No way in hell, Jon. This is government money. And a lot
more than we were willing to throw at it."

Smith nodded. The field of nanotechnology was fairly theoretical and while it would get some nominal funding from the
Pentagon, it was the kind of long-term, pie-in-the-sky project
that didn't tend to be a priority for the United States. He'd run
into the same problem himself over the years. The Department

of Defense tended to be most interested in developing ways to make existing technology tougher, faster, and more accurate. Politicians tended to be most interested in large, expensive systems that could be developed and manufactured in their districts. Nanotech fit neither bill.

"Okay, Greg. But specifically, who could have pulled this off? Who are the thinkers in the field?"

"Well, there's Gunter Heizenburg in Germany. He's doing interesting stuff at the University of Munich. And then you've got Sean Baxter at MIT. He's focused on creating new materials with nanotubes, though. I guarantee you that neither one of those guys is anywhere near doing something like this. You know how it is, Jon. They've got a bunch of grad students working for them and they fight tooth and nail for every research dollar."

"Then think harder!" Smith said, letting his frustration get the better of him. Asia was about to explode into a war that would drag in the entire world and now it seemed that someone had gotten hold of a goddamn doomsday weapon. "Sorry, Greg. It's been a long couple of weeks."

"Don't worry about it. I understand exactly what you're feeling. I can't even believe I'm looking at this. I keep thinking I'm going to wake up and find out it was just a nightmare. I mean, even if you *could* build something like this, you'd have to think long and hard about whether you should. You're messing with the forces of nature here. This is why guys like you spend your time figuring out how to cure diseases—not cause them. Once something like this gets out of control, you don't get that control back."

"Okay, Greg, let's take a step back for a second. This didn't just come out of thin air. Unless we want to start considering aliens, we can be confident that right now there are people working on this in a very well-equipped, well-funded, and well-secured lab. Who are they?"

"We should talk to Gunter and Sean. They—"

"No. No one else hears about this."

"Come on, Jon. I know a fair amount about nanotech, but it's not my field. I know both those guys and I can vouch for them."

"It's not just a matter of secrecy, Greg. Whoever did this knows I have those samples and they sure as hell have the resources to watch the obvious people in the field."

Maple sagged a bit and stared blankly at the diagram he'd created. "I keep coming back to the same answer."

"What's that?"

"Think about it. Who has the money, will, and access to talent that you'd need to get this done?"

Smith knew where this was going and shook his head. "It's not us, Greg."

"So you say. Look, I know you're a hell of a scientist and you're pretty well connected, but it's not hard to believe that something like this could go on way above your pay grade."

It was completely understandable and logical that Maple would head down this road, but Smith didn't have the luxury of letting his friend get trapped in a blind alley.

"I'm going to say this just once, Greg, and then we're going to leave it alone: there's no such thing as above my pay grade."

Maple looked at him skeptically but then quickly realized that Smith meant what he'd said.

"What if we cast a wider net? Maybe someone doing brilliant work in a related field?"

The engineer shrugged and shook his head.

"Okay. What about someone who worked in nanotech and died?"

Another shrug.

"Someone who worked in the field in the past but then moved on to something else?"

That seemed to get a glimmer.

"What?"

"Well," Maple started, chewing thoughtfully on his ragged thumbnail. "There was a guy, but it was a long time ago. And by a long time ago, I mean when you and I were still using Clearasil and chasing cheerleaders. He wasn't the theoretical father of nanotech—that was probably Richard Feynman—but he *was* the practical father. He was the first guy to make something actually work in the real world. But then he left his university position and started up a consulting company. As far as I know, he never worked in the field again."

"Name?"

"Ito."

Smith felt a jolt of adrenaline at the Asian-sounding name. "Chinese?"

"*Hideki* Ito," Maple said. "Japanese."

Smith began pacing around the lab again. "What's Ito done since he started consulting?"

The engineer frowned. "I honestly don't know. I mean, I assume he's still alive because I haven't heard otherwise but I'm not aware of any meaningful work coming out of him since the nanotech stuff early in his career."

A Japanese scientist. A Japanese reactor. As the pieces fell into place, the picture seemed to get hazier. Smith continued to pace, stopping short less than a minute later.

"What?" Maple said. "Do you have something?"

Smith looked him directly in the eye. "First of all, I want to reiterate that this is so far beyond top secret we don't even have a category for it. If this leaks, there would be consequences."

"Are you threatening me, Jon?"

"Yes. Look, I'm sorry I got you involved in this, Greg. But the fact is you *are* involved and there's nothing I can do about that now."

"Are you kidding? I have honest-to-God molecular factories in my lab. I wouldn't have missed this for the world. You've known me for a long time, Jon. This isn't my first rodeo. You can trust me."

"Okay. Then here's the rest of it. The radiation levels in Fukushima's Reactor Four were way too high to be explained by the damage done by the tsunami. That reactor was supposed to have been defueled."

Maple frowned. "After that buildup, I have to admit that I was hoping for something more interesting."

"Could radiation destroy these things?"

"At high enough levels, sure."

"So these little machines are basically just artificial viruses, right? They co-opt their host for fuel to replicate themselves. And the more there are of them, the more damage they do."

"Yeah, that's probably a good way of thinking about it for someone with your background. They're viruses that destroy the cellular structure of concrete, steel, and plastic."

"Well, I've worked with some of the most dangerous pathogens on the planet over the years. The first thing I think about when I'm doing it is containment. In my case a whole lot of stainless steel, four-inch-thick glass, air locks, and suits with separate oxygen supplies. And if all that fails, there's a toxic chemical shower that kills everything it touches."

From his expression, it was clear that Maple was starting to see where he was headed. "Of course! Why didn't I think of that? Reactor Four wasn't sabotaged with the nanobots. They were being developed there! The tsunami hit, containment was breached, and they flooded the lab with radiation. That's why there's no activity in the samples you gave me. They're dead!"

33

Prince George's County, Maryland
USA

When Jon Smith entered Klein's office, a young woman with tattoo-covered arms and a gold nose ring looked extraordinarily happy to see him. It was hard not to sympathize. Being stuck in a small room with Fred Klein and Randi Russell could be a little intense.

"How are you feeling?" she said with genuine concern.

"Better every day, Star. Thanks for asking."

Star Minctti was a thirty-something who looked like she'd spent most of her life dealing drugs from the back of a Harley. In fact, she was a former librarian and research genius. If you threw her in a warehouse full of unsorted government documents, she'd come up with the exact crumpled Post-it note you wanted inside of three hours. The fact that the old man was willing to overlook all the piercings and body art pretty much said it all about her skill level.

Klein greeted him with a subtle nod as he took a seat, but Randi ignored him in favor of fiddling with the lid of her travel mug. It was to be expected. Their conversation about Kaito Yoshima had strayed pretty far into the personal and after those kinds of exchanges, she always seemed to pull back a bit.

"Did you find Dr. Ito?" Smith asked.

"Not exactly," Star replied, standing against the wall in what seemed to be an effort to blend in with the artwork. "He does have an address, though. A nice house outside Ono. It's right there in the local phone book."

Smith started to ask a question but she anticipated it. "It's a few miles from the Fukushima plant."

"That's what I was afraid of. Can I assume he's not living there anymore?"

"It's closed up."

"And when did he move out?"

"It was one of the areas evacuated after the tsunami. He never came back."

Smith let out a long breath.

"Go on, Star," Klein prompted.

"Yes, sir. Dr. Ito started a private consulting company after leaving his research position at Kyoto University. He makes good money—around four hundred thousand US dollars according to his tax returns. All of it comes from three corporate clients."

"What corporations?" Randi said, finally looking up from her mug.

"I could give you the names but they wouldn't mean anything. As near as I can tell, they're just shells. They seem to have been set up solely to pay him."

"Does he have any employees?"

"None. It's a one-man show."

Smith pushed his chair back so he could see her better. "And what about that other thing I wanted you to look into?"

"General Takahashi? You were right. It's a bit of a maze, but it appears that his family has significant ownership in the company that operated the Fukushima plant."

Not what he wanted to hear. A few days ago he would have said that discovering the Chinese were behind the nanotech at Fukushima would have been a worst-case scenario. This, though, had the potential to be a hell of a lot worse.

"Great job as always, Star. Thanks."

She made a beeline for the door, obviously anxious to escape before Smith changed his mind and asked her to stay.

"Shut the door behind you, please," Klein called after her.

She did and they sat in silence for a few moments before Smith spoke. "The dangers involved with a weapon like this can't be overstated. And neither can the chances that it could go completely out of control."

"Are you sure it's meant as a weapon?" Klein said. "I read your report and looked into the technology. Is it possible that this was one of the Takahashi family's commercial pursuits? Nanotech is a growing field and I wouldn't be surprised if they were interested."

"It's possible," Smith admitted. "But why so much secrecy? And why self-replication across three materials that are critical to modern civilization and warfare? If I were working on this, I'd fuel it with some incredibly rare material. Then, if I lost containment, I wouldn't have to pump a bunch of radiation into it to keep it from wiping out the industrialized world."

Klein leaned back in his chair, staring for a moment at an antique map hanging on the wall. "There seems to be reasonable agreement that the Japanese are looking to expand their military capability and move out from under our umbrella. If I were an island nation with limited resources and manpower, this might be just the kind of weapon that would attract me."

Randi suddenly stood. "I know a couple of the analysts at

the agency who keep tabs on the Japanese. Maybe they could give us some context."

Klein gave her a brief nod. "Talk to them. Quietly."

She spun on her heels but then paused. "You look good, Jon. It's nice to see you not shuffling around like an old man."

A moment later she was through the door and gone.

Smith pulled a piece of paper from his pocket and slid it across the desk. "I've got a little shopping list for you, Fred. You know. Just in case."

Klein's eyes widened when he read the note. "Jesus, Jon. I'm not sure America even has one of these anymore."

"See what you can do."

"I assume you don't want it dropped in your garage."

Smith shook his head. "Send it to the Okinawa air base and put it under wraps. Then hope to God we never get a chance to use it."

34

CIA Headquarters
Langley, Virginia
USA

Randi Russell hustled down the hallway, already late because of a number of wrong turns. It never ceased to irritate her that she could flawlessly navigate the tangle of ancient streets and alleys crisscrossing the Middle East, but every time she came to headquarters, she got lost. Of course, she set foot in Virginia rarely and then only when there was no other option.

She spotted the conference room she'd been searching for and picked up her pace a bit. The men waiting for her were the agency's top minds on Japan and, in light of the shit storm going on in the Pacific, probably had better things to do.

Randi juggled her notepad and coffee, gripping the door handle and grimacing as she entered the room. She hated office buildings and everything about them. The smell, the fluorescent light, the cheesy artwork. But most of all, she hated the bureaucracy that incubated in them like bacteria.

The two men sitting next to each other behind the table didn't immediately react to her arrival other than to stare. Not an uncommon reaction in the scheme of things. She'd met them in passing years ago but, by design, she was a bit of a ghost. And she'd apparently built quite a reputation based on a bunch of outlandish stories quietly passed around Langley's back offices. Most weren't true, of course. The vast majority of the CIA's employees would never have the clearance to hear the even more outlandish real ones.

The man on the right suddenly leaped to his feet and strode around the table. The two analysts had picked up the nicknames Laurel and Hardy at some point, and the monikers seemed even more fitting now than when she'd first run across them.

"Randi, Randi..." Carl Rainsburg said, taking her hand and kissing it. "What a pleasure it is to see you again..."

He was probably 6 feet 6 and no more than 170 pounds dripping wet. A sandy-haired Caucasian who had a master's degree in Japanese literature from a school near Tokyo. His still-seated companion was of first-generation Japanese descent, a bit chubby, with an awful haircut and a habit of chewing his lower lip when he got nervous. At that moment, he was gnawing on it like he'd missed lunch.

"So smooth," Randi said, retrieving her hand and finding a chair. Rainsburg rushed to pull it out for her before rejoining his companion on the other side of the table.

"Nice to see you, Ms. Russell," Stephen Sato said, briefly interrupting his quest to ingest his lower lip.

"You, too. I appreciate both of you taking the time to meet with me. I'm guessing you're pretty busy right now."

"Not at all," Rainsburg said. "It's not every day we get to sit down with a beautiful legend like yourself."

"Uh-huh."

"You'll have to excuse my colleague," Sato said with a grin that came off a little slier than she'd have given him credit for.

"We always have time for the people hanging it out there in the field—beautiful or not. What can we do for you, Ms. Russell?"

"I'm concerned about what's going on in Asia."

"You and everyone else on the planet," Rainsburg said. "And take it from us, you should be. That's a pretty serious staring contest they've got going on right now."

"What I want to know is why. I understand what the Chinese are getting out of this, but what do the Japanese have to gain?"

Sato let out a loud breath. "How long do you have?"

"Give me the *Reader's Digest* version."

"It's all about history," Rainsburg started. "Thousands of years of it, culminating in some serious nastiness during World War Two. Let's just say that the two countries despise each other. You know that—you've worked in China."

She nodded. "But it seems like Masao Takahashi would be backing away from this thing like his ass was on fire. Why isn't he? Am I wrong when I say that the Japanese military is no match for the Chinese?"

"Japanese *self-defense forces*," Sato corrected. "Officially, the Japanese don't have a military because of the constitution we wrote for them after the war. Having said that, they do have the fifth-biggest defense budget on the planet."

"Still, she's right that they're no match for China," Rainsburg interjected.

"Not even close. Don't get me wrong now. Their people are well trained and they have some decent gear, but against the Chinese? No way. You're talking about a quarter million troops with conventional weapons versus two and a quarter million troops with a nuclear arsenal behind them. Last time I checked, those ain't good odds."

"But," Rainsburg said, "there's a rub."

"I know," Randi said. "We have a treaty saying we'll defend them."

"Exactly. And that makes the whole situation a lot more complicated. The Japanese people are understandably tired of taking it on the chin for things that happened before most of them were born. They want respect and they want to stand on their own two feet."

"But Takahashi courting a war and then letting us fight it for him isn't Japan standing on its own two feet. It's Japan stepping on ours."

"You make an interesting point," Sato said. "Takahashi's a complicated guy. He's nationalistic as hell, but he isn't stupid. And frankly he doesn't have any great love for the US. He blames us for his family having a hard time after the war. To be honest, Carl and I have been struggling to figure out what his endgame is here."

"Could he be starting to lose it? He's in his seventies, right? A little dementia, maybe?"

Sato shook his head. "No indication of that at all. Trust us when we tell you that Takahashi has an angle. Maybe he's changed his mind about politicians and he's looking to run for office. We haven't been able to figure it out yet."

Randi chose her next words carefully, not wanting to give away too much. "What if he thinks he can win?"

"What," Rainsburg said. "By dragging us in? What would—"

He fell silent when Randi shook her head. "What if he thinks he can win without us?"

They looked at each other and burst out laughing again.

"Sorry," Sato said, while Rainsburg continued to snicker. "Look, Takahashi's a little nuts and there's no question that his notion of Japanese superiority goes beyond disturbing. But that guy knows more about military strategy and history than most of our top generals combined. It doesn't take a genius to look at the Asian chessboard and see that Japan doesn't have any pieces."

"So you're saying that if he *did* believe that," Randi offered as innocuously as possible, "there's a chance that he would be right."

"Believe what? That the Japanese defense forces could defeat China? Why would he?"

"I'm just throwing it out there," Randi said. "What if, for the sake of argument, the Japanese defense forces have capabilities we're not aware of?"

Rainsburg rolled his eyes. "Sounds like we should introduce her to Eric."

"Who's Eric?"

"Eric Fujiyama," Rainsburg said. "He used to work here, but he let it get to him. You know how it is. We're all conspiracy theorists, but Eric went a little too far."

Sato pointed to his head. "Tinfoil-hat territory. He thinks Japan is in the process of taking over the universe."

"Interesting," Randi said. "Maybe you should."

"Should what?"

"Introduce us."

They looked at each other but this time without the laughter. Their sudden hesitance seemed to suggest there was more to this story, and Randi suspected she knew what it was.

"You still stay in touch with him, don't you?"

Both men stared guiltily down at the table. Sato was the first to speak. "He's a wacko, but he's also really smart. The guy's forgotten more about Japan than most people will ever know."

"Maybe even us," Rainsburg said.

"Okay," Randi said. "Sounds like he might be my man. You got a number?"

They both grinned.

"What?"

"He doesn't really like phones," Sato said.

"Carrier pigeon?"

Rainsburg scribbled something down on a sticky note and held it out to her. "This is his PO box in Portland. Handwrite a letter and send it there."

"Not certified or registered or anything," Sato interjected. "Just give him an anonymous PO to get back to, put a stamp on it, and drop it in a public box. If he's interested, you'll hear from him in a few days."

Randi looked down at the address.

Christ . . .

35

Tokyo
Japan

When Masao Takahashi entered, the four men in the room bowed respectfully and then took seats at the conference table. He returned their silent greeting before positioning himself at one end.

The commanders of the Japanese self defense forces and the director of the country's intelligence efforts had been called there by the prime minister to discuss China's continued hostile stance. The possibility that Japan could be forced to defend itself from its massive neighbor had finally become too obvious for even the politicians to ignore.

The meeting was supposed to start at precisely 1500 hours, but half an hour after that they were still waiting. It was to be expected—a cheap power play on Fumio Sanetomi's part, but one that would have no effect on the men in this room. Undoubtedly, someone on the prime minister's staff had been ordered to quietly watch them and report back any sign of discomfort. They were wasting their time. Each man sat in silence with eyes fixed straight ahead. They would do so for as long as was required.

Sanetomi finally entered forty-five minutes late.

"Good afternoon, Prime Minister," Takahashi said with a bow.

"My humble apologies, gentlemen," Sanetomi said, his refusal to acknowledge the general's greeting undoubtedly meant to signal his displeasure. "I received an unexpected call from President Castilla and our conversation only now finished."

Takahashi smiled passively at the intentional insult and then sat unbidden. The photos of Japan's dead sailors were being displayed on every news channel across the world and there was little doubt that the prime minister knew who had leaked them. But what could the politician do? As the threat to Japan grew, people looked away from the circus performers they had elected in favor of the military men who actually had the expertise and resolve to protect them.

"Everyone understands that this meeting is not officially happening," Sanetomi said as he took a chair at the head of the conference table. "Is that clear?"

All nodded. The prime minister locked his eyes on Takahashi. "No leaks will be tolerated."

The general bowed an acknowledgment, safe in the knowledge that he was untouchable. Sanetomi was completely ignorant of the inevitability of the path they were on. Even the men around him—men whose loyalty the prime minister thought he could count on—were not what he believed them to be. All had sworn their loyalty to Takahashi. And to an emergent Japan.

"We'll begin with the investigation into the sinking of the *Izumo*. Admiral?"

Sachio Inoue cleared his throat before beginning. "It was undoubtedly a torpedo, sir. Analysis of the damage and chemical residue, as well as the reports of the surviving sailors, are consistent with it being fired from the Chinese submarine that we know was in the area."

"And the Americans?"

"We turned over our data to them and they concur."

Takahashi watched the prime minister's face fall at the news. Of course, Admiral Inoue had altered the evidence as necessary before handing it over to the US Navy. The one factor they had struggled to control was the difference in the sound of their torpedo and that of the Chinese Yu-4. Those recordings had been modified after the fact and the Chinese were trying to use their own tapes to support their claim of innocence. The world, though, wasn't inclined to listen.

"Could it have been an accidental launch? Perhaps a rogue captain?"

"There is no way to know," Takahashi interjected. "And it makes little difference to the final outcome. Our sailors are dead and the Chinese military is on high alert."

Sanetomi glared at him for a moment and then turned back to the admiral. "Is there any other plausible explanation?"

Inoue shook his head.

"Why would they do this? What advantage is it to them?"

Akio Himura, the director of intelligence, responded. "We believe that the economic problems in China are worse than we and the rest of the world suspect. Their banking industry has been allowed to hide a great deal of debt, and it may be that they are on the verge of a financial catastrophe. Given that the collapse will be a direct result of the massive corruption of the Chinese political class, they could be facing a potential revolution. It may be that a physical confrontation is the only thing substantial enough to divert attention from their own crimes."

"But this isn't just a war with us. It's a war with America."

"Is it?" Takahashi said.

Sanetomi immediately held up a hand to silence him. "We're all fully aware of your childhood and your deep-seated issues with America, General. But I've spoken to their president and he's assured me that they intend to honor their treaty with us. At the very least, you must find some comfort in the fact that they've sent multiple carrier groups into Asian waters?"

"I don't, Prime Minister. China controls their debt, it holds over a billion potential customers for American companies, and Chinese sweatshops keep stores stocked with the cheap goods the American people demand. Our importance to the US pales by comparison."

"Enough! I'm not here to debate politics or economics. If I were, I would have invited people with knowledge of those disciplines. Your job is to defend this country should it become necessary. That's all. Am I understood?"

Takahashi gave a practiced nod. In all likelihood, the military would control the country after all this was done. The question was whether it would be more advantageous to let this little man continue on as a figurehead or whether his public execution for treason would be more beneficial.

"President Castilla has offered to personally host face-to-face talks between myself and China's leadership. I've agreed to attend, as has President Yandong. Every effort will be made to bring a peaceful solution to this situation, and I believe those efforts will be successful. However, I have to consider the possibility that they will not. In light of that, we need to discuss our readiness." He turned to Himura. "Let's begin with intelligence."

Himura gave a jerky nod and sat a bit straighter in his chair. "With regard to cyber warfare, our penetration into civilian and government systems is excellent. I expect to be able to shut

down seventy percent of the Chinese power grid within minutes of them launching an attack. The Internet will become
virtually useless and phone communication should see around
a forty percent degradation. We're hampered there due to the
archaic technology used in much of their landline network."

"And military computers?"

"Obviously, the systems are much more heavily guarded.
The access we have, combined with the loss of public power
to a number of the bases, should be enough to cause significant chaos in the chain of command. It will also reduce their
missile launch capacity by at least twenty percent."

Sanetomi turned to the head of their air defenses. "And
what will come of the other eighty percent?"

"Our missile shield has been a priority for obvious reasons,"
General Tadao Minami, the director of the country's air defenses, replied. "We expect to be able to intercept virtually all
of the incoming projectiles and to create a zone in which enemy aircraft—as well as our own, unfortunately—will not be
able to operate."

Sanetomi's reaction was understandably subdued despite
what, on the surface, seemed like an excellent prognosis.

The Americans had focused on the bullet-hitting-a-bullet
strategy of missile defense, but all of Ito's research suggested
that this was a dead end. Even if it could be made to work under idealized test conditions, effective countermeasures were
almost comically simple for the enemy to deploy. The only realistic solution was to create massive electromagnetic pulses
that short-circuited the electronics of anything entering Japanese airspace.

The only way they'd found to achieve that goal was with a
very specialized set of tactical nuclear weapons. The airbursts

themselves weren't particularly powerful—far less so than that of the bombs used to attack Hiroshima and Nagasaki—but the radioactive aftermath was quite innovative. Countless microscopic particles would persist in the atmosphere for days, shielding Japan in an impenetrable radioactive cloud.

"And the danger to civilians?"

"Acceptable," Takahashi said, once again cutting in. "Even when we suffered a nuclear attack during World War Two, radiation casualties were largely caused by people ingesting radioactive ash through drinking from the river. Our water supply is now protected from that kind of contamination. We expect to see twenty percent higher cancer rates nationwide for the next generation, as well as higher levels of birth defects, but this is unavoidable. And certainly preferable to the alternative."

"What about our air-to-air drones?" Sanetomi asked, unwilling to even look at his chief of staff.

"Of little use," General Minami replied. "We've only recently completed testing and there hasn't been time to ramp up manufacturing. Obviously, we have conventional fighters that will be able to patrol our territory when it's feasible to fly. Overall, we believe it will be enough to limit casualties to around a million."

"A million," Sanetomi said, seeming to have trouble processing the number. "That's a success?"

"In a country of one hundred and thirty-five million under attack by the second-largest military power in the world, yes," Minami said. "In fact, I consider it a near miracle."

Sanetomi turned again to Admiral Inoue. "What about our sea defenses?"

"As you know, our self-cavitating torpedoes are in their third generation and have proven extraordinarily effective. We have hundreds covering Japanese waters as well as Chinese ports and sea-lanes. We'll rule the sea within hours of your attack order."

"That's a great deal of confidence, Admiral."

"Well warranted, I assure you. Neither the Chinese nor the Americans are aware that this technology has been perfected, so they haven't developed any defense against it. Our system is virtually flawless in the face of current countermeasure technology."

Sanetomi turned to the only person in the room who hadn't yet spoken, a gray-haired man almost Takahashi's age. "And our ground forces?"

"Due to our sea and air capabilities, it is unlikely that we'll be in a position to have to fight an invading army," General Zenzo Kudo said. "Our preparations are primarily for disaster relief in the areas hit by Chinese weapons and for keeping civil order. On both counts, I'm confident that we will be extremely effective."

Sanetomi leaned back in his chair and stared blankly ahead for a few moments. "What if the Chinese decide to use their nuclear arsenal?"

"In that extremely unlikely event, our missile defense will defeat the majority of their attack," Takahashi said. "And even I agree that if we see a nuclear escalation, the Americans will intervene with whatever force is necessary."

"I wonder if it wouldn't be wise to announce to the world that we've created an electromagnetic pulse–based missile defense system. If we launch our shield, it could be misconstrued as a nuclear attack and prompt retaliation from the Chinese."

"It would be a serious breach of international treaties,"

Takahashi said. "And it could serve to escalate the situation further. I would recommend that we wait. If the situation escalates to the point where we might be forced to deploy our shield, we'll announce then."

Sanetomi nodded reluctantly but didn't immediately speak further.

Of course they had discussed only Japan's defensive systems, continuing the policy of keeping Sanetomi in the dark about their offensive capability. Ito's people had succeeded in shrinking a twenty-kiloton nuclear bomb—almost exactly the same power as the weapon used against Hiroshima and Nagasaki—into a container that could easily be carried by a single man. Thirty-three had been buried across China as well as in strategic points throughout America, Europe, and Asia.

In all likelihood, though, none of the weapons in Japan's nuclear arsenal—including its missile defense system—would ever be deployed. In the face of Ito's nanoscale weapon, atomic bombs were all but obsolete.

"What role would we need the Americans to take in all this?" Sanetomi asked.

"Limited," Takahashi said. "They're unlikely to take offensive action against the Chinese mainland in a conventional war, and their naval power is unnecessary in light of our torpedoes. Their fighter aircraft could potentially be useful in engaging Chinese sorties, but if our missile shield has been deployed they won't be able to approach our airspace."

"So the best-case scenario is a stalemate where a million of our people die. And the worst-case scenario is that this could descend into nuclear war in which millions on both sides die. All for no reason at all."

Takahashi remained expressionless, but inside he felt as

though an electrical current were running through every nerve in his body. It wouldn't be millions. It would be tens of millions. And it wouldn't be for no reason. China would be completely decimated—left scraping at the dirt like animals just to find enough food to survive.

At the same time, the rest of the world would enter a new age. The age of Japan.

36

T ry it again," Jon Smith said, leaning a little farther under the hood of the rusting AMC Gremlin.

Randi twisted the key and the engine turned over, but it wouldn't catch.

The wind picked up, tearing colorful leaves from the trees lining the empty rural road and depositing them in the dead motor. Smith brushed them off the air cleaner cover and began unscrewing the wing nut that held it in place.

"What's wrong with it?" Randi said, leaning out the open window.

"It's a forty-year-old piece of shit is what's wrong with it. Couldn't you steal a better car?"

Randi had gotten in the habit of taking cars from airport long-term parking when she needed something untraceable. She always got them back before the owners returned to find their vehicle detailed and full of premium gas.

"Fujiyama said that if I showed up in anything modern, he'd walk."

Smith let out a frustrated breath and dug around in the

carburetor with a stick. Eric Fujiyama had agreed to talk to them, but under conditions that even a paranoid schizophrenic would consider excessive. They couldn't just talk on the phone or get together at a Portland restaurant with a decent micro-brew selection. No, they had to drive an ancient car with shovels in the back to the middle of nowhere. And what about those shovels? Smith seemed to be the only person who was concerned that the host of their clandestine meeting in the woods requested that they bring tools suitable for digging graves.

"Kick it again."

This time the starter sounded a little sick but the engine caught. After replacing the air filter, Smith slammed the hood and ran around to the passenger seat.

"Whatever you do, don't stall it."

Randi scowled and pulled out with her eyes on a map taped to the dash. According to the highlighted route, their turn was just ahead. She eased right onto a rutted dirt road, the geriatric suspension protesting loudly enough to overcome the Steely Dan flowing from hidden speakers. Smith tried again to silence the stereo but the volume knob was broken and the eight track resisted every attempt at ejection.

"Slow down, Randi."

"What are you talking about? We could walk faster than this."

"And that's what we're going to be doing if you break what's left of this thing's axles."

"What's up your ass today?"

He flipped her off and turned toward the window to watch the trees creeping by. What was up his ass was that being crammed into this car had reinserted the dagger in his shoulder blade. But it was more than that. He'd been lucky enough to inherit a nearly ideal set of genes from two extremely athletic parents and had spent his life honing those natural gifts with a workout regimen that would make a Navy SEAL squirm. Feeling like Superman was his natural state and he was damn well ready to go back to it.

It took another twenty excruciating minutes, but they finally dead-ended into a small clearing. Smith slid a Sig Sauer from between the seats and scanned the shadows in the surrounding forest while Randi did the same. Fujiyama had insisted on no phones, GPS, or radios. So there wasn't going to be any backup should things go south.

"Does this seem inordinately stupid to you?" Smith said as they stepped out and crouched on either side of the vehicle.

"Come on, Jon. You love this stuff. You're just in a snit today."

He frowned and examined the clearing through the sights of his gun. Nothing but wilderness. Of course, that didn't mean anything. With the complexity of the terrain and the dense foliage, there could be an army out there and they wouldn't know it until the shooting started.

Instead of shots, though, an engine became audible on the road they'd come up. He and Randi both took cover in the trees and watched in silence as an Asian man in his late thirties pulled up in an open CJ5.

Eric Fujiyama released his seat belt and leaped out, doing a full turn in the middle of the clearing. "Randi! Where are you?"

Smith looked over at her and shrugged. The man was wearing jeans and a sweatshirt with no indication of a weapon.

"I'm here," Randi said, stepping out of the trees and walking casually toward Fujiyama with her gun tucked into the back of her pants.

"Hey," he said, nodding toward the Gremlin. "You can follow instructions. Good."

"Well, I can follow *some* instructions."

Smith appeared from the trees with his Sig Sauer hanging loosely from his hand. Fujiyama froze for a moment and turned to run but Randi grabbed him by the collar.

"Relax, Eric. We're just here to talk."

"Who the hell is he? I told you to come alone!"

"I know. And I apologize. He insisted on tagging along."

Smith took a seat on the bumper of the jeep and gave Fujiyama a disarming smile. "It's nice to meet you, Eric."

He didn't seem particularly happy about the change in the meeting's dynamic, but understood that there wasn't a lot he could do about it at this point.

"So, let me guess. Masao Takahashi is suddenly starting to look a little crazy and Laurel and Hardy can't figure out why. Now the CIA's worried and you need the help of the guy you fired because you thought he had a tinfoil hat in his desk drawer."

"I didn't fire you," Randi clarified. "I'd never even heard of you until a few days ago."

He folded his arms over his chest. "Fine. What do you want to know?"

Smith laid his gun down on the bumper and pushed it to a less intimidating distance. "You nailed it on the head, Eric. Takahashi seems to be almost anxious to start trading blows with an eight-hundred-pound gorilla. And sure, we're obligated to help out, but Japan's still going to get the shit kicked out of it. What's his angle?"

"What's his angle," Fujiyama repeated with a smirk. "Did you know that Japan, a country with no official military, has the fifth-largest defense budget in the world?"

"I did know that, actually."

"What you *don't* know is that the published figure is probably less than half of their actual expenditures. It's one of the reasons their recession lasted so much longer than anyone predicted."

"That would put it pretty close to equal with China," Randi pointed out. "Doesn't seem like they're getting value for their money."

"No it doesn't, does it? The Japanese are famous for their efficiency and yet they manage to spend over a hundred billion dollars a year on defense and not have much to show for it." His voice took on a sarcastic edge. "Who would have thought?"

"So you're saying that they *do* have the weapons," Smith said. "We just aren't aware of it."

"Seems like we'd notice all those ships and tanks," Randi said, baiting him. Based on what they knew about the nanotech, it was obvious where Fujiyama was headed with this.

"The Japanese don't have the option of building an old-school military. There's the cultural push-pull inside the country relating to what happened in World War Two, the constitution MacArthur wrote for them, the possibility that it would create an Asian arms race—"

"And they don't have the population base or natural resources to support it," Smith said, finishing his sentence.

"Ding! Give that man a cigar! So they had to create something new."

"What about the battleship they put to sea?" Randi said. "That was pretty standard stuff."

"The one that's on the bottom of the ocean now? It was just a diversion. Hell, I wouldn't be surprised if Takahashi sank that thing himself."

Smith opened his mouth to question him on that point, but the young analyst seemed to be warming up to his subject. Better to just let him talk.

"Look, do you remember back in the day when all the cool technology came out of Japan? Betamax, DVDs, video games, portable music players..."

"Sure," Randi said.

"What happened?" Fujiyama asked rhetorically. "Suddenly, right around the time Takahashi went to work as an aide to the former head of the Japanese defense forces, that innovation started to fade and America took over. Where did all those brilliant people go? The CIA seems to think they just went up in smoke."

"But you don't," Randi said. "You think Takahashi got hold of them and paid them to develop a next-generation arsenal."

Smith kept his face passive, but his mind was trying to churn through what he was hearing. The pieces were starting to fall into place. And the picture they created was terrifying.

"Let's talk Akito Maki," Fujiyama continued.

"Who?" Randi said.

"He's was a young chemical engineer who in the early nineties was on his way to increasing the stored energy in a given amount of rocket fuel by an order of magnitude. Then he went to work for one of the Takahashi family's companies and doesn't seem to have produced anything salable. Or Genjiro Ueda, a materials engineer who was combining carbon fiber and ceramics into incredibly tough materials. He went to work for a private contractor and makes an excellent living not producing anything. Then there's granddaddy of them all: Hideki Ito."

Smith glanced at Randi at the mention of the familiar name. To her credit, her expression didn't even flicker.

"Ito's one of the fathers of nanotech. Decades ago he was doing really interesting things with it and then he went to work for himself and no one really ever heard from him again. And that's only a *few* of the programmers, biologists, engineers, and nuclear physicists who've just kind of faded into Japan's woodwork over the last three decades."

"Do you have any evidence to back up what you're telling us?" Smith asked.

Fujiyama stared at him, looking a bit uncertain. Finally, he seemed to come to a decision and motioned with his head to a tall, tree-covered knoll to the east. "A bunch of files buried up there in a safe I designed myself."

"Files?" Randi said. "You mean, paper? Why wouldn't you just keep it on an encrypted disk?"

Fujiyama laughed. "Did you wonder why I wouldn't let you contact me over e-mail? Why I said no modern cars or electronics?"

"You think the Japanese are using them?"

"Are you kidding? I guarantee it. They say they really don't have much of an intelligence network, but Takahashi recognized how important computers would become when we were still churning out slide rules. What modern car or electronic device doesn't contain something either designed by or made by the Japanese? You know all this large-scale hacking that we blame on the Chinese?"

"You're saying that it's actually the Japanese intelligence network?"

"Of course it is! China is a mess—they still farm with donkeys, for Christ's sake. And while they're definitely starting to flex their muscles, they're an inward-looking people by nature. Not the Japanese, though. They're always peeking out from that little island of theirs at what their neighbors have that they can use."

"Okay then," Randi said. "Can we assume you asked us to bring the shovels because you're agreeable to letting us make some copies?"

Again his expression turned uncertain, and again his reticence didn't last long. "Yeah. I know your rep, Randi. But you didn't get any of this from me, right?"

"Never heard of you," she said, opening the hatch on the Gremlin and pulling out two of the three shovels inside. She handed one to Fujiyama, who immediately pointed at Smith. "What about him?"

"He's going to hang back, watch the cars, and keep an eye on our six."

She set off with Fujiyama hustling to keep up with her and Smith said a silent thanks. Normally, he'd think a knoll like that looked good for running a few laps. Today it looked like Mount Everest.

*   *   *

Randi knew she was going too hard up the steep grade but getting her blood pumping helped her think. She had one hand wrapped around a shovel and the other around a Beretta, but was still starting to wish she hadn't let Smith off the hook. They were exposed as hell—no electronics, no backup, and in terrain that favored an ambush.

That wasn't what scared her the most, though. What had her charging up the mountain at a pace few people could follow was the fact that the wild tale they'd just heard seemed completely plausible. She almost wanted to turn around and drive away. To never have to look at a stack of paper that told her World War III was winding up a few thousand miles to the east.

She couldn't hear Fujiyama's ragged breathing anymore and she slowed to let him catch up.

"Is it all the way at the top?" she asked as he dropped his shovel and bent at the waist to breathe. A weak nod.

"Why here?" she said, starting out again, this time at a slower pace.

"No reason," he managed to get out. "That's the point. No trail to lead here."

It took another fifteen minutes to cover what she estimated at about five minutes' worth of ground, but without him she wasn't going to find much. When they finally crested the top, Fujiyama pulled out a compass and a measuring tape, starting to make calculations based on a jagged rock set into the ground next to a stump.

Randi watched in silence as he crawled around, making marks in the dirt and then setting his bearing from them to get to the next point. A GPS would have sped things up, but he obviously wasn't interested in taking the risk that the device could be tracked.

It took about five minutes, but Fujiyama finally jammed a stick in the ground as a marker and went for his shovel.

"This is the spot?" Randi said, walking over to help.

"Yeah. It's about four feet down, though, and I remember the ground not being all that soft."

They each picked a side and started attacking the dirt. Unfortunately, he was right about the digging. Roots and grass had tangled the area since he'd buried his little treasure, slowing their progress.

The fall air wasn't cool enough to counteract the sun coming directly overhead. Sweat dripped off Randi's nose as she slammed the shovel repeatedly into the ground and tossed the dirt onto an ever-growing mound behind her.

Fujiyama was trying to keep up, but his side of the hole was barely enough to trip over, while she was down almost a foot and a half. As bad as the hike up had been, standing on top of this knoll under clear skies was making her feel even more exposed. Better to get this thing and get the hell out of Dodge.

She stuck the blade of the shovel in and jumped on the back of it, barely catching herself when she was suddenly thrown backward. It took a moment to figure out what had happened, but the fact that the blade was still in the dirt and the handle was still in her hand was a good clue.

"Damn it!" she said, throwing the broken handle aside.

"You can use mine," the young analyst said hopefully.

"No, we need to get this done and get the hell out of here. There's another shovel in the car. I'm going to run down and get it. Keep digging."

"I'm getting really tired, Randi. Maybe—"

"Would you rather go back to the clearing and then have to climb up again?"

He looked down the steep slope. "No, but—"

"Then shut up and dig. You're the one who buried the damn thing."

Randi set off at a hard jog, leaping rocks and fallen logs as she retraced their steps toward the cars. She kept an eye on the shadows and the Beretta in her hand but at the pace she was going, there was no way to make out much detail. Sometimes fast was better than cautious.

Randi was about a quarter of the way down the hill when

an unmistakable sound reached her. She bounced off a tree and turned just in time to see a pillar of flame rising from the top of the knoll. Burning debris, including charred pieces of Eric Fujiyama, arced across the blue sky.

She took a few steps uphill but then turned and started running toward Smith again. Whoever had planted that bomb would know they were there, and he wasn't in any condition to defend himself alone.

37

Tokyo
Japan

Takahashi followed Akio Himura through the heavy doors that led to the most secure part of the building. Officially Japan didn't have any significant intelligence capability, and the existence of this facility—ostensibly a division of the government's accounting office—was one of Japan's most closely guarded secrets.

The walls were lined with two-way mirrors, and Takahashi knew they were being watched from all sides by Himura's elite security. At the first sign of a breach, the multiple automatic doors they'd come through would lock down, trapping them and anyone else trying to gain access.

The encrypted text message had come during their pointless meeting with the prime minister but Takahashi had been unable to act on it, instead sitting obediently through another twenty excruciating minutes. With no helicopter available, he and Himura had been forced to go by car, spending almost another hour in Tokyo's heavy afternoon traffic.

They stopped in front of a white door with a visible carbon fiber weave and Himura raised his arms above his head. Takahashi did the same, submitting to the highly advanced body scan that would search not only for weapons but also for digital storage devices, cameras, and even pens—anything that could be used to record what transpired inside.

A green light flashed and the door slid open.

"Report," Himura said as they entered the inner sanctum of his intelligence apparatus. It was surprisingly unremarkable. No larger than twenty meters square with stark white walls and three stainless steel desks containing only computer terminals. Behind those terminals were men who seemed far too young to be working at this level of responsibility. The technical expertise necessary, though, eluded earlier generations.

"Two unknown people contacted Eric Fujiyama at the file site," the man closest to them said without looking up from his screen. Takahashi bristled a bit at his brusque demeanor but then reminded himself that the intelligence business was very different from the military. These were not people who snapped to attention when a superior entered the room.

"Do we have any idea who they are?" Himura asked, walking up behind the man.

"We've accessed an American satellite, but the angle isn't optimal. A blonde woman and a man with dark hair. The man stayed at the car while the woman went to the knoll with Fujiyama. She seemed to break her shovel and started down again while Fujiyama kept digging. She was halfway back to the clearing when the mine went off."

"Was she injured?" Himura asked.

"Not as near as I can tell."

"Russell and Smith," Takahashi said quietly. Himura nodded.

They'd been tracking Fujiyama for years and in fact had been subtly involved in discrediting him sufficiently for the CIA to fire him. After he was let go, though, he'd continued working on his theories and buried a cleverly designed safe with what they assumed was physical evidence supporting his ideas.

When Takahashi had discovered the existence of this buried treasure, he'd ordered it dug it up and replaced it with an explosive. The theory was that Fujiyama and anyone interested in what he'd compiled would be vaporized before they could do any damage. Obviously, that hadn't worked as planned. Leaving Fujiyama alive had proved to be a poor decision.

"Where are they now?" Himura said.

"Driving on Interstate Five in the American state of Oregon."

"Destination?"

"Our assumption is the airport. Russell has been known to steal vehicles from long-term parking and based on the make and model of the car, we know it's not a rental."

"Can we control it?" Takahashi asked.

"No. It's probably more than thirty years old."

"Have they contacted anyone?" Himura said.

"Doubtful. They haven't stopped and Fujiyama typically insists that people he meets with carry no electronics."

"Do we have human assets in the area? Anyone who could intercept them?" Takahashi said.

"None."

Takahashi took his intelligence director's arm and pulled him back toward the wall. "There's no way to know what Fujiyama told them before he died. We have to assume he gave them something—a thread to pull on."

Himura nodded. "If we're going to act, we need to act now. Before they can talk to their superiors. If we lose them again . . ." His voice faded.

"How?"

"We can't use their car, but we can use others. I must caution you, though, General. The risk of exposure is incredibly high. In fact, it's almost certain."

Takahashi looked across the room at the screen being used to monitor Smith and Russell's vehicle. Himura was right. It was impossibly dangerous. But doing nothing was equally dangerous. If they'd gone to Fujiyama, it seemed likely that they'd discovered the nanotech and suspected Japan of having a hand in its development.

"Do it," Takahashi ordered.

Himura gave a short bow and walked up behind the young man at the terminal. "Are there other vehicles available?"

"Yes. But we're going to lose the satellite image and the traffic around them is fairly light at this point. Their ETA to the airport is ten minutes. That's plenty of time for us to tie into the security cameras. We'll have good coverage and a higher density of modern vehicles."

Himura put a hand on the young man's shoulder. "Russell and Smith are not to enter the terminal. Is that understood?"

38

Portland International Airport
Portland, Oregon
USA

R andi Russell eased the Gremlin into long-term parking, keeping a close eye on the rearview mirror. The sun was still up in a cloudless sky, creating a distracting glare on the sea of cars in front of the terminal. Her well-trained eye couldn't spot anyone following, but she wasn't sure that meant much anymore.

"Wait a minute," Smith said, staring down at the notes he'd scrawled on a crumpled napkin from the glove box. "Was it Wedo?"

"Which one?"

He let out an exasperated breath. "Maki was the rocket fuel guy he told us about. His first name was something like Akido. This is the materials engineer. Genjiro Wedo?"

She shook her head. "Not Wedo. It ended in an *a*. Maybe Weda?"

"Yes!" he said, scribbling the name down. "That's it. Genjiro Weda. Now all we need to do it figure out a way to get this to Star."

She eased up to the parking kiosk and took a ticket before

driving through the gate. "We'll have our cell phones back in a few minutes, but even with Covert-One's encryption protocols, I'm not sure we should use them. Fujiyama's paranoia is rubbing off on me."

"I don't think it's technically paranoia if someone just blew the top off the mountain you were standing on and killed your informant."

"You make a valid point," she said, stopping in front of a space with a red cone emblazoned with the words "No Parking." She hopped out of the car and gave the cone a firm downward shove, collapsing it into a disk about the size of a Frisbee. When she got back in and pulled forward, Smith was already wiping down the interior to eradicate any fingerprints.

Randi retrieved a small backpack from the floor behind the seats and dug through its contents until she was able to release a hidden panel at the bottom. She handed Smith a wallet filled with well-worn IDs and credit cards, taking another for herself. "I assume you agree we should split up and buy return tickets under different names?"

"Hell yes," he replied, replacing the wallet in his pocket with the new one. "I'm having a hard time believing where this is leading, but for now we assume the worst."

"That the Japanese have spent the last thirty years quietly building a bunch of futuristic weapons that are now aimed directly at us?"

"When you put it that way, it sounds kind of bad, doesn't it?" Smith said with a weak smile.

Randi mumbled something under her breath and stepped out into the bright sunlight, turning slowly as she took in everything around her. There were a few widely scattered people pulling suitcases to and from the terminal, but no one closer than fifty yards. Beyond that, there was a couple in a BMW paying at the kiosk and a woman in a Prius driving slowly up their aisle looking for a space.

"I say we skip the airport transportation and walk," she said, slipping the backpack on. "We'll get our phones out of storage and head back on different airlines."

"Sounds about right," Smith said, getting out and slamming the door. "The Gremlin's not getting a detail and a full tank, huh?"

"First time ever," Randi said. "I must be slipping."

She started across the road toward the terminal and the moment she did, a high-pitched engine whine started to their right. Smith watched her spin, pulling a Beretta from beneath her jacket and bringing it level with the windshield of the Prius suddenly bearing down on them.

Randi had a gift for that kind of reaction. There was no time lag at all between her mind perceiving danger and her body dealing with that danger in the most efficient—and final—way possible. It was undoubtedly why she was still alive, but sometimes the speed of her instinct caused her to miss details.

Smith darted into the road, ignoring the pain in his back as he launched himself at her. He knew that her mind had transformed the human outline in the driver's seat into nothing more than a target and that she was thinking only about how to hit that target in the most effective way possible. What he saw, though, was a terrified woman jerking desperately on an unresponsive steering wheel.

It was over in less than two seconds. He hit Randi broadside and they both toppled toward the row of cars parked behind her. Smith got clipped by the Prius's front quarter panel, but the metal was so thin that it did little more than send him sprawling awkwardly onto the pavement.

Randi managed not to fall, instead slamming into the back of a Nissan Pathfinder just as the Prius jumped a sidewalk and rolled onto its top. She recovered quickly, turning a full 360 with her pistol held out in front of her, searching for a secondary attack. Around them, pedestrians were dropping their luggage and running in every direction, undoubtedly thinking this was the beginning of some kind of terrorist attack or mass shooting.

"What the hell, Jon!" Randi said, finally daring to glance down at him as he struggled to get back to his feet. "You could have—"

The empty Nissan she was standing behind suddenly started up and Smith saw the reverse lights flash on. This time her reactions were dulled by confusion and she was a split second too slow. The engine gunned and she went down, disappearing beneath the vehicle.

"Randi!" Smith shouted as the Nissan slammed into a Volkswagen in the next row. He bolted toward her, hearing the Pathfinder shift into drive for another try.

She was dazed and bleeding badly from one arm, but her thin frame combined with the Nissan's enhanced ground clearance had kept her from being killed. He grabbed her by the front of her jacket, not bothering to look back at the vehicle bearing down on them from behind.

Thank God she was light. He threw her across the hood of a low-slung Mazda and leaped after her just as the Nissan collided with its rear bumper. They both tumbled over the side and landed in the narrow gap between the Mazda and the minivan next to it.

Randi had managed to shake off the impact and aim over the hood, putting two rounds neatly into the windshield of the Nissan. Predictably, both were dead center on the driver's-seat headrest. Unfortunately, it was empty.

Smith grabbed her by the collar and yanked her back, pointing at the terminal building. "We've got to get out of here! Now!"

She took point and he realized he was coughing up blood again as he fought to keep up. Randi started to cut right in front of a brand-new Mercedes and he warned her off.

"No! Go left!"

She hesitated but then did as she was told, breaking into a sprint when the Mercedes started up and turned hard toward her. She barely managed to get in front of the old pickup Smith had been trying to direct her toward when the Mercedes rammed it. He dodged around the car and leaped into the truck's bed, throwing himself over the top of the cab and coming down next to her.

"Stay behind me!"

Smith crouched, running what must have seemed like a random pattern as he went for intermittent cover between older vehicles. She shadowed him with her pistol still at the ready but unsure what to shoot at.

"Go!" he shouted when they reached the road that ran directly in front of the terminal. It was clogged with cars and hotel shuttles, most stopped because of the panicked people fleeing in every direction.

A cab suddenly accelerated toward them, but it was too low-slung to chase them up onto the sidewalk. Instead it slammed into the curb and ripped off a good chunk of its front end in a shower of sparks. Smith went for the doors, fighting against the people flowing out of them.

Inside the terminal, armed guards had their weapons out but, like everyone else, had no idea what the threat was or where it was coming from. Most people were going for the doors out of instinct but others were running deeper into the building, spreading the hysteria.

Randi let the gun slide from her hand and took off her jacket, keeping her head down as they passed the security cameras that so were ubiquitous in modern airports. Smith stripped off his coat too, letting it fall to the floor amid the travelers darting around them. He threw an arm around Randi and pulled her close, partially in an effort not to get separated but mostly to try to camouflage her blood-soaked sleeve.

With nowhere to go, they stayed in the densest part of the crowd, mimicking their movements and trying to blend in. With a little luck, whoever was watching would lose them in the chaos.

39

D octor? The general is on a secure line for you. He says it's urgent."

Hideki Ito looked up from the computer terminal and saw the guard standing in the doorway. "I'm sorry. Did you say the general?"

The man nodded. "If you could follow me, please."

Ito stood and walked nervously down the corridor behind the man. Takahashi was a fanatic about security, particularly when it came to their primary research facility. He rarely came to the retasked nuclear waste dump and he *never* called there. The vulnerability of electronic communications had been made crystal clear to the old soldier.

What could have happened that would prompt Takahashi to ignore his own security protocols? Had the Chinese retreated in the face of world pressure? Ito began to sweat despite the cold emanating from the earthen walls. Had they attacked?

There were almost no connections to the outside world in this place—a lack of distraction that he normally appreciated. But he was beginning to ask himself if the general was taking advantage of his propensity to submerge himself in his work.

Ito had always known he was a pawn in Takahashi's grand plans. An important one, of course, but a pawn nonetheless. Now, though, he was wondering if he had allowed himself to become a prisoner.

"Through here, please, sir," the guard leading him said, indicating a door cut into the wall.

The communications room was understandably small and sparse. In his entire time working at the facility, this was the first time Ito had ever seen it open.

A lone computer screen was flashing a message requesting his password. He typed it in and slid a headset over the damaged skin stretched across his scalp.

"Hello? General?"

"We need to access the Fujiyama files," Takahashi said by way of greeting. The normally disciplined voice had an angry timbre that caused Ito's stomach to clench.

Eric Fujiyama had stored a series of paper files in an extremely clever lockbox that he'd buried in the American West. Takahashi had discovered its location and transported the box there, but accessing it had proved far more difficult than anyone would have expected. A careful examination using various advanced imaging systems had revealed a complex series of interlaced mechanisms measuring such things as vibration, changes in air pressure, and temperature fluctuation. Inside was a vial that spectrum analysis suggested was full of acid that would destroy the fragile paper the moment anyone attempted to breach the box.

"I'm not certain that they're accessible, General. One error and—"

"Just get them! You said you could use the nanotech."

"I said it was *possible* that the bots could weaken the structure sufficiently to safely open it, but there's no way to guarantee that it won't trigger—"

"Fujiyama talked with Smith and Russell. We don't know what he said, but it's likely that he gave them information that's in those files. We need to find out what he suspects so that we can anticipate their next move."

"Smith and Russell survived? How?"

While he had never been told directly, Ito had inferred that Takahashi had replaced the strongbox with a powerful mine.

"That's not your concern, Doctor. Your only concern is to retrieve those files without damaging them. I want to be clear that you're not to work on anything else until you've succeeded. Is that understood?"

"Yes, sir," Ito said reluctantly. What choice did he have?

The line went dead and he removed the headset before lowering himself unsteadily into the only chair in the room.

What if he failed? What if the files were destroyed in the process of trying to access them? Even isolated for so long, Ito could feel the change in Takahashi and the security men who prowled the facility. A storm was coming—one he himself had been unknowingly instrumental in creating. And when that tempest finally made landfall, it would consume them all.

40

Over Norfolk, Virginia
USA

J on Smith eased into the thick leather seat and looked out the window as Covert-One's G5 climbed out of the Norfolk airport. He and Randi had rendezvoused there in order to pick up the jet Fred Klein had sent for them. It seemed that the fake IDs, baseball hats, new clothes, and sunglasses had thrown off whoever had been tracking them. Most likely, General Masao Takahashi.

Randi fell into the facing seat, sliding a bottle of Tylenol and a can of Budweiser across the narrow table between them. "No microbrews in the fridge, but I thought Bud would still be better than water."

He used the beer to wash down a few pills before reclining and closing his eyes. The episode in the parking lot combined with hours of crisscrossing the country in the relative anonymity of economy class hadn't done his back any good. At least he'd stopped coughing up blood.

"Get some sleep, Jon. It's a long flight to Okinawa. Fred's cleared us for a nice quiet landing at our Kadena Air Base there, and then we can make our way to mainland Japan. I need you firing on all cylinders. Right now you look about a hundred years old."

"It's not the years," he said, not bothering to open his eyes. "It's the mileage."

She didn't respond immediately, but when she did she sounded unusually contrite. "Thanks back there. If it weren't for you, I'd have shot an innocent woman and gotten crushed by a jacked-up Nissan. Not the way I want to go out."

He smiled thinly. "I remembered what Fujiyama said about cars. He insisted we drive an old one."

"Sure, but I thought that was because modern ones can be tracked by satellite. I still don't understand what happened back there, Jon. How were those cars being controlled? It seems—"

The sound of insane laughter cut her off and forced Smith to look down at his phone. The extremely appropriate ringtone belonged to Marty Zellerbach, a high school friend of his who'd grown up to be a technological wizard and one of the world's top hackers. Occasionally very useful, he could also be incredibly exhausting. Zellerbach suffered from Asperger's syndrome and had a love-hate relationship with his medications that created wild pendulums in his mood.

"Are you going to pick up?" Randi asked.

"No."

"You know what he's calling about, Jon. And you know we're going to need to talk to him eventually."

"Eventually sounds good."

She flicked a hand out, putting his phone on speaker before he could intercept. "Marty. Sweetheart. How are you?"

"Randi? The question is, how are *you*?"

"I'm good, thank you."

"I noticed you're as gorgeous as ever. I'm glad to hear the arm wasn't serious."

Smith frowned. By the time he'd made it to Chicago, CNN was already running shaky cell phone footage of what had happened in Portland. He and Randi had both been vaguely recognizable, but in the chaos it was doubtful that anyone would come to the conclusion that they were the target of the attack. Or even that it was an attack at all.

"Jon? Are you there? Are you all right? You looked a little slow out there."

"I'm fine, Marty."

"Can I assume those cars were after the two of you and not the woman with the Baby Jogger?"

Randi looked down at the phone's screen and confirmed that the call was encrypted. Not that Marty was in the habit of talking on open lines. He was extremely suspicious of the NSA and lately had become concerned about space aliens.

"I think that's safe to say," she responded. "What the hell happened out there, Marty? How were those cars being controlled?"

"It's really not all that hard. Modern cars don't have mechanical linkages anymore. They're computer controlled. All you have to do is get into the onboard system. You know that asshole neighbor I have who keeps calling the cops on me? I got into his Lexus through the tire pressure sensor. Now his heat is on full blast all summer and his AC runs all winter. If I wanted to, I could take control and make him drive through his garage door. In fact, that's not a bad idea..."

"Okay," Smith said before Zellerbach could embark on one of his legendary tangents. "But you had physical access to the car. You plugged your laptop into it and if you wanted to drive it remotely you'd have to have either a cable connected or some kind of a radio controller, right?"

There was a long pause. "That's true. Yes."

"There's no way someone could have gotten to all those cars to hack them, Marty. And I'd be willing to bet there was no one within radio controller distance either. Explain that."

Silence. Clearly, this was a problem he couldn't entirely figure out. And if there was one thing that Zellerbach couldn't stand, it was a technological issue on which he couldn't pontificate endlessly.

"Maybe someone got access during the manufacturing process. Radio control could be handled by hijacking cell towers or even satellites. The airport would be an ideal location—lots of security cameras to tie in to so you could see what you were doing."

"They were different makes and models," Randi said.

"Yeah, but parts for those cars are built all over the world. It doesn't matter who upholstered the seats and made the shift knob. What you need to know is who made the engine control unit."

"So how hard would this be, Marty?"

"That's kind of a vague question. It would depend on —"

"Okay, let me rephrase. How much would it cost me to hire you to do it?"

"I'd probably ask for a fifty-million-dollar retainer and five years. No guarantees, though. I mean, I'd have to infiltrate the manufacturing and design companies that make the ECUs and figure out how to hide some very sophisticated software in their systems. Then I'd have to figure out a way to communicate with it..." His voice faded as he became lost in thought.

"You know all these guys," Smith said. "Who do you think did it? Give me some names."

"I doubt we're talking about an individual hacker," Zellerbach admitted. "Or even a group like Anonymous. I think we're talking about a government."

Smith and Randi looked at each other, clearly thinking the same thing: The Japanese did a lot of design and manufacture work for the auto industry. And they'd have the technological ability to hijack cell towers and satellite networks.

"Okay," Smith said. "Thanks, Marty."

"Do you want me to dig into this?"

"Absolutely not," Randi said. "We don't know what we're into here, but whatever it is, it's dangerous. We can't scrape up enough of the last guy who helped us to fill a shoe box."

"I'm not afraid."

"We know," Smith said. "But you've already given us what we were looking for. We'll call you if we need more. Talk later…"

He reached over and cut off the phone, then closed his eyes again to the sound of Randi tapping on her laptop. He was just about to drift off when she spoke.

"Star got the names we asked for, Jon. Odd woman, but you have to respect the skills."

"And?"

"We were close. The rocket fuel guy is Akito Maki with a *t*, not a *d*. The materials guy is Genjiro Ueda. Both are still alive and both work as private consultants. We've got life stories, tax returns, home addresses, phone numbers, you name it."

Smith let out a long breath. "If they knew enough to blow the top off that mountain, we have to assume they've got Fujiyama's files. They'll circle their wagons around anyone who was mentioned in them."

"I don't see that we have much of a choice. We're talking about Japan spending the last thirty years building a clandestine military and now purposely courting a war with China. The president can't march into the UN with a bunch of conjecture. We need something concrete."

Smith just couldn't stay awake anymore. His body was draining his normally limitless reserves to heal itself and it wouldn't be denied any longer. As he started to drift off, his mind began to project images of war. He'd been through too many. Seen too much. But what he'd experienced was nothing compared with the scale of a confrontation between the two Asian giants.

What would that look like?

Not anything anyone had seen before. Takahashi was too smart to let China overwhelm him with its superior numbers and the sheer weight of its hardware. No, much more likely the first shots fired in this conflict would be silent. Takahashi would simply have a handful of men fly to China and deploy his nanoscale weapon. The country would quietly rot from within. Eventually, the power grid would falter, machinery would crumble, buildings would collapse.

By the time the Chinese figured out what was happening, they'd be living in the Stone Age. No food, no transportation, no heat. Not even help from the outside because any relief effort would be attacked by the same nanotech that had destroyed China.

And in truth, that was a best-case scenario. Based on what he'd seen of Takahashi's technology, Smith wasn't confident that it could be controlled. A few minor mutations and it could run amok, spreading across the planet and destroying everything in its path.

41

S tatus report," General Takahashi said as he entered the expansive lab.

Dr. Hideki Ito was standing in front of a thick glass wall using a set of mechanical hands to pry open a metal box on the other side.

The scientist started to turn, but Takahashi motioned toward the glass. "Continue what you're doing."

After an awkward bow, he returned his attention to the box. "The nanobots have significantly weakened the structure of the safe, General, and we've confirmed that they have fully penetrated. The vial that we believe contains acid is made of glass so it's still intact. The papers are unharmed for the same reason—paper can't be used as fuel."

"But you're not in yet."

"No. These arms were designed for structural testing, not trying to perform delicate operations like this. It's a slow process."

"Then why not go inside and use conventional tools?" Takahashi said impatiently.

"The safe has been irradiated to destroy the bots. Levels are above safety thresholds, even for someone in a suit."

Takahashi's jaw tightened as he watched Ito's clumsy attempts to get a firm grip on the lockbox's combination dial. His people had lost contact with Smith and Russell in the Portland airport and so far had been unable to reacquire them.

What did they know?

It seemed likely that they were on their way to Japan via either private or military aircraft, and he had to assume that Fujiyama had discussed what was in his files to some extent. Perhaps he'd relayed only general suspicions, but he could just as well have given them specific names, projects, and locations. There was no way to know, and Takahashi didn't have enough men he trusted to cover every possibility.

The mechanical hand slipped off the dial and Ito let out a frustrated grunt before lining up again.

"How much longer, Doctor?"

"It's impossible to say, General. Even if the arms had been designed for this, I'd have to go slowly. There's no way to be certain that the linkages connecting the acid to the triggers have weakened enough. I—"

"Open the enclosure."

Ito turned toward him, obviously not sure he'd heard correctly. "Sir?"

Takahashi went to the far side of the lab and began putting on the radiation suit hanging on the wall. "Open it."

"General, the levels are far beyond what that suit was designed to handle. I—"

"Your objections are duly noted," Takahashi said.

Fear was etched deep in the scientist's ravaged face. After what had happened to him at Fukushima it wasn't difficult to determine why.

"Enter your access code to open the enclosure and leave the laboratory," Takahashi ordered.

"But, General. You ca—"

"Do it now!"

Ito stood frozen as Takahashi put the headgear on and linked to a small air tank.

Finally, the scientist punched his code into a keypad next to the air lock and then hurried for the exit.

Takahashi passed through the air lock and walked directly to the box centered in the enclosure. There were a number of tools designed to be used with the mechanical arms and he picked up the heaviest, struggling to control it in the thick gloves. His breath fogged the suit's faceplate as he swung the instrument repeatedly into the combination dial. On the fifth try, it shattered and pieces of it scattered across the stone floor. Selecting a more delicate tool, he dug into the exposed mechanism, carefully breaking off the various linkages and wires.

He tried to push back memories of the radiation victims the Americans had left in Hiroshima and Nagasaki, but was unable to keep them fully at bay. He'd been only a small child when he'd first seen the burns—similar to Ito's, but fundamentally different from the war injuries that had been so common at the time. A number of years had passed before the cancers had set in, but he could remember occasionally glimpsing people shamed by massive tumors and hearing tales of their slow, agonizing deaths.

With the last of the latches crumbling, Takahashi used a carbon fiber screwdriver to pry at the lockbox's seams. He couldn't hear anything beyond his own breathing, but felt the steel beginning to give as he drove the tool deeper. Sweat was stinging his eyes now and he tried to blink it away as the door finally released.

The documents were intact.

The tension in his shoulders and back relaxed somewhat and he carefully removed the thick stack of manila files.

Fate, it seemed, was once again favoring the Japanese people.

42

Outside Yaita
Japan

Jon Smith eased the car along the suburban Japanese street at precisely the speed limit. The houses on either side were a mix of styles, a bit more colorful than he'd expected and all borrowing to some extent from traditional Asian architecture. Most lots were at least an acre, and the overall landscape was too wide open to offer much cover.

He'd managed to find a rental car with tinted windows that, combined with his dark hair and complexion, would prevent him from attracting too much attention. Not that the neighborhood was exactly awash with pedestrians. He'd seen a group of kids playing soccer in a school playground about two miles back, but beyond that the area looked almost deserted. Everyone was still at work.

His target, the materials engineer Genjiro Ueda, lived directly ahead on a wooded hill rising a few hundred feet into the overcast sky. Sun glinted from the windows of widely spaced houses, and a narrow road was intermittently visible through the trees. It was a much more workable setting for what he was there to do. The lots expanded to an even more generous three acres and the foliage grew in density with elevation. The question was whether to go now or to wait for darkness.

It didn't take long to arrive at a decision. When he and Randi had split up so she could go after Akito Maki, they'd agreed that speed would have to take precedence over discretion. If they were right about Takahashi, he'd be circling the wagons around his people as fast as he could.

Smith kept a close watch on his rearview mirror as he ran through the details Star had uncovered about his target. Ueda was in his late forties and a little thinner and more fit than Smith would have preferred. He'd been a postdoc at the Tokyo Institute of Technology studying carbon fiber technology when he'd suddenly left to start his own firm. He made a good wage—the equivalent of low four hundreds in US dollars—but even the inestimable Star had been unable to get a good bead on who his clients were.

Satellite photos and a few street views from Google showed an elegant two-story house with a fence that was more form than function and lacked a gate. Star had been able to find no evidence that Ueda and his wife of fifteen years had any kind of security system. Also, no kids, no pets, and no neighbors within view. The engineer seemed to work largely out of an office in his house, and his wife didn't have a job. So the hope was that he'd be there. Smith wasn't particularly anxious to have to sit around and wait.

The grade of the road started to steepen and he maintained his speed, counting driveways as he went up. The idyllic neighborhood wasn't exactly Afghanistan but that didn't stop the adrenaline from pumping. Normally, Covert-One ops were planned to the very last detail. By comparison, this one felt hopelessly half-assed. He was still suffering badly from his injuries and probably only functioning at 60 percent of peak. There had been no time to insert a surveillance team to recon the area, he had no backup, and the sum total of his operational experience in Japan consisted of getting shot in the back with a crossbow bolt.

Smith reached for a compact Taser lying in the passenger seat as he turned into Ueda's driveway. The plan was to shock him, stuff him in the trunk, and get the hell out of there. Three minutes tops, depending on the situation with his wife. As Randi was fond of saying, what could possibly go wrong?

Smith's normal bias would be to park down the road and go quietly over the wall, but someone was bound to notice a six-foot American wandering around the neighborhood. Particularly when he started climbing fences in broad daylight. Better to try to stay a little closer to the natural rhythms of the area.

He parked behind a Toyota SUV and slipped the Taser into his pocket before stepping from the car. Nice house, nice yard. Nothing out of place.

Not that appearances meant much. If he'd been fighting for the other side, he'd make sure everything looked as normal as possible to draw his opponent in.

There was no bell in evidence next to the door, so Smith gave it a few hard raps with one hand, keeping the other wrapped around the Taser in his jacket.

When footsteps became audible on the other side, he moved back a pace and checked behind him again. A moment later the door was opened by an attractive Japanese woman who looked to be in her midthirties. She seemed genuinely surprised to see an American on her porch, and Smith cautiously took it as a good sign.

According to Star, she'd taken five years of English in secondary school. Based on her grades, though, he decided to
enunciate carefully.

"Hello. I'm Professor Jon Richards from the Massachusetts
Institute of Technology. Is your husband at home?"

Her brow knitted a bit but she seemed to understand.
"Please come in. He is here. He is in his…office."

Smith smiled easily and stepped across the threshold, closing the door behind him.

"Please stay," she said deliberately, then started toward the
back of the house.

He waited for her to disappear and then followed silently,
still clutching the Taser. It would have been preferable for her
not to be home, but that had probably been too much to hope
for. Nothing a little duct tape couldn't solve.

He saw her pass through a doorway at the back and decided
this was his best chance. According to the architectural plans,
there was only one way in and out of the room. They'd be easier to control in the confined space.

He could hear Genjiro's voice, slightly elevated in volume
but completely unintelligible.

"Good afternoon," Smith said, trying to sound cheerful as
he entered the medium-sized home office.

"Who are you?" Genjiro said, standing up from behind his
desk. His English was solid and so was his body. According to
Star, he'd been involved in the martial arts since he was five
years old.

"I'm an engineer with MIT," Smith said with another disarming smile. "I was in the neighborhood and Bob Darren said
I should come by and introduce myself."

He maintained eye contact with Genjiro, making certain

that he wasn't looking toward the Taser sliding out of Smith's pocket. Unfortunately, his wife was paying more attention.

Instead of running or shouting, though, she whipped around and aimed an extremely well-executed spinning back kick right at Smith's head. He ducked, feeling her foot pass through the top of his hair as her husband leaped across his desk.

If he lived through this, Star was going to get a serious ass chewing for missing the woman's fighting skills.

There was no question that he was losing control of the situation, and he had only a few seconds to get it back. The woman recovered quickly and transitioned smoothly into a front kick aimed directly at his testicles. If he was 100 percent, he'd have foot-swept her, Tasered her husband, and been on his way. But those days were over for a while.

There was no choice but to use the Taser on her. She stiffened and dropped like a stone just as Genjiro launched a brutal side kick. His background was in tae kwon do, so he'd be heavy on foot techniques—a game Smith had no interest in playing. He slipped the kick and grabbed hold of the man, going for his neck, but mostly trying to stay close enough to shut down his offense.

Genjiro managed to swing an elbow, but Smith moved even closer and was struck by the man's triceps. He took a vicious stomp to his right foot, but the light hiking boots he was wearing absorbed the brunt of it and gave him time to snake an arm around the engineer's throat.

After decades of training, though, Genjiro wasn't going to make it that easy. He went for Smith's fingers and almost got hold of one before Smith could close his fist. The Japanese was off balance and Smith managed to spin him to the ground, landing hard on his back with both knees. That dazed the man enough for Smith to sink the choke hold deeper and tighten it as much as his injured back would allow. Genjiro clawed blindly behind him and Smith buried his face into the man's back to protect his eyes. After thirty seconds the engineer started to weaken. Smith kept the pressure on, not easing off until Genjiro was on the verge of slipping into unconsciousness.

When Smith rolled the man over, he reached out weakly but stopped when he felt the suppressor of Smith's Sig Sauer pressed up under his chin.

"We can all walk away from this no worse for the wear, Genjiro. I just want to talk to you about your work."

"I'm a consultant. I—"

"You work for Masao Takahashi."

Smith realized he'd been hoping that Genjiro wouldn't have any idea what he was talking about—that he and Randi were wrong about all this. It was clear from the man's eyes, though, that he knew exactly what was being asked.

"Who?" the Japanese said, obviously too panicked and oxygen deprived to come up with a more elaborate denial.

"You're telling me you don't know who Takahashi is?"

"I...of course. But—"

"Your country's on the brink of war, Genjiro. And Takahashi's doing everything he can to make sure it happens."

"Make sure it happens?" the man said as his head cleared. "The Chinese attack our ships, they try to kill him. We have a right to defend ourselves!"

"What if I tell you that I think Takahashi sank the *Izumo*? That he *wants* this war."

"Impossible! We can't defeat China. The Americans would

get involved and we would end up in a bloody stalemate that
serves no one. Takahashi knows this better than anyone."

Smith nodded imperceptibly. Of course Genjiro wouldn't
have the big picture. He was just a soldier. A brilliant one, but
a soldier nonetheless.

"Do you think you're the only one he recruited? What about
Japan's other geniuses? The ones who used to make your coun-
try the world's technological capital. Where is Hideki Ito?
Where is Akito Maki?"

Genjiro didn't respond, considering what he'd just heard.

"Takahashi has an army of men like you designing weapons
for him," Smith pressed. "But you've done too good a job. Mu-
tual assured destruction no longer applies. Takahashi thinks he
can win."

Genjiro opened his mouth to speak but whatever he said
was drowned out by the sound of shattering glass.

Smith dropped and rolled to his side with his pistol held
out in front of him. A large projectile had come through the
east window and slammed into the back wall. It shattered on
impact, sending what looked like a bunch of finned .50-caliber
rounds cascading to the floor.

Genjiro used the confusion to pull away and struggle to his
feet amid a sound that reminded Smith of the Independence
Day bottle rockets his father used to buy on the black market.

"Get your ass down!" Smith shouted as tiny jets of flame
erupted from the backs of the objects lying around the room.
A moment later they began to skitter across the floor and take
to the air.

Smith managed to grab Genjiro's ankle but it was too late.
One of the projectiles hit him in the right side, puncturing his
heart and both his lungs before erupting from his back in a

spray of blood, tissue, and bone. It cartwheeled out of control, finally hitting a wall and going dead.

Most of the others hadn't gotten off the ground yet and Smith stayed low, going for Genjiro's wife. He had no idea what the hell these things were or what their capabilities were. Did they have a targeting system or did they just fly at random and cut down everything in range? Either way, he wasn't planning on hanging around to find out.

Smith heard a loud whoosh behind him and he dived, rolling over the top of the woman who was just starting to shake off the effects of the Taser. The projectile barely missed him, rocketing past his right shoulder and sticking in the heavy wood molding near the ceiling.

If all these things managed to get into the air, Smith knew that his survival would be measured in seconds. He grabbed the dazed woman, dragging her toward the heavy desk that dominated the room. She screamed and he felt the warmth of blood splattering across his face. When he looked back, a chunk the size of a baseball was missing from her right thigh.

His plan to get beneath the desk and pull it toward the wall as cover was starting to look completely pointless. It was quickly becoming clear that these things weren't just high-tech shrapnel—they had some kind of command and control structure. If they weren't able to get around the desk, they'd go right through it.

Smith lifted the struggling woman into a fireman's carry and went for the broken window, falling through it and bringing what glass was left in the frame down on them.

He rolled on top of the woman, lying on his back with his Sig Sauer aimed toward the open window—more out of habit and training than an expectation that it would do any good. After an excruciatingly long two-count, he came to the realization that they weren't following. He could still hear the bottle-rocket sound of their engines, but whoever programmed them had obviously set them up to stay within the confines of the house.

He moved off the moaning woman and into a crouch, sweeping his weapon from left to right. They were sandwiched between the house and a dense, blossom-covered hedge. He couldn't see out, but that probably meant no one could see in either. His vehicle would be to the right at about twenty yards, but it might as well have been a mile. Genjiro's wife was going into shock and his injuries were going to make carrying her that distance a slow and painful process.

Smith pulled his cell from his pocket and dialed Randi, sliding cautiously along the rough-hewn boards that sided the house.

"Yeah," she said, picking up on the second ring.

"Abort! Do you understand me? Abort!"

"Jon? What the hell—"

His body was suddenly racked with a kind of pain he'd never felt before. Randi's voice turned to static and he felt his legs buckle. The gun fell from his hand as he fought to stay upright. Then everything went dark.

43

Utsunomiya
Japan

J on!" Randi shouted into the phone. "Jon, can you hear
me?"

It was obvious he couldn't. The static was so loud that she
had to hold the phone more than a foot from her ear. And then
it went silent.

She resisted the urge to slam the cell repeatedly into
the dashboard of her rented car and instead threw it on
the passenger seat. The traffic was bumper-to-bumper and
she gunned the car into oncoming traffic, turning onto a
slightly less crowded street lined with high-rise apartment
buildings.

As expected, there were no empty spaces, so she pulled
into a loading dock decorated with emphatic signs that she assumed said "No Parking."

"Calm down," she said in the empty confines of the car.

People walking by on the sidewalk started looking at her
with vague concern, probably based on her expression. She
picked up the phone again and pretended to be in the midst
of a cheerful conversation. A few moments later, no one was
giving her a second thought.

What the hell had happened? She'd seen Smith bleeding from an artery, getting shot at, and playing with viruses that could wipe out half of humanity. He always sounded like he was speaking at a PTA meeting. This call had been different and it unnerved her. He'd sounded desperate.

She turned the wheel to pull back out into the street but then stopped before releasing the brake. Her first instinct was to try to make it to him, but what was the point? It would be almost an hour's drive, and that was only if the GPS in her phone stopped inexplicably switching into Japanese.

Her target was only about a mile away and her second instinct was to go for him despite Smith's warning. Akito Maki was the last lead they had, and if they blew it what was the next step? Snatching random Japanese scientists, hooking them up to car batteries, and asking if they'd been spending their weekends building a science fiction army?

She looked across the street and saw an Imperial Japanese war flag flying over the entrance to an apartment building. It was one of probably twenty she'd seen that day. And then there were the demonstrations, T-shirts, banners, and barricades erected in front of Japan's government buildings. Grocery stores were having a hard time keeping their shelves stocked as people squirreled away supplies to get them through what everyone seemed certain was coming.

She slammed a hand into the wheel and it felt so good she did it a few more times. Normally she'd assume that Smith had escaped whatever he'd gotten himself into, but his injuries were slowing him down badly. More likely he was dead or captured.

A man in a police uniform was approaching from the north

and he pointed sternly at her. She gave an apologetic nod and eased back into traffic. The GPS in her phone warned her in Japanese that she was headed away from her destination. She turned it off and dialed Fred Klein.

If they ever needed one of his miracles, it was now.

44

Northeastern Japan

Jon Smith opened his eyes and stared up at the fluorescent light hanging above him. Beyond it was an earthen ceiling, and judging from the rock jammed into his spine, the floor was similarly constructed.

He eased into a sitting position and made a quick survey of his surroundings: a small cave that, based on the uniform striations in the walls, had been created by machine. The space was no bigger than ten by ten feet and there was a single door built out of a reddish material with a visible carbon fiber weave. Other than that, there was only a simple wood table and a couple of matching chairs.

He stood unsteadily, focusing for a moment on his physical condition. His back wasn't as bad as it could be—thank God Ueda's office had been on the first floor. Not that it had done the engineer much good.

He remembered hitting the ground with the man's injured wife and calling Randi. After that, there was nothing until he'd woken up in this place.

Smith took a seat in one of the chairs and saw that a cut on the back of his hand had been patched up. Better than the alternative, he supposed, but waking up in unidentifiable places with a bunch of doctored wounds hadn't been working out all that well for him lately.

He considered going to work on the door with one of the chairs, but after a few moments decided it would be a waste of time. Instead, his thoughts turned to Randi. Had she done what he'd told her? Had she turned tail and run?

He hoped the fact that she wasn't there with him suggested yes, but she could just as easily be dead. Or imprisoned at a facility closer to her target.

The door began to slide back and Smith rose from the chair and took a step back. He put a hand on the chair, but as weapons went it wasn't exactly state of the art. For now it might be better to just figure out where he stood. If an opportunity arose, he could always take it.

The man who came in was immediately recognizable. A full five inches shorter than Smith, he had a solid, stocky build and a weathered face beneath military-cut gray hair.

"General Takahashi," Smith said, bowing subtly. It was vaguely possible that he could kill the man before anyone came to his aid, but there was no way to know if that would solve problems or create more. Civility seemed to be a wiser course of action at this point.

Takahashi returned the bow as the door closed automatically behind him. "Colonel Smith." He motioned toward the table. "Please sit. It's my understanding that that you're injured."

It would have been disrespectful to refuse, so Smith took a chair and watched the general as he did the same.

"Randi Russell?" Takahashi said simply.

His first reaction was to lie, but that would just insult the old soldier's intelligence. "She was on a similar mission. I told

250   Robert Ludlum and Kyle Mills

her to abort after I ran into your...toys."

The old man nodded. "A self-propelled, self-directed antipersonnel weapon. As yet a bit unsophisticated. We can limit them to a certain area but beyond that they just seek out body-heat signatures. I'm told that more advanced targeting computers are too heavy."

That explained why they hadn't gone for him specifically and why they hadn't chased him through the window. Lack of sophistication notwithstanding, the weapon had terrifying potential if dropped into the middle of an advancing infantry. And as far as Smith knew, nothing even remotely similar was under development by the United States.

"But that's not what got me, is it, General?"

"No. Genjiro's house was surrounded by tiny grains of silicon that are very similar to sand but charged by solar radiation. When a certain remote signal is given, they rearrange themselves into a circuit and can deliver quite an electric shock. Think of it as a twenty-first-century minefield. Depending on the circuit created, it can kill or incapacitate. More important, though, it can be permanently shut down after hostilities end. No more generations of children having their limbs blown off by mines left behind. A significant improvement, don't you think?"

Smith actually did, but decided not to admit it. "Ironic that Genjiro would be killed by something he had a hand in designing."

Takahashi nodded. "And unfortunate. He made significant contributions over the years. Having said that, his time was coming to an end. As a soldier and scientist, I imagine that you've discovered the same thing I have: War favors the wise and experienced. Science prefers the young and inspired."

Smith didn't respond.

"Do you know where you are, Colonel?"

"I can only speculate."

Takahashi leaned back in his chair and waved him on. "Please do."

"After losing Reactor Four, you'd need a new venue to work on your nanotech weapon that eats metal, concrete, and plastic. I notice none of those materials are present in this room. You'd still need radiation to kill it just in case, though. So, I'd have to guess an underground nuclear waste storage facility."

The old soldier smiled. "I would say that you live up to your reputation, but I have to admit that I know surprisingly little about it. We have excellent penetration into America's military computers as well as those at the CIA and NSA. They all seem to indicate that you're a microbiologist. I think you'd say virus hunter."

"Maybe your access isn't as good as you think, General."

"I believe it is. We've been developing supercomputer and cyber warfare technology since the early eighties. Your own NSA is about ten years behind us. A much more likely explanation is that you're not here at the behest of any of those organizations."

Fred Klein insisted that Covert-One's computers be completely cut off from the outside world. If you wanted to access them, you had to be physically sitting behind one of the terminals at the marina. And getting to one of those terminals without Klein's permission would be a challenge for the Eighty-Second Airborne.

"Knowledge is power," Smith said noncommittally.

Takahashi smiled, obviously not expecting him to just roll over and give up his employer. "As is technology. You directed the military's development of Dresner's Merge unit, did you not?"

"Yes, sir." It was more or less public knowledge, so he didn't see any harm in admitting it.

"A fascinating system. Limited, of course. But I was very interested to see where you were taking it." He looked at Smith as though he were a gifted child. "I greatly regret that you weren't born Japanese, Colonel. You would have done very well on my staff."

Smith accepted the compliment with a respectful nod. The endless pages of information he'd gone through on Takahashi had painted a picture of an extremely formidable soldier. But sitting there across from him, Smith realized they hadn't captured the full extent of the man.

"So you weren't as impressed by the Merge as I was," Smith said, trying to draw him into saying more about the technologies his people had developed. Surprisingly, Takahashi seemed completely unguarded on the subject.

"What you were working on was already obsolete, Colonel. There's no way to improve the soldier. No matter how well equipped he is, he's still flesh and blood, driven by unpredictable and unstable emotions."

"Obsolete," Smith repeated, thoughtfully. "Like your battleship?"

From his expression, it was clear that Takahashi knew he was being baited. He just didn't seem to care. "The *Izumo* was just a piece of military theater. Something for our people to rally around and to keep the Chinese off balance."

"But you've obviously done better."

"Unquestionably. My predecessor started with a blank page. He threw out everything we thought we knew about warfare and brought in philosophers and scientists who'd never had anything to do with the battlefield. Together they imagined something completely new."

"And you managed to find the talent to build it."

"Young people in America are quite self-absorbed, don't you think? The Japanese are nationalistic by their very nature. Most of the people I approached were honored to be asked to serve their country. The rest were convinced by my financial resources."

"Convinced to do what, though, sir? Start a war with China?"

Takahashi's face became a mask. "At your country's insistence, the Japanese people gave up their right to project power militarily. We made up for that somewhat with the strength of our economy, but a superpower needs both. Certainly you understand that. You're a soldier serving the second-most-powerful military in history."

Smith ignored the sudden demotion to runner-up. "I can't help thinking that you're telling me a great deal, General."

It was likely that it didn't matter because he was going to be tortured for information and then killed afterward, but it seemed sensible to bring up the subject.

"Our countries are allies, Colonel. Nothing I've done is intended to harm our close relationship."

Smith noticed the lack of emotion in Takahashi's voice. At best, he saw the United States as a necessary evil. At worst, a problem that he hadn't yet figured out how to solve.

"Can I assume, then, that I'm free to go?"

Takahashi actually laughed. "I think that can eventually be arranged, Colonel. But first, I'd ask a favor."

"Sir?"

"Your president is personally hosting a meeting between

China's leadership and our prime minister. It begins tomorrow in Australia. I'd like you to contact your superiors and request a private meeting between him and me while he's there."

Takahashi reached into his pocket and retrieved a phone, sliding it across the table.

"Take me at my word that this summit is meaningless, Colonel. We're entering a new era and it's time our countries discuss how it can be brought in with the minimum chaos."

"You mean how the world will be divided up between us."

"If you prefer."

Takahashi stood and gave a short bow before walking to the door. A moment later Smith was alone again in the locked cave.

There was no way to know for certain the capabilities of Takahashi's military, but even if it was just what Smith had experienced firsthand, the face of war would be changed forever. If the man had actually found a way to control his nanotech to the point that he could deploy it as a weapon, then the US military and the rest of the world's militaries combined were now irrelevant.

He reached for the phone and dialed one of many emergency numbers he'd committed to memory long ago. It would be routed through the analog phone system of Myanmar, passing through a house with two handsets literally taped together. And when the conversation was over, that house would conveniently burn down.

Not surprisingly, Klein picked up on the first ring.

"Yes."

"We have a bit of a situation, sir."

"Are you all right?"

"For now."

"But you managed to get to a phone."

"A phone was provided."

"I see. To what end?"

"The general would like a private meeting with our friend while he's on his southern vacation."

"Understood. And are you recommending that our friend take the meeting?"

"I think it would be wise."

"Can he contact the general directly with his response?"

"I imagine so. He doesn't seem particularly concerned about confidentiality."

"And you? Is there anything we can do to help you?"

It was an interesting question. In the end, though, he appeared to be inside the facility where the nanoweapon was being developed. While the chances were remote, it was possible that he could figure out some way to cause trouble.

"No. I'll be fine."

"Thank you for the call. And good luck."

45

Tokyo
Japan

Randi Russell slung the bag over her shoulder and dodged along the crowded sidewalk, watching her reflection in the store windows for anyone taking undue notice. Beyond a few admiring glances from the men she passed, her practiced eye spotted nothing. By design, she wasn't the only Caucasian on the street. Covert-One didn't keep a safe house in Tokyo, and Klein had been forced to set one up with less time and forethought than he usually brought to the task. They'd agreed that the best bet would be to hide in plain sight—to rent an apartment in a part of the city heavily frequented by foreign tourists and businessmen.

Randi cut right and jogged up a stairway leading to a set of glass doors. She pressed her hand against a palm reader—the Japanese loved technology—and heard the lock buzz. A moment later she was striding across a tastefully minimalist lobby toward a bank of elevators.

The one on the right was open and she ducked inside, keeping an eye on the glass front of the condo building as she punched in her floor number. Still nothing, but it didn't mean much. In that kind of a crowd, a professional surveillance team would be virtually impossible to detect. And that didn't even take into consideration probable hacks into the surveillance cameras that bristled from just about every wall in Tokyo. At this point, pretty much everything had become a roll of the dice. And those dice were most likely loaded.

The elevator rose smoothly to her floor without anyone else getting on. Randi put a hand on the Beretta under her jacket as she stepped into the hallway. Empty.

She moved quickly, feeling uncomfortable out in the open. A wave of her key card in front of a door near the back of the corridor caused it to pop open and she stepped through.

A man jumped up from the sofa that was nearly all the furniture that would fit in the tiny space, watching her with a startled expression.

"You're not Jon."

"They told me you were smart," Randi said, entering the kitchen to empty her bag of the ramen and beer it contained. As expected, the refrigerator was no bigger than the one she'd had in college. Space in Tokyo was at an incredible premium, and while she would have liked to go with something a bit roomier, those kinds of condos tended to attract attention. Better to be just another one of the anonymous millions wedged into three hundred square feet.

"Who are you?"

"That's not really important," she said, tossing him a beer and taking one for herself. She came out of the kitchen and went straight for the couch. "Now, let's have a chat about nanotechnology."

Greg Maple looked down at her. "I don't know what you're talking about."

Instead of looking away after the lie, he kept staring—

studying her face with an enigmatic expression that was more complicated than the fear she expected under the circumstances.

"What?" Randi said, popping open her beer and taking a swig.

"You..." Maple started. "You look like someone I used to know."

Randi didn't immediately react. Maple and Smith had been friends for a long time. Long enough for him to have met her sister.

"You mean Sophie."

His eyes widened. They looked enough alike that Randi had become used to the reaction. It was still gut-wrenching to think about her dead sister—Jon's dead fiancée—but at least she was practiced at it now.

"You're Randi Russell?" Maple said.

"In the flesh."

"CIA."

She nodded.

"I knew it!" Maple said, pulling up a folding chair. Their knees almost touched in the tiny space. "He's military intelligence. You're working together."

"That's right," she said. It was the obvious assumption and she decided to run with it.

"Where is he? Is he okay?"

That was a hard question to answer because she honestly didn't know. According to Klein, when Smith had called to set up a meeting between the president and Takahashi, he'd sounded fine. There was no way to know if that was still the case, though.

"We've lost him."

"Lost?"

"Misplaced," she corrected. "Temporarily. And in the mean-time, I'm filling in."

"Is that why you had me kidnapped?" he said with a little understandable anger coming to the surface.

She decided not to acknowledge it. "It's my understanding that you've taken the lead on this nanotech problem. I need to know what you've learned."

"You could have picked up a phone instead of dragging me all the way to Japan."

"Phones are too hard to secure, Greg. I prefer to have my conversations face-to-face. Now drink your beer before it gets warm."

He popped open the can obediently and took a swig, but it didn't seem to make him any less nervous.

"So? Have you figured out anything that can help me?"

He shook his head. "Probably not that can help you, but things that are . . . amazing."

"Let's hear those, then. Keeping in mind that I'm not Jon. I'm not a scientist."

"Okay. I found a couple of structures that didn't seem to have anything to do with the machine's ability to copy itself."

"Jon told me about them. You didn't know what they were for. Have you figured it out?"

"I think so. The first is to control the number of times the individual unit can replicate. So you take one nanobot and you set the replication counter to ten. It makes ten new bots, but each of those can only make nine. And in turn, each of those can only make eight. When you get to zero, replication ends. In that example, you'd end up with millions of bots before it's all over. If you were to set that initial parameter at a thousand instead of ten, you're talking numbers that are hard to even imagine."

Randi frowned and set her beer down. "You said a couple. What about the other structure?"

"That seems to relate to magnetism."

"They attract each other?"

He shook his head. "I think they measure the earth's magnetic field."

"What for?"

"Probably to locate themselves—like birds."

She let that process for a moment and didn't like the conclusion she was coming to. "So, if they know where they are, it's possible that they could be programmed to work only in a certain geographic area and to go dormant outside that area."

"Very possible."

They had known the technology worked—the machines were clearly able to self-replicate using steel, plastic, and concrete as fuel. What Jon hadn't been sure of was whether it could be weaponized. Weapons had to be deadly, but just as important they had to be controllable. If you had a gun, you had to be able to aim it. And that's exactly what Maple was talking about.

She wanted to ask more, but was unsure how much to reveal. In the end, though, Maple wasn't an idiot. With the facts he already had, it seemed reasonable to assume that he'd already considered the scenario she was interested in.

"Then you're telling me I could make it so these things only worked, say, in China. When they crossed over the border into another country, they'd just stop reproducing."

"Assuming that the system is foolproof. The problem with replication is that it's hard not to introduce errors. *Mutations* is probably a better word. Usually, those mutations are neither here nor there. Sometimes they kill the organism, or in this case break the machine. But every once in a while, they could make the machine better."

"And by 'better,' you mean better at reproduction. There could be a mutation that turns off the control system."

"Exactly. Theoretically, errors could be introduced that would allow the machines to replicate indefinitely or operate outside the programmed geographic borders. Even worse, though, you could get changes to the type of fuel the bots use. What if they became capable of eating rock? Or water? Or flesh? That's potentially end-of-the world stuff."

"What if that happened? How would we stop them?"

"Radiation. And a lot of it. That's the only thing I'm aware of that can kill these things."

She let out a long breath and picked up her beer again. "That's why it was developed in Fukushima, right, Doc? So they'd have a way to kill it if they lost control."

"That would be my guess. Everything was probably going along fine and then the tsunami caused a containment breach. It forced them to irradiate Reactor Four."

"Okay. Let's assume they're still working on this thing— either developing it or manufacturing it. They'd still need that safeguard, right? Access to radiation."

"I assume so."

"Okay. Then put yourself in their shoes. Where would you be?"

"A nuclear sub would be ideal. Easy to irradiate and even if you didn't get them all, they'd end up at the bottom of the ocean. With no fuel chain, they'd corrode in the salt water before they could make it to civilization."

"It's a little hard to make pronouncements about the Japanese military right now, but building something as big as a nuclear sub without anyone knowing doesn't seem plausible. Even for Takahashi."

"Yeah, I thought of that too," Maple said. "But I have a theory. Do you want to hear it?"

"Hell yes, I want to hear it."

"A few years ago, the Japanese built a facility to store the nuclear waste from their reactors. It's carved out of a mountain in the northeast. That's it. If I was working on this thing, that's where I'd be set up."

46

Outside Melbourne
Australia

President Sam Adams Castilla stood at the massive window and looked out over the rows of vines stretching to the horizon. The sun had just set, casting long shadows across the landscape and obscuring all but one man patrolling the grounds with a German shepherd.

The house was on loan from an Australian manufacturing magnate whom he'd known since he was the governor of New Mexico. Its relative isolation made it easier for the Secret Service to secure as well as a more appealing venue for the negotiations he was hosting. Setting was more important than most people realized. Warm, comfortable, and serene. Those were things that put people in the mood to compromise.

A quick glance at his watch confirmed that it was time. As the president of the United States it was his prerogative to keep people waiting, but he sensed it would be a mistake in this case.

He walked across the expansive bedroom suite and into the long second-floor hallway. Two Secret Service men fell in behind, talking quietly into microphones hidden near their wrists to tell their team that he was on the move.

Normally he would have greeted them by name, but not today. Today he was lost in his own thoughts.

The direct talks between Prime Minister Sanetomi and President Yandong of China had been going surprisingly well. Or maybe it wasn't so surprising. Both men had a nasty nationalistic streak, but both also seemed to understand that they had taken this particular drama a little too far. That it wouldn't be long before the situation metastasized beyond anything that either country could handle.

It was only the first day of the summit and the six-hour meeting that had ended earlier that afternoon already was generating compromises from both sides. Of course, the question of the Senkaku Islands was still open, but Castilla was convinced that it could be resolved in principle over the next few days.

What he wasn't sure of, though, was whether it mattered.

He continued around the corner, blind to the expensive artwork and historical pieces that normally would have caught his eye. Instead, he focused on a closed door at the end of the seemingly endless corridor. Were the prime minister of Japan and the president of China even relevant anymore? Or had the power to control this situation shifted into the hands of a single man? The man he was about to meet.

Castilla paused, taking a deep breath as his two guards took up positions along the wall. One of the surprisingly few meaningful benefits to being the president of the United States was that he was generally better informed than the people he met with. In this instance that edge had been lost. Badly.

Castilla pushed through the door and closed it behind him. A Japanese man in a dark-blue business suit immediately rose from one of two wingback chair set up in front of a fireplace.

The electric lights had been dimmed and the flames gave off a warm glow, though it didn't feel as tranquil as Castilla had hoped.

General Masao Takahashi gave a respectful bow, and Castilla strode across the room to offer his hand. The soldier's grip was predictably firm and they locked eyes, neither man attempting to assert dominance, but neither willing to cede it.

"Please," Castilla said, indicating the chair Takahashi had risen from.

The soldier sat after another short bow and the president took the chair next to him. "It's my understanding that you have valuable information relating to the negotiations between your country and China," Castilla said.

"I'm very grateful and honored that you agreed to see me," Takahashi said. "I understand the demands on your time."

The famous Japanese politeness. Castilla wanted to take the man by the throat and scream, *What the hell are you doing, you crazy son of a bitch! Trying to start World War Three?*

Instead he smiled and reached for a pot on a table next to him. "Tea?"

"Thank you."

Takahashi appraised the man in front of him as he poured two cups and held one out. Once again fate had smiled on him. Most politicians were dim and one-dimensional. Not so, Castilla. He was an extremely intelligent man who didn't need to rely on others for knowledge of history, geopolitics, and economics. Even war. While he would resist, the man would at least be capable of understanding.

The Americans were an interesting people. While there was little doubt that they were inferior to the Japanese, their genetic impurity was in many ways their advantage. Originally America had attracted only those who had the ability to make the difficult ocean crossing and, perhaps more important, those who wanted to. Individuals who had the courage, mental capacity, and discipline to throw off the yoke of Europe's repressive aristocracies and carve out a better life on their own.

The president didn't seem inclined to speak further, so Takahashi decided to take the initiative. "I assume that Colonel Smith and his people have fully briefed you on Fukushima?"

"That you were using Reactor Four to develop a weapon based on molecular manufacturing?"

Takahashi nodded.

"They have. It's my understanding that it can destabilize concrete, plastic, and steel—the building blocks of modern civilization. But it's also my understanding that it will be almost impossible to control. And that if it should run wild..." Castilla's voice trailed off.

"It's been extensively tested with one hundred percent success," Takahashi said. "We can control it."

"By using the earth's magnetic field to localize it and limiting its ability to reproduce," Castilla said.

"You are indeed well informed."

"The problem is that my people aren't convinced. They believe there's a big difference between a lab setting and the real world. The consequences of using this type of weapon go well beyond anything developed by humanity thus far. The only analogy I can come up with would be a full-scale nuclear war between the US and the Soviet Union."

Takahashi took a sip of his tea. As formidable as this politician was, he was, at his core, a hypocrite. When it was the

American people who were threatened, the United States threw its values of freedom, human rights, and privacy into the trash bin. It indiscriminately wiped out civilians via robotic drones. It imprisoned countless people without charge and then tortured them for information. It dropped atomic bombs. But when another country was in the crosshairs, the Americans were always the first to call for moderation and restraint.

"Our development efforts over the last decade have been quite varied, Mr. President. The nanotech is only one component."

"And what are the other components?"

Takahashi didn't respond, instead taking a sip of his tea.

"Surely, one of the benefits of having an incredible arsenal is letting your enemies know that it exists and that you're willing to use it."

"But we aren't enemies, Mr. President. I'm here out of friendship."

Castilla didn't bother to hide his skepticism. "Japan is an island. Can I assume your first order of business was to control the sea?"

"Our first priority was in fact cyber warfare. Naval superiority was our second."

"But your new battleship was sunk."

"The battleship was a showpiece. Our defenses are based on self-cavitating torpedoes."

"Like the Soviet Shkval?"

"In the same way as a computer is like a handheld calculator. Our units are significantly faster, have vastly greater range, and are artificially intelligent."

"But that wouldn't protect you from China's missile batteries or air force."

"We've developed an extremely effective air defense system based on electromagnetic pulses."

Castilla's brow furrowed. "Nuclear."

"Yes. Our system creates a long-lasting radioactive cloud that destroys the electronics of anything moving into our airspace."

"I would have thought that your history would make you understand the seriousness of that kind of weapon."

"On an emotional level, yes. But on a logical level, it had the opposite effect. The casualties in Hiroshima and Nagasaki were much lower than most people realize. There are people who were within a few meters of ground zero who are still alive today. Obviously this isn't an ideal solution, but my people tell me that America's approach to missile intercept is ultimately a dead end."

"If the Chinese were to see nuclear weapons detonated..." Castilla paused for a moment. "This could escalate into a full-scale nuclear war."

"As you mentioned earlier, we would tell them about our missile defense network so that they don't misinterpret it as an offensive strike. But if they choose to escalate, it's unlikely any of their weapons would reach us."

The president had gone noticeably pale, even in the warm light coming from the flames. A sensible response in Takahashi's estimation. Again, Castilla proved that he was no fool.

"Biological?" the president said in a careful, even voice.

"We have significant stockpiles of a modified version of the SARS virus. Of course, this is a weapon that would be used only in the event of a significant ground force invasion. It's extraordinarily contagious and fast acting, though not particularly deadly. The illness lasts two weeks on average. Quite incapacitating, I'm told."

"Can I assume that your population is fully protected?"

"Of course. It was done quietly through our national vaccination program." Takahashi waved a hand dismissively. "We also have armor that is thirty times lighter and nineteen times thinner than steel. Rocket fuel nine times more potent per kilogram than what you have access to. Computers that are an order of magnitude more powerful than those available to your NSA. The list goes on, but I assume you understand my point."

Again the skepticism crept into the president's expression.

"You think I'm exaggerating," Takahashi said. "That even with double our public budget, we could have never gotten this far ahead of you. What you don't understand is that it's not about budget."

"It's not?"

Takahashi shook his head. "The problem you have is that the purpose of the US military isn't to win wars."

"I think that would come as a surprise to the Joint Chiefs."

"You'll have to excuse my English, Mr. President. Perhaps 'purpose' was the wrong word. Let me change it to 'priority.' First and foremost, the US military is used to bolster employment through active military, support personnel, and so on. It enriches defense contracting companies. It gets politicians reelected through the acquisition and protection of projects in their districts. And admittedly, it strokes the egos and nostalgia of aging generals like myself. With all due respect, sir, you've pumped trillions into a military that hasn't been able to deliver a clear win since you defeated us. Afghanistan, Iraq, Vietnam, Korea, Somalia. Your soldiers are courageous and well trained, but the motto of the US military-industrial complex seems to be, 'If it hasn't worked in the past, make it more expensive.'"

"But that's not your motto."

Takahashi shrugged noncommittally. "The US completely destroyed my country's military capability during World War Two. It created a blank slate for us to work from. You, though, had created a massive military by the end of that war and it was in many people's best interest to maintain and grow it. Your F-35 program is an interesting example. A trillion dollars for a fighter that has no clear mission, is nothing more than an incremental improvement over prior planes, and is so complex that it doesn't even reliably fly. And then there are the billions in weapons that go straight from the factory into long-term storage because your military has no use for them. I'm buffeted by no such winds."

Castilla picked up his tea, warming hands that had gone cold while listening to the man across from him. "Can I assume you'll be publicly announcing what you've just told me and perhaps giving the world a demonstration? I suspect that you'd see a very quick change in attitude from the Chinese. And that's your goal, right? Peace?"

Takahashi watched the man in front of him drink from his cup. He was surprisingly formidable, this politician. A worthy ally. Or a very dangerous enemy. "I'm not sure that would be in my country's best interest, Mr. President."

Castilla had obviously been prepared for this response, and no emotion showed on his face. "You want this war."

"That's a gross overstatement. But I think you have to agree that the Chinese present numerous challenges to both Japan and the world. They steal other countries' intellectual property. They manipulate their currency. They use de facto slave labor to take critical manufacturing jobs from places like the United States. They are creating border disputes with virtually every country in the region and are building a military to press those claims. They protect the North Koreans. Their environmental problems are scaling to the point that they're causing damage outside their borders. And their demand for resources is becoming almost limitless. Obviously, I could go on, but the basic point is that they aren't contributors to the world. They're leeches. A billion tiny leeches."

This time Castilla was unable to hide his feelings: the blood drained visibly from his face. Takahashi leaned forward, putting his cup on the table and meeting the eye of the man who had once been the most powerful in the world. "I tell you all this as a courtesy, Mr. President. Japan neither wants nor needs your protection. Finish your summit if you must, but pull your carrier groups back and stay out of this. It's none of your affair."

"What if the American people are unwilling to just stand by while you perpetrate genocide?"

Castilla expected Takahashi to take offense at his characterization and his horror grew when the soldier's expression didn't even flicker. "Make no mistake, Mr. President. I will protect my country's interests at all costs. And against all enemies."

47

Northeastern Japan

Randi Russell ducked under the branches of a tree and continued upward toward the intermittent flashes of blue sky. The mountain was just one in the endless rolling carpet of green that covered this remote part of the island. The complete lack of trails was comforting from an anonymity standpoint, but not ideal for speed. The foliage was nearly as dense as she'd run into in Laos, though it wasn't as hot, thank God.

She put her back against a tree and lifted the nozzle of her CamelBak to her mouth. Visibility was only about ten feet but she was confident she wasn't being followed. In order to even approximate silence, someone would have to slow to a rate of no more than a couple hundred yards an hour, and that would have left them crawling along the canyon below.

She'd decided that plausible deniability was completely lost—no one was going to believe that an American bushwhacking toward a nuclear storage facility was a lost hiker. In light of that, Randi had equipped herself with ultralight hiking boots, fatigues dyed specifically for the environment, and a silenced Beretta with two spare clips. If anyone spotted her, there would be no doubt about her purpose, but at least there would be a reasonable chance for escape.

She started out again, weaving between trees and crawling under bushes as she made her way methodically to the summit. Hopefully, this one wouldn't blow up like the last.

When the terrain started to level out, she dropped to her stomach and slid across the dead leaves and sticks, scanning for surveillance equipment and booby traps. Not that she really had any idea what to look for. Based on the latest from Fred Klein, goddamn space-based lasers and genetically modified, glow-in-the-dark rottweilers weren't out of the question.

Randi slowed further, slithering through the tall grass until the slope turned downward. It took a few moments to mat down a hole sufficient to see though, but when she did, she was pleased to learn that her map-and-compass skills hadn't entirely disappeared in the GPS era. Below, at a distance of about a mile, was exactly what she'd come to see.

It looked pretty much like the pictures she'd found on the Internet. The entrance was a natural cavern about twenty yards high and a bit less in width. According to the publicly available plans, it descended into the mountain for nearly two-thirds of a mile before dead-ending into a set of blast doors. Beyond those doors, the cavern was human made, leading into the main nuclear waste storage area.

There was one access road, paved to allow heavy trucks to travel along it safely. The entrance was ringed with a not particularly formidable-looking chain-link fence, creating a courtyard large enough for a semi to be unloaded in. Steel tracks were visible going into the cave entrance, but none of the transportation carts that traveled along them were in evidence. She guessed that they were stored just inside to keep them out of the weather. Other than that, there was nothing but a tiny guardhouse with a single guard.

Randi let out a long breath and retrieved her binoculars, studying the area in more detail. Even magnified, there wasn't much to see. Or, more precisely, she was seeing exactly what someone would expect at this type of installation. Either Takahashi was as clever as he was given credit for or this really was nothing more than a radioactive trash heap.

Randi focused her lenses on the guard and felt a glimmer of hope for the first time in days. He looked too hard to be of the hourly variety. She waited for him to exit the guardhouse and watched as he walked the fence line, peering into trees that had been cut back about seventy-five yards. No gut hanging over his pants. No wheezing or waddling. He moved with graceful efficiency and was carrying a Belgian assault rifle. Not a particularly common weapon and one that she herself had taken a liking to a few years back.

Randi shifted her gaze back to the cavern entrance, but all she could see was darkness and shadow. Was Smith in there? Was he alive? And if so, what was his condition?

Her gut told her that this was it. Takahashi was all about efficiency and it was a hell of a lot more efficient to commandeer an existing facility than to build one from scratch. Case in point: Fukushima's Reactor Four. Add to that the decidedly non-doughnut-eating guard and she had a reasonable leg to stand on. A thin, weak leg to be sure, but there weren't a hell of a lot of other options at this point.

Based on what she was hearing from Klein and what she was reading in the papers, there wasn't any more time for hand-wringing. The shit was about to hit the fan in Asia and it wasn't clear whether even the full diplomatic and military might of the United States was going to be able to do anything about it.

So, that left her. A lone woman lying in soggy grass. Outstanding.

She pulled back slowly, covering about fifty yards before she stood and started back down the way she'd come. What wasn't she seeing? What had Takahashi's scientists been doing for the past three decades? Sure, the nanotech, torpedoes, EMPs, and germs. But that was just the big stuff. What kind of defenses had he set up around that entrance? Had he built things that she'd never even dreamed of, let alone trained for?

And what about the nanotech? If it was indeed being developed and stored inside, was it possible that an assault on the facility could release it? According to Greg Maple, that had the potential to be an end-of-days scenario.

Bottom line? She was screwed. Takahashi had won.

Randi jumped off a boulder, dropping to the dirt five feet below. When she landed, she shook her head violently and forced a few deep breaths of the mountain air.

This wasn't the time to start feeling sorry for herself. Nothing was impossible.

48

Outside Melbourne
Australia

Fred Klein moved across the carefully manicured lawn, following David McClellan as he skirted the mansion and tried to avoid the light bleeding from its windows. The rest of the president's security detail had been pulled back for Klein's arrival. It was well-known that he and Castilla had been friends since college and that they got together regularly based on that relationship. It also seemed likely that people assumed he gave the president occasional advice based on his background with the CIA and NSA. Showing up in Australia, though, would push those assumptions a little too far. Better to make his entrance and exit as quiet as possible.

McClellan pointed toward a set of stairs carved into the ground between two enormous flowering bushes. Klein could feel an uncharacteristic film of sweat forming between his palm and the handle of his briefcase as he descended toward an unlocked steel door.

The basement beyond was dim and only partially finished, a fittingly clandestine place for this particular piece of business. President Sam Adams Castilla sat alone at a folding table next to the wall, gazing into the crystal glass in his hand. He didn't acknowledge his old friend's arrival and Klein understood. The man was under almost unimaginable pressure. And it was about to get worse.

"I understand the negotiations are going well," Klein said, deciding to try to start the meeting on a positive note.

"Doesn't matter," Castilla replied, continuing to stare at the two fingers of bourbon in his glass. Generally, the man was a force of nature. Now, though, something fundamental had changed. For the first time since they'd known each other, Castilla looked... broken.

Klein sat and slid a thick file marked "President's Eyes Only" across the table.

"I don't have the energy, Fred. Just hit me with the highlights."

Castilla had given him a detailed account of his meeting with Takahashi and asked him to evaluate the man's claims. As far as Klein knew, no one else was even aware that the meeting had taken place.

"In a nutshell?" Klein, said, reaching for the bottle of Black Widow and pouring himself a short glass. "Assuming thirty-plus years of research and development focused on the systems Takahashi told you about, my people think it's largely doable."

Castilla let out a long breath.

Klein opened the folder so he could go over the points in order. "Obviously, we know that the nanotech exists. We still aren't sure that the control systems are robust enough to make it a viable weapon, though."

"But you're telling me they might be. That it's potentially deployable."

"I believe so, yes."

Castilla took a healthy slug of his drink and then topped it off from the bottle. "Where do your people stand on tracking this thing down?"

"Randi is working on options, but they're limited."

"So you're nowhere."

Klein hated to fail his old friend but there was just no sugarcoating the current situation. "I'm sorry, Sam. My top man has been captured and I'm up against a brilliant general who's been laying these plans since you and I were in school."

"I'm not blaming you or your people, Fred. No one could do more. I know that."

Klein gave a short nod, though the vote of confidence made him feel even more powerless.

"We're convinced that he has the torpedoes he told you about. The technology's been around since the Soviet era and the artificial intelligence needed to operate them isn't that much more advanced than what we see in modern video games. Also, because this would have been a priority for him, we can assume that he's deployed a significant number of them."

"So tell me this, Fred. Why the hell don't *we* have three-hundred-knot, artificially intelligent underwater missiles?"

"We're actually working on the technology, but the program hasn't seen much funding. We have a level of naval superiority that makes them a bit moot. Besides, as a country, we've shied away from putting life-and-death decisions in the hands of computers. Our strong bias is to have a human in the loop."

"But the Japanese don't have that bias."

"No. What they have is a limited population base and limited resources. There are records of Takahashi's predecessor talking about his philosophy of small, cheap, and independent. It seems like they've stuck with that."

"How would they launch them? They don't have much of a navy. I mean, I assume the intelligence community that I keep writing billion-dollar checks to would notice if the Japanese were building a fleet of submarines."

"We assume that they reside on the bottom of the ocean, waiting for a go signal."

"Great," Castilla said.

"With regard to missile defense, my people also think Takahashi is telling the truth."

"So, the US has spent God knows how much on our system and we can't hit the broad side of a barn. But a little island in the Pacific has completely nailed it."

"We've looked into a similar EMP-based shield in the past but decided not to pursue it. I don't have to tell you that we have to tread carefully on missile defense in order not to skew the balance of power so much that it could prompt an attack. And to be clear, Sam, these are *nuclear* weapons. The US has never looked to acquire this kind of tactical nuclear capability. Once you start down that road, things can escalate pretty quickly."

Klein flipped a page in the file. "The biological weapon is a simple matter. As you know we—"

"Have a moral objection to biological weapons," Castilla said, finishing his sentence. "It's unbelievable that we even have a defense industry with all these caveats."

Klein leaned back in his chair, examining the side of his friend's face. It would have been bad enough if he stopped there, but the president of the United States had to have the whole story.

"We also need to talk about what Takahashi didn't say, Sam."

Castilla finally looked directly at him. "What he didn't say?"

"We have to assume that they have autonomous fighter drones based on their torpedo technology and that our planes would be no match for them."

"It just keeps getting better and better."

"We also have to assume that if they have nuclear defensive capability, they have nuclear offensive capability."

"Missiles?"

"We don't think so. It would be extremely hard to hide those kinds of installations. More likely suitcase nukes. My people believe that the Japanese could have easily developed something in the twenty-to-fifty-kiloton range."

"Terrific."

"Also, if they have a bioweapons program, I think it's safe to assume that it's not just defensive like Takahashi told you."

"Any good news?" Castilla said. "Anything at all?"

"There is, actually. While we think they've developed the technology for all these weapons, manufacturing them in any large quantity would be extremely difficult. Not only because it would be hard to keep it under wraps, but because of the cost."

Castilla suddenly stood and began pacing back and forth across the stone floor. "I sat three feet from Takahashi, Fred. I looked into his eyes. He didn't build his army to defend Japan. He built it to annihilate China and to turn his country into a superpower. The government there will end up a military puppet and Takahashi will start his march across the East."

He turned and looked back at Klein. "Wielding power is hard, Fred, but the US has struck a pretty good balance. Now, I'm not going to stand here and blow sunshine up your skirt. It's true that some of our restraint has been because we have a strong belief in freedom—both our own and others'—but that's not the whole story. A big part of it is that we live in a massive country blessed with enormous natural resources. For the most part, we haven't *had* to go out and take what we need. Japan is different. It's a small island with an aging population and a debt problem that makes ours look mild. Take my word for it—Takahashi wants to expand."

Castilla started pacing again. "I've been thinking about this nanoweapon ever since you first told me about it. Have you considered what will happen if Takahashi actually uses it? Have you really thought it through? The entire Chinese power grid will go down when the plastic gets eaten off the wires. Dams will collapse and flood entire regions. Building will implode, machines will fall apart. And not just cars and tractors. Even the shovels people might be able to use to eke out an existence will crumble. We're heading into winter and a billion people could be without heat, without shelter, without food. Six million Jews died in World War Two. This could make that look like a historical blip. There's no way to spin this that we aren't talking hundreds of millions of casualties, Fred. *Hundreds of millions.*"

"You spoke with him," Klein said. "And like you say, you looked into his eyes. Where do we fit into all this?"

"That's just it, Fred. For the first time in three-quarters of a century, we don't. Takahashi has no particular love for the US—he blames us for a lot of Japan's problems. He's not stupid, though. He knows that we account for more than a fifth of the world's economic activity. We're necessary to keep the world from complete economic collapse and to maintain the status quo to the degree it's possible. All he asks of us is that we stand back and watch him butcher millions of women and children. Simple, right?"

Castilla reached into his pocket and pulled out a small case, retrieving a single cigarette from it. The president had been carrying that cigarette around since he quit smoking twelve years ago. For emergencies, he liked to say.

Klein was going to voice his disapproval but instead remained silent as his old friend flicked a lighter to life.

"I don't sleep too well," Castilla said, letting the smoke roll from his mouth. "But one of the few things that let me catch a few hours here and there was knowing that if everything went pear-shaped, I had the most powerful military on the planet. Now you're telling me that it was all bullshit."

Klein put his palms flat on the table in front of him. "We still do, Sam. A modern military isn't just a tool to destroy an enemy. We use ours to rebuild countries after they've been devastated. We're the most effective disaster relief organization in the world. We provide security, we promote stability. We create technology that trickles down to private industry and moves the world forward. And let's face it, Takahashi has a point. We provide jobs and fund defense contractors. What you have to understand is that Japan hasn't built a twenty-first-century military. They've built a twenty-first-century war machine."

49

Northeastern Japan

Randi Russell paused at the entrance to the kitchen and looked around. The shades were drawn and the only light was coming from a lamp hanging over a tiled island in the room's center. The house was a bit dilapidated, but also large and isolated, which was what she'd asked for. Besides, it had power and heat, so it was one step above most of the places she'd haunted over the last decade.

She watched the four people inside run their fingers along a map spread out on the island and talk in hushed tones. On the left were Eric and Karen Ivers, Covert-One operatives she'd known since she'd first signed up. In fact, they'd snatched her at gunpoint and taken her to her first meeting with Fred Klein.

The man in the middle was probably six feet five, blond, and wiry. Since Klein had sent him despite the fact that he would stick out like a sore thumb in Japan, it seemed likely that he had serious skills.

The man to his right was a good foot shorter, but Japanese, thank God. While Randi had redyed her hair black and used makeup to color the skin on her face, it was only enough to fool a casual observer with very bad eyesight. He'd have to be their point man for all things public. The rest of them would be forced to move around at night, keeping to secondary roads. If spotted in this rural setting, they'd garner a lot of interest from the widely scattered locals.

"Any brilliant ideas?" she asked, continuing into the room.

Everyone turned toward her and she shook hands with the tall blond man. "You must be Vanya. Pleasure."

"The pleasure is mine, Randi. I am looking forward to working with you." His accent was a little vague. Eastern European for certain, but she couldn't place the region. Probably by design.

Turning to the man next to him, she gave a short bow. "And you're Reiji. An honor."

He returned the bow but didn't say anything. Hopefully because he was the quiet type and not because Japanese was his only language.

Finally, she gave a nod to the Iverses. "Congratulations on the wedding. Sorry I couldn't be there."

They both responded with an understanding shrug.

As she looked into their faces, she wasn't really sure what to think. They were only five in all and two were completely unknown to her. The fact that they had Fred Klein's confidence meant a lot but she still preferred working with people she'd seen in action. Or at least knew by reputation.

"I take it you've all been briefed on the nanotech we're concerned with?"

Nods all around.

She leaned over the map and tapped a red dot in the center of the island. "We believe that the weapon's being developed here at a nuclear storage facility bored through the side of a mountain." She slid her finger along a thin line. "This represents the only road in. Everything else is steep and densely wooded. There's a relatively flat section to the south of the facility that's bordered by a deep canyon, with steep but negotiable walls. The nearest population center is a small village about forty miles east."

She pulled out her phone and brought up a photo. "This is the entrance. Call it five meters in diameter. The bottom's been flattened and there are rails leading inside. It's about a kilometer through the cavern before you get to the main blast doors."

She swiped to a second photo. "Here you can see the chain-link fence that surrounds the facility. Four meters high, topped with razor wire. Beyond the obvious cameras, the one guard is the only security visible."

"Can we assume that there's a lot that's not so visible?" Karen asked.

"Definitely. But I can't say what it is."

"Certainly, that tunnel is a shooting gallery," Vanya said. "I'd put chain guns in the walls and operate them remotely. In a matter of seconds the air would be so full of bullets you wouldn't be able to breathe."

"Don't forget mines," Reiji said in respectable English. "Antipersonnel mines would be extremely effective in that confined space."

"And that's just the conventional stuff," Randi said. "The Japanese military seems to have spent the last thirty-plus years developing whole new classes of weapons. The truth is we have no idea what to expect. If we're right about this place, we could be facing things we've never seen before."

"And if we're wrong, we're going to be facing a lot of very confused forklift operators," Eric said.

That actually got a round of subdued laughter. Not enough to break the tension, but enough to at least take it down a notch.

"Do we know anything about the blast doors?" Karen asked.

"The specs call for a foot of steel, but we think it might be stronger than that."

"Stronger than a foot of steel?"

Klein's military brain trust had been going through Taka-hashi's claims and had recently come upon something that everyone—including her—had missed: the good general's limo. Everyone attributed his surviving Yoshima's assassination attempt to luck, but if you looked at the tape with no preconceived notions, it was clear that luck had nothing to do with it. His car should have been completely vaporized. Instead, it seemed to have suffered barely a scratch before being whisked away by helicopters never to be seen again.

"Maybe a lot stronger, actually."

"It sounds like it would be easier to just go through the damn rock," Eric said.

"It doesn't matter if the door is made of paper," Vanya said. "The likelihood of anyone surviving an incursion into that tunnel is very remote, no?"

"I know that I don't want to be the poor son of a bitch standing there with his dick in one hand and a power drill in the other," Eric said. Everyone seemed to agree.

"Okay," Randi said. "So we forget the front door."

"I hate to point out the obvious here, but a bunker buster," Karen offered. "Quick, effective, and it should get around whatever ground defenses they've dreamed up. We could fly it in from our base on Okinawa. They'd have zero time to react."

Reiji's brow furrowed. "Bomb Japan? This cannot happen, yes?"

Randi looked up at him. The man was undoubtedly a patriot and she was hesitant to talk freely on this subject in front of him. Having said that, Klein had specifically cleared everyone standing around this table. As far as he was concerned, their loyalty to Covert-One was above suspicion.

"Unfortunately, it can happen, Reiji. Based on what I'm being told, nothing is off the table. The problem here isn't approvals so much as the nanotech we suspect is being housed at the facility. There's no way to overstate how dangerous it could be if it got out. We can't risk blowing it into the atmosphere."

"Deliveries?" Eric said.

"What little intel we have suggests that everything going in and out is examined with some kind of particle scanner. You couldn't smuggle in a cockroach."

"The Cask of Amontillado," Vanya said. Everyone just stared at him.

"Three Americans here and none of you read Poe? Your education system is as bad as I have been led to believe. My point is this: We don't really want to get in here. We just don't want them to get out. Why not seal it up?"

"That's the kind of out-of-the-box thinking we need," Randi said. "But in this case, I don't think it's workable. We believe that there's a lot of mental horsepower and equipment in there..."

"She's right," Reiji interjected. "When the workers and scientists realize what we're trying to do, they will panic and try to get out any way they can. If they succeed, their weapon could get out with them."

Everyone fell silent and that silence stretched out a depressingly long time.

"I don't read much Poe, but I like movies," Eric said finally. "This thing reminds me of the alien in those Sigourney Weaver flicks. In the unlikely event you find a way to hurt it, it bleeds acid all over you."

Randi ran over the map again, trying to come up with something—anything—they were missing. "Come on, people. We're supposed to be the best at this kind of thing. Get me into that damn facility."

50

Northeastern Japan

From his position on the cot, Jon Smith studied the room for what must have been the thousandth time. Clearly Takahashi hadn't considered the necessity of housing prisoners in this facility and had been forced to repurpose what appeared to be a break room. The kitchenette was still there, including a refrigerator stocked with food. Furniture was utilitarian, and a small bathroom with a sink was on the other side of a pocket door.

More interesting was the construction. The walls were natural rock and hardened mud, while fixtures— even the fridge— were a mix of ceramic, carbon fiber, and wood. His clothes had been taken and he was now wearing the same white cotton jumpsuit as the two workers he'd glimpsed when he'd been moved to this cell. Buttons appeared to be bone and there was no belt that would necessitate a buckle. Shoes were slip-on and contained no nails that he could discern.

So, while he couldn't be 100 percent certain that the nanotech was being developed here, the lack of materials it could consume suggested that it was at least being stored here.

The question was, what could he do about it? The door wasn't budging and the best tools he had for tunneling were a few plastic spoons left in one of the drawers.

Even if he could escape, what would he be escaping to? For all he knew, World War III was already being fought on the other side of the millions of tons of earth above him.

Smith stood and picked up one of the folding chairs with his right hand. He lifted it carefully out to his side, the searing pain behind his shoulder blade not quite as bad as it had been the day before. He wasn't sure if he'd survive long enough for it to matter, but he might as well use the idle time to get some of his strength back.

Halfway into his third set, the door leading to the corridor outside slid back. He dropped the chair and turned, expecting Takahashi but instead seeing someone very different.

The man who entered was probably no more than five feet six, but the fact that he walked slightly stooped made him seem smaller. His hair was long, but growing only in intermittent patches on a damaged scalp. The discolored skin on his face seemed to have collapsed in places, but his eyes were surprisingly clear.

Despite the disfigurement, there was little question as to his identity. And there was even less question that he had been working in Reactor Four on the day of the tsunami.

"Dr. Ito," Smith said, indicating the chair he had just put down.

The scientist nodded gratefully and took a seat without speaking. His expression was hard to read due to the intermittent paralysis of his facial muscles, but his body language suggested fear. Of what, though?

"My compliments," Smith said as he took a chair on the other side of the table. "Your nanotechnology is half a century ahead of anything else I've seen."

Ito gave a barely perceptible bow to acknowledge the compliment. "Molecular engineering. It was my dream. Can you imagine the possibilities? Skyscrapers building themselves. The repair, and perhaps even creation, of organs without surg—"

"But that's not what you created," Smith interjected.

"No," he said, a hint of misery mixed with his thick accent. "The closer I got, the more afraid people became."

"Of the dangers?" Smith prompted.

Ito nodded. "A scientist such as yourself will recognize the irony. The more success I had, the harder it was to get funding. No one wanted to be associated with a potential accident."

"No one but Takahashi."

This time the nod was more of a head jerk. Strangely violent.

"He had virtually unlimited resources. And he was very generous with them."

"But there are always strings attached, aren't there?"

Ito leaned forward, suddenly seeming to need the table for support. "He wanted my invention to consume concrete, metal, and plastic. This wasn't ideal from a safety standpoint, but the dangers were acceptable. After I made self-replication work, of course I wanted to branch out in other directions. To find practical uses for the technology. Takahashi, though, wasn't interested."

As a scientist, Smith could sympathize. It was easy to become blinded to everything but that next breakthrough. Discovering something capable of changing the world, the opportunity to take a place alongside the great minds of history—all things that could be more intoxicating than any drug.

"So when it became clear that your invention destabilized the materials it fed on, Takahashi wanted you to focus on controlling it."

Ito looked at him suspiciously.

"I'm not just a scientist, Doctor. I'm a soldier. And I wouldn't be a very good one if I didn't understand that weapons that can't be controlled aren't very useful."

Ito was silent for a few moments before speaking again. "I didn't start my life intending to make weapons, Colonel Smith. But I wanted to create. I wanted to explore my theories."

"And this was the only way to do it," Smith prompted. "Takahashi was your only source of reliable funding so you did what he asked."

Another jerky nod. "I built in limitations to their ability to replicate from the beginning for obvious reasons. Takahashi asked that I also create limitations based on geographic position—so they would shut down outside a preset area. It seemed like a prudent additional measure."

"And do those measures work?"

"Flawlessly in our tests," he said with discomfort that Smith understood perfectly.

"How many replications did you perform in your tests, Doctor?"

He seemed to want to stand, but didn't have the energy. "Tens of millions."

"And how many replications would you expect if this was used as a weapon?"

"The number is nearly incalculable. Larger than the number of stars in the universe. I've explained this to the general many times—that as the number of replications increases, so do the chances of a disastrous mutation. But he seems less inclined to listen with every passing day. He's changed, Colonel. You're still a young man, so you wouldn't understand. Takahashi doesn't have many more years left. He's dedicated his life to this. He—"

"Dedicated his life to *what?*"

Ito looked around him as though someone might be watching. "I thought it was to create a new Japan—one that could rival or perhaps even surpass America. Imagine what the weapons we've developed could accomplish. We could destroy North Korea's military-industrial complex without harming its citizens. Or even specific weapons in precisely defined regions. Can you imagine? There's no limit to where our technological and military power could have led the world."

In many ways, Ito was right. What if his nanotech could be targeted at bomb-making materials or even gunpowder in the Middle East and Africa? Hell, in certain neighborhoods in inner-city America. How many lives would be saved? How many countries could be stabilized? The problem, though, was one of intent. America had done shockingly well in wielding its overwhelming power. While imperfect, the US had a stable government with built-in checks and balances, a deep-rooted culture of democracy, and a general reticence to project power unless it was absolutely necessary.

Takahashi, it appeared, had none of those virtues.

"I understand that this isn't what you intended, Dr. Ito. But you know as well as I do that what you intended doesn't matter. Takahashi's provoking a war with China and he plans on demonstrating Japan's new military superiority by wiping that country off the map."

Ito nodded miserably. "And he won't stop there. His vision is the same as his father's: the rebirth of Imperial Japan. But this time, because of me, he will succeed."

51

Outside Tokyo
Japan

General Masao Takahashi walked alone through the stone-and-earth corridor, feeling a familiar resentment. It was an insult to him and the men loyal to him that they had been literally forced underground. It wouldn't be long, though. Soon, the Japanese people would understand what he had accomplished.

The door in front of him slid open without his bidding, having read various biometric markers as he approached. Inside, he found the heads of the three branches of his defense forces as well as Akio Himura, the director of Japanese intelligence.

Takahashi chose not to sit and indicated for his men to dispense with the customary greeting of their superior. The meeting was, after all, a formality. Plans for the attack on China had been carefully laid over years, and every detail of those plans was being meticulously adhered to. As the day finally approached, though, it was appropriate—even in the new technological era he had ushered in—for the men leading the war effort to meet face-to-face. Perhaps for the last time in this place.

"It's my understanding that all defensive measures are in

place and ready to be deployed. That includes civilian rescue missions in the event an attack reaches our soil."

The men seated around the table in front of him all nodded.

"To reiterate. There are no problems that I'm unaware of?"

More nods. Despite having known the answers to his question already, seeing his staff's acknowledgment allowed him to relax a bit.

"Then we're waiting on Ito. He's completing the individual canisters containing specifically targeted nanotechnology. They'll be smuggled into China and released in all major cities, military bases, and power installations."

"Do we have an updated estimate of the time to failure on the dam?" Admiral Inoue asked.

The Three Gorges Dam across the Yangtze River would be the first structure attacked. Its collapse would unleash a flood that they projected would kill millions as well as cutting electricity to critical sections of the country. The catastrophe would overwhelm China's military and civilian network as they carried out rescue efforts and tried to determine the cause of the failure.

While the country was consumed with that disaster, the rest of their infrastructure would quietly disintegrate. When their machines began to fail and their cities crumbled, the Chinese would have no idea of the cause. And even if they did, it would be too late.

"We expect a full breach within six weeks of deployment," Takahashi said. "The rest of China will be three weeks behind that."

"And the Americans? What of your meeting with President Castilla?" Tadao Minami asked. He was too brilliant a soldier to remove as head of the air defenses, but Takahashi considered him the weakest of the group. He saw Japan's future as one of the most powerful members of the international community, while the others shared a vision of Japanese dominance.

Takahashi crossed his arms over his still-powerful chest. "Their reaction is difficult to predict. While their president seems intelligent enough to understand his country's new subordinate position, I'm not sure of the depth of that understanding. Further, we have to acknowledge that he's only one facet of the American government and that the congress he answers to is largely populated with half-wits and fanatics. In light of that, we have to be prepared for America to act stupidly."

The faces of the men in the room darkened. Some carried more than a hint of apprehension, but it was something Takahashi was prepared to tolerate. History created a powerful current in Japan, and they all remembered the consequences of the attack on Pearl Harbor.

"Don't misunderstand me, gentlemen. I've made it abundantly clear to the president that this is not an attack on America and that we have no intention of mounting one unless we're provoked."

"And if we are?" Minami said. "They're the cornerstone of the current world order and account for almost a quarter of the world's gross domestic product—something that will be even more important to us when China's economic output disappears. How much damage can we really afford to inflict on them?"

Takahashi was unaccustomed to being challenged and stiffened perceptibly at what he saw as an attack. "If the Americans side with the Chinese, we *will* respond. Is that understood?"

His men all responded in the affirmative, but the concern persisted on their faces. While he would deeply enjoy crushing the United States for what it had done to Japan, it was admittedly impractical. In the end, the pleasure of slowly bleeding it of its power and influence—watching its arrogant population face the reality that their every action was subject to approval from Tokyo—would be so much more satisfying.

"As you well know, I understand and appreciate the importance of America to Japanese interests," he continued, making an effort to moderate his tone. "I've created a slowly escalating battle plan against them that should prove a sufficient deterrent without the use of Ito's weapon."

"And does that plan involve an attack on their mainland? Against their civilian population?"

Again Takahashi stiffened. He had responded to Minami's concerns but now the man was courting insubordination. "We'll destroy America's naval capability in the Pacific. If they don't immediately disengage, yes, we'll move against their homeland. The American people are weak and unable to endure even the mildest discomfort. We've identified a series of fourteen individual power stations that are protected by nothing more than chain-link fences. If destroyed, virtually the entire country will go dark for a minimum of three weeks. After only a few hours of that, the country's citizens will be demanding that their politicians agree to an unconditional surrender."

"And if they're stronger than you give them credit for?" Minami pressed.

"Then America will cease to exist!" Takahashi shouted. "We will release Ito's weapon there and watch it rot! Is that understood?"

Minami looked down at the floor, unwilling to meet his superior officer's glare. "Of course, General. I understand completely."

Takahashi looked around the room and, finding no further dissent, gave a short bow before leaving. There was no more to say. He'd chosen his men well. Even Minami would die before he failed to carry out his duty to Japan.

The general hesitated at a T in the corridor. He had matters in Tokyo that demanded his attention, but instead of turning left toward the exit, he turned right. The grade steepened, sinking farther into the earth as he traveled its considerable length.

The door at the end didn't automatically slide open at his approach like the other. He had to put his hand against a glass plate and punch his personal code into a keypad.

Inside, the walls were painted stark white with the exception of the one at the back, which was floor-to-ceiling glass. Through it, Takahashi could see what appeared to be sixteen normal thermoses, each containing millions of Ito's nanoscale weapon. In the next few days the scientist would fill another ninety-six. One for every target in China.

Takahashi moved forward reverently, finally stopping and leaning in close to the transparent barrier. The political summit in Australia was complete, and President Castilla had done his job admirably. Tensions between China and Japan were calming. Prime Minister Sanetomi had been to the Japanese news outlets and convinced them that the profits they were generating by whipping up hysteria would be of no use with a sky full of missiles. And China was following suit, using its iron-fisted control of its media to moderate anti-Japanese messages.

Sanetomi had even scheduled a trip to Beijing. The rumor was that he would make yet another apology for World War II atrocities and that China would formally accept that apology.

Takahashi continued to stare at the innocent-looking thermoses, his breath rhythmically fogging the glass in front of his mouth. He'd hoped to provoke an outright attack by China in order to provide a plausible defensive motive for its annihilation. But it wasn't to be.

In the end, it was unimportant. The rules of engagement, illusions of morality, and international law were irrelevant to war. They were institutions of the weak. And Japan would feign weakness no longer.

52

Northeastern Japan

Y ou can't just kidnap me, throw me in the back of a plane, and steal my invention!" Max Wilson said, pulling the collar of his leather jacket tighter around his neck and looking into the dense forest surrounding them.

"I don't understand why you keep saying that to me when it's pretty clear that I can," Randi replied impatiently.

That man was a good four inches shorter than her, with a heavy build, callused hands, and a nose that looked like it had been broken more than a few times. Not a person you'd guess had PhDs from both Stanford and Cal Tech.

His father had died in an accident in a West Virginia mine when Wilson was only twelve. Out of what seemed like an extremely misguided sense of loyalty, he'd followed in the old man's footsteps—dropping out of high school and descending into those same shafts.

It hadn't taken long before the mining company's engineers noticed that young Max seemed able to come up with solutions to problems that were cheaper, more workable, and more elegant than their own. And then there was the matter of his hobbies: number theory, quantum mechanics, and paleomagnetism. Apparently, he was a pretty fair bowler too.

One of the company's geologists recommended Wilson to his alma mater, and he was immediately accepted. He spent the next ten years in academia but eventually returned—in his own way—to the mines.

"Well, you *are* smoking hot. So I suppose that's some consolation."

"Thank you, Dr. Wilson. That's very kind of you to say."

"Call me Max. And you are?"

"Randi."

"Randi…"

"Just Randi."

"Government," he muttered.

"You came highly recommended by Greg Maple."

This time his words were too low to fully understand but she was pretty sure they had something to do with kicking his colleague's ass when he got back to the States.

Randi put a hand on his back and led him deeper into the trees, winding along until they reached an area that had been covered with a camouflage canopy.

"Where are we anyway?"

"The woods," Randi replied.

"Not American, though. Too long a flight."

"It's not important."

"That's because you know where you are. And you weren't kidnapped."

She shrugged. Hard to argue the logic.

They came over a rise and Wilson stopped short. Just ahead was a silver cylinder about twenty yards long and a little less than two in diameter. It had been in multiple pieces when it arrived, making it a hell of a lot easier to smuggle into the mountains of middle-of-nowhere, Japan, but the five kids swarming around it almost had it back together.

"Hey!" Wilson said. "Those are my grad students!"

"I thought you might appreciate the help."

He spun toward her, obviously infuriated, and she countered with what she hoped was a disarming smile. It would have to do. Her normal methods of persuasion were completely off limits with civilian academics.

"Help with what?" he said, his voice straining with anger.

Randi pointed north. "Tunneling through that mountain."

His face went blank. "You can't be serious."

"Don't I look serious?"

"It's a goddamn prototype! It's never even gotten dirty."

"Yeah, but your last version got dirty and worked pretty well from what I hear. It's my understanding that this model's even better."

Wilson's invention was a next-generation tunneling machine. On the surface, it didn't seem much different from the ones currently in use, but the similarities ended pretty quickly when you looked deeper. Traditionally designed machines ejected enormous amounts of dirt that had to be hauled away, and braces had to be placed at intervals to keep the shaft from collapsing. And then there were the massive power cables necessary to keep them running.

Wilson's system did away with all those complexities. It had a nuclear core that powered the diggers. The excess reactor heat was used to fuse the earth lining the tunnel into a substance stronger than concrete. The unit he was ultimately working toward would be larger than a locomotive, but this much smaller prototype was perfect for the very stupid idea she and her team had settled on.

"There's no way to power it," Wilson protested. "You wouldn't believe the red tape I have to deal with to get nuclear fuel from the government."

"I had it gassed up before it was shipped."

"Bullshit."

Again, Randi shrugged. "When I ask for something, I get it, Max. You should keep that in mind."

He eyed her suspiciously for a moment and then jogged toward his invention. When his students saw their professor approaching, they abandoned what they were doing and surrounded him, all talking at once in panicked voices that were a little too loud.

Randi watched for a few seconds and then turned and started back through the trees, angling toward a small table where Eric Ivers and Vanya were poring over a topographic map. Reiji had taken Karen on another of their endless supply runs. Everything had to arrive in small shipments so as not to attract attention.

"How are we looking?"

Vanya gave her a worried glance and Ivers just laughed.

Neither reaction was difficult to understand. They were halfway up the side of a mountain that contained a nuclear storage facility that they believed housed the most dangerous weapon ever built by human hands. Their plan? If you can't get in the front door, bust a window and go in the back.

"So not good?"

"No, no," Ivers said. "We've got this by the ass. All we have to do is crawl through two miles of extremely hot tunnel, hand-dig the last bit so no one in the facility hears Wilson's little underground nuclear missile, and then leap out and yell

Freeze! You're under arrest!"

"What could possibly go wrong?" Randi said.

Vanya winced. Obviously, her attempt at humor had fallen flat. "What couldn't? You think that a prototype digging machine put together by a bunch of students in the woods isn't going to break down? You think Takahashi doesn't have seismic sensors that are going to lock onto us a mile away? And how are we going to hand-dig the last portion? Half that mountain is solid rock. But let's, for a moment, ascribe to the fantasy that we actually get into that facility. How many guards are we going to be up against? Is the layout still what's on the original plans we have or has Takahashi changed it? What weapons are they armed with?"

He fell silent, though Randi knew he probably could have gone on for another hour.

No one spoke for a long time. Vanya had said what they were all thinking, but what alternatives did they have? As inconceivable as it was, Klein had been clear that her team was the best hope of averting the greatest humanitarian disaster in history. She knew herself well enough to know that she wouldn't be able to live with stepping to the sidelines. For her, it would be better to go down fighting. But that wasn't necessarily true of the people who had gotten stuck with this detail.

"Look," Randi started. "Normally when I say this I don't mean it. But today, I do. If you want out, no one's going to think any less of you. Hell, most likely no one's going to be around to think any less of you."

Vanya thought about it for a few moments. "I'd be dead twice over if it weren't for Mr. Klein. I will see this through. No matter how it ends."

"Eric?"

His normally broad grin faltered. "I knew this was a shitty job when I signed on, Randi, but that thing Wilson built is a grave digger and you know it. We're going to die in that tunnel and no one's ever even going to know. No parades or newspaper articles or statues at the academy. Just a cozy hole in the side of a Japanese mountain and a few friends to share it with."

"So you're out."

He shook his head. "Karen says she won't leave. And since she's the only family I have, I figure we might as well die together."

53

Oval Office
Washington, DC
USA

When Castilla entered the Oval Office, General Keith Morrison, the chairman of the Joint Chiefs, leaped to attention. The president noted that he looked a little dazed and hoped it was just the fact that he probably hadn't slept for days.

Castilla offered his hand and nodded toward the thick dossier the soldier was holding. "Are you bringing me good news, Keith?"

Morrison's expression turned from dazed to a bit ill.

"Sit," Castilla said, pointing to the sofa. "Please."

Three days ago, he'd personally handed the general a full account of his meeting with Takahashi, Covert-One's analysis of that meeting, and everything Greg Maple had come up with on Hideki Ito's weapon. His orders had been for Morrison to very quietly double-check and flesh out the analyses. No one beyond a few select experts was to be told—not the secretary of defense, not the CIA, and sure as hell not the NSA. At this point, secrecy was paramount, and with the exception of Fred Klein, Morrison was the only person he felt he could trust. Not only was the man an honest-to-God war hero, but he also had a master's from Harvard and seemed physically incapable of not following the orders of his commander in chief. Perhaps even more important, he had known Masao Takahashi for over twenty years.

Morrison started to open the folder in his hand but then seemed to lose strength. Finally, he just laid it on the table between them. "May I ask where you got the analysis you gave me, sir?"

"No," Castilla responded simply.

The soldier nodded. "Well, it was a hell of a job. I wish whoever did it worked for me."

The president had had plenty of time to prepare for this meeting so he was able to keep his expression impassive. He'd hoped that Morrison was here to tell him that Klein and Takahashi were completely full of shit, but the truth was that neither man ever had been before.

"Tell me about Takahashi," Castilla said. This was one of Klein's few blind spots. He could lay out the intel better than anyone, but he'd never worked with the Japanese general. Never gotten drunk with him.

Morrison chewed his lip for a moment. "Masao is a complicated man. He's brilliant—there's no question of that. He has an encyclopedic knowledge of history but manages to avoid getting bogged down in it. He's always leaned toward a progressive view of the military..." His voice faded for a moment. "But I wasn't aware it was this progressive."

"Let me ask you a question, Keith. Do you like the man? Do you consider him a friend?"

Morrison shook his head. "I've always admired Masao, but when you get to know him, you come to understand that he has a dark side."

"Explain."

"First of all, let's be clear that he blames the US not only for the defeat of Japan, but for what he sees as Japan's weakness over the last three-quarters of a century. And on a personal level he holds us responsible for the deaths of a number of his family members during and after war, including his mother."

"So the fact that after everything the Japanese did, we helped rebuild them into a major economic power doesn't hold any water with him at all?"

"He doesn't see that as generosity. He sees it as fear."

"Fear of what?"

Morrison didn't respond immediately, obviously wanting to choose his words carefully. "In addition to history, Masao has a keen interest in genetics. And while he's never come out and said it directly, I can tell you that he believes the Japanese people are—"

"Please don't say the master race," Castilla said, starting to feel a little ill. The world had been down this path before.

"As much as I want to say no, that's an accurate portrayal. In his mind, we singled out Japanese Americans for internment during World War Two because we subconsciously acknowledge that they're a homogeneous, superior group that has to be suppressed. He sees our rebuilding of their country as a desperate attempt to control them. To make them dependent on us and prevent them from reestablishing a military capability."

"Jesus, Keith. Why am I just hearing this now?"

"Because Takahashi's personal feelings were never important before. He doesn't run the country and Japan is an ally with virtually no offensive capability. Or so we believed."

Castilla didn't immediately respond. The thought of Takahashi using his new arsenal against the American mainland had made his mouth go dry. "If he thinks the Japanese are at the top of the genetic hierarchy, can I assume that he thinks the Chinese are at the bottom?"

"Unquestionably."

"So where do we slot in, Keith?"

"I'm afraid I don't know the answer to that, sir. My gut says that we aren't in his crosshairs. The Chinese have a deep hatred for the Japanese and they're pushing the entire region hard."

Castilla nodded knowingly. If he'd been the prime minister of Japan instead of the president of the United States, it would be an issue that consumed him. The situation between China and Japan was starting to parallel that of the United States and Soviet Union during the Cold War. Except that Japan had to trust the US to intervene on its behalf. A very precarious position to be in.

"Okay. But why escalate this, Keith? Why not demonstrate their capabilities publicly—put China in its place?"

"That would just maintain the status quo, sir. Takahashi is more ambitious than that. With his only real rival in Asia out of the way and a demonstration of his military superiority, he has the ability to take control of the entire region. Japan is a resource-poor island with a relatively small, aging population. He needs territory, people, and raw materials."

"What's his endgame?"

"Based on what I know about the man, I would say that his goal is to wipe out China and overtake the US as the world's primary superpower."

It was time for a drink. Castilla walked to his desk and pulled out a bottle. Morrison was a devout Mormon, so he didn't offer, though the man looked like he could use it.

"Then it's your opinion that he will attack."

"Yes, sir."

"How?"

"There's no question in my mind that he'll lead with the nanotech. I'd introduce it quietly and by the time the Chinese realize what's happening, their military and civilian infrastructure will be in full collapse. Assuming they discover who's behind it and they're still capable of mounting a counterattack, it'll be easily handled by Japan's defenses."

Castilla poured himself a glass of bourbon and leaned against his desk for support. It was hard to even comprehend. Hundreds of millions of people going into winter with no electricity or shelter, no food or transportation. Cities full of people fighting for whatever scraps they could find in the rubble. And a planet suddenly robbed of a massive economic power that manufactured an enormous amount of its goods and consumed trillions of dollars' worth of products and services. In all likelihood the world would be plunged into a massive depression and the United States and Japan would spend the next fifty years battling for supremacy.

"We're talking about the extermination of hundreds of millions of people, Keith. Of civilians. Women and children. How do we stop him?"

"Militarily?"

Castilla nodded.

"We can't, sir. I'm sorry."

"That's not acceptable. America isn't going to sit by while people are slaughtered. That's not who we are as a country."

"I understand, sir. But it's my duty to give you my unvarnished opinion."

"And that is?"

"We can't win. But we can lose big."

"You're telling me that a country that spends more on its military than the next ten countries combined is helpless?"

"Essentially, yes. We have a number of insurmountable problems in a confrontation with Japan. The first is that we would have to rely heavily on our navy and I don't think there's any question that their self-cavitating torpedo technology is what Takahashi says it is."

"So all those aircraft carriers the admirals keep telling me I need are useless because of a few video game controlled torpedoes?"

"Our fleet wasn't designed to defend against a swarm of autonomous torpedoes traveling at three hundred knots, sir. In the end, our carriers are as big as cities and move just about as fast. We'd have to keep them well out of range and we aren't certain what that range is. In a worst-case scenario, all of our carrier groups could be taken out within a few hours."

"Submarines?"

"We assume that these would be much harder for Takahashi to neutralize."

"Then we could use their missiles?"

Morrison nodded. "The only chance I can see of defeating Japan would be a preemptive nuclear strike done in waves, preferably from land and sea and preferably in a coordinated effort with China."

Castilla took a long pull on his drink, focusing for a moment on the sensation of it burning down his throat. What Morrison was talking about was the annihilation of every living thing on the island of Japan in an attack that the world would see as completely unprovoked. All on the assumption that Takahashi was indeed going to move against China and that he had the weapons he said he did.

"There could be drawbacks we'd need to consider, though, sir."

"Really?" Castilla said, his voice rising uncontrollably. "Drawbacks to turning Japan into a radioactive cinder? Who would have thought?"

He caught himself and let out a long, slow breath. "I'm sorry, Keith."

"I understand, sir. I think I yelled almost the exact same thing at one of my staff just this morning."

"I assume you're talking about Japan's retaliation?"

"Yes, sir."

"The nanotech."

"I'm not so sure that would be in Takahashi's best interest. The destruction of the US would be devastating to the civil and economic stability of the world—something Japan would feel the effects of for the next century."

"Then what?"

"You have to understand that the US is completely undefended against an attack by a sophisticated enemy. We can assume that Takahashi would know the moment we launched, and based on what he told us we can surmise that his missile defense system will protect Japan for at least a few days."

"And in those few days, what could we expect?"

"Certainly an extremely sophisticated cyber attack. We'd lose communications, Internet, and most of our power grid. If it were me, I'd also have charges set up at strategic points in our grid to make sure it would take months to get power back to the entire country. Further, if Takahashi has a nuclear weapons program, we can assume he's created suitcase nukes and has brought a number of them into the US."

"What the hell makes you think that?" Castilla said. "He never said anything about suitcase nukes."

"Because it's what I'd do, sir. We developed them years ago but abandoned the technology because we have an incredibly effective intercontinental delivery system. Miniaturized nukes dovetail perfectly with Takahashi's philosophy of small, cheap, and independent."

"Do we have any way to find them? Where would they be?"

"There is no practical way to find them," Morrison responded. "And as far as where they'd be, certainly Washington. In order to make it convenient for lobbyists and bureaucrats, we've chosen to concentrate our entire government in a very small geographic location. Of course, he'd cover other major cities and major military facilities. Then, too, there's the possibility of a biological attack, though I would bet against it for strategic reasons. Not fast acting enough."

"Jesus" was all Castilla could manage to get out. He was starting to feel numb. "So you're telling me that we just have to sit back and watch?"

"We've known each other for a long time, Mr. President. You know how hard this is for me to say, but yes. We can't win this fight. And even if we could, we can't be certain it would do anything to help the Chinese. The nanotech may already have been deployed. The best thing we can do is start drawing up plans for humanitarian efforts in the aftermath. Beyond that, our hands are tied."

54

Northeastern Japan

The door slid open and Jon Smith watched it carefully. The procedure was the same as it had been every time before: a single guard standing with his back against the far wall of the corridor, one hand buried suggestively in his jacket. It was always the same man—stocky, rock hard, with a weathered face and dead eyes. Smith owed his life many times over to his gift for sizing up the competition, and this guy was one nasty piece of work. Almost certainly Special Forces, probably significant combat experience, and clearly serious about his job.

Smith expected—or more accurately hoped—that this was the beginning of another visit from the very conflicted Dr. Ito, but instead Masao Takahashi strode in. The door closed behind him and Smith bowed respectfully. Pretty much everything that could be used as a weapon had been removed from the room, and fashioning one out of the materials at hand was impossible with two cameras watching him.

"Colonel Smith," the man said, taking a seat and sliding an Android tablet across the table. "I have something to show you that I think you'll find interesting."

Smith looked down at the tablet. It was split into four

videos with touchscreen controls at the bottom. The top left feed depicted a table set up in the woods with camouflage screening above it. Two men were leaning over it, silently discussing something that appeared to be a map. The second feed showed a massive silver cylinder being worked on by a group of young people. A woman stood about ten yards from them, leaning against a tree and watching. The image was too small to make out facial features, but he knew the body language. Randi Russell.

The other two feeds were just shots of dense foliage. One of them had a few out-of-focus feathers in the foreground.

"The activity is just on the other side of the mountain this facility is built into. I'm told that the machine you're looking at is a new kind of nuclear-powered tunneling system. It appears that Ms. Russell is wise enough not to mount a frontal assault and is instead going to try to come up on our flank. I have to admit that I admire her tenacity. And the machine itself is really quite ingenious."

"But her plan isn't going to work," Smith said.

"No. And I can't imagine she doesn't know that. Ms. Russell has a duty to perform and she intends to do so to the best of her ability. I would expect no less from a woman of her reputation."

"So you have the entire mountain wired with cameras?" Smith said, really just to stall. But for what? A sudden bolt of inspiration that would allow him to stroll out of there and warn Randi that her operation had been compromised?

"No, that wouldn't be practical," Takahashi said, tapping the tablet with a finger. "Actually, I think you'll be quite intrigued by this technology. Your own military has put a great deal of money into small, stealthy surveillance drones. We did the same more than a decade ago but they're frankly not a very good solution."

"No?" Smith said, still desperately trying to calculate a way to stop what was starting to look inevitable.

Takahashi shook his head. "They're not particularly stealthy, they're difficult to land and maneuver, and they have very limited range. Birds, though, have none of those failings. When one of my people came to me with the idea of mounting fiberoptic cameras to birds of prey and controlling them with mild electric shocks, I have to admit I was skeptical. Twelve years later, though, we've turned it into an incredibly versatile battlefield surveillance platform. And better yet, even with training the animals, our costs are under three thousand US dollars per unit."

"Impressive," Smith said absently, unable to take his eyes off Randi. The woman was a witch when it came to recognizing that she was in danger. Yet there she was, completely oblivious. He tried to will her to look up but what good would it do? All she'd see was a goddamn bird perched in a tree.

"I have to admit that I'm not quite sure how to react to Ms. Russell's efforts and thought I'd ask your advice. My assumption is that by now Keith Morrison has told your president that siding with the Chinese would be suicidal. But is he listening? Is what you're looking at on that tablet a last, futile attempt to stop me? Or is it the first salvo in a full-scale attack by your country? Is Castilla willing to sacrifice the lives of millions of Americans in order to protect a country that every day becomes more of a threat to you and your standing in the world? From my perspective, that seems ... insane."

Smith stared down at the video feeds, trying to decide what to say. He'd had a great deal of time to think, and much of it had been spent on how the US would fare in a confrontation with Takahashi's new military. The conclusion that he'd come to was that America would be decimated and the world would descend into chaos in the aftermath.

"President Castilla isn't a stupid man and neither are the people advising him, General. Here's what I can tell you. If Randi is involved, this is a very quiet, small-scale operation. Virtually no one knows about it and if it doesn't work, no one ever will."

"Then, in your opinion, your country will back down."

"In my opinion, yes," Smith said honestly. "There's a big difference between sacrificing a handful of operatives and sacrificing three hundred and fifty million civilians."

Takahashi leaned back in his chair and nodded thoughtfully. "Perhaps he just can't face the idea that you are no longer the world's preeminent power."

"He's a realist, General. We've known for decades that the era of wars between major powers was over. The destructive force of modern weapons is just too great. There would only be losers."

Takahashi smiled thinly. "Until now."

It was clear that he was referring to his nanoscale weapon and its ability to throw off the balance of power enough for him to get the upper hand.

"No, sir," Smith said. "I believe the potential for blowback from your weapon goes well beyond anything we saw during the Cold War. And I suspect that if you ask Dr. Ito, he'll tell you the same thing."

"Scientists are never certain of anything, Colonel. They hedge, they equivocate, they overcomplicate. As a soldier, I expected more of you."

"I'm sorry to disappoint, General, but I'm not just a scientist, I'm one of the world's leading experts on the consequences of biowarfare. That's basically what you're doing here. You're creating artificial life and weaponizing it. You won't be able to control it, sir. I guarantee that. If you feel you have to attack China, do it. Nuke them. I imagine you've built quite an arsenal and have a way to deploy it that they'll never see coming. But destroy Ito's weapon and everything relating to it."

Takahashi didn't react other than to tap one of the feeds on the tablet. It depicted an empty meadow probably only twenty yards in diameter. Smith focused on it but wasn't sure what he was supposed to be looking for. A moment later a projectile flashed into view at the top of the frame. Dirt and rock were thrown into the air when it impacted the ground and the dust clouded the image.

For a moment, he wasn't sure what had happened, but then he noticed the broken metal parts strewn across the clearing: fins, a nose cone, broken chunks of a fuselage. It had been some kind of bomb, probably dropped from a high-altitude drone. But it hadn't exploded. A dud? Had his side finally gotten a lucky break? Randi sure as hell couldn't have missed that. She'd know that her operation was blown and get her people the hell out of there.

It didn't take long to realize that he had fallen victim to wishful thinking. Tiny jets of flame became visible throughout the clearing and he stared down in silence as they began to take to the air.

55

Northeastern Japan

E verybody get down!" Randi shouted, shoving the students off the digger as the low whistle from above grew louder. Max Wilson was standing frozen on top of the machine's titanium shell, a bloom of colorful wires in one hand and a set of pliers in the other. She yanked his ankle, pulling his feet out from beneath him and following him to the ground.

The whistle was earsplitting now, and she had to shout to be heard. "Faces in the dirt! Hands on the backs of your heads!"

All but one complied, a panicked kid who barely looked eighteen. "Bruce! Get your ass—"

The impact was a hell of a lot closer than Randi had hoped. She buried her face in the grass and waited for the flames to wash over her, but nothing happened. After staying motionless for a full three-count, she pulled out her silenced Beretta and ran for the closest tree.

Eric Ivers appeared to her left, taking similar cover about ten yards away. He gave her an inquisitive look but all she could do was shrug. Vanya was a little farther ahead, moving methodically toward the impact site with an MP5 clutched in his hands.

"Reiji. Karen," Randi said, activating her throat mike. "Are you all right?"

They'd returned from their supply run about an hour ago, and she had no idea where they were.

"We're fine," Karen responded after a few seconds. "Reiji and I are approaching from the south. Whatever it was, we think it landed in that little clearing where we first unloaded the digger."

"Roger that. Vanya's closing from the north and he's about fifty meters out. Eric and I are covering him."

"Understood."

"Be careful, Karen. Remember that we aren't sure what we're dealing with here."

Randi indicated that she was going to advance and Ivers gave her a nod before easing his Glock around the thick tree trunk. When she made it to cover, she waved him forward.

They continued to leapfrog like that, stopping every few seconds to listen to the silence and to see if they could make out anything through the trees. Vanya was nearing the edge of the clearing when Randi heard a quiet hissing that seemed to be originating just in front of him. It grew in volume as she poked her head around the tree, but the foliage was too dense for her to make out a source. What was visible, though, was some kind of artificial light flickering in the shadows.

She glanced over at Ivers, who knitted his brow and mouthed, *Bottle rockets?*

The truth was, she had no idea. But she suspected it wasn't going to turn out to be anything as benign as fireworks.

"Vanya," she said into her throat mike. "Stop where you are. There's something I don't li—"

The Eastern European suddenly broke cover, dropping his

rifle as he raced toward them at a full sprint. She held her gun out in front of her, searching over the sites for a target, but he seemed to be running from a ghost. A moment later, though, she saw them. A swarm of thin contrails overtaking him from behind.

"Vanya! Drop!" she screamed.

He did as she ordered, throwing himself headfirst over a fallen log. Instead of all of them passing harmlessly overhead, though, a few changed trajectory. One slammed into the log with enough force to split it in the middle. Four more hit her man, thudding sickeningly into his body and splattering the leaves above him with blood.

"Pull back!" Randi shouted. "Karen! Reiji! Do you hear me? Get the hell away from the clearing!"

She and Ivers ran, weaving through the trees with the hissing sound trailing them. The projectiles were clearly guided, but there was no way to know by what method. She broke left, hoping that she could lead them away from Wilson and his students. Ivers appeared to have the same idea and broke right, trying to confuse the tiny machines.

Randi dodged behind a tree and heard the crunch of wood as one of them impacted the trunk. She dared a look back and saw at least three more flying in a loose formation, all clearly locked onto her.

Breaking cover, she leaped over a large boulder. On the other side, the ground seemed to disappear from beneath her and she found herself cartwheeling down the steep side of the canyon.

56

J on Smith paced back and forth across the tiny room, feeling the overwhelming urge to throw something. Unfortunately he hadn't been left with anything heavy or breakable enough to give him any satisfaction.

Takahashi had departed an hour ago and taken the tablet with him. Before he did, though, they'd watched one of Randi's men go down and her disappear over a boulder. He couldn't be certain what happened after that, but having had experience with those projectiles, he could guess. The only reason he was alive was that the ones attacking him had been programmed to stay within the confines of Genjiro Ueda's house.

The door began sliding open and Smith moved quickly toward it, standing in a position where he could lunge through and snap Takahashi's neck before the soldier knew what was happening. He had no illusions that it would do much to save Randi or prevent the coming world war, but at least he'd have some revenge before they put a bullet in his head.

Instead of Takahashi, the stooped figure of Hideki Ito appeared. Smith looked past the scientist at the man standing against the corridor wall. Still the same one—taking in every-thing with black eyes and a hand in his jacket. The distance was only five yards but it might as well have been a mile.

The door slid closed after Ito passed through, and he moved close to Smith. "We have to talk."

"About what?"

Ito pointed to the cameras looking down on them. "I've initiated a software upgrade to our security system. The cameras are rebooting. We have seven and a half minutes."

Smith looked up at a clock on the wall and took note of the time before stepping back to examine the man. He was sweating where his ravaged skin would allow, creating a glistening patchwork across his face. "You have my attention."

"What I built was never meant as an offensive weapon. My expectation was that the general would publicly demonstrate its capabilities in some nonlethal way. That it would make us safe from our enemies and perhaps even be a positive contribution to society."

"But instead he's going to use it to exterminate the Chinese."

"It's..." Ito's voice faltered. "Is *ironic* the correct word? My technology is useful because it can be carefully targeted. Certain materials, certain locations. We could destroy China's entire military capability without harming a single human being. But he's going to use it in a way that's completely indiscriminate. He'll kill everyone. Civilians, women. Even children."

Was Ito just running on at the mouth to try to assuage his guilt or was he there to suggest some kind of action? Smith glanced up at the dead cameras, painfully aware that the clock was ticking.

"Can he be stopped?"

"The prime minister is flying to China today, and he's ordered Takahashi to go with him. Both Sanetomi and President Yandong have made it clear that they will find a way to come to terms. That this situation will be de-escalated."

"But Takahashi doesn't want that."

"No. He's ordered me to finish making the weapons, and when I'm done he plans to deploy them."

"I assume you're here because you don't want that blood on your hands, Doctor. Do you have a course of action in mind?"

Ito reached beneath his smock and pulled out a screwdriver made of what looked like carbon fiber.

Smith almost laughed when the scientist held it out to him. He'd hoped for something a bit more clever from the man who had cracked molecular manufacturing.

Ito obviously sensed his disappointment. "As I'm sure you're aware from your investigation of Fukushima, we have sterilization protocols in place that are similar to what you use in your lab at Fort Detrick."

"Radiation," Smith said.

Ito gave a short nod.

"And as the lead researcher, do you have the ability to unilaterally initiate sterilization?"

"Yes. However, this is Takahashi's facility. The procedure takes time to implement, and he has the ability to override."

"Will he?"

"I guarantee it. I've seen how twisted the man has become. He will never allow his weapon to be destroyed."

"So what are you proposing?"

"If we can access one of the server rooms, there is a chance that I can block his attempt to shut down the sterilization protocol."

"Then why don't you do it?"

"Because I don't have access to those particular servers without his express permission."

"And that's where I come in."

"Yes."

Smith looked down at the screwdriver in the scientist's hand. "There's a problem with your plan."

"What?"

"On my best day, I couldn't close the distance to that guard before he gets his gun out. And believe me when I tell you that this isn't my best day."

"But we have to—"

"What we have to do is deal with reality, Doctor. I have a lot of ground to cover and the guard just has to move his gun a few inches. It's not going to happen."

Ito started to panic. "There's no time! The cameras are going to come back online in only a few minutes. You have to help me!"

"Calm down, Doctor. I will help you, but there's going to have to be a minor change in plan. When you leave here, does the guard follow you or do you follow him?"

Ito's bloodshot eyes darted back and forth as he tried to remember. "He follows me."

"Okay. Fine," Smith said, trying to keep his tone soothing. "Do the guards wear body armor?"

"I don't think so. No. I've never seen it."

"Good. Then you're going to walk out of here like you always do. And when you get close"—Smith touched a place on his upper stomach—"put that screwdriver right here."

"What?" Ito said, eyes widening. "You want—"

"Listen to me!" Smith said, raising his voice enough to silence the man. "You need to drive it upward and to your right. Toward his heart."

"But—"

"He has no reason to expect this," Smith said. "But when you do it, he's going to try to get his gun out and he'll probably try to grab you. Stay right up against him. Be calm and don't give him room to maneuver. In two seconds it'll be over."

"No," Ito said. "I . . . I cannot do this."

"You're either going to have the figurative blood of millions of innocent people on your hands or the literal blood of one trained killer. As moral dilemmas go, that one seems pretty straightforward."

"But . . . but I'm a scientist. An old man. What if he kills me?"

"Then all your worries will be over, won't they?"

The scientist wiped his mouth with the sleeve of his lab coat and then, surprisingly, turned and pressed his hand against the palm reader next to the door.

His gait was a little too fast and stiff, but it didn't matter. The guard's eyes were locked on his American prisoner as they had been every time before.

Smith just stood there watching, calculating the odds that Ito would just keep on walking at about 99 percent. Again, though, the scientist surprised him.

He struck just as the door started to slide shut, pressing himself up against the man and pinning him to the wall. Smith rushed the door and grabbed its edge, but the mechanism was too powerful. The last thing he saw was the guard wrapping a hand around Ito's fragile neck.

His heart was pounding far harder than it would have been if he'd taken the man himself, nearly audible in the silence that had descended on the room. There had been no gunshot, but what did that mean? Had Ito managed to hold on? Were the two men lying dead on the floor, one with a screwdriver beneath his rib cage and the other with a broken spine?

The door slid back again and Ito stood in front of it, his face frozen into a distorted mask.

"Well done," Smith said as he brushed by the scientist and crouched next to the body. The screwdriver was still lodged in it and he retrieved the tool, wiping the blood off and stashing it in one of the pockets of the jumpsuit he'd been provided.

Unfortunately, there was no equally practical place to store the man's Glock. In the end, Smith had to unzip the front of the jumpsuit and stuff it in the waistband of his boxer shorts. Not exactly at his fingertips but it would have to do.

"Dr. Ito," he said, standing and putting a hand on the still-dazed scientist's shoulder. "The server room. Where is it? We don't have much time before the cameras come back online."

57

Northeastern Japan

The layout of the facility was predictably simple—nothing more than a set of wide corridors carved from the earth, most of which emanated from a massive central cavern. Individual shafts occasionally split off, leading to storage areas. Some were filled with fifty-gallon drums containing nuclear waste, but most were empty. Others had been hijacked by Takahashi's organization and were guarded by the familiar composite doors.

Smith and Ito moved along at an excruciatingly casual pace, with Smith's head bowed submissively. Just another worker on his way to make some trivial repair for management.

Of course, that cover story would bear precisely no scrutiny at all but his dark complexion and black hair would be enough to dampen the interest of anyone more than twenty paces away. Thankfully, no one had come anywhere near that close so far.

They crossed the main artery leading to the loading area and Smith subtly shifted his gaze to the massive blast doors and the smaller adjacent door dedicated to pedestrian traffic. Two men were standing guard in front of the exits, both with compact assault rifles hanging across their chests.

Ito ducked into another corridor and Smith felt himself relax a bit when they left the guards' line of sight. The passage dead-ended into a door after about another fifty yards, and Ito stopped to speak to a camera bolted above it.

Smith didn't understand anything that was said, but they'd settled on a story about a problem with the rebooting of the security system. Specifically, a couple of physical connections that weren't responding. Not exactly a stroke of genius, but reasonably credible and it went a long way toward explaining why Ito was accompanied by a large man with a screwdriver.

Smith kept his head down, trying to relax. They had one chance at this and he couldn't afford to blow it. According to Ito, there was one systems administrator and one security man inside. What the scientist couldn't tell him was which of those men would come to the door. It was precisely these kinds of operational unknowns that Smith spent his life trying to avoid.

After an endless thirty seconds of back and forth, the door finally slid aside. Ito glanced back at him and gave a gruff order before walking inside. Smith followed along obediently, head still bowed, but eyes straining upward.

The room was as described, no more than twenty feet square with walls mostly hidden by computer equipment. There was a single desk with a terminal on it to the right and two rolling chairs—only one of which was currently occupied.

The tech was a young man with an artificial reddish tint to his hair and the air of having downed a few too many espressos that morning. He was talking a mile a minute, gesturing maniacally toward his screen as Ito approached and put a hand on the back of his chair.

The security man was lifting his wrist to his face, undoubtedly to report the unusual situation into a radio microphone secured there. Smith backed toward him slowly, pretending to watch Ito, but really focused on the guard.

The angle of Smith's body would make it hard to for the man to get a clear view of his face, but this wasn't just some rent-a-cop. He wasn't going to be fooled for more than a few seconds.

It turned out to be even less than that. The man's left hand suddenly stopped rising toward his mouth and his right went for a gun in an exposed shoulder holster.

Smith spun, going for the man's throat with the screwdriver but knowing there was no way in hell he'd connect. At the last moment he let his knees collapse and redirected the blade to the man's upper thigh. It sank halfway to the hilt but the guard barely seemed to notice, smoothly wrapping his hand around the grip of a Sig Sauer P226.

Smith ignored the shouts coming from behind him, forced to rely on the dying scientist to handle the computer tech. The gun was nearly free now and Smith lunged, slamming his shoulder into the man's elbow with the full force of his 180-pound frame. The pain flared in his injured back, but the impact had its intended effect—the gun was rammed back into its holster.

The screwdriver had hit the guard's femur and was stuck there. Smith tried to get hold of it again as the man drew back a hand to drive down into the crouched American's neck. He didn't fully compensate for the weakness in his thigh, though, and the brief hesitation was all Smith needed. He leaped up-ward, slamming the back of his head into the man's chin. He staggered to the side as Smith used his superior weight to drive him toward the wall and buckle his injured leg. He put his hand over the man's face and shoved downward as they fell, ramming the back of his head into the flagstone floor. The give was noticeable as his skull collapsed.

Smith grabbed the Sig Sauer and spun to see the computer tech trying to escape through the door. Ito had his arms wrapped around the younger man from behind and while it wasn't a particularly powerful effort, it was enough to keep the tech's hand from making firm contact with the palm reader.

Smith went for them, grabbing the young man by the hair and dragging him to the floor. He squirmed wildly, shouting unintelligibly in a panicked voice.

"Do we need him?" Smith said, gritting against the pain in his back while the computer tech clawed at him.

"No."

Smith slammed the butt of the gun into the man's forehead and he went completely still.

"Are you all right?" he said, staying on his knees for a moment to let a wave of pain and nausea subside.

"Yes," Ito replied. "Are you?"

Smith gave a short nod and the scientist took a seat behind the terminal.

"Once I activate the sterilization process, the system will initiate a general lockdown. It will take a few minutes for that to be completed, and then the entire facility will be flooded with radiation. If you can get past the guards at the entrance, you still have time to escape."

It was a tempting offer. To not die of a massive dose of radiation in a dark hole. To smell the forest and see the sky again. But when Ito fired this thing up, Takahashi could be counted on to do everything in his considerable power to stop it.

"No. I'll stay and make sure nothing goes wrong."

Ito was visibly relieved. He'd already gone through this

once and knew that he wouldn't survive this time. Dying alone, for some reason, was so much more terrifying than dying with someone else. Even a stranger.

The scientist tapped a few commands into the terminal and hit the "enter" button. A moment later the wail of an alarm began echoing through the facility.

58

Northeastern Japan

General Masao Takahashi walked into the empty lab and glanced at his watch. The prime minister had insisted that he accompany him to meet with the Chinese president at his retreat outside Hanzhong. They were to fly out of Japan in a few hours and at this rate, he would barely make it to the airport in time for their scheduled departure.

It mattered little, though. What could Sanetomi do other than demonstrate his displeasure in the careful, ambiguous way of all frightened politicians? His anger would quickly dissipate when he saw how contrite and deferential his highest-ranking soldier was in the presence of President Yandong.

Takahashi smiled. Of course, Sanetomi would see this as an indication that the power of his office had been reasserted, but the truth was very much the opposite. Submissiveness was easy to feign when talking to the dead leader of a dead civilization.

When he looked through the lead glass wall at the containers filled with nanoweapons, his brow furrowed. Sixteen. No more than there were last time he'd been there. Ito had promised that all 120 were on the verge of completion, and no one had informed him of a delay.

Takahashi pulled out his radio and entered the code for

Hideki Ito. For the first time in their decades-long association, there was no answer.

His jaw clenched as he stared at the empty rows in front of him. Ito had always been weak. His single-mindedness and addiction to research funding had made him easy to manipulate, but recently his focus had begun to waver. It was something that would not be tolerated.

Takahashi switched channels to connect with the head of his security detail. A moment later his man's voice crackled to life over his earpiece.

"What can I do for you, General?"

"Ito isn't answering his page. Locate him."

"I'm sorry, sir. We're rebooting some of our security systems and won't have that capability for a few more minutes. It's possible that his communications have been affected."

"If you can't do it electronically, then send your men out. I want him found and brought to the storage lab. Is that clear?"

"Yes, sir. I'll do it immediately."

Takahashi felt a familiar knot tying itself in the back of his shoulders. While the technological explanation was plausible, his gut said it was something more. He was losing control of the scientist.

His hunch was confirmed a moment later when the silence was broken by the deafening screech of the containment breach alarm.

He put his radio to his mouth again, reconnecting to security. "Report!"

"We're on with the main lab and they say they have no breach," came the frightened reply. "We have people on their way to check the storage lab. It may have—"

"I'm in the storage lab!" Takahashi shouted. "It's secure."

If the alarm was going off, that meant the facility was in the process of lockdown. When complete, the entire space would be flooded with radiation. The weapon would be destroyed along with every living thing trapped inside.

"Sir, I don't—"

"Shut up and listen! Shut down the breach protocols. Do you understand me?"

Relief was audible in the man's voice. "Yes, sir. We're initiating the override now."

Takahashi stared at the glass in front of him, turning the situation over in his head—the missing canisters, the reboot of the security system. The phantom breach.

Ito.

He pressed his palm against the reader next to the portal that allowed access to the weapon. As expected it just pulsed red, indicating that it had been frozen by the alarm. Takahashi pulled the cover from a keypad and punched in his override code—one of many Ito had not been told about. The bolts securing the portal retracted and he ducked through, grabbing two of the canisters and starting back into the corridor.

His earpiece came to life a moment later. "Sir, the shutdown sequence isn't responding."

Takahashi started to run, feeling his rage increasing to the point that even he found it hard to control.

"*Why* isn't it responding?" he asked, suspecting that he already knew the answer.

"We're being blocked by the central computer, sir. It's Dr. Ito. The cameras have come back online and we can see him in the server room. He's with the American."

59

Northeastern Japan

I t's done," Dr. Hideki Ito said over the drone of the alarm. "The facility is locked down and the sterilization process has begun."

He leaned back in his chair and stared blankly at the computer screen in front of him. A red bar graph indicating the ambient radiation levels dominated it. Twenty-three rads and rising.

Smith leaned over the scientist's shoulder, ignoring the graphical illustration of his slow death and focusing on the security camera feeds. Three men had reached the main cavern and were coming full tilt in their direction.

"Can they get through the door?" Smith asked, tapping the image with his index finger.

"It's virtually indestructible," Ito responded. "And even if they do, it wouldn't matter. The system is designed with the idea that the servers would be attacked by the nanotech—there was no way to construct them without using vulnerable materials. So even if they gain entry and destroy everything, it will have no effect. The sterilization protocols have the ability to operate independently from the mainframe."

Smith backed against the stone-and-dirt wall, looking down

at the two men lying motionless on the floor. What would it be like to die from radiation poisoning? How long would it take? It wasn't exactly something they went into in medical school.

A light started flashing on-screen but Smith was too lost in his own thoughts to notice until he saw Ito jerk straight in his chair.

"What is it?" Smith said, coming up behind the man again.

"It appears to be a malfunction. There are a number of doors that haven't locked down." The scientist sucked in a frightened breath as he scanned through various screens of text that Smith couldn't read.

"Talk to me, Doctor."

"It's ... it's the storage lab." He tapped in a few commands and the screen began flickering through security camera stills.

"There!" Ito said, jabbing a finger at the monitor. Smith leaned in closer. The image depicted Masao Takahashi running with two thermos-size containers.

"Tell me those aren't what I think they are."

Ito just kept watching the stream of images. Finally he found one of Takahashi time-stamped only a few seconds before, and he switched to video. The general was still running but he'd been joined by two guards—one in front and one behind.

"He's going for the exterior doors," Ito said, spinning his chair toward Smith. "He must have an override code that I wasn't told about. If he escapes with those canisters..." The scientist fell silent.

"If he escapes with those canisters, what?"

"The nanobots inside are programmed for trillions of divisions and are designed to operate within the borders of China. The collapse of the country will be slower, but the end result will be the same."

"Hundreds of millions of people freezing and starving."

Ito nodded.

"Shit!" Smith shouted, slamming a fist down on the table next to the keyboard. "Can we get an outside line?"

"No. You can't feel it, but the radiation is getting fairly intense. It makes our communications system useless."

"Can you open this door?" Smith said, pointing to the one leading back out into the corridor.

Ito nodded.

"Where are the security guards that were coming our way?"

Ito typed a few more commands into his keyboard and located them. They were just outside.

Smith stepped back, trying to think. Takahashi would know the door was indestructible. Did he send the guards just to stand there and make sure Smith couldn't get out? Or did they have an access code that Ito had been kept in the dark about?

His question was answered a moment later when one of the men retrieved a piece of paper from his pocket and pulled the cover off the keypad.

"Open it!" Smith said, crouching and extending the Sig Sauer out in front of him.

"But they'll—"

"Now, goddamn it!"

The man was beginning to enter the code, but his progress was slowed by the fact that he had to keep referring to the paper in his hand. They had less than five seconds before the advantage swung heavily in the direction of the three men outside. Until then, though, Smith had the edge. He knew their positions from the security camera images, and they wouldn't expect the door to open until the override was fully entered.

"Come on!" Smith prompted. "Hurry!"

Two of the armed men were standing one slightly behind the other, partially overlapping in the narrow passageway. Both had guns drawn and both were trained on the door.

Smith dropped to the floor and aimed at the right jamb about waist height. With luck, their first shots would go over his head.

The door began to slide open and he could hear the surprised shouts of the men outside. He followed the widening crack through the sights of the handgun he'd taken from the dead guard. One of the security men fired, but it was a blind shot that went well wide and slammed into the bank of computers against the back wall.

A little more...

Smith squeezed off a round, hitting the lead man in the side, just above his belt. Not a fatal wound, but that wasn't the goal. It was a soft part of the body with no bone to deflect the bullet. The man buckled at the waist and was thrown back into the man behind him as Smith leaped to his feet.

His gamble worked. The bullet passed right through and hit the man behind, interrupting his aim and sending a bullet hissing past Smith's right ear. He ignored the sound, sprinting forward and firing at the two men struggling to stay on their feet. He hit the front one in the chest and then slammed into them before pressing the Sig's barrel to the second man's forehead and squeezing the trigger.

The back of the guard's skull sprayed across the dirt wall and Smith spun, lining up on the man at the keypad. He'd dropped the piece of paper containing the access code and was going for his gun, but the barrel hadn't even cleared his leather shoulder holster when a round from Smith's weapon hit him in the face.

Smith ran down the corridor, stopping just before it opened into the main cavern. It looked clear to the right, so he stepped out, holding his pistol in front of him with both hands.

Takahashi was about fifty yards away—running toward the exit a hell of a lot faster than a man his age should have been able to. It was a relatively easy shot made impossible by the trailing guard who was directly in the line of fire.

Smith squeezed off a round and the man went down, rag-dolling across the ground before coming to a stop on his back.

The second man turned at the sound of the shot, returning fire accurately enough to force Smith to protect his eyes against the spray of dirt and shattered rock exploding from the wall next to him. The guard came to a full stop about sixty-five yards away and was walking his shots toward Smith as he concentrated on Takahashi's receding back.

Again, though, the guard had put himself in a position to disrupt the line of sight to the fleeing soldier.

A round passed just over Smith's head and he was forced to duck back into the corridor. There was no time for this. He immediately moved back into the open and raised the pistol. Its dead owner had done a meticulous job of sighting it in, and Smith's first attempt spun the guard halfway around but didn't knock him down.

Smith ran at him, covering the distance at a full sprint as the injured man struggled to stay on his feet. By the time the guard was able to raise his weapon, Smith was only about ten yards out and easily put a round directly center of mass.

The thud of the man's body hitting the ground was audible as Smith continued forward, eyes locked again on Takahashi as the soldier arrived at a small door adjacent to the main blast doors.

He'd obviously taken the precaution of memorizing the override code and a moment later the door slid open. Smith began emptying his gun in the man's direction. Takahashi turned sideways to present the smallest target profile possible and slipped through the gap into the exterior cavern.

"No!" Smith shouted, trying to will his legs to pump faster. His injuries made it impossible for him to get in a full breath, and his vision was starting to swim as the door began to close again.

He was a good two seconds too slow and instead of passing through, he hit it still running full speed. The pain in his back flared and he dropped to the ground just as a series of rounds slammed into the wall above him.

Smith rolled to his stomach and saw the men coming his way. All were armed and this time there were more than three. This time he counted nine.

They were running in a tight group, creating an easy target. He took out two in quick succession, thinking it would cause the others to scatter, but that didn't happen. They just kept racing straight at him. He squeezed the trigger again, but the magazine was empty. Smith unzipped the front of his jumpsuit and went for the Glock. They were too close for him to stop them all but at least he could take a few with him.

Maybe it was best this way. The death they planned for him would be a lot quicker than the radiation and a lot more pleasant than living with the knowledge that he'd failed to prevent the murder of tens of millions of innocent people.

There was a quiet hissing behind him and he glanced back to see the door sliding open again. It took him a moment to process what had happened, but when he did a thin smile spread across his face.

Ito, you beautiful son of a bitch...

The men in front of him were only seconds from overrunning his position, a few firing wildly in his direction, hoping to get lucky. The Glock was sighted in just as meticulously as the Sig and the lead man went down, slowing the group's progress as they were forced to leap over their fallen comrade.

Smith slithered backward and wasn't quite through when the door reversed itself. He put a hand against the cavern wall and shoved, barely getting his head clear before it closed. The dull thud of men hitting the other side was audible as he rolled onto his back and gulped at the cool air. A moment later that sound was replaced by the far less comforting roar of an engine starting up. Struggling to his knees, he squinted into the sun coming from the cavern entrance. An open jeep was racing toward the light with a familiar outline hunched over the wheel. Masao Takahashi.

Smith got to his feet and started running again, but he couldn't manage anything more than a staggering jog. His broken ribs were preventing him from taking in full breaths and he'd used up the last of his adrenaline. All he could do was watch helplessly as the jeep disappeared.

He was about forty yards from the cavern entrance when he spotted a human outline slip into view. Smith dived to the ground just as man opened up with a submachine gun. The shooter's eyes were adjusted to the bright sunlight so instead of trying to aim he just hosed the place down.

Smith rested the butt of the Glock in the dirt to try to isolate it from his heaving chest. The gun jerked in his grip but the man kept firing. Smith lined up again and squeezed the trigger, this time forcing himself to hold his breath despite desperately needing oxygen.

The assault rifle kept sparking but the position of the barrel faltered and finally dropped, kicking up a cloud of dust as the rounds pounded the ground. A moment later the man was down.

Smith tried to stand but only made it to his knees before he collapsed. He lay there on his stomach, choking quietly on the dust until the burning in his lungs and limbs started to subside. Finally, he pushed himself to his feet and lurched forward. He had to get to a phone. He had to talk to Klein.

60

Northeastern Japan

Randi Russell's eyes snapped open, but she couldn't see much. Just spinning green set to the sound track of the ringing in her ears. She remained completely motionless, moderating her breathing to the point that it was completely inaudible and picking a fixed point to stare at.

Slowly the spinning stopped, but the ringing persisted with enough intensity to make her virtually deaf. Were the projectiles gone or were they all around her, waiting for any sign of motion that they could target?

She moved only her eyes, finding nothing but dense foliage intermittently broken by a darkening sky. The slope she'd cartwheeled down was to her left and the river was maybe another fifty yards downslope to her right. She was in a fair amount of pain but none of it was localized in a way that suggested serious injury—just the depressingly familiar feeling of having spent half an hour in a clothes dryer with a bunch of bowling balls.

She lay like that for a few more minutes, trying to find any sign of the things that had killed Vanya and chased her into the canyon. Soon, though, thoughts of her team and Wilson's students began to overwhelm her. What had happened to them? Were any still alive? Did they need her help?

Lying there was pointless, she concluded. She didn't know anything about the weapon that had been used against her. It might key on motion, but it could just as easily track heat or the shape of human outlines. The more interesting question was, did it just search for targets until it ran out of fuel or could it power down and lie in wait?

In the end, there was only one way to find out.

Randi grabbed a tree branch and used it to pull herself into a sitting position. She was in no condition to run and there was nowhere to go anyway, so she just sat there for a moment, waiting.

Nothing.

"Report," she said into her throat mike but got no response.

Finally she risked standing. Miraculously, the damage to her body was limited to countless scrapes and gashes peeking out from tears in her clothing. Most of them had clotted and the shadows were lengthening, suggesting she'd been unconscious for the better part of an hour. Too long.

Randi started back up the slope, using trees and bushes to help propel her along the steep grade. Her progress was uncharacteristically slow but her balance was way off and the fact that she couldn't hear much was making it worse.

It took fifteen minutes to cover the ground she'd careened down in only a few seconds, and she finally stopped just below the canyon's lip. Crouched beneath a tree, she looked for any sign of danger or life. There was nothing, though. Just a light breeze rattling the leaves.

"Randi."

She spun, snatching a rock from the ground since she hadn't been able to find the gun she'd dropped.

"Stop! It's me!"

Eric Ivers had prudently chosen to put a solid five feet between them before calling out. Now he crawled up next to her. "What the hell's wrong with you? I've been trying to get your attention for the last five minutes."

She pointed to her ear and he nodded his understanding.

"You okay?" he said, bringing his mouth close to the side of her head in order to be heard.

"Yeah. You?"

"I've been better but I'm still breathing."

"Have you ever seen anything like those things?"

"I've never even heard of anything like those things."

"Why aren't we dead?"

"I think I can answer that," he said. "I rolled about halfway down the canyon and when I stopped, one of those goddamn things had me dead to rights. Nothing I could do, so I just laid there. Then the contrail disappeared and it started to lose altitude."

"It ran out of gas?"

"That's what it looked like to me."

"Did you pick it up? Do you have it?"

"Unfortunately, yes," he said, pointing down. The projectile was lodged in his shin.

"Shit," Randi said. "Can we get it out?"

"I tried. It's barbed. The goddamn Japanese think of everything."

"Okay. You wait here," Randi said. "Let me go scope things out."

"Fuck that."

She'd anticipated his response and wasn't prepared to argue. His wife was up there and she wasn't responding to the radio.

Randi crept forward with Ivers right behind. Normal tactics seemed pointless—there was no way to provide each other cover from those things. Better to stay close and maybe one of them could draw fire while the other went for another ride down the canyon.

She came over the crest in first position and still there was nothing but empty wilderness. They angled left, stopping every few seconds for Ivers to listen for the telltale hiss of the projectiles' engines.

Finally they came upon the digger and Randi felt the breath catch in her chest.

She'd lost people before. More than she wanted to remember. The difference was that they were all pros who had signed on of their own free will. This was very different.

She stood straight and walked toward the shredded bodies of Wilson and his students. Not a single one was even worth crouching down and checking for a pulse. Their dead eyes stared accusingly at her, and the weight of those stares left her bracing herself against the blood-spattered tunneling machine.

After a few moments, Randi started in the direction Ivers had gone, no longer concerned about the projectiles or anything else Takahashi could throw at her. The team she'd put together was down, a bunch of innocent kids were dead, and pretty soon that genocidal maniac was going to go on a rampage through the most populous country in the world.

Yet she kept on breathing. It was her greatest talent. Sometimes she wondered if it was her only talent.

Reiji was lying facedown, penetrated by no fewer than four of Takahashi's projectiles. Ivers was up another twenty yards, kneeling over his dead wife. Randi gave him a wide berth. What could she possibly do? What could she say?

Instead she headed for the table they'd been using as a command center. The secure satellite link was undamaged and she put the headset on, opening an encrypted channel to Fred Klein.

"Go ahead," said the familiar voice.

"We're shut down."

"Casualties?"

"Two survivors including me."

"The professor and his stu—"

"Gone."

"Understood. I have an extraction team on alert at the Okinawa air base. They'll be in the air in—"

"No. I don't know what we're dealing with and I'm not going to put any more of our people in the line of fire. Eric and I will find our way home by ourselves."

61

General Masao Takahashi sat silently in the back of the limousine as his driver weaved through the small, private airport. It had been three hours since he'd been chased from his own facility by the American and the traitor Hideki Ito. Communications had been lost and according to the team he'd sent to the site, the blast doors were sealed. With no sign of life inside and exterior radiation levels well above normal, it appeared that the emergency sterilization protocol had been carried out.

Takahashi glanced down at his briefcase, confirming once again that it was resting safely on the seat next to him. The two canisters inside were all that was left of the weapon. Its creator was dead, the development facility would be uninhabitable for a thousand years, and the fourteen other canisters had been irradiated.

It didn't matter, though. Ito and the American had failed. While the destruction of China's infrastructure would be slower and more haphazard than he had planned, it would be just as complete. That was the genius of the weapon. It had a life of its own.

The private jet ahead was the only one in view on the tarmac and was surrounded by Sanetomi's security detail. The prime minister's impending visit to China had been widely publicized, but turned out to be less popular than the politician's advisers had calculated. The remote airport had been chosen to avoid the inevitable protests by Japanese citizens opposed to further appeasement of their enemy to the west. Patriots who were willing to rise up and defend the honor of their homeland while self-serving cowards like Fumio Sanetomi cowered.

The limousine glided to a stop and Takahashi stepped out with his briefcase gripped firmly in his hand. The prime minister's men watched through dark glasses as he approached the steps leading into the plane, finally moving to block his path.

"Are you armed, General?" one asked.

"Of course not."

"You'll excuse us if we check."

The man was understandably nervous. Normally, Takahashi wouldn't take this intentional insult so easily. But today he held his arms out at his sides with a smile, letting the man use his metal detector as Sanetomi watched from one of the jet's windows.

They didn't bother to check the briefcase because this had nothing to do with security and everything to do with putting him in his place. Of course, the prime minister had no idea what that place was.

When the infantile display of power was over, Takahashi entered the plane and walked immediately to the back.

"Sit," Prime Minister Sanetomi said.

The old soldier took a place across a small table and laid his briefcase on top of it.

"In a few hours we'll be landing at President Yandong's retreat," Sanetomi said. "During our time there, you will speak only when spoken to and your responses will be short, respectful, and contrite. You do not represent Japan and you will not take part in any discussions of policy or our relationship with the Chinese. Am I understood?"

"Very clearly," Takahashi said. "But if this is the case, may I ask why I'm being included on this excursion?"

"In order to publicly apologize for your aggressive behavior and to offer your resignation as head of our self-defense forces."

"I see," Takahashi said, looking out the window as they taxied toward the runway. The security detail was already packing up and moving toward an SUV parked nearby. Four more guards were on the plane, one sitting near the cockpit and three more strapped in midfuselage. Apparently, Sanetomi's negotiating team had taken a commercial flight earlier that day.

"And who will be accepting my resignation, Prime Minister? You or your Chinese master?"

The politician suffered a rare moment of visible anger as his face reddened and the muscles in his jaw tensed.

"You've always been a twisted man, General—obsessed with a world that's been gone for more than half a century. I should never have let you remain in a position of responsibility. I and my predecessors believed that it was time to relieve the Americans of their responsibilities toward us and to create a Japan that could be a positive force in the world. But it's clear that you see things very differently and that we allowed you to drain money from our economy for too long. You seem to believe that we can actually win a war with China. That is a delusion, General. Even with the weapons you've developed

and the help of the Americans, our country would be decimated. Millions would die on both sides to achieve an even
more acrimonious stalemate. The time for war—the time for
men like you—is past."

"And so we're left with men like you. Men who will give
away our country piece by piece. First to be run from Washington and now to be run from Beijing. Men who will turn our
people into slaves in order to cling to their own false sense of
power and prestige."

"This conversation is over!" Sanetomi said, the volume of
his voice rising. "You will—"

"I will do nothing!" Takahashi responded, slamming a hand
down on the table hard enough to turn the heads of the security men on the jet. "You are an arrogant and stupid child. You
think I've told you and the pitiful men who preceded you the
full extent of what I've accomplished? You think I would trust
the future of my country to speech makers and whores?"

Sanetomi shrank back in his seat. Takahashi was, at his
core, a man of violence. But on the surface he had always been
careful to maintain the appearance of placidity.

"We will not fly to your ally Yandong's retreat," Takahashi
continued. "Nor will I be resigning my commission. We will
fly to Chengdu where I will release the weapon I have in my
briefcase. And then either you will decide to preside over a vic-
torious Japan or you will be tried and executed as a traitor."

Sanetomi looked at the black leather briefcase, and then
back to Takahashi. "You . . . you brought a nuclear weapon on
board this plane?"

The soldier laughed. "Nothing so crude, Prime Minister.
What I have inside is a nanoscale weapon that will take hold in
Chengdu and then spread throughout China, quietly destroy-

ing everything in its path. All you have to do is continue to be convincing in the role of frightened appeaser. By the time the Chinese understand what's happening and who's responsible, it will be too late."

Sanetomi just stared at him, frozen. He was aware of Hideki Ito's early experiments and their military potential, but his predecessor had seen the almost infinite danger of this class of weapon and shut down the program. Sanetomi himself had reaffirmed that decision when he'd taken office.

"Ito..." he stammered. "Ito succeeded?"

Takahashi nodded.

"That weapon isn't a weapon of war," Sanetomi said, licking his lips nervously. "It's a weapon of extermination. And not just of an opposing force. Of women and children. Millions of them."

"Chinese children grow into adults, Prime Minister. And Chinese women breed like stray dogs."

Sanetomi's mouth hung open for a moment, and then his eyes shifted past his military commander. "Guards! Take the general into custody immediately!"

Takahashi looked behind him at the four men rushing in their direction. They surrounded him and the prime minister, hands hidden suggestively in their jackets.

"Take the general to the front of the plane and subdue him," Sanetomi said and then looked at the briefcase on the table between them. He didn't understand the full capabilities of the weapon inside, nor was he confident that he understood his position in Tokyo anymore. Clearly Takahashi had been able to create this monstrosity without his knowledge, but it was impossible that he had been able to hide it from everyone. There was no question that other high-level officials had been involved in its development, funding, and testing. Who were those people? Certainly key military leaders, but what about other politicians? Sanetomi was a proud patriot but had always been careful not to cross the line into full-fledged nationalism. Many in his government weren't as cautious. Whom could he trust?

In the end, there was only one choice.

"Tell the pilot to turn around. He's to set a course for the American base on Okinawa. Get President Castilla's office on the phone. Tell them it's critical that I speak to him immediately."

The Americans had found evidence of this weapon at Fukushima and had top people studying it. More important, he was confident that there was no one in their government who had any desire to see Asia descend into a genocidal war.

The guards just stared at him, apparently uncertain that they'd heard their orders correctly. Takahashi had been a fixture in the self-defense forces for decades and was increasingly a symbol of Japanese sovereignty and strength.

"You heard me," Sanetomi growled. "Do it now!"

The security man next to him seemed to wake from his stupor and pulled a gun from his jacket.

Probably unnecessary in light of their superior numbers and Takahashi's age, but it would be hard not to take pleasure in seeing the man secured to a seat with a gun to his head.

The guard moved his pistol toward an almost preternaturally calm Takahashi but at the last moment, swung it in the direction of the guard next to him. The sound of the shot was deafening in the confines of the small jet and warm blood was flung across Sanetomi's cheek. He clawed at the buckle of his seat belt in an effort to get to his feet but was stopped when one of his remaining guards grabbed his wrist in a vise-like grip.

The security man closest to the cockpit broke away and ran toward it. A moment later two more shots rang out and Sanetomi saw the body of the copilot sag over the edge of his seat.

"Takahashi! What is this?" he heard himself say. But he knew quite well.

"It seems that the former soldiers you use in your security detail aren't as loyal to you as you thought."

"Stop this, General. There's still time. You can't—"

Sanetomi was silenced when a clear plastic bag was pulled over his head. He thrashed wildly, but there was no way to overcome the strength of the guards and the seat belt pulled tight across his lap. Finally, he went still, staring at Takahashi through the fogging plastic as his vision began to swim from lack of oxygen.

Takahashi returned his stare for a moment before twisting in his seat to shout to the guard who had taken control of the plane. "Contact the Chinese and tell them that we believe the prime minister has had a heart attack and request permission to divert to Chengdu in order to get him medical attention."

The world around Sanetomi began to go dark but he wouldn't allow himself to start fighting again. It would be futile and he refused to give the man casually watching him die the satisfaction. He forced his expression into a mask, giving away none of the fear he felt—for the Japanese people, for his family. For the horrors that Takahashi would soon unleash on China and the world.

It was his responsibility. His fault for not seeing what was happening in time to stop it. And for that, he deserved to die.

62

The helicopter touched down about twenty-five yards from the hangar. Jon Smith immediately jumped out, running crouched toward the base commander, who was trying to stay clear of the powerful rotor wash.

"Colonel Smith," he yelled in a heavy Southern drawl as they shook hands. "Steve Baron."

"Nice to meet you, sir. Have you been briefed?"

Baron put a hand on his back and led him toward the hangar as the chopper started to lift off again. "I'm not sure I'd call it a briefing, but we're ready for you. And I'm real anxious to hear what the hell all this is about."

When they entered through the massive doors, Smith found a group of men sitting in front of an easel containing a map of China. Next to the easel was something much more intriguing—a warhead about a foot and a half in diameter and a yard long resting on a wheeled cart. It had a new coat of paint, though beneath it bubbles suggesting rust could be seen. Not surprising for a weapon that had been retired when he was still in grade school.

Smith had to admit that he'd had doubts when he asked

Klein to track down the warhead, but the man had once again come through. It was hard to believe that the only hope they had to stop the most advanced weapon ever developed was this dilapidated Cold War relic.

With one exception, the men were wearing flight suits similar to the one he'd been given, though theirs included insignias denoting name and rank. The exception was a craggy-looking man in mechanic's coveralls. They all stood and saluted, but Smith didn't return the salute, instead walking past them to stand next to the map. While Baron knew who he was and undoubtedly assumed he was working for military intelligence, it was better to remain anonymous to the others.

"You can call me Jon," Smith said, making eye contact with the men in front of him. Baron had been personally ordered by the chairman of the Joint Chiefs to put together the best men the Eighteenth Fighter Wing had to offer, and Smith had to admit they were an impressive crew. Whether it would be enough to prevent the greatest genocide in human history, though, remained to be seen.

He patted the warhead with his right hand and then pointed to the man in coveralls. "Where do you stand on getting this thing loaded underneath a plane?"

The man rose, looking more than a little uncomfortable. "Sir, that thing is an antique and the best thing we've got to carry it is a two-seater F-15 trainer that wasn't designed for it."

"I don't want to hear problems," Smith said. "I want to hear solutions."

"Understood, sir. I'm going to get it done for you, but it ain't going to be pretty. My guys are rigging up something in place of one of the fuel tanks. And there are no onboard systems to release it so we're having to rig something up."

"The only thing I'm interested in is if it's going to work."

"It'll work. You've got my word on that, sir. But she's gonna fly like a hog and you aren't gonna have any missiles."

"What about the Gatling gun?" Smith said.

"Yes, sir. The gun will be hot."

"How much longer?"

"We're making a few tweaks and then we're going to do a third round of tests. We can have you in the air in twenty minutes."

"Make it fifteen. You're dismissed."

The man slid out of the row and went for the warhead, pushing it toward the back of the hangar. Smith watched him go, not wanting to continue until he was out of earshot.

"The prime minister of Japan is currently on his way to a diplomatic meeting in China. According to my sources, he entered Chinese airspace about ten minutes ago. Our mission is simple. We're going to intercept his plane over an uninhabited area and we're going to shoot it down. Missiles are strictly off limits. The plane will be taken out using guns only. We'll then drop the warhead that you just saw, centering it on the wreckage. That's it. Any questions?"

They all just stared at him in stunned silence. General Baron was the first to break it. "You heard the man. Let's saddle up."

The pilots looked at each other and finally stood, slowly gaining momentum as they started for their aircraft. Baron waited for a few moments and then approached, moving alongside Smith and speaking in a hushed tone. "Colonel, I was told in very clear terms that what you say goes. What I wasn't told is that you were going to use my men to start World War Three."

"We're hoping to avoid that."

"You're hoping to avoid that," Baron repeated with understandable incredulity. "Look, Colonel, I understand that all this is classified and you're some kind of golden boy but there are some questions I need to ask here."

Smith frowned, but he didn't want to come down too hard on the man. He had an excellent reputation and in his position Smith would be looking for the same kind of assurances.

"What questions, sir?"

"Is the prime minister on that plane?"

"Yes."

"Do we have permission to fly over Chinese territory?"

"No."

The general let out a long breath. "That's what I was afraid of. I'm sorry, Colonel, but I'm going to need confirmation of these orders."

"Then I suggest you get on the horn, sir. Because make no mistake. In less than twenty minutes, we *will* be in the air."

63

Over Eastern China

Y ou have penetrated our air defense zone and are approaching Chinese territory," a heavily accented voice stated over the speakers in Smith's helmet. "Reverse course immediately."

He squinted through the canopy at the F-15s escorting him. The sun was still an hour from setting, creating a blinding glare in the sky to the west. The pilot in front of him was holding the plane steady but it seemed to take a fair amount of effort due to the modifications made back at the base. Below, the East China Sea glittered with tiny whitecaps, reminding him that they hadn't yet reached the point of no return.

It was close, though. The jutting shoreline of mainland China was visible ahead in the distance.

"This is Commander Jones of the Eighteenth Fighter Wing," Smith said, picking a random alias and speaking into his radio microphone. "Our aircraft has suffered a computer failure and I'm unable to turn. We're rebooting and expect to have the problem corrected soon."

When the Chinese air force man came back on, he seemed

to have not heard the admittedly lame excuse. "Do not cross into Chinese territory, Commander. I repeat, do not cross into Chinese territory."

"We may not have any choice," Smith said, trying to stall the Chinese military's response as long as possible. "We're doing everything we can. Please contact General Baron at Kadena for confirmation."

There was no response this time and Smith decided to take it as a positive sign that the Chinese were running it up the chain of command. With a little luck, they'd contact Baron and he would tell them the exact same thing in the slowest possible way. Every second he could give them might be the difference between success and failure.

"ETA?" Smith asked the pilot.

"Thirty-one minutes to intercept. Three minutes to incursion into Chinese territory."

Smith nodded to himself and again wondered exactly what orders the pilot had been given. General Baron had never reappeared and it seemed likely that he was still trying to get confirmation of Smith's authority. Had he told his pilots to hold in international airspace until he gave them direct authorization to continue? Smith ran his fingers over his sidearm. If so, things were going to get real interesting real fast.

For once, luck was with him and Baron's voice crackled to life over an encrypted frequency. "I have just spoken personally to the president and I'd like to quote him directly. 'If you see Jesus Christ himself coming out of the sky in a fiery chariot and Jon tells you to fire on him, you will do so without hesitation.' Are those orders crystal clear?"

Smith let out a quiet sigh of relief as the affirmative responses came from all the pilots in his formation. A moment ago there had been a thousand things that could go wrong with this particular Hail Mary. Only 999 left.

"Are we aware of any Chinese response yet?" Smith said.

"It looks like they're scrambling fighters for an intercept, but we're still trying to solidify the intel on that. My Chinese counterpart is trying to reach me through back channels but I'm under orders not to respond to him."

"Understood." The president and Klein would undoubtedly be trying to work through this at much higher levels.

"I'll update you as soon as we get any information you can use, Jon. In the meantime, good luck."

* * *

"Contact! Ten bogeys closing fast from the south."

The voice coming over the radio was expected, but Smith still felt a jolt of adrenaline. It hadn't taken General Baron long to confirm that the Chinese air force wasn't going to take this lying down. With the escalating tensions throughout Asia, a sudden incursion by an ostensibly crippled US aircraft and its escorts would seem more than a little suspicious.

"What's the plan, Jon?" his pilot said.

This was no time for hesitation, but Smith was having a hard time giving the order. The Chinese were understandably frightened by this invasion of their airspace—just as the Americans would be if the shoe was on the other foot. But deep down, they would be finding it hard to believe that the United States would unilaterally attack the second-largest military in the world with a handful of F-15s. It was unlikely that their pilots were authorized to take offensive action—and the Chinese didn't sneeze without authorization.

"Sir?" the pilot prompted, but still Smith didn't speak. There were hundreds of millions of lives at stake but this still felt like murder. He would never be able to wash the blood off his hands. The blood of honorable men defending their country.

"ETA to the prime minister's plane?"

"Just under five minutes, sir."

Smith looked down at the dead landscape thousands of feet below. There was nothing for hundreds of miles in any direction. It was exactly what he'd hoped for. Exactly what he needed.

"American aircraft," said an accented voice over his earphones. "Turn around immediately and prepare to be escorted out of Chinese territory."

There was no more time. Smith switched his radio to communicate with all six pilots under his command. "Take them out."

The two seconds of silence that ensued seemed excruciatingly long.

"Sir, would you repeat that order?"

"We have the element of surprise but it isn't going to last. Take as many of them out as possible with the initial attack. We'll continue on to intercept the prime minister's plane. The rest of you keep the surviving Chinese fighters off us at all costs. Is that clear? There are no other considerations. Keep them off us *at all costs*."

64

Oval Office
Washington, DC
USA

I understand that, but—"

Sam Adams Castilla held the phone's receiver away from his ear as the president of China went on another panicked tirade. His English wasn't bad, but tinged with hysteria it was hard to follow everything he said. Not that the details mattered. The bottom line was that there were six American F-15s over his country with Chinese fighters nearing intercept. And Castilla hadn't even gotten to the bad news yet.

"Mr. President, we need to—"

Yandong just kept talking over him—demanding that the aircraft reverse course immediately, railing against the absurdity of the disabled flight computer story, and projecting the impending devastation that would be the result of a war between their nations.

General Keith Morrison, the chairman of the Joint Chiefs, was the only other man in the room. He was sitting in one of the chairs in front of Castilla's desk, talking quietly into a secure phone. After a moment he stood and wrote upside down on a legal pad in front of the president.

4m 30 sec

It was the countdown to when the two groups of fighters would come within weapons range. To when the world could potentially change forever.

"MR. PRESIDENT!" Castilla shouted at the top of his lungs. "LET ME SPEAK, DAMN IT!"

Yandong fell into a stunned silence just as a Secret Service man burst through the door with his gun drawn. He retreated when Keith Morrison waved him off.

"Mr. President," Castilla said, moderating his tone. "The aircraft is not disabled. I want to tell you exactly what's happening and why. Please, sir, let me fully explain the situation to you before it's too late."

The silence on the other end of the line extended for a few seconds. Finally, Yandong spoke. "You have one minute."

It seemed like an arbitrary deadline to avert one of the worst humanitarian disasters in history but he'd have to work with it.

Castilla looked again at the numbers Morrison had written on the pad. Of course he wasn't going to tell his Chinese counterpart the full, unvarnished truth. Instead, he'd use the cocktail of facts, diversions, and lies that Fred Klein had come up with. When it came to this kind of thing, Klein was the best who ever lived.

"Masao Takahashi has gone insane," Castilla said deliberately. "We recently learned that he's developed a new kind of biological weapon and that he's planning on releasing it in China."

This time the screaming at the other end was completely unintelligible. Some was in Chinese and obviously not aimed at him. Castilla tried to stay calm, praying that he hadn't just opened the gates for a nuclear attack on Japan.

"President Yandong! Let me finish."

The shouting on the other end died down and Castilla could hear the man's elevated breathing over the line. It was a good sign. Yandong was understandably scared, and scared people were usually looking for a way out. Unless they panicked, in which case everyone was screwed.

General Morrison stood again and wrote *2m 30 sec* on the pad. Castilla ran a hand across his throat, signaling him to stop with the updates. The pressure was bad enough as it was.

"We believe that Prime Minister Sanetomi and his government are completely ignorant of Takahashi's pla—"

"Is Takahashi on the plane with Sanetomi?" Yandong interjected.

"Yes, but—"

"And does Takahashi have the biological weapon with him?"

"We believe he does. We also think it's likely that he's either subdued or murdered the prime minister."

"We have received a call from the plane saying that Sanetomi suffered a heart attack. We've approved rerouting to Chengdu."

Castilla's jaw tightened. It made perfect sense. While the nanotech wasn't technically a biological weapon, it behaved almost exactly as if it were. Takahashi needed to unleash it in civilization for it to take hold. Yandong's rural retreat would be too isolated to ensure its spread.

"Mr. President, I have the US Army's top microbiologist on one of those F-15s with orders to shoot Sanetomi's plane down."

"You're going to shoot down the Japanese prime minister's plane?" Yandong said, suspicion starting to overshadow the fear in his voice. "Over Chinese territory?"

"Those are the orders I've given," Castilla said and then took a deep breath. "There's more, though. My man's plane is also carrying an enhanced radiation weapon."

"A...a what?"

"They're more commonly known as..." Castilla winced as Keith Morrison looked on. "Neutron bombs."

"You've flown a nuclear bomb into my country?" Yandong shouted, followed by more yelling in Chinese.

"Mr. President! We don't know exactly what we're dealing with in regard to this genetically engineered disease. My man has recommended that the wreckage of the prime minister's plane be irradiated to make absolutely certain that the pathogen is killed and can't be picked up by the wind."

He could hear more muffled shouts that he didn't understand, but this time he didn't interrupt. The carrier groups in the Pacific were all on high alert, and America's subs were converging on the Chinese coast. Morrison had moved the military to DEFCON 3 and was holding there so as not to add more fuel to the fire. The secretary of state was in Japan, talking with the leaders in Sanetomi's government and trying to figure out just who the hell was in charge.

Beyond that, there was nothing Castilla could do. His cards were on the table and his only option now was to wait for Yandong to lay down his own hand.

65

Over Eastern China

As the five F-15s under his command broke off and started on a course to intercept the ten Chinese Shenyang J-11s, Smith realized he was holding his breath. And that he couldn't seem to get it going again.

In his helmet, he could hear the broken English of one of the Chinese pilots warning them off. Undoubtedly another was on the radio to their base, trying to get rules of engagement from a long, complex, and confused chain of command.

For better or worse, Smith's people had no such issues. The buck stopped with him.

General Baron was right about his pilots. They were flawless. They flew in perfect formation, holding until they were at the edge of missile range and then all firing simultaneously.

The moment the contrails became visible, they broke formation and went after the Chinese aircraft that hadn't been targeted. Four of five missiles hit home, with the last passing over the top of one of the Chinese fighters as it dived desperately toward the ground.

There were now six J-11s against the five Americans. Smith twisted in his seat, watching through the canopy while his pilot pushed the trainer's engines to the very edge.

His combat career had been with the infantry and Special Forces, leaving him with a limited knowledge of aerial warfare. In the end, though, it seemed pretty much the same as the frenzied chaos of ground battles—just a hell of a lot faster and in three dimensions.

It was impossible to pick out individual confrontations in something that looked like a swarm of bees crisscrossed with contrails. One of the F-15s took a series of rounds to its tail, but managed to stay on target and launch one of its missiles at the aircraft in front of it. The AIM-120 hit, but then the damaged American fighter lost control and went into a flat spin that wasn't recoverable. A fireball erupted to the east, too distant for Smith to tell whether the plane was one of his or one of theirs. A moment later a Chinese aircraft broke from the melee and began streaking in their direction.

"We've got an incoming plane," Smith said, twisting a bit more in his harness to keep his eyes on it.

"I know," the pilot responded, but other than that he didn't seem inclined to take any action at all.

"Can we outrun it?" Smith said.

"No way in hell, sir. We're too heavy and your little toy is compromising our aerodynamics."

"Can we outmaneuver it?"

"It's like flying a pig with wings, sir."

And they were carrying no missiles. Only the Gatling gun.

"ETA to the target?"

"About two and a half minutes."

It wasn't enough time—the Chinese fighter was coming up on them fast and none of the F-15s was in a position to break away and engage it.

His pilot rammed the stick forward and Smith found himself pinned to the seat as they dived. The jet shook like it was going to come apart as the Chinese fighter swung in behind.

Smith wanted to look back at the warplane hunting them but the g-forces made it impossible. How close was it? Had it been able to match the ferocity of their dive? Did its pilot have a shot?

His questions were answered a moment later when the cockpit was filled with the dull screech of an alarm. The aircraft behind them had radar lock.

Smith braced himself and managed to find enough leverage to turn slightly in his seat. Out of the corner of his eye, he could see the plane only a few hundred yards back, using its superior maneuverability to counter their pathetic attempts to shake it. In the distance he could see the contrails of the ongoing dogfight, but individual planes were impossible to make out.

Smith faced forward again, staring blankly at the back of the pilot's seat. Did Takahashi know what was happening? Was he laughing while he watched the Chinese destroy their last hope?

Smith's teeth were clenched so tightly that he could hear them grinding together in his head. He closed his eyes and waited, but nothing happened. He assumed that waiting helplessly to be incinerated had thrown off his ability to mark time but eventually the seconds stretched out long enough to suggest that this wasn't it. Finally, he opened his eyes and twisted around. The plane was still there, lined up right behind them.

"Why isn't he firing?"

"I'm not sure, sir."

"Could he have a weapons malfunction?"

"Maybe. But I don't think so."

They leveled out and the J-11 disengaged, setting a course back to help his comrades.

The first thing that came to Smith's mind was that it was a trick. But to what end? That pilot could have killed them with the flip of a switch. Had Castilla managed to get through to his Chinese counterpart? Convince him to pull back?

Smith looked past the plane hurtling away from them and squinted at the dogfight still in progress. As near as he could tell, there were only two Chinese aircraft remaining and both were being double-teamed by the surviving F-15s. It was time to make a decision. The J-11s weren't going to last much longer, even with the plane coming to their aid.

"Disengage!" Smith said, opening a channel to his men. "I repeat: disengage. Defensive actions only."

66

Over Eastern China

General Masao Takahashi adjusted the focus on his binoculars and panned them slowly across the jet's side window. On both sides of him his men were doing the same with their naked eye—silently watching the events unfolding in the sky to the south.

It was impossible to follow the chaos of the dogfight, or even to reliably differentiate between the US F-15s and the Chinese J-11s. What he could say with certainty, though, was that the Americans' surprise attack had been successful. The odds were roughly even now.

He dropped the binoculars and went forward to the cockpit where he grabbed a headset. "Connect me to Chengdu tower."

The pilot flipped a switch on the radio and then returned his attention to the windscreen, leaning into it and scanning the tangled contrails being created by the warplanes.

"Chengdu tower. This is General Masao Takahashi in Prime Minister Sanetomi's plane. Your aircraft have engaged a group of American fighters to our south. Please advise. What is the situation?"

These communications were undoubtedly being monitored at the highest levels, and he could use that to keep the Chinese off balance. It seemed likely that President Castilla had already informed them that Takahashi was attempting to deliver some kind of weapon, using that as cover for the incursion into China's airspace. Clearly they didn't trust the Americans and had decided to stop them. All he had to do was make sure they stayed the course and unwittingly destroyed their only chance at survival.

"Stand by, General," a voice over the radio responded.

"Tower, is this an exercise? Please advise. We appear to be within missile range. Should we change course?"

"Stand by."

Takahashi isolated the mike and spoke to his pilot. "What is our ETA to Chengdu?"

"We should be at the outskirts in fifty-three minutes, sir."

Takahashi looked out at the dogfight, now barely discernible on the horizon. The distance was nothing more than an illusion, he knew. The fighters' superior speed would allow them to close it in a matter of seconds.

Squinting into the sunlight, he focused on a contrail near the center of the chaos. There was something strange about it. Something different about the way it reflected the sunlight.

"Binoculars!"

One of his men rushed to bring him the pair he'd left on the seat and Takahashi put them to his eyes. A jolt of adrenaline coursed through him as he saw that a lone fighter had broken away and was on course to intercept them. He kept the lenses trained on it long enough to analyze the profile and confirm that it was American.

"Tower, this is Takahashi," he said into his headset. "One of the F-15s has broken away and is on course to intercept us. Connect me immediately to President Yandong. We are on a diplomatic mission and the prime minister is gravely ill."

"We are connecting you, General," the voice responded. "Please stand by."

Another fighter broke away and gave chase. Takahashi watched, feeling the pounding of his heart ease slightly. It was Chinese and it was overtaking the F-15 at a rate that would put it behind the American fighter well before it got within range of Takahashi's jet.

Nothing could stop him now. Not the Americans. Not the Chinese. This was his destiny. They would land in Chengdu and while the doctors pronounced Sanetomi dead, he would release the weapon that would exterminate their entire useless race.

Of course the Japanese government would insist on the immediate return of the prime minister's body, and Takahashi would solemnly accompany it on its journey back to home soil. He would make speeches about his admiration for the politician, about his patriotism and dedication. In reality, though, he would be waiting for the first subtle signs of weakness in Chengdu's infrastructure. For the confused and typically secretive reaction from the Chinese government as it tried to protect its power. And finally for the country to descend into chaos.

The general watched the F-15 begin evasive action, but its maneuvers seemed awkward and heavy in comparison with the fighter hunting it. Any moment now the American threat—and indeed America's domination of the world—would be over. The question was, what should he do about this affront? Would he magnanimously ignore it? No, that would demonstrate weakness. Perhaps the sinking of an aircraft carrier. A demonstration of not only Japan's ability to defeat the American navy but its willingness to act in the face of aggression.

The J-11 was locked in behind its prey now and Takahashi watched the American pilot futilely try to shake it off. Nothing he did, though, had any effect. Nothing could save the aircraft now.

Takahashi counted the seconds in his mind as they ticked past, but the Chinese pilot didn't fire.

"Chengdu tower," he said, trying to keep his sudden uncertainty from creeping into his voice. "The American aircraft is still on an intercept course. Are we connected to President Yandong?"

No response.

"Chengdu tower, I—"

He fell silent when the Chinese fighter suddenly broke off and swept south.

"Where is the nearest population center?" he said to the pilot.

"I don't know, sir."

"Find out and change course for it!" Takahashi said. He brought the binoculars to his eyes again but couldn't find the F-15. Running to the back of the plane, he pressed the side of his face to one of the windows, trying to get a line of sight.

The fighter was close and continuing to overtake them. Its gray paint scheme and dual tail fins were fully distinguishable despite the sun's glare.

"Sir!" the pilot shouted from the cockpit. "The closest significant population concentration is approximately fifteen minutes to the north."

Takahashi ran forward again and picked up a headset as his security men kept their eyes locked on the windows. "Put me on a channel monitored by the F-15 and change course for that city.

"US military aircraft. This is General Masao Takahashi

of the Japanese self-defense forces. We are diverting from Chengdu. What are your intentions?"

Silence.

"US military aircraft!" Takahashi repeated, starting to feel the unfamiliar sensation of panic rising in him. "I repeat, this is General—"

He was thrown backward, slamming his head into the back of the empty copilot's seat as the pilot suddenly banked right. For a moment, he thought the buzz filling his ears was a result of the impact, but it didn't take long for him to recognize it for what it really was: the F-15's Gatling gun.

Takahashi crawled back to the headset on the floor, but the cable connecting it to the control panel had been severed. When he looked up, he saw the American fighter coming in from the east, the flash of the twenty-millimeter rounds fully visible through the windscreen. This time there was nothing the pilot could do. The bullets ripped through their wing, causing the jet to buck wildly. Takahashi managed to get into the copilot's seat but a moment later the metallic screech of the wing's structure tearing away filled the cockpit.

The jet lurched sideways and Takahashi tried to get hold of the seat's harness as the whistle of the air passing over the damaged aircraft grew deafening.

The pilot wrestled with the stick for a moment but then just gave up and allowed the plane to spin toward the earth.

67

Over Eastern China

Their first pass had been unsuccessful due to Smith's insistence on micromanaging the targeted area. On the second, the pilot stitched a perfect line into the Japanese plane's wing. As they streaked by, Smith twisted in his seat to watch the aircraft lurch violently and then begin to cartwheel.

"Swing around!" he said and the pilot arced the F-15 north, allowing them an uninterrupted view of the crippled plane as it dropped toward the empty landscape below. The wing finally gave way, leaving a trail of shredded metal in the sky. The fuselage held together until impact, thank God. The wreckage—and presumably Ito's weapon—remained confined to an area only a couple hundred yards in diameter.

"Let's do it," Smith said.

The pilot obliged by putting the plane into a dive, aiming at what was left of Sanetomi's plane. There was no way to maneuver the weapon they carried once it was away, forcing them to get dangerously close to the target. They only had one shot at this and a miss—even a near one—wasn't an option.

"On my mark, sir."

Smith clutched the radio remote control in his hand. It looked like something better suited to a video game than dropping a thermonuclear weapon, but it was the best the mechanics back at Kadena had been able to come up with. If it worked the way they said it would, Ito's weapon would theoretically be annihilated. The blast radius of the weapon was relatively small—no more than five hundred yards, with radiation strong enough to destroy the nanotech extending out another two miles. What could go wrong? Pretty much everything. The makeshift bomb release mechanism could jam. The antique weapon could fail to detonate. They could simply miss the crash site. Worst, though, was the possibility that a few of Ito's bots could be blown clear with enough velocity to survive the radiation zone.

Smith flipped the cover off the remote's button. His stomach felt like it was trying to escape through his throat, and he knew it wasn't just the speed of their descent unnerving him. It was the knowledge that millions of lives depended on a single movement of his thumb.

"Now!" the pilot said and Smith depressed the button.

There was a brief grinding sound and then the right side of the plane sprang upward as the weight beneath it disappeared.

"It's away!" the pilot said as he yanked back on the stick. Smith felt his G suit inflate, working to keep the blood from draining from his head with the force of the climb. His vision began to blur as the view transformed from the brown of the dead landscape to the unbroken blue of the sky.

The flash was followed by a roar that drowned out the sound of the two Pratt & Whitney engines. The plane bucked violently in the turbulence and the sensation changed from one of flying to one of being thrown through the sky. Warning alarms that didn't mean anything to Smith sounded as the pilot fought for control. The tail end of the aircraft pulled left, then right, and a moment later they were flipping end over end. The pilot continued to strain the engines, but they were useless in the air blast from the weapon. The g-forces subsided, as did the roar of the hot wind around them, but that was all Smith could be sure of as they continued to tumble.

New alarms were added to the ones already sounding as more of the plane's systems failed. Finally, the engines sputtered out. In that moment everything went strangely silent. There was nothing but the world spinning around them and the rhythmic thud of his own heartbeat.

"We're not going to make it," the pilot said with admirable calm. "Good luck, sir."

The canopy above Smith blew open and he felt himself being ripped from the cockpit. The tail just missed him as the plane continued to go end over end. The pilot wasn't so lucky. The back of his ejection seat was struck and both it and he were cut in two.

Epilogue

Arlington National Cemetery
USA

Jon Smith looked away from the young family crying over a flag-draped casket and instead gazed out on the tombstones gleaming in the sunlight. With the help of a quietly grateful Chinese government, his pilot's remains and those of the other airman killed in the dogfight had been recovered. Both were being interred with full military honors.

Of course, President Castilla couldn't be here—it would have been suspicious for the commander in chief to show up to the funerals of two men killed in yet another vaguely described training accident. Fred Klein was absent too. As always, he preferred to remain in the darkness.

And then there was Randi. No one knew where she was. The deaths of the people on her team—particularly Professor Wilson and his students—had hit her hard. She'd been last seen somewhere near the border of Cambodia and Laos, but since then there had been no word. Not that it mattered. She always reappeared eventually.

That left him, or more accurately what remained of him, to quietly represent Covert-One. Mixed in with all the other uniformed servicemen, no one would pay much attention to a lone light colonel leaning on his cane for support.

He turned back and watched as the flag was removed from the casket and carefully folded for presentation to the pilot's wife. She would never know that her husband was directly responsible for saving the lives of millions of innocent people.

One day, many years from now, the incident would be declassified so that historians could write theses and argue about its finer points over stylish drinks in stylish bars. He hoped someone would also have the presence of mind to formally recognize the people who had died. In his estimation, it was worth a few taxpayer dollars.

Until then, though, Klein's carefully laid plans for the cover-up were working. The crash of Prime Minister Sanetomi's plane had been explained away as a bird strike, and the inevitable demonstrations by Japanese and Chinese conspiracy theorists had been quickly broken up by their governments. Asian newspapers were now dominated by pictures of Sanetomi's successor smiling and shaking hands with President Yandong. Everyone seemed to understand that the xenophobia angle had been pushed too far, and compromise was beginning to carry the day.

Ito's facility was sealed off and would remain that way for centuries in order to let radiation levels subside. When the press noticed the rather uninteresting fact that Japan's nuclear storage facility had been abandoned, the government would provide a bland story about concerns over structural instability.

Greg Maple was in China searching desperately for any sign of Ito's nanoweapon in cooperation with Chinese scientists. So far their luck was holding and he'd come up empty. The Chinese had restricted the area of the neutron bomb blast for miles in every direction and were calling it an accident at an underground nuclear energy lab. Of course, the world was suspicious that it was an atomic weapons factory but the fact that President Castilla was publicly backing the Chinese version of the story ensured that the controversy would blow over quickly.

The only matter left to deal with was Takahashi's military. Prime Minister Sanetomi's successor had provided the United States unlimited access, and the commanders of the self-defense forces had little choice but to cooperate. It would take years to sort out what had been done, how it had been done, and what it would mean to the balance of power going forward. What really mattered, though, was that Ito's weapon appeared to be dead and gone. Smith was happy to let the details be handled by others. He and his people had already sacrificed enough.

Despite the cool weather, a sweat broke across Smith's forehead and he felt his stomach start to roll over. It was a sensation that had become depressingly familiar and he had to concentrate to keep from vomiting. A few days ago, it was a battle he would have lost, but the intensity of the bouts was subsiding.

The ceremony wrapped up and Smith mixed in with the crowd as it dispersed, relying on his cane to keep him moving forward. The radiation sickness brought about by his exposure at Ito's lab and at the neutron bomb detonation site had been one of the most miserable experiences of his life. He'd been assured, though, that the acute effects would be behind him in less than a month. Of course his chance of getting cancer as he aged had risen to near 100 percent, but he'd never really pictured a future of golf, rocking chairs, and sunny porches. A shallow grave and a bullet in the back of his head seemed a hell of a lot more likely.

That left the hole in his shoulder blade and his mending ribs. He'd been given a six-month leave to get his body back where it needed to be and had already started the slow, painful process. His physical therapist—an unflaggingly enthusiastic young woman who appeared to be well shy of her thirtieth birthday—had assured him that one day soon he'd be back putting the hurt on the Special Forces operatives he ran with on weekends.

Smith had to admit that he didn't share her confidence, but in an effort to get her to stop referring to him as "Colonel Negativity" he'd decided to just follow her orders and try to enjoy the ride.

To prevent a war in Asia—one that could quickly
spread to the rest of the world—Paul Janson and
Jessica Kincaid must learn the truth behind a young
woman's murder...

Robert Ludlum's™

THE JANSON EQUATION

WRITTEN BY DOUGLAS CORLEONE

Please turn this page for a preview.

1

Joint Base Pearl Harbor—Hickam
Adjacent to Honolulu, Hawaii

Ten minutes after the Embraer Legacy 650 touched down at Hickam Field on the island of Oahu, Paul Janson stepped onto the warm tarmac and was immediately greeted by Lawrence Hammond, the senator's chief of staff.

"Thank you for coming," Hammond said.

As the men shook hands, Janson breathed deeply of the fresh tropical air and savored the gentle touch of the Hawaiian sun on his face. After six months under Shanghai's polluted sky, smog as thick as tissue paper had become Janson's new normal. Only now, as he inhaled freely, did he fully realize the extent to which he'd spent the past half-year breathing poison.

Behind his Wayfarers, Janson closed his eyes for a moment and listened. Although Hickam buzzed with the typical sounds of an operational airfield, Janson instantly relished the relative tranquility. Vividly, he imagined the coastal white sand beaches and azure blue waters awaiting him and Jessie just beyond the confines of the U.S. Air Force base.

Hammond, a tall man with slicked-back hair the color of straw, directed Janson to an idling olive-green Jeep driven by a private first class who couldn't possibly have been old enough to legally drink. As Janson belted himself into the passenger seat, Hammond leaned forward and said, "Air Force One landed on this runway not too long ago."

"Is that right?" Janson said as the Jeep pulled away from the jet.

Hammond mistook Janson's politeness for genuine interest. "This past Christmas, as a matter of fact. The First Family vacations on the windward side of the island, in the small beach town of Kailua."

The three remained silent for the rest of the ten-minute drive. Janson's original plan upon leaving Shanghai had been to land at nearby Honolulu International, where he'd meet Jessie and be driven to Waikiki for an evening of dinner and drinks and a steamy night at the iconic Pink Palace before boarding a puddle jumper to Maui the next day. But a phone call Janson received thirty thousand miles above the Pacific changed all that.

Janson had been resting in his cabin, on the verge of sleep, when his lone flight attendant, Kayla, buzzed him over the intercom and announced that he had a call from the mainland.

"It's a U.S. senator," Kayla said. "I thought you might want to take it."

"Which senator?" Janson asked groggily. He knew only a handful personally and liked even fewer.

"Senator James Wyckoff," she said. "Of North Carolina."

Wyckoff was neither one of the handful Janson knew per-

sonally nor one of the few that he liked. But before Janson
could ask her to take a call-back number, Kayla told him that
Wyckoff had been referred by his current client, Jeremy Beck,
CEO of Edgerton-Gertz.

Grudgingly, Janson decided to take the call.

As the Jeep pulled into the parking lot of a small administrative
building, Janson turned to Hammond and said, "The senator
beat me here?"

The flight from Shanghai was just over nine hours and
Janson had already been in the air two hours when Wyckoff
phoned. From D.C., even under the best conditions, it was
nearly a ten-hour flight to Honolulu, and Janson was fairly sure
there was snow and ice on the ground in Washington this time
of year.

"The senator actually called you from California," Hammond
said. "He'd been holding a fund-raiser at Exchange in downtown
Los Angeles when he received the news about his son."

Janson didn't say anything else. He stepped out of the Jeep
and followed Hammond and the private first class to the building. The baby-faced PFC used a key to open the door then
stepped aside as Janson and Hammond entered. The dissonant
rumble of an ancient air conditioner emanated from overhead
vents, and the sun's natural light was instantly replaced by the
harsh glow of buzzing fluorescent bulbs.

Hammond ushered Janson down a bleak hallway of marred
linoleum into a spacious yet utilitarian office in the rear of the
building, then quietly excused himself, saying, "Senator Wyckoff will be right with you."

Two minutes later a toilet flushed and the senator himself
stepped out of a back room with his hand already extended.

"Paul Janson, I presume."

"A pleasure, Senator."

Janson removed his Wayfarers and took the proffered seat in front of the room's lone streaked and dented metal desk, while Senator Wyckoff situated himself on the opposite side, crossing his right leg over his left before taking a deep breath and launching into the facts.

"As I said over the phone, Mr. Janson, the details of my son's disappearance are still sketchy. What we do know is that Gregory's girlfriend of three years, a beautiful young lady named Lynell Yi, was found murdered in the *hanok* she and Gregory were staying at in central Seoul yesterday morning. She'd evidently been strangled."

The senator appeared roughly fifty years old, well groomed, and dressed in an expensive, tailored suit, but the bags under his eyes told the story of someone who'd lived through hell over the past twenty-four hours.

"The Seoul Metropolitan Police," Wyckoff continued, "have named Gregory their primary suspect in Lynell's death, which, if you knew my son, you'd know is preposterous. But of course my wife and I are concerned. Gregory's just a teenager. We don't know whether he's been kidnapped or is on the run because he's frightened. Being falsely accused of murder in a foreign country must be terrifying. Even though South Korea is our ally, it'll take time to get things sorted out through the proper channels." The senator leaned forward, planting his elbows on the desk. "I'd like for you to travel to Seoul and find him. That's our first priority. Second, and nearly as important, I'd like you to conduct an independent investigation into Lynell's murder. Now may be our only opportunity. I'm a former trial lawyer, and I can tell you from experience that evidence disappears fast. Witnesses vanish. Memories become fuzzy. If we don't clear Gregory's name in the next ninety-six hours, we may never be able to do so."

Janson held up his hand. "Let me stop you right there, Senator. I sympathize with you, I do. I'm very sorry that your family is going through this. And I hope that your son turns up unharmed sooner rather than later. I'm sure you're right. I'm sure he's being wrongly accused, and I'm sincerely hopeful that you can prove it and bring him home to grieve for his girlfriend. But I'm afraid that I can't help you with this. I'm not a private investigator."

"I'm not suggesting you are. But this is no ordinary investigation."

"Please, Senator, let me continue. I'm here as a courtesy to my client Jeremy Beck. But as I attempted to tell you over the phone, this simply isn't something I can take on." Janson reached into his jacket pocket and unfolded a piece of paper. "While I was in the air, I took the liberty of contacting a few old friends, and I have the names and telephone numbers of a handful of top-notch private investigators in Seoul. They know the city inside and out, and they can obtain information directly from the police without having to navigate through miles of red tape. According to my contacts, these men and women are the best investigators in all of South Korea."

Wyckoff accepted the piece of paper and set it down on the desk without looking at it. He narrowed his eyes, confirming Janson's initial impression that the senator wasn't a man who was told *no* very often. And that he seldom accepted the word for an answer.

"Mr. Janson, do you have children?"

As Wyckoff said it there was a firm knock on the door. The

senator pushed himself out of his chair and trudged toward the sound.

Meanwhile, Janson frowned. He didn't like to be asked personal questions. Not by clients and not by prospective clients. Certainly not after he'd already declined to take the job. And this was no innocuous question. It was a subject that burned Janson deep in his stomach. No, he did not have children. He did not have a family—only the memory of one. Only the stabbing recollection of a pregnant wife and the dashed dreams of their unborn child, their future obliterated by a terrorist's bomb. They'd perished almost a decade ago, yet it still felt like yesterday.

From behind, Janson heard Hammond's sonorous voice followed by a far softer one and the unmistakable sound of a woman's sobs.

"Mr. Janson," the senator said, "I'd like you to meet my wife, Alicia. Gregory's mother."

Janson stood and turned toward the couple as Hammond stepped out, closing the door gently behind him.

Alicia Wyckoff stood before Janson visibly trembling, her eyes wet with mascara tears. She appeared to be a few years younger than her husband, but her handling of the present crisis threatened to make her look his age in no time flat.

"Thank you so much for coming," she said, ignoring Janson's hand and instead gripping him in an awkward hug. He felt the warmth of her tears through his shirt, her long nails burrowing into his upper back.

If Janson were slightly more cynical, he'd have thought her entry had been meticulously timed in advance.

Wyckoff brushed some papers aside and sat on the front edge of the desk. "I know your professional history," he said to Janson. "As soon as Jeremy gave me your name I contacted State and obtained a complete dossier. While a good many parts of the document were redacted, what I *was* able to read was very impressive. You are uniquely qualified for this job, Mr. Janson." He paused for effect. "Please, don't turn us away."

"Turn us away?" Alicia Wyckoff interjected. "What are you talking about?" She turned to Janson. "Are you seriously considering refusing to help us?"

Janson remained standing. "As I told your husband a few moments ago, I'm simply not the person you need."

"But you *are*." She spun toward her husband. "Haven't you *told* him?"

Wyckoff shook his head.

"Told me what?"

Janson couldn't imagine a scenario that might possibly change his mind. He'd just left Asia behind. He needed some downtime. Jessica needed some downtime. In the past couple years they'd taken on one mission after another, almost without pause. Following two successive missions off the coast of Africa, Janson and Kincaid had promised themselves a break. But when Jeremy Beck called about the perpetual cyber espionage being perpetrated by the Chinese government, Janson became intrigued. This was what his post–Cons Ops life was all about: changing the world, one mission at a time.

Wyckoff pushed off the desk and sighed deeply, as though he'd been hoping he wouldn't have to divulge what he was about to. At least not until *after* Janson had accepted the case.

"We don't think Lynell's murder was a crime of passion or a random killing," Wyckoff said. "And we don't think the Seoul Metropolitan Police came to suspect our son by themselves; we think they were deliberately led there."

Janson watched the senator's eyes and said, "By whom?"

Wyckoff pursed his lips. He looked as if he were about to sign a deal for his soul. Or something of even greater importance to a successful U.S. politician. "What I say next stays between us, Mr. Janson."

"Of course."

The senator placed his hands on his hips and exhaled. "We think Gregory was framed by your former employer."

Janson hesitated. "I'm not sure I understand."

"The victim, Lynell Yi, my son's girlfriend, is—*was*, I should say—a Korean-English translator. She'd been working on sensitive talks in the Korean demilitarized zone. Talks between the North and the South and other interested parties, namely the United States and China. We think she overheard something she shouldn't have. We think she shared it with our son, and that they were both subsequently targeted by someone in the U.S. government. Or to be more specific, someone in the U.S. State Department."

"And you think this murder was carried out by Consular Operations?" Janson said.

Wyckoff bowed his head. "The murder and the subsequent frame—all of it is just too neat. Our son is not stupid. If he *were* somehow involved in Lynell's murder—an utter impossibility in and of itself—he would not have left behind a glaring trail of evidence pointing directly at him."

"In a crime of passion," Janson said, "by definition, the killer isn't thinking or acting rationally. His intellect would have little to do with what occurred during or immediately after the event."

"Granted," Wyckoff said. "But according to the information released by the Seoul police, this killer would have had plenty of time to clean up after himself."

"Or time to get a running head start," Janson countered.

Wyckoff ignored him. "Lynell's body wasn't found until morning. She was discovered by a maid. There wasn't even a DO NOT DISTURB sign on the door. Whoever killed Lynell *wanted* her body to be found quickly. *Wanted* it to look like a crime of passion."

Janson said nothing. He knew Wyckoff's alternative theory was based solely on a parent's wishful thinking. But what else could a father do under the circumstances? What would Janson himself be doing if the accused was *his* teenage son?

"Tell me, Paul," Wyckoff said, dispensing with the formalities, "do you *honestly* believe that powers within the U.S. government aren't capable of something like this?"

Janson could say no such thing. He *knew* what his government was capable of. He'd carried out operations not so different from the one Wyckoff was describing. And he would be spending the rest of his life atoning for them.

"Before I became a U.S. senator," Wyckoff continued, "I was a Charlotte trial lawyer. I specialized in mass torts. Made my fortune suing pharmaceutical companies for manufacturing and selling dangerous drugs that had been pre-approved by the FDA. I made tens of millions of dollars, and I would be willing to part with all of it if you would agree to take this case. Name your fee, Paul, and it's yours."

For something as involved as this, Janson could easily ask for seven or eight million dollars. And it would all go to the Phoenix Foundation. A payday this size could help dozens of former covert government operators take their lives back.

And Janson had to admit, he liked the idea of looking closely at his former employer.

And if by some stretch of the imagination the U.S. State

Department was indeed involved in framing the son of a prominent U.S. senator for murder, the government's ultimate objective would likely have widespread repercussions for the entire region, if not the world.

"I have one condition," Janson finally said.

"Name it."

"If I find your son and uncover the truth, you'll have to promise to accept it, regardless of what that truth is. Even if it ultimately leads to your son's conviction for murder."

Wyckoff glanced at his wife, who bowed her head. He turned back to Janson and said, "You have our word."

2

Dosan Park
Sinsa-dong, Gangnam-gu, Seoul

As the brutal cold burrowed deep into her bones, Jessica Kincaid couldn't shake the feeling that she was being followed. She lowered her head against the gusting wind and stole another glance over her left shoulder but saw no one.

You're being paranoid. You're the one doing the following.

Across the way, Ambassador Young's chief aide entered an upscale Korean restaurant named Jung Sikdang. Kincaid cursed under her breath. She couldn't very well walk into the restaurant; Jonathan would recognize her right away. And she sure as hell didn't want to wait around outside in the bitter cold for an hour while Jonathan enjoyed his evening meal. *Damn.* She'd been so sure he was heading straight to his apartment, where Kincaid could knock on the door and hopefully corner him alone. But no. An hour of surveillance, wasted.

After leaving the U.S. Embassy, Kincaid had headed north to the Sophia Guesthouse in Sogyeok-dong. It was her first time visiting a traditional *hanok* and she was instantly charmed. Fewer than a dozen rooms surrounded a spartan courtyard with a simple garden and young trees that stood completely bare in solidarity with the season.

Rather than poke around uninvited, she went straight to the proprietors, a husband and wife of indistinguishable age. Both spoke fluent English. Although wary at first, they gradually opened up to Kincaid once she agreed to join them for afternoon tea.

Seated on low, comfortable cushions, Kincaid asked the couple whether they had ever seen Lynell Yi or Gregory Wyckoff before their recent visit. Neither of them had. Nor had they personally overheard the loud argument that was alleged to have taken place the night of the murder. The guests who *had* overheard the argument—a young Korean couple from Busan—had already checked out. Kincaid had seen their home addresses listed in the police file Janson had obtained on the plane, so she moved on.

After tea, Kincaid asked if she might have a look around, and the couple readily acquiesced. As they walked through the courtyard toward the room where Lynell Yi's body was found, the husband launched into a semicomposed rant about the disappearance of the *hanok* in South Korean culture. The one-story homes crafted entirely of wood, he said, were victims of the South's "obsession with modernization." As he pointed out the craftsmanship of the clay-tiled roof, he noticed Kincaid's chattering teeth and explained that the rooms were well insulated with mud and straw, and heated by a system called *ondol,* which lay beneath the floor.

The wife took a key from her pocket and opened the door to number 9, the room in which Wyckoff and Yi had stayed. It was located in the newer section of the *hanok*. Kincaid was surprised to find that the two-day-old crime scene was already immaculate. There was no yellow police tape, no blood or footprints or any other evidence to be seen. According to the husband, a team had rushed in and cleaned the place up and down the moment the police indicated they were finished. Kincaid made a mental note to check whether this was normal procedure in the Republic of Korea.

The room itself was cozy, about half the size of a one-car garage. But it was also elegant in an understated way. There were no beds or chairs, just traditional mats, a pair of locked trunks, and a small color television set you probably couldn't purchase in stores anymore. She'd seen the room in evidence photos, but the pictures didn't do the place justice.

Kincaid walked to the window, which was made of a thin translucent paper that allowed in natural light. She placed her hand on one of the speckled walls and thought that if she gave it a solid punch, her fist would land in the next room. So much for proving that fellow guests couldn't possibly have overheard an argument between the victim and the accused. But what truly puzzled her was that the police noted no signs of a struggle. Given the size of the room, that seemed all but impossible, especially considering the fact that Lynell Yi had apparently been the victim of manual strangulation.

"Tourists from the West still love to stay in *hanok*," the husband said, collapsing her thoughts. "They do not come to Seoul to stay in a high-rise they can see in New York City or London."

Kincaid nodded. She understood his passion, and unlike

Janson, she could certainly understand why the young lovers might have slipped away from their modern apartment nearby to experience an amorous night in a traditional Korean home. Maybe she was just more romantic than Paul—or maybe Paul had previously been inside a *hanok* and had been reminded of the six-by-four-foot cage he'd been kept in during the eighteen months he spent as a prisoner of the Taliban in Afghanistan. That would certainly be reason enough for him to dismiss the *hanok* as a desirable place to stay. Either way, Kincaid didn't think Janson's theory that the young couple had been on the run held much water.

Following her visit to the Sophia Guesthouse, Kincaid waited in line for a dish of spicy chili beef then headed south back to the U.S. Embassy. By then it was nearing five o'clock Korean time, and she was hoping to catch Jonathan exiting the embassy after calling it a day. Jonathan was probably in his mid- to late twenties, not a teenager but certainly closer to Lynell Yi in age than most people employed at the embassy. And when Kincaid asked if there was anyone in the office who knew Lynell Yi well, the ambassador's glance toward the doorway made her suspect that Jonathan might hold some of the answers to questions she had about Yi's job, maybe even her relationship with Gregory Wyckoff.

Jonathan exited the embassy at a quarter after five and walked to the subway station at Chongyak. There he took the 1 line, and Kincaid hopped into the subway car trailing his. He got off just two stops later and boarded the 3. On the 3 train, he seemed to settle in for a lengthy ride. And lengthy it was; he didn't step off the train again until they were south of the Han River in Gangnam-gu, the district made famous—or infamous—by that obnoxious pop song Kincaid heard over and over at clubs around the world.

Sweet Jesus. Now that she'd thought about it, she couldn't get the damned song out of her head.

Kincaid continued to watch the restaurant. As she held her arms across her chest against the cold, she experienced that feeling again. That odd sensation that while she was watching Jonathan, she too was being watched. *But by whom?*

She searched the faces of the few people on the street braving the freezing weather. She eyed a group of teenagers huddled at the far corner of the park. She counted four males and two females, all probably under the age of eighteen. An unlikely bunch of spies, to say the least.

To her left, she spotted a vagrant hunched over on a park bench.

A vagrant? In these temperatures? How could he possibly survive the night?

The sun was dipping low behind the mountain; dark was falling fast. If she didn't identify her stalker soon, it would be all but impossible. She reached into her pocket for her phone to call Janson but then thought better of it. She'd already informed him that she'd followed Jonathan to the restaurant. She could handle this on her own.

She turned away from the restaurant, retreating back into the park. The group of teens paid her no attention. The vagrant didn't stir. Two males were walking fast straight toward her, but as they approached she noted they were holding hands, exposing their fingers to the cold. In this weather, that was true love.

A minute later she moved past the couple, deeper into the park. She stole another look over her shoulder. Had any of the people she'd seen earlier followed her? None that she could tell. But she felt a pair of eyes on her nevertheless.

Kincaid quickened her pace as her pulse sped up and her head filled with images of men in fedoras and dark trench coats, with handguns hanging at their sides.

In the center of the park, she spun around and spotted movement in a copse of trees. An animal? No. Unless a grizzly bear escaped from the Seoul Zoo, this creature was too large to be anything but a human being.

She continued moving forward as though she'd seen nothing. But she heard a rustle and was suddenly sure that whoever was following her knew he'd been made. Which meant that he was probably a professional.

With no one else in sight and the cover of dusk protecting him, her attacker finally made his move and launched himself out of the shadows.

Kincaid didn't hesitate, didn't bother looking back, just took off in a sprint across the park in the direction of the river. Over the shrieking gusts of wind she heard her pursuer make contact with bushes and low tree branches as he cut a parallel course north toward the Han, attempting to overtake her.

But Kincaid was fast. Fastest in her class at Quantico, where her professional life began. In the time since she'd left Virginia to join the FBI's National Security Division, she'd put on a few years but not a single extra pound. And her world hadn't paused since she'd been stolen away by the State Department after catching the eyes of some spooks from Consular Operations.

It was times like this when brimming with confidence counted, and that was a trait she'd had in spades all the way back to her childhood in Red Creek, Kentucky. She'd taken that confidence with her when she'd boarded a Greyhound bus, leaving her daddy behind for the first time in her life. And over the years that confidence had been refined, first by the Bureau, then by Cons Ops, and most recently by Paul Janson.

She charged through a row of bushes and found herself back on a street. She paused a moment to catch her breath, which was billowing in large white puffs before her eyes. Through the mist she eyed a taxi, and her arm shot up almost instinctively.

The orange taxi slowed and pulled to the curb and Kincaid opened the door and dove into the backseat, shouting, "Go, go, go."

As the taxi peeled away Kincaid raised her head just in time to see a tall Korean man breaking through the bushes, stopping on a dime, then raising his arms with a gun in his hands. She watched him take aim and nervously waited for the sound of a gunshot, the shattering of window glass, the buzz of a bullet as it streaked by within inches of her face.

Mercifully, the assassin never fired.

ABOUT THE AUTHORS

ROBERT LUDLUM was the author of twenty-seven novels, each one a *New York Times* bestseller. There are more than 225 million of his books in print, and they have been translated into thirty-two languages. He is the author of *The Scarlatti Inheritance*, *The Chancellor Manuscript*, and the Jason Bourne series—*The Bourne Identity*, *The Bourne Supremacy*, and *The Bourne Ultimatum*—among others. Mr. Ludlum passed away in March 2001. To learn more, visit www.Robert-Ludlum.com.

KYLE MILLS is the *New York Times* bestselling author of over a dozen novels including *Rising Phoenix* and *Lords of Corruption*. He lives with his wife in Jackson Hole, Wyoming, where they spend their off hours skiing, rock climbing, and mountain biking. To learn more, you can visit his website at www.KyleMills.com or e-mail him at author@kylemills.com.